Magic in a Glass

―――――

Love, Life & the Quest for a Perfect Wine

Garry Scholz

Taurus Press
Alexandria, Virginia

Magic in a Glass

Published by Taurus Press
Alexandria, Virginia
February 2014

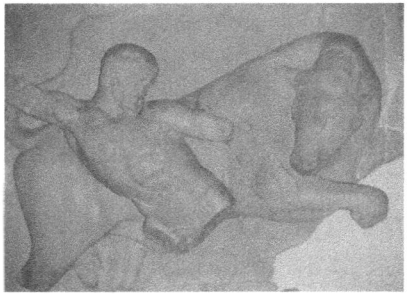

Contact: gscholz1950@gmail.com

The Taurus Press logo is a copyrighted photo taken by the author in Olympia, Greece.

ISBN-13: 978-0983757832

Dedication

For my wife Donna, my companion wine enthusiast with whom I've visited many of the great wine regions of the world. Thanks for an incredible life's journey.

Author's Note

This is a work of fiction and all characters are a product of my imagination. That being said, the story was inspired by my admiration of a real wine region and its relatively recent development. Please read the story first, then read the author's story notes at the end.

Prologue

Looking Back

Watilla, Washington
2012

Michael Ross, a wine glass cradled in one hand, walked through wide French doors and out onto the home's second story deck. At 62 he was still a tall, handsome man with a slightly weathered and sun-burned face, although his chestnut-colored hair was well on its way towards turning gray. His lean physique had taken on a little weight over the years as well, but, all-in-all, he could still attract a lady's admiring glance.

He stopped at the railing and stood for a moment, gazing with satisfaction over acres of green vineyards spread out before him. Taking a sip of the red wine in his glass, he reflected back over his life, thinking about the major events and people that had shaped his adulthood.

First, of course, there had been his dream—his vision—of creating an entirely new wine district where none had previously existed. Almost everyone had thought him crazy at the time. Everyone, that is, except Professor Cline. Based on his studies, the researcher had enthusiastically encouraged Michael. Still…it had seemed like something of a long shot. But Michael had never given up, his dream always driving him, year after year, decade after decade.

Then there had been the people in his life, and here he reflected back on the memories of those who had impacted him most. Of course there had been a number of women. Oh, yes, those wonderful, beautiful creatures who had loved him, and whom he had loved in return.

The first had been slim, tall, vivacious Jacqui with her raven black hair and bright, mischievous eyes. God, he thought, every man should experience a French girl speaking to him with that sexy accent all French women had.

And then, next, Jancy, and here Michael ceased to smile. Beautiful, sexy, blue-eyed Jancy with her brilliant blonde hair. He had fallen hard for her and had loved her intensely. But then he had…no, he refused to think about that anymore. He would not allow himself to wallow in self-reproach and self-recrimination. He had put that dark episode of his life behind him years ago.

It was good enough that her daughter Jana accepted him and respected him. That Jana should have been his daughter was one of those twists and turns of life that are a product of what might have been if only…

Michael doubted that a single day had gone by in his life when he had not thought about Jancy. She had always been there, back in one corner of his mind, haunting him. He sighed heavily and moved on with his thoughts.

Lastly, Maggie. Michael smiled slightly at the bittersweet memory of such an extraordinary woman. Because of the circumstances, he had loved her with a special love that few men and women experience. She had turned him into a better man, and he was thankful for that.

He took another sip of the wine, savoring the deep flavors of the Syrah grape. It had been his specialty – Syrah. And he had been good at making it - very good. That old fox R.R. Parkston had profited handsomely off Michael. He wondered, how many hundreds of thousands of dollars had that man made from my wine before he died? Quite a few, quite a few. Not that Michael had minded, though. He smiled broadly thinking about the sly craftiness of the legendary wine critic. Rest in peace, R.R., he thought, rest in peace. You were one-of-a-kind and the wine world misses you.

Finally, there had always been the eternal cycle of earth and climate, birth and death. The cycle of life, he thought, the cycle of life. The vineyard gave birth in spring to new buds; the buds created new growth and grape clusters; the clusters matured and ripened; the clusters were harvested; then the period of dormancy before the whole cycle began anew. Yes, there had always been that rhythm of life, year after year, going on seemingly forever.

The cycle of life caused Michael to reflect on his best friend, Tommy. Off in the distance he could see Tommy's vineyard. He raised his glass and mentally said, "Here's to you, old friend. Here's to you."

Just then, Michael's thoughts were interrupted by the voice of his wife coming from inside the house. She was calling for him, asking if he was already out on the deck. He turned and answered back that he was, and a moment later she came through the French doors, wine glass in hand, ready to join him in their daily ritual of sitting on the deck in the evening and enjoying quiet time together. Michael smiled at her, his eyes taking in once again what to him was the most beautiful woman in the world. Who could have predicted that he and she would ever have ended up together? It was quite an incredible story.

Chapter 1

A Dream is Born

Watilla, Washington
July 1975

The biggest surprise about southeastern Washington for Michael Ross was that it was desert. Real, honest-to-goodness desert. "Hell, when folks from out of state ask me about the weather in summer," chuckled the middle-aged farmer driving the worn F-150 pickup Michael was hitch-hiking in, "I tell them, 'Well, light showers ending in June, temperatures in the 80s and 90s, and a 50% chance of rain by the middle of October.'"

Michael smiled and shook his head. "Crazy, man."

Just twenty-five, his six foot frame was as lean and lanky as it had been 10 years earlier, giving Michael an almost teenage appearance. Intense, chestnut-brown eyes were matched by his light-brown, chestnut-colored hair that he wore nearly shoulder length. His face frequently sported an infectious grin because of his good-humored nature. Girls would readily use the word cute to describe him.

Mile after mile of sun-burnt, rolling hills passed by his window, most dotted with sagebrush and bunch grass, but occasionally they were interspersed with wheat fields. It was an uninspiring landscape as the farmer drove along the empty highway that led from the foothills of the Blue Mountains to the small, rural town of Watilla situated smack in the middle of nowhere.

"Mostly grazing and wheat country," the farmer commented, "except where there's irrigation and then you'll see alfalfa and some orchards, or maybe even a dairy operation. A little further west from here, up on top of Horse Heaven Hills, you've got mile after mile of dry land wheat farming."

Michael shook his head as he chuckled "Dry land farming? That sounds appropriate from what I'm looking at out my window."

"Yeah," the farmer agreed before explaining, "You raise a crop of wheat one year, then plow up or disk the land and leave it lie fallow the next year so rain and melting snow can soak in. That way, you have enough moisture for another crop. It's a rotation system - wheat in the odd years; fallow in the even years."

"That sounds like my college roommate's farm," Michael commented.

"You mean the guy you're visiting?"

"Yeah. I promised him I'd stop in and see him after I got done bumming around Europe."

*   *   *

What a glorious two years it had been! Graduating from UC Santa Cruz where he had majored in liberal arts, Michael had received a graduation present of enough cash to allow him to spend six months in Europe. His father was a professor at the university, and his mother was college educated as well, so they had always emphasized learning and travel as a way to enlightened living.

But Michael was an enterprising young man, so hell, it had been no big deal to stretch six months into two whole years. He knew a thing or two about making wine and taking care of vineyards, so he had hitchhiked his way from one great wine region to another. Sometimes he had stayed a week or two, sometimes a month, exchanging room and board for his temporary help.

Back in Santa Cruz County there was a budding wine region in the foothills and valleys of the Santa Cruz Mountains. When he had turned 12, Michael had started working summers at a local winery, being what was affectionately called a cellar rat. He enthusiastically did every wet, dirty, gofer job they had thrown at him. By the time he had turned 16, he was working part-time the entire year round and had, in effect, become the assistant winemaker and vineyard manager.

After graduating from college, he had started his European adventure in Paris, which was a neat place to hang out in summer, but after a couple months he was in Champagne where he had happily labored performing the back-breaking work of harvesting Chardonnay and Pinot Noir grapes from the traditional three-foot high cordons of vines.

Two weeks later he had gone south to Bordeaux where he also helped with the harvest, and where he had savored what was considered the best Cabernet Sauvignon and Merlot on earth. One of the numerous chateaux in the famous Medoc region had allowed him to continue working an extra month in the cellar, mostly punching down the fermenting juice. It wasn't fun; it was hard work and anything but glamorous. But he had learned even more about winemaking, not to mention making great strides in perfecting his French.

More importantly, he had learned how finicky the best French winemakers were in making their wine. It was their passion, their obsession, their whole life wrapped up in the pursuit of crafting a perfect bottle of wine.

"It is more than *terroir*," one elderly winemaker had told him, referring to the influence of soil and climate. "It is your very soul wrapped up in the wine. It expresses your love, your passion, the very essence of your being. If not, then you cannot make a great wine."

Michael had nodded sagely as he had listened, pretending to understand. But later, when he had drifted down to the Loire Valley, he had begun to understand what the old man had meant. Wine was so different from one varietal to another, from one vineyard to another, from one winemaker to another. Great wine really did express both the effects of locality and the passion and skill of the winemaker.

He had started at the mouth of the river and had worked, eaten, and drank his way on up the valley. In the lower part, there had been the pleasant surprise of Muscadet, made from the crisp, white *melon* grape, and so wonderful when enjoyed with the local seafood. Then he had traveled to mid-valley and discovered the almost intoxicating aromas of a ripe bowl of fruit wrapped up in a bottle of wine called Chenin Blanc, as well as a wonderful red made from Cabernet Franc. Finally, in the high valley region where it was colder, he had been knocked over by the sharp, crisp, refreshing Sauvignon Blanc.

After that he had spent a month in Burgundy sampling first the incredible Chardonnay of Chablis, then the mineral, almost tart Pinots made in the Cote de Or region from grapes grown on chalk. Hell, in Europe, grapevines more often than not grew in gravel, cobbles, or nearly right in bedrock. They certainly didn't seem to miss the lack of topsoil. And he had learned that this affected the resulting wine, that you could detect the minerality of the land with each sniff and taste.

"You cannot make great wine from bad grapes," one Burgundy winemaker had informed him. "You must have great grapes to begin with because great wine starts in the vineyard." Then the man had chuckled as he had added, "A good winemaker insists on the best quality grapes and then he tries to not ruin what nature has blessed him with!"

A month later Michael had headed further south , arriving in the Northern Rhone Valley. It was a land where Syrah was king and he had an epiphany. In the Côte Rôtie, St-Joseph, and the Hermitage regions, he had encountered the wonderful, inky dark wines that smelled of bacon, leather, white pepper, and pipe tobacco. Their taste was rich—even silky—and was an intriguing mix of red and dark fruit, highlighted by a sassy spiciness. Each sip produced a long lingering finish as if the wine were reluctant to say goodbye. Right then and there, Michael had developed an intense interest in crafting this red wine – an interest that would turn into a lifelong passion.

He had lingered in the valley, working an entire year at one of the wineries in the Côte Rotie region. After that, he had hitch-hiked further south into the Southern Rhone valley, another world class wine district. Here he had encountered a bewildering array of grape varieties—nearly 20 in all—grown and blended into the most intriguing wines, especially the reds. Vacquyras, Gigondas, and Chateauneuf-du-Pape were the most famous of the numerous appellations.

Those days in France had been the most wonderful of his life to date. And in more ways than one.

*   *   *

The year he had spent in the Northern Rhone had been at a classic Rhone winery by the name of Domaine Garçon. There he had learned the nuts and bolts of making world-class Syrah. The winemaking family that owned the Domaine had found him to be a quick learner and a hard worker, but the main reason he was thankful they had allowed him to stay on was due to his involvement with their daughter. It had been his first true love affair with a young woman and she had captured his heart. He had been truly smitten.

His lovemaking with slim and slender, brown-eyed Jacqueline— affectionately called Jacqui—had been frequent and intense. Eventually, however, she had broken his heart. Her family had tolerated him for just so long, but in the end they had desired someone better for her, someone with good financial prospects, not an American itinerant who would one day move on.

Michael's stay with the family, however, had produced a lasting and profound impact on his life in another way. The grandfather—old and wise Jacques—had taught him that winemaking was more than grapes, earth, and weather.

"To make a truly great wine," he had lectured Michael in his soft, fatherly voice, "you must put your heart into it. The wine must express who you are as a winemaker, and it will demand all the skill you can bring to your craft. It is more than a labor of love; it is a spiritual journey. A perfect bottle of wine has much love in it, and a piece of your very soul as well. You must love the wine as you make it as you would love the most wonderful woman in the world. The wine will then be truly incredible. It will be the perfect bottle."

Michael had found the elderly man's advice almost amusing. But Jacques had been so passionate, so earnest, when he had given it that it was easy to believe the old man put everything he had into each and every bottle. A perfect wine? Yes, he could believe that such a thing existed after listening to Jacques.

The year spent at the Domaine had allowed Michael to observe and learn Jacques's method for making his so-called perfect wines. In the vineyard in spring, Michael's eyes had popped when the old man had shown him just how severely the vines needed to be pruned.

"They must be under stress," he had informed Michael. "Only in this manner will they produce a yield that is small but intensely flavorful, and with just the right amount of sugar and acidity."

That was the whole point – producing grapes with just the right balance of sugar and intense, complex flavors. The sugar in the juice, of course, was needed for fermentation; the basic winemaking equation being sugar plus yeast equaled alcohol plus carbon dioxide.

And so, he had learned much in his year at Domaine Garçon, both in the cellar and in the vineyard. After his sojourn there, and his time in the Southern Rhone, Michael had drifted over into Northern Italy, sampling the robust reds of the Piedmont, as well as the delightful sparkling wines of the Veneto region that were called Prosecco. And, naturally, his curiosity had led him to explore the highly complex, fascinating wine called Amarone, made entirely from the juice of raisins.

Then he had wandered down the spine of Italy, savoring the wonderful diversity of wines he encountered before finally hopping over to Greece. His last stop had been on the Greek island of Santorini where he had been dumbfounded by the vineyards. In order to protect the grapes from the harsh, dry winds, vines were trained to grow as short, circular baskets on the ground, allowing the grapes clusters to hang inside them. It was the most amazing sight.

*   *   *

About 10 miles outside Watilla, Michael noticed that the loess deposits exposed by road cuts became increasing thinner and were underlain by gravelly materials, what geologists called alluvium. He had been thinking about this geology for some time, so he turned to the farmer to ask, "Anyone around here grow grapes?"

The farmer glanced at him in surprise. "Grapes? No, not that I know of. Why would we grow grapes? With refrigerated trucks these days, we get grapes and all kinds of produce from California."

Michael smiled at the misunderstanding. "No, I don't mean table grapes. I'm talking about wine grapes."

"Wine grapes?" the farmer asked, incredulously. "Why on earth would anyone want to try to grow wine grapes? You can't do that in this type of country."

"I'm not so sure," Michael replied. "You have some nice alluvial deposits here."

"You mean the silt?"

"Well, the sand and gravel materials beneath it. I've noticed lots of silt deposits exposed in these road cuts. It's technically called loess. And lying beneath it is alluvium."

The farmer shifted in his seat and explained that the locals called the topsoil, The Silt. "It's good for growing wheat."

"I think it'd be good for vineyards, too," Michael offered.

But the farmer pooh-poohed him. "Never heard of any such thing. Not in this climate. It's too hot in summer and too cold in winter. Besides, there ain't enough rain unless you irrigated."

Michael knew better but chose to drop the subject since they were rolling into Watilla and this was his stop. He hopped out of the pickup, grabbed his duffle bag, and thanked the farmer for the ride.

After checking into a local motel, he used a pay phone at the street corner to call his former college roommate, Lawrence. It was dinner time, so he hoped to catch his friend at home. A lady answered the phone whom Michael assumed was Larry's mom. She informed him that his friend was indeed in the house. A moment later he said hello.

"Larry! This is Michael! How the heck are you?"

"Hey, buddy, how's it going? You in town now?"

"Yeah, just got in. Are you free tonight?"

Larry replied that he was just sitting down to dinner but would be free in an hour. He suggested a place to meet. "There's a local place right downtown called The Roundup Saloon. You can get a bite to eat there without dropping a lot of money. Why don't I meet you there at 7:00 and we can have a beer or two?"

Michael agreed and the two friends said good-bye. Since it was only 6:00, he decided to unpack first and head on over to the saloon.

The Roundup was a typical Western small town bar with a faded, once gorgeous, ornately carved back bar. But the establishment had seen better days and was now just a well-worn local hangout filled with cigarette smoke.

Michael slid into an empty booth and a few minutes later ordered a beer and a burger, not bothering to ask the middle-aged serving lady if the bar carried any wine. After she left, he noted with interest a sign hanging on one wall: White Caucasian Appreciation Society Meets Here.

What the hell is that all about, he wondered. Shrugging it off, he finished eating and ordered another beer as he was forced to kill time listening to slow, sad country-western tunes playing from the jukebox. Right at 7:00 his friend showed up and Michael stood to shake hands. As the two friends greeted each other warmly.

After sitting down, Larry waved the server over and ordered a beer for himself. Turning back to Michael, he said, "So, you're back from your grand European vacation!"

"Yeah, I guess so," Michael replied, grinning. "You should go over there yourself and see some of the sights."

But Larry simply shrugged off the suggestion. "Well, maybe I will sometime," he answered without conviction. "In the meantime, I've got a farm to run." Then, joshing his friend, he added, "Not like some people I know who gallivant around the world!"

"Hey, that's not fair, man!" Michael protested good-naturedly. He knew that Larry's folks hoped he would take over the family farm one day. Then he added, "I'm going to go to work! I'm done traveling for now."

Larry's curiosity was aroused. "What're you going to do?"

Michael blew out a breathe of air and ran his fingers through his hair before answering. "Well, actually, you know what I'd really like to do?"

Larry leaned forward, his arms resting on the table of the booth. "No, what?"

"Run a winery and make wine," Michael answered. "Preferably my own winery. So I could do it right, you know?"

Larry chuckled. "Still have your head in the clouds, eh?"

"No, I'm serious!" Michael protested. "I know one hell of a lot about making wine now."

Shaking his head, Larry replied, "Well, winemaking is certainly fitting for a lib art major."

Michael brushed the comment aside. "It's as much science now as art," he pointed out. "Running a world class operation is a business, you'd better believe. I learned that in France. You have to make great wine and earn a reputation for quality. Year after year after year."

Larry leaned back in the booth and drained his bottle of beer. "Well, where in California would you make your wine?"

Michael pondered the question for a moment, frowning. "You know, I'm not sure I'd do it in California."

"Really!" Larry was taken a little aback.

"Yeah, land is starting to get expensive and my folks say it's only going to get worse."

"Okay then, where?"

Michael cleared his throat. "Maybe here," he ventured.

Larry's eyes popped at this news. "Here!" he exclaimed in disbelief. "In Washington? Are you serious, man?"

Shrugging his shoulders, Michael slowly nodded. "I think so. The soil conditions look good right here in Watilla. And, the desert-like climate should be good for wine grapes, so I don't know, maybe it's not such a crazy idea."

Now it was Larry's turn to ponder a reply. After a moment, he said, "Man, that's heavy. You'd be way out there, that's for sure. One hell of a risk."

Michael cracked a little smile thinking about it, of doing something no one else had done. Before he could speak again, though, Larry held up a hand.

"You know, come to think of it, I've heard something about growing wine grapes in the Yakima Valley west of here. There's some old coot professor at Wash State who's been mentioned in the local paper a couple times this past year. I think he runs an experimental ag station over in the Prosser area with some experimental plots. In the Rattlesnake Hills area, I think. Not sure, though."

Michael brightened at this news. "Do you happen to remember his name?"

Larry scoffed. "Hell, there can't be but one person at WSU looking into this! Shouldn't be hard to find out. Just call them up and ask. Probably in the Plant Sciences department I would think."

*   *   *

The next morning Michael called Washington State University in Pullman from his motel room. When he mentioned an experimental Ag station in the Prosser area, the operator said, "You're probably looking for Dr. Wilbur Cline. Here's his number."

Michael wrote the number down, thanked the lady, hung up, and then dialed the research station. It was early enough in the morning that he caught the professor in his office.

"Will Cline. Can I help you?" the voice answered.

Michael was somewhat taken aback. The voice on the other end was not that of an old man; it was strong and sounded like a middle-aged guy.

"Uh, Dr. Cline, my name's Michael Ross and I'm calling from Watilla. A friend of mine thought that you were looking into the possibility of growing wine grapes in this part of Washington."

The voice on the other end chuckled. "I've been doing more than looking into it, sir. I've been experimenting for the better part of 20 years now. With more than 300 varieties. Mostly *Vitus vinifera.*"

"Wow!" Michael was impressed.

Cline, however, was a busy man and not in the mood to pass the time chatting. "Do you know what *Vitus vinifera* is?" he asked, testing Michael.

"Sure, it's the grape species that most wine is made from, especially all the great grape varieties in France and most of the rest of Europe. In California they call them the French varietals."

Cline was suitably impressed with Michael's knowledge. Almost no one in the U.S. outside of the California wine industry knew that nearly all wine made in the world came from a single grape species. Over thousands of years humans had gradually developed an amazing array of grape varieties from a single ancestor grape.

"You seem to know your grapes, Mr. Rogers," Cline complimented him. "But tell me, why are you calling from Watilla interested in wine grapes?"

Michael took a deep breath and said, "Because I'm interested in planting a vineyard. Ten, maybe 20 acres."

"What grapes?" Cline immediately asked, his curiosity piqued.

"You tell me," Michael shot back.

"Can you meet for lunch tomorrow?" Cline asked, direct and to the point.

"Sure," Michael replied. "Where are you located at exactly?"

He had only a general idea of where Prosser was, just that it was somewhere an hour and a half west of Watilla.

"I'll come to you," Cline countered. "Give me the name of a place to eat and I'll be there around noon."

"Okay, how about the Roundup Saloon? It's downtown. Main and 2nd."

"I'll see you then."

*   *   *

Michael judged that Professor Will Cline looked to be in his late forties when the man walked into the Roundup, introduced himself, and then slid into the booth. He was average height, had close cropped brown hair, and his face sported a few sunburned wrinkles from a lifetime spent in the outdoors.

"You're younger than I thought you'd be," Cline commented.

"And you're younger than I expected, as well," Michael countered with a grin. "I was led to believe at first that you were a little old white-haired man laboring in the halls of academia."

Cline chuckled. "A lot of people have the wrong impression of me when they learn I study grapes. Sounds boring to them, so they assume I can't be an active, normal person."

After a few more minutes of small talk, the two men ordered lunch; Cline went for the French dip while Michael ordered a club sandwich.

"God, I love these small town western bars!" the researcher exclaimed as he gazed around at the room. "Just look at that back bar! You don't see that kind of hand-carved craftsmanship anymore these days."

Michael agreed, then was hit with a question to which he had only learned the answer the previous day. "What's that all about?" Cline asked, gesturing to the White Caucasian Society sign.

Michael shifted in his seat and explained. "My friend Larry says that the sign used to read, 'Spics Not Welcome.' Someone must have complained because one day last year a guy showed up from Olympia from the Governor's office on civil rights and informed the owner that his license would get pulled if he didn't take the sign down."

"I should think so," Cline commented. "The bar's license is issued by the state and the state has nondiscriminatory laws. So, if you want a liquor license, you can't discriminate."

"But the new sign has the same message," Michael observed. "If I were Hispanic, I wouldn't show my face in here."

Cline nodded. "There's probably a small population of them locally, mostly for the fruit orchards. If so, then I'd guess there's a cantina around here somewhere where they hang out."

Shifting the topic of conversation, Michael asked, "So, what have you learned about growing grapes in Washington?"

"Not the entire state," Cline replied. "I've only studied the eastern half, the portion encompassing the Columbia-Snake River area which also includes the Yakima and Watilla Valleys."

"Why just this part of the state?" Michael wanted to know.

Cline shook his head as he explained. "The western part of the state—especially the Cascade Range and Puget Sound—is just too wet and humid. You can grow wine grapes, but not the traditional varieties that most people associate with fine table wine. My research over the years has really come to concentrate these days on the so-called French varieties."

Michael nodded in understanding. "And you think this area of the state is suitable for those?"

"Oh my, yes!" Cline exclaimed with enthusiasm. "Cabernet, Merlot, Petit Verdot – even Chardonnay. But you know what? I think the grapes that will put Washington State on the map will be Syrah and Vigonier."

Michael smiled. "Rhone grapes!"

"Yes, indeed," Cline replied, nodding and smiling. "You can add Marsanne and Roussanne to the list, and perhaps some of the reds found in the southern Rhone as well."

The researcher proceeded to explain his opinion. "You see, we actually have a Mediterranean type climate here. Very warm summer days with cool nights. Plus, there's almost no rain in summer, so you have lots and lots of sunshine which is ideal for the grapes we're talking about."

Michael was puzzled, though. "We're a lot farther north than California, so the growing season has to be a lot shorter. I can hardly believe that you can grow and ripen something like Cab here."

Cline broke out with a little Cheshire cat smile as he leaned forward as if to share a secret. "Yes, the growing season is shorter in terms of days," he confided. "But not in terms of hours of sunshine. We're further north alright, so that means more hours of daylight during the growing season."

"The same number of hours of sun!" Michael marveled, realizing that his hunch about the area was turning out to be correct. "What about soil conditions?" he wanted to know. "Seems like I've seen some promising areas around here."

"Yes, indeed," Cline confirmed, leaning back in his booth seat. "The state of Washington has been blessed with glaciations," he explained. "That means the surficial geology consists of unconsolidated deposits in many places. Sand, gravel, silt, and combinations thereof."

"Yeah, I've seen some of that," Michael told the researcher. "Especially south of town."

Just then their lunch orders arrived, so Cline said, "Let's eat lunch and afterward we can take a drive south of town so you can show me what you're talking about. We'll see if there's any potential for vineyards."

                            *   *   *

That afternoon Cline and Michael drove around a 10 square mile area south of Watilla in the researcher's pickup, making a number of stops to examine different road cuts and evaluate the nearby land. As they did, Cline peppered Michael with questions about his background, especially his qualifications for making wine and growing a vineyard. He was impressed by Michael's year at Domaine Garçon.

"Well, you certainly should know a thing or two about making wine," he commented approvingly.

At one point they stopped on top of a hill that overlooked a section of the Watilla River. Getting out of the pickup, they walked up a short slope to the top of the roadcut, noting along the way that the exposed soil consisted of several feet of silt over mixed sand and gravel. Viewing the property before them, they saw that it was torn up and overgrown in weeds.

"Probably was an orchard," Cline commented as he scanned the scene. "Most likely apple trees, I'd guess judging by that old fruit barn over there. For some reason it was abandoned and the trees torn out."

He turned and fixed his gaze ahead on the river which was roughly a quarter mile in the near distance. It was spanned by an iron bridge that allowed the county road to cross over to the opposite side. Before the bridge, though, a three story, brick schoolhouse stood by the road.

"That looks abandoned as well," Michael commented.

"Yeah, I think you're right," Cline agreed. "There's been a lot of consolidation of small school districts going on, especially in rural areas like this. I'd guess that the kids around here all go into town now for school."

The two men got down to discussing the prospect for a vineyard. Pointing towards the river, Cline said, "You see the little floodplain along the river?"

"Yeah," Michael replied.

"Now, you see how the land rises up to where we're standing? This is called a terrace. We're standing on a terrace deposited by the Watilla River back at the end of the last glaciation. Roughly 10,000 years ago. This should be well-drained ground with not much organic matter. It's good for orchards, so it's no surprise somebody planted one here once."

"But a vineyard?" Michael asked hopefully.

"It's my opinion that it'd be an ideal location for a vineyard as well," Cline responded with conviction."You've got the right soil conditions, plus a southern exposure on a descending slope. Perfect!"

As the wheels of Michael's mind were turning, Cline added, "You know, if no one is going to take care of this property, then you should look into buying it." Then he quickly added, "If you're really serious about a vineyard, that is."

"Oh yeah, I'm serious!" Michael assured him. "Ultimately, I'd need 20 acres or so to have any chance of running a commercial winery, but that's a hell of a lot of vines. I'm not sure I can afford to buy both the land and thousands of vine starts. I'd have to begin pretty small and slowly expand."

Cline, however, had a ready answer. "You plant at least five acres to start with, Michael, and I'll give you the vines," he assured the young man. "And if you plant additional acres later on, then that would be even better."

"You'd just give me the vines? For free?" Michael asked in disbelief.

"Sure," Cline immediately replied. "I'd love to have an experimental plot over here in the Watilla Valley. You purchase a plot of ground that I approve of and the university will provide you the starts. But, and this is important, you have to take the varieties I give you. You can decide on how many rows of each, but I have to approve the varieties."

The researcher quickly added an additional enticement, " Plus, if you eventually plant more than 10 acres, I'll sell you the extra vines at wholesale. At the cost to me which, by the way, isn't that much."

Michael was stunned by his good fortune; it seemed too good to be true. But the more Cline talked to him and explained his research, the more Michael understood that the professor badly wanted to get a wine industry underway somewhere in eastern Washington. And the sooner, the better.

Chapter 2

The Pioneer

Watilla, Washington
September 1975

Over the next several days, Michael made his way back to California to his parent's home in Santa Cruz. There he excitedly told them about his plans to plant a vineyard and start making wine. He told them all about Dr. Cline and his research. Of how the climate was perfect. Of how the soil conditions were ideal. How the land he was interested in was south facing, ideal for a vineyard. And he talked about the old school building

Not surprisingly, his folks were skeptical and tried to dissuade him. "Michael," his mother said one evening over dinner, "why do you want to move to Washington? We'll never hardly ever see you! Goodness knows, you were gone in Europe for two whole years!"

"Because it would be like being a pioneer," he countered, trying to explain how he felt. "There's no one there now doing it! I'd be the first to start making wine in a perfect place for it."

Dismayed, his mother tried another angle. "You know we love you and think so much of you. You're an intelligent young man with his whole future ahead of him. Don't rush into this! Please. Think it over more. If you really want to be a winemaker, then go back to the local winery where you used to work. Spend a year or two there and then maybe think about starting something of your own around here. Or even next door in Monterey County."

Michael knew exactly what his mother was really concerned about, though. "You're worried I'll blow Uncle Bill's money, aren't you?" he asked accusingly. "You're afraid I'm going to waste it on my dream."

Three years earlier, his mother's brother had suddenly died of a heart attack. He had left Michael quite a nice sum of money in his will with the provision that Michael's mother had to approve any amounts spent until he turned 30. That was still five years away.

His mother sighed. "We just don't want you to throw away a lot of money on something that's unproven."

She glanced across the dinner table at her husband, her eyes asking him to intercede. Taking his cue, he cleared his throat and offered another counter argument. "Michael, we don't doubt you know how to make wine. It's just that we're concerned about how or where you would sell it. Now, I'm not a businessman, but I do know that any product has to have a market."

"You don't think people drink wine in Washington?" Michael asked, frowning.

"No, no, I'm not saying that!" his father had protested. "It's just that places like Napa and Sonoma Counties are successful because of San Francisco and the whole Bay area being in their backyards. It's a built-in market of a couple million people. People with disposable income."

Silence followed for several seconds, and then his father asked, "What would be your market?"

Michael grew defensive, uncomfortable. He rubbed his forehead before answering. "Besides Watilla, I guess the closest area would be the Tri Cities – Kennewick, Pasco, and Richland. Beyond that, Pullman to the northeast with its university, and Yakima to the northwest. They're within a reasonable drive. Plus, there's Boise across the state line. It's about a 4 hour drive."

His father pondered his son's answer for a moment before responding. "Is that enough of a market?"

Michael shrugged. "Look, I'm only talking about a couple thousand cases a year to start with. That's small time. I'll sell my wine to restaurants throughout the region and I'll hold tasting events in any town or city within a couple hours drive. Word will spread."

Slowly nodding his head, his father admitted, "Word of mouth is the most powerful advertising of all, that's for sure. Plus, I'm sure you'll be a novelty in that part of the country. People will seek you out just to see what the heck you're doing."

Michael had immediately perked up at these words and his mother suddenly had a look of alarm on her face. "Does this mean you'll give me a chance?" he asked hopefully.

Clearing his throat, his father replied, "Let's crack open a good bottle of Napa Cab and discuss this further." Then, smiling, he added, "I want to hear in detail how you'll go about pulling off this crazy scheme of yours."

In the end, his father was inclined to allow Michael to proceed with his dream. Since his mother looked to his father for advice on anything financial, she reluctantly gave her blessing as well. As a result, Michael was free to use his uncle's money to get started.

*   *   *

Less than two months later, Michael found himself standing at the same spot where he and Cline had surveyed the landscape overlooking the Watilla River back in July. A real estate agent stood next to him this time, talking about the abandoned orchard land.

"Old man Swenson owned and managed this for most of his adult life, nearly 40 years," he explained. "It was planted in four or five kinds of apples. When he died, his two daughters and their husbands didn't want anything to do with it. One's in Seattle and the other's down in L.A., so after a couple years they decided to put it up for sale."

Michael nodded as he listened. The agent continued, pointing a finger to a nearby power pole along the road. "Now that line coming off that power pole goes over to a water well. It's that little shack over there. See it?"

Michael confirmed he saw what the agent was indicating.

"You'll have to get a water well contractor out here to look at it," the agent advised. "Might need to pull the pipe and replace it. Maybe the pump motor, too."

"Hmm, I think I'll have that done before making an offer," he informed the man. "It could affect the selling price."

"That it could," the agent agreed. "And we'll get a survey of course. Supposed to be 25 acres, more or less. Looks like about 20 was planted in trees."

After a moment of silence, Michael asked, "What's the story with the old school down there?"

"Built in 1915 as a general school for grades one through eight," the agent explained. "Later on, they included high school. Operated till 1958 when it was converted to just being an elementary. That lasted until the consolidation in '64 when the new school in town was finished. Been empty ever since."

"It's an interesting building," Michael commented. "I was down there the other day and looked it over. Very unusual for the era in which it was built. There are a lot of nice architectural elements on the front."

The agent nodded. "Yep, the story goes that the county was competing for settlers with the town across the border 10 miles from here. The county built a fancy school to attract folks to farm here in Watilla County instead of settling across the state line in Oregon."

Michael frowned. "Do you suppose a fellow might be able to buy it?"

"The school?" the real estate agent asked in surprise.

"Yeah. I'm wondering if a guy could pick it up pretty cheap. Shame to just let it sit there and slowly deteriorate."

The agent scratched his head. "Well now, that's a good question. Depends on what you'd do with it. The county's already turned down a couple offers. They want someone to restore it and keep it historically accurate."

"I see. And the price?"

The agent cleared his throat before replying. "We'll ask and see. We can come in pretty cheap if you're willing to commit to restoring it."

The wheels were turning in Michael's mind. "That's a two story building—three if you count the basement level—and it appears to have been pretty solidly built," he told the agent, thinking out loud. "I could make my wine in the fruit barn, store inventory in the basement of the schoolhouse, eventually make a tasting room for the public on the main level, and live in the top level."

The agent chuckled and shook his head at hearing this. "Boy, I'll say one thing about you – you got big plans! You're really serious about having a winery, aren't you?"

"Yes, I am."

"Well, I'll tell you, that's the dog-gonest thing I ever heard of! At least for these parts. But more power to you if you can pull it off."

Michael smiled. "You can have one of the first bottles of wine I make!"

The agent laughed. "Ok! I'll look forward to that!"

Michael was silent for a moment as he pondered the situation. He was either in or out. He would either take the first momentous step on an incredible but risky journey, or he would return to California and work for someone else.

Making a snap decision on the spot, he turned to the agent and said enthusiastically, "Let's go get started making an offer!"

* * *

Several weeks later he was the proud new owner of 25 acres of land that Dr. Cline considered a prime location for growing wine grapes. Michael arranged to meet again with the researcher, this time at the man's office. Cline was elated to hear the news.

"What are you going to call your vineyard?" he asked Michael at one point during their visit.

"You mean give it a name?"

"Yes! Of course!" Cline responded enthusiastically. "All great vineyards have names!"

Michael thought it over for a moment as his mind pictured the site. He saw the schoolhouse and, just beyond it, the iron bridge over the Watilla River.

"I think I'll call it the Schoolhouse Bridge Vineyard," he declared. "It borders Schoolhouse Road and the bridge nearby is called Schoolhouse Bridge."

"Hmm, makes sense," the researcher agreed. Then he added, "Let's get down to work and figure out what you're going to plant!"

Over the next hour the two men discussed the pros and cons of over two dozen common grapes for table wine. Michael initially agreed to Syrah—his favorite—as well as Cabernet Sauvignon and Merlot. Those were no-brainers for red wines.

"Let's add Cabernet Franc and Petit Verdot," Cline urged. "I'm convinced both will do well at your site. That way, you can make

Bordeaux style blends as well as straight varietals like Cab Sauv and Merlot."

"Ok," Michael agreed, looking forward to the fun he would have designing red blends.

"You know Michael," Cline commented at one point, looking up from his order form. "Let's add Malbec, too. Even though it's a minor grape of Bordeaux, I think it'll do well out here as a varietal. I've read some very encouraging things about what they're doing with Malbec down in Argentina, and my own experimental plantings have shown that it seems to thrive here as well."

"Argentina?" Michael was surprised at this information.

"Oh yeah," Cline answered. "They're growing it in the high desert of the foothills of the Andes. Pretty much the same climatic conditions as here in the Columbia Valley."

Michael shrugged. "Sure, why not?"

Cline then plunged into a different aspect of the project. "Okay, Michael, what about white grapes?"

The young man shifted in his chair and answered, "Well, you said that Viognier is particularly well suited for this area, so I should grow some of that, both for blending with my Syrah and to sell as a straight varietal." After a moment's reflection, he added, "And, of course, Chardonnay is mandatory. I'm not sure if Americans are aware of any other white wine besides Chardonnay."

Cline chuckled. "Pinot Grigio in a jug!" he joked, poking fun of cheap jug wine commonly available in American stores. Michael had to give a small laugh over that comment.

Turning serious once again, the researcher cleared his throat, and said, "Well, we'll have to see about educating the public's palate. We need to introduce them to Roussanne and Marsanne."

Michael nodded. He was well familiar with those two grapes from his time in the Rhone Valley. He had been amazed at the large variety of great wines—both red and white—that the French enjoyed but that most Americans had no clue existed.

"Okay," he agreed, "let's add those two. I'll figure out something to do with them, especially in the beginning. White wine will be the foundation of my cash flow."

"That's right," Cline confirmed. "Once the vines start producing, you'll need at least two additional years before the reds will be properly aged. In the meantime, you can be selling the whites to bring in some cash."

Cline's comment raised a question in Michael's mind. "How long do figure before I can make wine? Two, three years?"

The researcher leaned back in his chair and glanced up at the ceiling of his small office. "Well, that's a good question. Based on the years I've spent so far with my little experimental plots, I've found that most varieties start bearing small amounts of fruit in their third year. And certainly, by the fourth year you'll be making serious amounts of wine. But it'll be the fifth or sixth year that the vines really come into their own."

Michael sighed. "I'm so eager to get going right now. Three years will seem like forever!"

Cline nodded. "It's like the old saying in the Army: Hurry up and wait!"

Michael chuckled, "Yeah, I'll just have to be patient. But, God, I can't wait to get going!"

Cline smiled knowingly. He leaned forward and fixed his gaze on Michael. "Young man, if things go as I expect, then you'll have one hell of a lot of work on your hands four or five years from now. You'd better be ready."

Michael nodded. "I'll be ready," he vowed.

"Good! I'm getting tired of promoting winemaking in the Columbia Valley. It's time we got a number of commercial wineries in operation and actually making wine!"

With that, Cline had Michael sign off on some paperwork after decisions on how many starts he wanted of each grape variety.

"The vines will be delivered next spring," Cline informed him. "Probably in April. I'll let you know two or three weeks ahead of time."

*   *   *

Michael accomplished one other major task that fall – he bought the old schoolhouse. He arranged for his real estate agent to let him inside for an inspection prior to making an offer. Meeting the man out front, they walked together up to the grand old building. Michael glanced upward up at the small belfry perched on top of the second story.

"If memory serves me right," the agent said to him, "the school district gave the bell to the local historical society."

"Hmm, I'm glad they saved it," Michael commented.

The agent unlocked the double front doors and they stepped inside into a small foyer. Immediately in front of them was a grand and gorgeous wooden staircase that led up to the main floor. Michael marveled at it as he stared. The steps were worn, yes, from the feet of thousands of children over the decades. And the wooden hand railings were equally worn from countless hands sliding along on them. But, oh my god, did the staircase ever have character!

Off on either side of the staircase two other smaller sets of steps led down into the basement of the building. "Let's go upstairs first!" Michael said enthusiastically.

He and the agent climbed the steps up to the main floor. They found a number of small rooms that obviously served as classrooms. In the back, however, they discovered a much larger and open room. Built in place wooden shelving lined three of the walls.

"Looks like the library," the agent commented.

"Yeah, I think you're right," Michael agreed. "What a neat room!"

A doorway on one side of the library opened into another room that was larger than a classroom. The two men puzzled over its former function.

"I'll be danged if I know what this was used for," the agent said, frowning as he glanced around the room.

But Michael suddenly brightened. "I bet it's a study hall or something like that!"

"Yeah, I think you're right," the agent agreed. "They probably created this room after the school was turned into one for all 12 grades."

The two men returned to the main staircase and took one of the side stairways up to the next level. Here they found the same gorgeous woodwork and wood floors as in the rest of the building. The rooms consisted of a dozen small classrooms with the exception of one room that was slightly larger and contained several work benches with small sinks.

"The science lab," the agent commented. "Probably biology. Maybe chemistry, too."

Michael agreed. "I like the fact that it's plumbed for water. Makes it easier to convert this to a place to live."

The men retreated back down to the main floor and then on down into the basement. Here they found two small restrooms, one marked 'Boys' and the other 'Girls.' There were several classrooms as well, plus a two larger rooms that were unfinished, their walls composed of brick tile building blocks mortared together.

"This one looks like the old coal room," the agent observed, peering into an empty space. "Good place for storage."

The other larger room contained an old boiler and associated piping that moved steam through the radiators in all of the other rooms throughout the building. After inspecting the boiler out of curiosity, Michael and the agent exited the building through the back door located in the rear of the basement. Once outside, they got a better feel for how the structure was built partially underground – like a walkout basement of a house.

"There's the playground," the agent pointed out as they looked at a bare area not far from where they stood. "No swings or anything else now, though."

But in Michael's mind, he saw the ghosts of children from the past laughing and running and swinging and using a slide. He smiled as he thought about all the children who had enjoyed recess here. He really liked the schoolhouse. It simply oozed character.

*   *   *

In October Michael was put on the agenda of a meeting of the Watilla County commissioners. He and his real estate agent made their offer for the schoolhouse. He was careful to make clear his plans, that he intended to use the building for storing and selling wine, as well as to live in it.

After a lot of questioning—which included a number of incredulous comments about the craziness of trying to grow vineyards and make wine in southeastern Washington—the commissioners approved the sale on certain conditions. First, Michael had to pursue registering the building as an historic structure. Second, he needed to keep it historically accurate for any renovations he might plan. And finally, he could store wine in the basement but not make it. He would have to do that elsewhere.

Michael accepted the conditions. There was that large old fruit storage barn on his property which was insulated for storing apples after they had been picked, so he would use that for making his wine. The basement of the schoolhouse would be his inventory room for storage of cases of wine.

Excited at the prospect of launching his enterprise, Michael returned to California to spend the winter with his parents in Santa Cruz. When spring came, he would return to Watilla, plant his vineyard, and renovate the schoolhouse.

Chapter 3

Eight Amigos

Schoolhouse Bridge Vineyard
April 1976

Michael surveyed the growing stacks of grape vine starts with alarm as they were unloaded from the motor carrier truck. Each bundle of burlap contained dozens of vines, all bare root and dormant. He checked the label on each bundle and placed them in different piles, each pile a different variety. The Viognier here, the Syrah there, Cabernet Sauvignon next to the Syrah, and so on.

He had rashly wanted to go whole hog the previous fall and order 10 acres worth of starts when he had met with Cline to finalize his order. But the researcher had wisely declined.

"I want to see if you'll hold up your end of the bargain first," he had informed Michael. "So, let's begin with five acres worth and if they do well after a year, I'll get you the second five acres."

Now, today, five acres worth of vine starts seemed like an immense amount of work. He ruefully remembered Cline telling him that the vines would number between 6,000 and 7,000. Was he sure he could handle that much?

"Shouldn't be a problem," Michael had answered, cocksure of himself. Now, he mentally thought to himself, Lordy, Lordy, I hope some help shows up!

The previous Saturday he had drove into Watilla to the Mexican cantina La Buena Tierra—The Good Earth—to post a help wanted ad. Carrying a blank piece of paper, he had walked in before the dinner crowd and found the bar and café to be warm, cozy, and noisy despite not being at capacity yet.

He had been a little uncomfortable when the conversations had died away, knowing full well that he was the only white person in the place and that all eyes were on him, wondering just what the heck he was doing there.

Approaching the small bar, he had asked the man behind it if he spoke English. Shaking his head and answering, "No," the man had turned away and disappeared into the kitchen behind the bar.

A pretty, petite Mexican woman, middle-aged, emerged a moment later and walked up to him. "Si? May I help you, Señor?"

"Yes, I need some translation help," he had informed her."I'd like to put up a help wanted ad in this establishment. Is that possible?"

"Si," the woman had replied, slowly nodding her head.

Michael had then introduced himself and had asked her to write the ad on his piece of paper. He then had dictated a short ad for laborers to help plant a five acre vineyard. Before finishing her writing, the woman had stopped, looked up skeptically at him.

"A vineyard, Señor? Do you perhaps mean to say an orchard?"

But Michael had reassured her it was grapevines he would be planting, so she finished writing the ad in Spanish. "And the wages?" she had then inquired.

Michael had forgotten to ask around beforehand what the going rate was in the area for Mexican laborers. Thinking a moment, he had answered, "Please put down that the pay will be standard orchard rate."

But the woman had hesitated. "It would be better if it was a little more," she had quietly informed him.

Clearing his throat, Michael had quickly thought on his feet. "Please say that if the work is done well, then I will pay a 10% bonus."

The woman had nodded approval before finishing the ad. Michael had then thanked her with one of the few words he knew in Spanish, "Gracias."

"Con gusto," she had answered. He would learn later that she had used the more formal version of "You're welcome."

*   *   *

After the motor carrier had driven off, Michael had a few moments to contemplate the huge amount of burlap bundles lying on the floor of the fruit barn. The insulated structure would still keep the interior temperature cool this time of year, but still, he would have to start to wet down the roots and get the starts in the ground as quickly as possible.

A few moments later, he heard the sound of a vehicle slowly driving down the access road to the barn. He walked outside and saw an older model white pickup with what looked like three men inside. As the pickup rolled to a stop, Michael saw that the back of the vehicle held four or five additional men.

A Mexican man, small in stature, got out of the driver's side and walked around the front of the truck. "Amigo!" he called out, greeting Michael. "Hello!"

Michael said hello back and thought to himself, this guy is a dead ringer for Charles Bronson! The Mexican had the same build, facial appearance, and pencil thin mustache as the well-known actor. Michael was amused at the similarity and instantly liked the guy.

"I am Jorge," he announced, pronouncing his name in the Spanish manner and forcefully rolling the r.

"I'm Michael," Michael replied, extending his hand. The man seemed somewhat surprised at this but readily shook hands.

The other men did not get out of the pickup, so Michael assumed they were waiting for a sign from Jorge. "You are planting a vineyard, no?" the Mexican asked.

"Yes, I am," Michael answered. "The vines are in here."

He led Jorge into the barn where the Mexican looked over the huge amount of burlap bundles. "Many, many vines," he had simply observed. "Much work."

"Yes, a lot of work," Michael agreed.

Jorge nodded as he continued looking things over. "Many days," he added.

"Yes, probably at least a week."

Jorge kept slowly nodding as he thought things over. "I have some amigos," he announced. "Me and my amigos can work. If you can pay, we can work."

"Okay," Michael replied. "I'd like to hire you. I saw your friends in the pickup. Looked like seven or eight."

"Seven," Jorge replied. "Seven plus me."

Michael was feeling much better about the task ahead of him. If the Mexicans were dependable workers, then he had eight laborers to assist him. He told Jorge to go get his men. A couple minutes later, the group was assembled in front of him. All were much shorter than Michael but looked sturdy and strong, as if they were used to doing manual labor.

"Do they speak English?" he asked Jorge.

The Mexican shook his head. "Not so good."

"Alright, you can translate for me."

"Si."

Michael cleared his throat and addressed the men. He explained that they would plant five acres of grape vines. He told them roughly how the process would work and emphasized that the rows had to be perfectly straight and spaced just so. He told them that the vineyard would be there forever, that anyone who drove by would see the vineyard and if it wasn't planted in an orderly manner, then they would think whoever had planted it was sloppy and lazy.

Jorge, however, refused to translate this last part. "We will plant like you say," he informed Michael. "If it is not so good, then it will be because of how you tell us, not because of our work. My amigos and me are good workers."

Taken a little aback, Michael's face colored slightly at the slight rebuke from Jorge. Evidently, these were proud men. That was good. That would come in useful.

When Michael was finished, he informed Jorge, "I'd like to meet each man and learn his name."

Jorge translated as Michael stepped up to the first man and extended his hand, "I'm Michael," he simply said.

"Antonio," the man replied as they shook hands.

Michael went down the line, shaking hands with each man and learning his name. Jorge seemed amused.

"An Americano who shakes hands with Mexicanos," he said. "That is very interesting."

Michael shrugged. "It's the decent thing to do."

"Si," Jorge agreed.

Then Michael made a request of the Mexican before he started the men to work. "I'm fluent in French," he informed Jorge. "But I don't know Spanish. As the days go by, perhaps you and your men can teach me some Spanish."

"Si, con mucho gusto!" Jorge replied, smiling widely. Then he translated, "With much pleasure."

*   *   *

And so, the first five acres of Michael's vineyard were planted that week. Jorge and his gang worked from Monday through Friday, laboring with posthole diggers, shovels, rakes, and watering buckets. Rows were sighted in and string stretched along where each row would go. Each two to three foot long vine went into a hole that had been wetted with some water. Then the start went in and the hole filled. A special fertilizer, recommended by Dr. Cline, was worked by hand into the soil around the vine, and then more water given until the loose soil was saturated with just the right amount. Finally, a plastic guard was placed around the start to protect it from rabbits, mice or whatever else might want to gnaw on it.

On the second day of work, Cline himself showed up, anxious to see what progress Michael was making. "Looking good!" the researcher exclaimed, eyeing the vines already planted. Watching the workers, he commented favorably on the work being done.

"This is the second commercial vineyard I'm involved with," he informed the young man. "A third one is going in over west of Benton City and then I'll have enough data to gather for my research paper. I can't wait to prove wine can be made in this part of the country!"

By Wednesday Jorge wasn't asking for payment at the end of each day. "We know now you will pay us," he told Michael. "We can wait until Friday."

It was a sign that the Mexicans and Michael were getting along well. He was picking up some Spanish and they were proving to be steady, reliable workers. And, in fact, the work went on through Saturday in order to finish up the entire five acres. Then the Mexicans were back on the following Monday for several more days of work to install the drip irrigation system that Cline had specified. Support stakes were driven in and tubing run along each row. Connections to a manifold were made back near the pump by the barn that pumped water up from the well. A timer was installed and wired in so the vineyard could be watered automatically on a fixed schedule.

Michael didn't commit yet to installing posts and wires for training the vines. He wanted to be assured first that the vines would grow. Once they budded out and tendrils emerged, then he would have Jorge and his men out once again to install the system so the vines could be trained into horizontal cordons.

After two long, hard weeks of work, Michael had his vineyard established. He gazed upon it with a great deal of satisfaction. He had major blocks of Syrah, Cabernet Sauvignon, Merlot, Chardonnay, and Viognier, as well as a couple rows each of Cabernet Franc, Petit Verdot, Malbec, Roussanne, and Marsanne.

This is the real deal, he thought to himself, somewhat amazed by the reality of the situation. This is a promising vineyard with some great varieties of grapes. Now, I have to be up to the task of making good wine from them when the time comes.

*   *   *

As spring turned into summer, the vineyard achieved a 98% success rate of growth which made for very little work replanting new starts. In June, Jorge's men installed the training system under Michael's direction, and tied the young tendrils to the first horizontal wire. The irrigation system was fined tuned under Dr. Cline's supervision after the spring rains stopped. The researcher thoroughly enjoyed each of his periodic visits, excited to see the vineyard turn more and more green.

One Friday in late June, Jorge surprised Michael with a suggestion. "You should come to the cantina this evening," he said. "Very big celebration."

"Why? What's up?" Michael asked, curious.

"The vineyard!" Jorge answered with a big smile. "We celebrate the vineyard!"

Seeing the look of perplexity on Michael's face, he explained. "The vineyard means more work in the future. It must be cared for, and in a few years, there will be harvests every fall. And, if the vineyard is successful this year, then you have said you will plant another five acres next year. Even more work!"

Michael suddenly realized a fundamental truth he hadn't thought of. His vineyard was the start of a significant enterprise. Jorge was absolutely right. There would be a tremendous amount of work in the years ahead, work that the Mexicans would gladly do. Michael was becoming, in effect, an employer with guaranteed work.

At the end of the day, it was no surprise to him that he was the only non-Latino at the cantina, and he told Jorge how gratified he was to be so honored. The Mexican was dismissive, however. "You are a good man," he informed Michael. "Any good man is welcome here."

Michael stayed for two hours, enjoying the music of a live Latino band from somewhere, and trying to understand what was being said to him in the noise of the jam-packed place. His limited Spanish wasn't good enough to keep up with the others, but either Jorge or his wife, Maria, was there to translate, especially when either he or the vineyard were being toasted, which became more and more frequent as everyone had more and more to drink.

He understood now the reason the cantina had been named La Buena Tierra - The Good Earth. The Mexicans made their living primarily from agricultural products that were grown in the area. Yes, the good earth, he thought. May it bless my vineyard and bring me good fortune.

Chapter 4

The Banker & The Accountant

Kennewick, Washington
August 1977

Michael sat, fidgeting, in a chair in front of the expansive and highly polished desk of Bill Burton, Jr. who was intently reading through the pages of Michael's business plan. The thirty year old banker would turn a page, read for a moment, and then a "Hmmm," would emanate from his throat as he frowned. Then on to the next page and another "Hmmm" and another deep frown.

Oh my God, Michael thought to himself, he's actually pretending to understand it! Is this what I'm reduced to: a guy who appears to be a dumb jock holding my fate in his hands?

Over the past winter, Michael had stayed with his parents in Santa Cruz and worked full-time at the local winery, fine-tuning his skills and asking many questions about why they did so and so exactly this way, and why didn't they do this, and so forth.

The owners eagerly complied, excited about Michael's project in southeastern Washington state. Although they had thought he was a little crazy, they were determined he not fail because of any misunderstanding of the finer points of winemaking. All in all, it had been a pleasant winter and it had gone by quickly.

When spring had arrived, he was back in Watilla to plant another five acres of vines. Jorge, of course, was only too glad to bring his gang of amigos back once again to get the job done. Plus, the Mexican was intensely interested in a new chore that had been created – pruning. The first year's vines needed to be pruned before sending out new tendrils.

Jorge had thought Michael's method was too severe, but Michael tried to instill in him the basic premise of creating a great wine vineyard. "Too much fruit ruins everything," he told the Mexican. "A truly great vineyard must bear a reduced crop. Perhaps as low as only three tons per acre."

The Mexican was amazed. He had friends and relatives in California working in table grape vineyards where the goal was upwards to as much as eight to ten tons per acre. The more fruit, the better. But Michael taught him that, in a wine vineyard, the opposite tended to be true, that less could be better.

And so, the first five acres of vines had been pruned back to Michael's satisfaction, and the next five acres had been planted to both Michael's and Dr. Cline's satisfaction. The researcher had been extremely pleased with the survival rate of the first year's planting – almost 95% had survived the winter..

"This is absolutely great!" he enthusiastically informed Michael. "These guys are loving it here!" he exclaimed in reference to the vines. "They're as happy as hogs in mud!"

This was all to the good for Michael, but there was a problem. Money. Michael was out of money. He had used his uncle's inheritance to buy the 25 acres of land and the schoolhouse, and then pay the Mexicans for all their work. In addition, he had done basic renovation to the upper floor of the schoolhouse so he could live in it. But now the money had basically run out.

Over the winter he had enlisted the aid of a college friend who had majored in business to help him prepare a business plan. The reason was that Michael had one serious problem with his overall scheme to make wine in the Watilla Valley: he was the first. There was no one else whose equipment he could rent, or whose facilities he could use in order to get started. He was the first pioneer and he would have to provide everything. There wasn't a single soul that he could call on for assistance.

That meant buying crushing, de-stemming, and fermenting equipment, even if some or all of it was used. He still had to buy it and have it shipped to his location. It also meant buying oak barrels, stainless steel tanks, and his own bottling, corking, and labeling machine. It would have been immensely easier, and far cheaper, if there had been other wineries in the area he could have paid a reasonable fee to in order to use their equipment and facilities. At least in the early years.

To his dismay, the local Watilla bank had turned him down. "Don't know about vineyards," the banker had told him. "Sounds a little far-fetched to me. Now, if you were to do an orchard, or grow onions, then we could talk about it."

Unfortunately, the Watilla Valley was known far and wide for its sweet onions, so the local bank had been reluctant to back a new enterprise of growing grapes. Onions were a known quantity. This attitude, in particular, drove Dr. Cline nuts. "The onions grow on a completely different type of soil!" he had exclaimed. "They don't realize what a gold mine they're sitting on with the soils that grapes like!"

So, Michael had no other choice than to travel to the Tri Cities area, the cities of Pasco, Richland, and Kennewick clustered together – Pasco on the north bank of the great Columbia River and the other two cities on the south bank. They were an hour's drive west of Watilla, so, in a way, they were sort of local.

Michael had gone to three banks there, including one that Cline had mentioned that specialized in SBA lending. That would be the Federal government's Small Business Administration which guaranteed 90% of qualified loans to small businesses. But even this bank had turned him down. Now he was reduced to a last hope with the Tri Cities National Bank.

*   *   *

Bill Burton Jr. had ushered him into his luxurious office. "My grandfather started the bank," he had informed Michael. "Made it through the Great Depression without failing, a fact he was always intensely proud of. Now, my dad runs it and says he's retiring any day, but I don't believe it." Then, chucking, he had added, "He'll die in his office chair reviewing a loan application."

Michael had immediately spotted the large, framed photograph on Bill's office wall. It was a photo of the stout, burly banker in a football uniform and in a three point football stance. "Is that a Niners uniform!" Michael had asked, astonished.

"Yep, I played for the 49ers for two years," Bill had replied with pride in his voice. "Well, more correctly, I should say that I was with the organization for two years. Only played in a handful of games."

"Wow!" Michael had replied in awe.

Bill had chuckled. "I played right tackle for UCLA but blew out a knee. I was rehabbed enough by my senior year to play full time, and then the 49ers drafted me in the last round. I was on their practice squad the first year, but got to play in five games the second year. Until the knee went bad again. Then I resigned myself to fulfilling the family destiny of being a banker."

"What did you major in at UCLA," Michael asked, curios, expecting an answer of physical education or something like that. He was surprised when Bill had answered, "Business Finance."

Okay, so maybe Bill wasn't just a dumb jock, but Michael was still depressed as he sat waiting for the banker to pass judgment. After another five long minutes ticked by, Bill suddenly cleared his throat and looked up at Michael. "To tell you the truth, I don't know beans about winemaking," he announced. Michael's heart sank.

The banker reached over to his Rolodex and flipped it to a certain page. Then, taking a pen and a piece of paper, he wrote out something. Handing the paper to Michael, he said, "This is a local CPA the bank has a lot of confidence in. I'd like you to retain him to conduct a feasibility study of your proposed project. Then we'll talk again."

"But he probably has no idea about winemaking, either," Michael protested.

Bill, however, was firm. "Jonas Bringhurst is a sharp operator. He'll figure it out."

Dejected, Michael tried to put on a happy face. "Okay, I'll give Mr. Bringhurst a call."

"Fine!" Bill replied as he smiled, then stood up and extended his hand. The interview was over.

*   *   *

Jonas Bringhurst didn't exactly look like a CPA. He was short and stout, was mostly bald on top, and had a short, neatly trimmed beard.

In the course of their time together, Michael learned that he was in his mid-forties and had five kids.

"Good Mormons have five children," he joked good-naturedly at their first meeting in his office. "Three to ensure that you and your wife replace yourself, and a fourth to help propagate the faith. Any more than that and you're just going for bragging rights!" And then he gave a hearty chuckle.

Oh no! Michael thought to himself, his heart sinking. He couldn't believe he was paying $500 to a Mormon to do a feasibility study of winemaking.

"Don't Mormons believe in not drinking alcohol?" he asked in dismay.

"Oh, yes," Bringhurst replied, confirming Michael's fears. "Why, is that a problem?"

Clearing his throat, Michael said, "Well, you hold my fate in your hands. Don't you have a conflict of interest?"

But Bringhurst waved his hand dismissively. "Nah, not a problem." Then he added, "I don't believe in drinking coffee, either. That doesn't prevent me from doing business with coffee drinkers."

Michael wasn't so sure but he had no choice. Bill Burton had specified Bringhurst, so Michael was stuck with him. He sat silent as the accountant read through his business plan. After ten minutes, he looked up at Michael.

"You're asking for a loan of $75,000, but I'm wondering if that's sufficient."

Michael shrugged. "I've kept it barebones."

He explained how there was no one else that he could rent equipment from, or who had facilities to rent out for the first couple years. "I'm the pioneer, so to speak," he said. "I can't rely on anyone else. It's a major liability."

Bringhurst, however, surprised Michael by commenting, "That may not be a total liability. If you scheme to make wine succeeds, I'm assuming others will follow. Won't they be in the same boat? They'll need the same equipment and facilities. And there you'll be with everything they would require. You could rent out to them and recover part of your initial investment."

Michael perked up. "I never thought of that!" he confessed.

From that point on, Michael had a newfound respect for the accountant.

*   *   *

Two days later Bringhurst came out to the vineyard. He walked the 10 acres of vines as Michael talked about the importance of soil and climate on growing wine grapes. He spoke of his time in France, especially in the Rhone Valley, and how some of the famous French wine regions were at the same general latitude as southeastern Washington.

"Is that a fact!" Bringhurst exclaimed, surprised. "I never would have thought of that."

The accountant was impressed as well with the fact that Professor Cline was using Michael's vineyard for a research paper to be published in two or three years.

"I'll have to talk to him," he told Michael.

Bringhurst spent a couple hours in and around the fruit barn as Michael explained the nuts and bolts of winemaking and how he would use the facility. He went over all the equipment and supplies he would need as the accountant constantly wrote it all down in a small notebook he carried.

Michael was heartened by the questions Bringhurst asked. They were intelligent, probing ones indicating the accountant was taking a keen interest in the whole process of raising grapes and turning them into wine.

At one point, Bringhurst mentioned that Michael's business plan only provided for a hand operated filling and corking machine. "You'll be ramping up to more than a thousand cases in just a couple years," he pointed out. "It strikes me that such a crude process is severely impractical."

In his defense, Michael could only say, "I was just trying to keep costs to a minimum."

But Bringhurst lectured Michael on the need for adequate resources. "You'd be surprised at how many businesses start out undercapitalized," he said. "There almost always is no making up for that. It's the number one cause of failure of new businesses as far as I'm concerned."

After a brief moment of thinking things through, he declared, "You need to include in your plan one of those automated bottling and corking machines you've mentioned. Not a huge one, but one capable of, say, at least a couple cases a minute."

Michael blew out a breath of air. "Wow, that's going to cost some serious money!"

Bringhurst, however, was firm. "That's the name of the game. A serious business enterprise requires serious money. Besides, major capital investments will provide large depreciation write-offs and that, in turn, will mean major tax losses in the early years."

"Oh, no!" Michael replied, suddenly alarmed.

But the accountant smiled as he countered, "No, no, that's good! Very good! You can eliminate any tax liabilities plus carry excess losses forward into years when you become profitable. At least for several years, anyway."

"Oh, okay," Michael replied, a look of relief on his face. Who knew tax losses were good?

Bringhurst reached out and squeezed Michael on the shoulder. "I've pretty good at creating tax losses," he confided, smiling slyly.

Michael was beginning to really like this guy.

*   *   *

Three weeks later he was back in the accountant's office. After exchanging greetings, Michael settled into his chair and Bringhurst handed him an official looking report bound in an attractive blue cover. Michael accepted it and opened it to peruse it.

"Your new business plan," Bringhurst informed him.

As Michael read the introductory page, he suddenly exclaimed, "$125,000! Good God, are you serious?"

Bringhurst nodded. "Yes, that's my estimate of your capital needs over five years. Actually, the total is more than that. That's just the base loan amount. The total startup costs are around $175,000, so you'll have to supply the difference, either with cash or collateral."

Stunned, Michael could only reply, "I don't have any money. You're talking $50,000!"

"But you have property," the accountant countered. "You have 25 acres, ten of which are planted in vines."

"But the property isn't worth that much," Michael pointed out, dejected. His entire project was turning into an impossible dream. His parents had already helped him out with living expenses and modest amounts of money for basic renovation of the schoolhouse. They wouldn't provide much more.

Bringhurst, however, sat in his office chair with a Cheshire cat grin on his face. "You're correct when you're talking about your property as bare land. But you have 10 of the acres with growing vines on them. Although they may have been acquired at no cost through Dr. Cline's grant, they represent a valuable asset to you."

"They do?"

"Yes, certainly," Bringhurst confirmed. "I called several accountants in California who do the books for wineries. Napa, Sonoma, Santa Barbara Counties, places like that. After talking to them, believe me, those vines of yours are valuable. You'll have no problem covering your part of the total financing package with them as collateral."

"Okay, great!" Michael replied, relieved once again.

"I've already sent a copy of my report over to Bill Burton. You should be hearing from him in a few days."

But Michael frowned and slowly shook his head. "He'll fall out of his chair when he sees how much money is needed."

Bringhurst, however, dismissed Michael's fear with a wave of his hand. "He wanted me to do a study of your proposed project. I've done that and I've concluded it's feasible. What's he going to do now, say that I don't what I'm talking about?"

"Well, he could, couldn't he?"

Bringhurst's eyebrows shot up. "I hardly think so!" he exclaimed. "My firm has many business clients and I always refer them to his bank for all their banking needs."

Michael nodded in understanding. The world of business was certainly revealing itself to be very intriguing. Write-offs, tax losses, carry forward items, and now this network concept of you-do-me-a-favor-and-I'll-do-one-for-you.

Bringhurst suddenly smiled and said with enthusiasm, "I can't wait to start doing your books and financial statements! I've never been involved with this kind of business before. That's what gets an accountant's juices flowing: learning an entirely new type of business and all the details of its costs and revenues."

Michael chuckled. "And tax losses," he joked.

"Oh, yes, there'll be lots of those!" the accountant added with enthusiasm.

A humorous thought suddenly struck Michael. "You know, this is going to be a business relationship where a teetotalling CPA does the books for a winery."

Both men gave a small laugh. Then Bringhurst leaned forward as if to convey something in a conspiratorial manner. "On the record, I'm a good, abstaining Mormon," he said in a low voice. "Strictly off the record, be sure and save one of your first bottles for me."

"I will," Michael assured him, smiling broadly.

*   *   *

Two days later when Michael had come in for a noon break from working in his vineyard, he saw he had a voicemail message blinking on his phone. He went over to it and punched a button to play it back.

"Hello, Michael, this is Bill Burton at Tri Cities National. I wanted to let you know that our loan committee met earlier this morning to review your application and they approved it. So, congratulations! Please give me a call at your convenience to arrange a time to come in. I have a lot of paperwork for you to sign."

After listening to the message, Michael sat down at his simple kitchen table and thought about what was about to happen. Everything seemed to be coming together, and in a bigger fashion than he had ever envisioned. It started to hit him that this was all very serious business. God, he couldn't fail! He would go so bankrupt he would never recover.

After a moment, however, he glanced at the most recent copy of *Wine Explorer* magazine lying on the table across from him. A slight smile flickered on his lips as he wondered if, years from now, he would ever be mentioned in it. Perhaps one of his wines would be reviewed someday. What a nice fantasy!

Then, shaking the thought from his head, he began to dwell on the more sobering thought of obligating himself to a substantial business loan. He would have to sell one hell of a lot of wine to be able to ever pay it back.

Chapter 5

Making Wine

Olde Schoolhouse Cellars
Early Autumn, 1979

Two years had flown by for Michael. He had closed on the loan with Bill Burton and acquired a substantial amount of funds to draw on as he needed them. First, he had purchased enough vines the previous year to plant yet another five acre block. Dr. Cline had been true to his word and had made it possible for Michael to buy them wholesale.

By this time, Jorge had become Michael's de facto vineyard manager, and the industrious Mexican needed no instructions any longer on how to plant and set up the new block of vines. He and his amigos got the job done efficiently and with enthusiasm. Every vine they planted guaranteed that much more work for them in the future.

In addition, the Mexicans were eager learners for pruning and training the existing vines. The initial block of five acres had truly taken on the look of a flourishing vineyard one would see in typical wine country, and the second block was coming along nicely. In addition, several additional grape varieties had been added: Sémillon and Pinot Gris for whites; Sangiovese and Tempranillo for reds.

"I think they all have a fair chance of doing well," Cline had commented to Michael. "I believe you'll be able to make wine from all of them."

In the interest of learning what would thrive best, Michael had consented to incorporating at least several rows each of these new grapes. But he kept adding more of the so-called standard ones: Chardonnay, Cabernet Sauvignon, Syrah, and Merlot.

Then, just this past spring, Michael and the amigos had planted the last and final block of five acres. Now, the vineyard was at its maximum of 20 acres of usable land, the few remaining acres being judged too low for production by Cline.

"You need to be mindful of early or late frosts," he had informed Michael. "Cold air is like water; it flows downhill and settles in any low areas. Even though you have a few more spots here and there that you could plant, I advise you not too. You'd be asking for trouble."

Michael was content to quit at 20 acres. If he was going to succeed as a commercial winery, then the vines he had planted would be more than sufficient. When all 20 acres reached maturity in a few years, he would theoretically have the juice to make nearly 10,000 gallons of wine, assuming an average crop of four tons per acre. That amount of wine would translate into at least 4,000 cases of twelve 750 ml bottles.

Those kinds of numbers gave him pause for thought. Marketing would be crucial. If he were to sell his total production at an average of $5 to $6 per bottle, then he was looking at roughly $300,000 of gross revenue.

Michael would lie awake at night thinking about that tantalizing possibility, of making that kind of money. Of course, he would also have tremendous costs. But still, a profit margin of 10% or 20% would give him more than enough to live his simple lifestyle. In fact, this being the late 1970s, he would become comfortably well off with an income of that much.

But it all depended on selling the wine, one of the fundamental facts of successful winemaking that he was now only beginning to fully appreciate.

*   *   *

From September through October of 1979, Michael harvested his first block of vines. He purchased and equipped the Mexicans with small, curved knives for cutting the clusters of grapes from the vines. The harvest was progressive, extending over the weeks as each grape variety became mature.

The amigos would harvest them under Michael's direction, placing the clusters in small bins. Their kids joined in, helping to carry the bins over to a small trailer with sideboards. When the trailer would become half full, one of the amigos would drive it with a tractor over to the winery barn.

Actually, despite the fact that the fruit barn was now fully converted into a winemaking facility, everyone continued calling it simply, 'The Barn.' So, as grapes were harvested, they were taken to the barn for processing.

In cooperation with Jonas—the two men were on a friendly first name basis now—Michael and he had planned the setup of equipment and the flow of the production process. In fact, Jonas was quite the process expert these days. He had surprised Michael the previous year with his newfound knowledge.

"I took the family along to San Francisco a couple weeks ago when I attended a CPA seminar on changes to Federal tax law," he had informed Michael one day during a visit. "We visited Fisherman's Wharf, China Town, Little Italy, places like that. But when they flew back home, I stayed behind and did a little wine touring in Napa and Sonoma."

"Really!"

"Oh, yeah. I visited a number of wineries," he had informed the surprised Michael. "Tasted a lot of wine. Spitting of course. But whenever I spoke to someone in charge and told them what we're doing up here in Watilla, they usually gave me a personal tour of their production facilities. Let me tell you, I filled three notebooks with notes! Took a bunch of photos, too."

Michael had been impressed. Although he certainly knew how to make wine and how to use the equipment needed, he had found Jonas's suggestions invaluable when the equipment had actually been delivered. The accountant had a keen sense of how to lay out the production process for maximum efficiency.

And so, the spacious fruit barn had been totally converted into a winemaking and storage facility. Outside, a large, concrete crush pad had been poured and a de-stemmer, crush machine, and press installed. Inside, stainless steel tanks had been set up, newly delivered oak barrels stowed away, and a little cozy room built for a simple lab.

And, of course, a small but impressive looking bottling line had been set up. Antonio, one of the original amigos, was a natural mechanic, and in a little under a week he and another amigo had assembled and completed the installation of the complex machinery, and then another day to tinker with it to get it running just right.

After installation, Michael had the capacity to automatically sterilize, fill, and cork bottles fed onto the line at its beginning. Plus, the machinery also installed a foil capsule around each bottle's neck, and then glued on a front and back label.

On the outside of the barn, there was now a newly painted sign proclaiming it as Olde Schoolhouse Cellars, the official name Michael had chosen for his winery.

*   *   *

This first autumn of harvest was the initial fulfillment of Michael's dream. The oldest block of the vineyard was being harvested, which meant the vines that had been planted in 1976. At three years of age, the vines yielded small amounts of Chardonnay, Viognier, Syrah, Merlot, and Cabernet Sauvignon. Plus, there were even smaller amounts of Cabernet Franc, Malbec, and Petit Verdot, but that didn't matter because they would only be used as minor blending constituents.

Michael's intent this first harvest had been just to practice his hand at making wine from his own grapes, but Jonas immediately set him straight. During one of the first days of harvest, the CPA was on hand to take it all in. When he heard Michael's plan, he protested.

"You're going to make wine for real and try to sell it," he lectured the young man. "You need to have bottles on a retail shelf somewhere so we can count everything you're doing as legitimate business expenses. Otherwise, the IRS will say that it's just a hobby. The government has approved you as a bonded winery, so you're legal. You might as well make wine for real, even if you're only experimenting at first."

"But I won't have anything to sell until spring, and then it'll only be the two whites. The reds won't be ready for another year and a half at the earliest," Michael replied.

"Then get the whites on a shelf somewhere next spring," Jonas said firmly. "And, open up your tasting room then as well. Maybe in April, or May at the latest. It's okay if you're just open on weekends and only during warm months the first couple years."

Michael nodded. "Okay."

"And get together with a distributor," Jonas added. "That'll help a lot."

*   *   *

With Jorge and a couple of amigos as assistants, Michael got down to the business of making small batches of wine. The Chardonnay came in first, followed weeks later by Viognier and the first of the reds. Michael preferred to put the whites through the press in whole clusters, then the juice, now called must, went into three foot cubic fermentation bins where the must would undergo a transformation over the next couple weeks.

The clusters of red grapes, however, were first put through a de-stemming machine to separate the grapes from their stems. After that, they were sent through a press that exerted just enough pressure to split open the skins of the grape berries. Next, whole grapes went into fermentation bins but, instead of fermenting, Michael held them for up to a week in what was called a cold soak. He couldn't afford expensive steel tanks with cooling coil jackets, but simply adding dry ice to the fermentation bins worked nearly as well.

Cold soaking was a well known technique that extracted more color from the skins and enabled Michael to make a wine with a bright fruit character. After cold soaking, the grape berries and the liquid must was allowed to undergo fermentation.

Michael also practiced a technique he had been taught in France that involved what was called free run juice. That was the juice that came out of the grapes prior to pressing. The weight of the grapes placed into a press caused a lot of juice to come out naturally. Michael kept this free run separate and, in fact, fermented it separately. Later, he would blend the wine made from the free run with the non-free run wine to create what he thought was a superior product.

The two white wines went into both stainless steel tanks and used oak barrels. Michael would later mix the two batches together in order that his whites retain their crispness and acidity, but yet have a little influence from the properties of the oak.

The reds, however, went into mostly new French oak barrels whose insides were lightly toasted where they would age for a year or more before bottling. True to Rhone tradition, he mixed 5% of the white Viognier into his red Syrah to stabilize the color and produce an intriguing, deep-colored red wine.

The other reds were made into two different type of wines. He made small batches of the Cabernet Sauvignon and Merlot as 100% varietals, while he made a small batch of Bordeaux style wine by taking the Cabernet Sauvignon and mixing it with smaller amounts of Merlot, Cabernet Franc, Malbec, and Petit Verdot.

*   *   *

Michael stayed in Watilla that winter due to the needs of overseeing his wines. There was racking, fining, and filtering to be performed periodically as time went by to clarify the young wine. Once March arrived, he, Antonio, Jorge, and two other amigos spent several days running the bottling line and bottling the Chardonnay and Viognier. He had his first wine ready for sale and he was immensely proud that finally he had reached this point.

When he tried to sell it, however, he ran into resistance. The largest grocery store in Watilla did agree to stock his Chardonnay, but only if they were able to pay after it sold, and if he would take back any that didn't sell after a couple months. But still…he did have some bottles on a retail shelf and that satisfied Jonas.

Michael also visited the local Watilla beer distributor, but the owner turned him down. "I carry a few California wines," he informed Michael. "Not much call for wine here locally. Mostly Chablis and stuff like White Zinfandel. That's what folks drink here."

It grated on Michael for California Chardonnay to be called Chablis. It was demeaning to the French who made true Chablis. And as for White Zinfandel, he was well aware of the growing popularity of that cheap wine. It disgusted him.

"I have Chardonnay," Michael informed the man hopefully.

But the guy put Michael off. "Chardonnay is Chardonnay," he shrugged. "And I already have the Chablis stuff."

"Mine is different. Here, let me open up a bottle and you can try it," Michael offered.

"Naw, I'm a beer drinker," the distributor replied. "Can't stand wine." Then he added, "Except if it's sweet, then I might drink some once in a while. Why don't you make some sweet wine? Maybe I'd carry a little of that and see what happens."

As far as Michael was concerned, though, this was an insult. It was true that many Americans preferred sweet wine rather than dry. He would not, however, give in and make sweet wine. He would succeed or fail on what he considered to be true table wine.

Dejected, he left the distributor with a standing offer to come out to his tasting room the next month and try his whites. The man said he just might, but Michael knew he wouldn't.

*   *   *

There was another aspect of Michael's life that wasn't working too well, either – his love life. He had no one steady in his life other than a sometimes on, sometimes off, girlfriend named Sandy. She was a local girl who Michael considered a hippie refugee from the late 60s. She fancied herself a flower child and free love advocate. And she was all for hanging out with Michael, sampling his wine and getting a little drunk.

After a month or so, however, Sandy would inevitably take off again for Seattle or Portland to hang out with other hippie types until a month or two later, she would run out of money and then come back home to her parents in Watilla. She would then once again drop by Olde Schoolhouse Cellars for some sex and free wine. Finally, after a year of this, Michael dropped her completely.

But on the bright side, he opened his tasting room to the public in May. Only on Saturday and Sunday afternoons, though. A few curious folks came out on Saturdays to see what he was all about, and they bought a few bottles of wine. And, most would suggest to him that he should sell sweet wine as well.

Virtually no one, however, came out on Sunday afternoons. Michael found out that he was, in essence, being boycotted since a large portion of Watilla's population went to church and frowned very much on the sale of alcohol on Sunday.

All in all, it was rather depressing and Michael now realized the enormity of the challenge facing him.

Chapter 6

Jancy

Santa Cruz, California
Thanksgiving, 1981

Michael made a quick trip home to enjoy Thanksgiving in 1981 with his parents before returning to Watilla, a place he now referred to as home.

"Although I'm normally closed for the winter, I'm reopening the tasting room for the holiday season now that I have some reds to sell," he explained to his parents as they enjoyed Thanksgiving dinner. "I'll be open weekends until Christmas."

"That's great, dear," his mom replied, pleased. "Seems like your business is picking up."

Michael, however, shrugged. "I'm not selling enough to make Jonas happy."

"I'm sure everything will turn out alright in the end," she said in that motherly way that's artificially optimistic. Then she added, "I really like this Syrah you made, so I know others will, too."

Michael had brought with him two mixed cases of wine to leave with his folks, one of whites and one of reds. Today they were enjoying his Syrah from the 1979 vintage with lamb after having first opened up and enjoyed one of his 1980 Chardonnays with appetizers before dinner.

"Yes, Michael," his father chimed in, "this Syrah is very good. It's rich and powerful with a wonderful, smoky, bacon-like aroma. It goes perfect with the lamb. Nice change of pace from always having turkey for Thanksgiving. I'm glad you suggested it."

"Very French," Michael simply replied.

His father nodded. He swirled the wine around in his glass another time, a deep furrow creasing his forehead. Raising the glass to his nose, he sniffed it yet again before taking his third sip.

"In fact," he announced, "it's damn good. I can't think the last time I've had a red wine this good."

Michael suddenly sat up ramrod straight in his chair, his face beaming with pride. "Thanks, Dad! That's quite a compliment. I must be doing something right!"

"Yes, indeed."

A moment passed while his mother added her compliments as well before his father spoke again.

"You know, son, the annual San Francisco International Wine Competition takes place in January. Why don't you enter this wine in it?"

"Enter my Syrah in the competition?" Michael asked, taken by surprise.

"Sure. They have both domestic and international divisions," his father explained. Chuckling, he added, "And an open division for those high end Napa wineries who want to go head-to-head with the French."

Michael thought for a second, pondering the suggestion. "So, you're saying I should enter the domestic division?"

"Uh huh," his father confirmed. "You could leave a couple bottles and I'll run them out to the local winery for them to deliver in January when they take their own wine in. I'm sure they'd do that for you since they know you so well."

And that's what Michael did. He pulled out two bottles of his Syrah from one of the cases and left them for his father to take out to the winery where Michael used to work.

*   *   *

The holiday season passed with lackluster sales. A distributor in the Tri Cities whose books Jonas kept agreed to carry a couple of Michael's wines. Jonas, however, was becoming concerned.

"You'll only have the upcoming year remaining to harvest and make wine," the accountant warned. "If sales don't increase to a higher level, then your cash flow situation will become dire by the end of the year."

Inventory was beginning to pile up, and the new releases during 1982 would increase substantially the amount of unsold wine on hand. This dark prospect was weighing on Michael's mind late one cold January morning. Looking out a window from his tasting room where he was doing a little sprucing up, he saw his dormant vineyard covered with a light dusting of snow. It was a pretty sight and he thought of grabbing his camera and going outside to photograph it.

Just then the phone rang. He walked over and picked up the receiver. Since it wasn't his personal line upstairs, he answered, "Hello, Olde Schoolhouse Cellars."

"May I speak to Mr. Michael Ross?" the voice on the other end asked.

Expecting the usual sales call from some vendor or other wishing to sell him something, Michael answered, "Speaking," with no emotion in his voice.

To his great surprise, however, the voice on the other end identified itself as Mr. So-and-so, one of the organizers of the San Francisco International Wine Competition. "I'm calling all the wineries that won major awards before we send out a press release to the media," he informed Michael. "That way, you can be prepared with your own press release when the news hits locally."

A little stunned, Michael managed to ask, "I won an award?"

"Oh my, yes, Mr. Ross, I should say so," the man replied, chuckling. He went on to explain. "Your '79 Washington State Syrah won a gold medal. The judges awarded a total of five golds in the domestic Syrah category and yours was one of them."

"Wow!" was all Michael could muster to say.

"Not only that," the man continued, "but it also won a double gold because it was judged to be the best of the five Syrahs that won gold. So, congratulations again!"

"Thanks!" Michael replied, both amazed and pleased by this news.

"Now, Mr. Ross, I'll also tell you something on the side as an FYI," the man continued. "At the end of the competition we take all the double gold winners and judge them to determine best of show. A best of the best, if you will. Well, we only make one award – the best of show. There's no silver or bronze. But I can tell you that your Syrah came in third in the balloting, Ahead of a Napa Cab, actually."

"Oh," Michael simply replied, at a loss for words. All this surprising news was nearly overwhelming.

The man on the other end chuckled again. "That's making quite a statement, Mr. Ross, when a Washington State wine shows up a Napa Cab. There was quite a bit of buzz over that, I can tell you. There were many incredulous winemakers scratching their heads and saying, 'What the hell is going on?'"

A smile spread across Michael's lips. "I suppose so," he agreed.

"Anyway, Mr. Ross, we'll be mailing out the medals tomorrow." Then, as an afterthought, the man added, "Whatever you're doing up there in Watilla, Mr. Ross, keep it up because you're definitely doing something right."

After thanking the man and hanging up, Michael thought to himself, Damn! Wish I had entered some of my other wines, too!

*   *   *

Although wine is a highly subjective commodity when it comes to individual preferences, Michael found out just how fixated the public was in regard to gold medals. The results of the competition were released to newspapers all over the Northwest. In Washington alone, newspapers in Seattle, Tacoma, Olympia, the Tri Cities, Spokane, and Pullman all received the news. And, of course, the local Watilla newspaper as well.

Suddenly, overnight, Olde Schoolhouse Cellars was an object of intense curiosity. Michael received phone calls from newspapers all over the state that wanted to do a telephone interview with him for a story. A reporter from the Watilla paper came out in person to talk to him and take a number of photos.

A professional photographer from the Tri Cities also arranged to come out. "The Seattle paper hired me," he explained to Michael. "A guy there says he interviewed you recently over the phone for a story and he wants a photo or two to go with it."

The following week, the story came out, titled, 'Something Good is Fermenting in Eastern Washington.' It more or less accurately described Olde Schoolhouse Cellars and how Michael was gambling that the greater Columbia River Valley was a great place to grow wine grapes and make wine.

"Mr. Ross has stumbled upon what may well turn out to be a gold mine in the Watilla Valley, a gold mine of wine, that is," part of the story read. "When a winemaker from our great state can go to California and beat the pants off the local boys, well, not only does it make us feel mighty proud, but it tells you that some of the best wine in the country might just be right here in Washington."

As Michael continued reading the article, he was relieved that the reporter included some of the background information that Michael had given him about Dr. Cline and his groundbreaking research. "Dr. Wilbur Cline may ultimately turn out to be the godfather of Washington wine, watching over and nurturing the birth of what one day could well be a thriving wine region. Time will tell."

One of the most glaring errors in the story was the information about his tasting room. "Open daily 12 -5, or by appointment," the story said.

"Idiot!" Michael blurted out loud. "I'm not open every day!"

Oh well, he thought, it's a rather minor misstatement. At least he got my name right and spelled Olde with an 'e.'

Business picked up as the next two months passed by. Professors and other faculty and staff from the university at Pullman made the drive down to check him out, and more folks from the Tri Cities stopped in.

Michael was surprised as well that people were now stopping in from Portland and Seattle. They usually had relatives somewhere in eastern Washington and made it a point to swing by Olde Schoolhouse Cellars to check it out whenever they visited.

Everyone wanted the gold medal wine, whatever it was. Sometimes they didn't even know, just that Michael had a gold medal something or other. By this time in his business career, he was savvy enough to steer visitors to his other wines as well. He made it a point of pride to convince each visitor to purchase more than just one bottle.

And despite his disdain for making sweet wine, he compromised with the Viognier. "I make an off-dry version in addition to the regular," he would inform visitors. He had mixed emotions about it because it was disconcerting that it became his most popular selling wine. On the other hand, that helped the cash flow situation.

Jonas, of course, was pleased as punch over the publicity and the increase in sales. He urged Michael to expand his tasting room hours. "Why don't you open on Fridays, too?" he suggested.

Michael followed up and changed his hours. In fact, he expanded them on all three days. Now he was open Friday, Saturday, and Sundays from noon to 6:00 p.m. In addition, his distributor in the Tri Cities made arrangements with a Tacoma area distributor to handle three of Michael's wines in the Tacoma-Seattle region. Things were looking up.

*   *   *

After spring had set in for earnest, Michael was out in the vineyard on a pleasant late April day helping the amigos prune the vines. His walkie-talkie that he carried suddenly crackled to life with a message from Luis who was working in the barn unloading a new delivery of oak barrels.

In Spanish he told Michael that he had a visitor. After a brief pause, he chuckled and added, "Una buenota!"

Michael's eyebrows shot in surprise at this piece of information. Well, well, today was promising to be interesting. His visitor had struck Luis as being a hot chick. Probably a reporter, Michael thought, or else a saleslady.

He replied to Luis that he was on his way. After five minutes he arrived at the barn, went inside, and found Luis nearby in animated conversation with a young lady. Michael inspected her from behind for a moment while Luis conversed with her.

She was rather tall and slender with a blonde ponytail sticking out from a dark baseball cap. She had a loose fitting white tee shirt on and wore shorts which revealed nicely her long, slim legs. She also wore low cut hiking boots.

An outdoor girl, definitely, he thought to himself.

Luis evidently was giving her a quick tour and explaining the operation of the winery. The young lady asked questions and made comments in fluent Spanish which was another surprise for Michael.

Since they were turned away from him, he spent a minute listening to the conversation. It seemed the young lady was knowledgeable about the layout of a winery. Who the heck could she be, he wondered. Finally, he cleared his throat and said, "Hola!" as he walked up to them.

When the young lady turned around, Michael was nearly struck dumb by her good looks. The most incredibly intense and piercing blue eyes meet his as she smiled sweetly, revealing perfect, bright white teeth. She said, "Hello," in English and added, "You must be Michael Ross."

"Uh, yeah, yeah I am," he managed to say, trying to recover from coming face to face with such an attractive girl. He immediately liked her natural, refreshing look. She used no makeup except a touch of eyeliner. Her face was a long oval with a prominent chin and a long, sloping, equally prominent nose. He couldn't guess exactly what her ancestry was. Scandinavian? Whatever she was, though, she looked damn good.

She stuck out her hand. "I'm Jancis Phillips," she simply said, introducing herself. "Friends call me Jancy."

"Michael Ross," he replied as he shook hands with her. Jancy's handshake was confident but feminine; not strong, but not weak, either.

Another aspect of her struck Michael favorably. She was actually shorter than she had initially appeared. From a short distance away, she had appeared taller; perhaps it was an optical illusion due to her slimness. Now, standing right in front of him, she was really several inches shorter than he, a fact he liked.

As Luis scuttled by and left the building, Jancy smiled and confided to Michael, "After he referred to me as a hot babe, he was quite embarrassed when I replied in Spanish, 'Oh, thank you for the compliment, Señor.'"

Chuckling, she added, "He was so mortified that I had to ask him to show me around to get him moving and talking again!"

Michael smiled. He was beginning to enjoy this Jancy Phillips, whoever she was. Nobody local, that was for sure. She quickly let him know what she wanted.

"I had to come here to see for myself what Olde Schoolhouse Cellars was all about," she began to explain. "After you won double gold at the San Francisco competition, I said to myself that something unusual had to be happening in Washington."

"You were at the competition?" he asked, convinced more than ever that Jancy was a reporter.

"Yes, I was one of the judges," she replied, her brilliant blue eyes engaging his.

"Wow, I'm impressed!" Michael confessed, taken a little aback. "How did you get to be a judge?"

Jancy told him that at the time she had been working for a certain Napa winery, the name of which Michael immediately recognized. It was one of the most prominent in the entire Napa Valley. Wow.

Recovering from his surprise, he asked, "What did you do for them? Work in the tasting room?"

Those incredible eyes of hers instantly flashed cold as if in anger. "Why do you assume that I had to be working in the tasting room?" she snapped.

Startled, Michael threw up his hands in mock surrender. "Hey, it was just a question! I've never known a woman in the wine business who actually worked in the cellar. They're always in marketing or the tasting room."

Jancy relaxed a little. "I was the assistant winemaker," she proudly stated.

Michael let out a low whistle. "That's impressive! Especially for such a well known winery."

But Jancy just shrugged. "Yeah, well, being the assistant winemaker meant that I did all the actual work. The head winemaker got all the credit, but I did all the hard work."

Michael nodded sympathetically. "Yeah, that's the pits." Then a thought popped into his head. "You said you used to work there. Are you working somewhere else right now?"

Jancy shook her head as she said, "Nope. Out of a job right now." Her blue eyes had turned angry again. "The head winemaker was a fucking chauvinist bastard!"

Her use of the f word shocked Michael. She continued, "He was pretty worthless. A fifty something guy resting on his past laurels. His main pastime was 'barrel sampling.' By the end of most days, he would go home fairly smashed. I often wondered how much of the profit he drank up with all that damn barrel sampling."

Michael slowly shook his head at this news. "You have to spit," he declared. "You can't be barrel sampling and swallow. Your sense of taste goes to hell pretty quickly."

Jancy's eyes opened wide as she replied emphatically, "No kidding!" Then she continued with her story. "After he would have four or five or six swallows, he would be in the mood to try and grope me. He used to try to get me cornered somewhere in the cellar and grope or kiss me. The bastard actually used to laugh when I squirmed away. It was just a fucking game with him."

Boy, oh boy, Michael thought to himself. This girl is something else. She's sexy as all get out but she can certainly swear a blue streak.

"Then one day," Jancy continued, "it got to be too much and I smacked him as goddamn hard as I could. I ran like hell and got out of there because I think he would have killed me."

Michael listened in disbelief. "Didn't the owners ever do anything?"

Jancy's eyes were blazing brilliant blue with an icy fire. "Hello! Male chauvinist pigs!" she spit out. "To them, girls only exist for ogling and screwing."

Michael's eyes held their ground with hers as he softly said, "Well, I personally think otherwise."

He immediately saw her relax again, the iciness leaving her eyes. "Good!" she said emphatically. "I was hoping you wouldn't turn out to be a chauvinist!"

"I'm not," he assured her.

*   *   *

Jancy asked to be shown around, so Michael spent an hour with her as he explained his production flow process, and what wines were aging in the horizontal barrels stacked in his storage system. He was impressed when she caught on right away to the shorthand codes he had written on the ends of barrels.

"81 – M – B -7/8 – 10%," she read off one barrel end. Then she quickly translated, "1981 Merlot from Block B, rows 7 and 8, and with 10% maleolactic."

"That's right," Michael confirmed. "That's last year's Merlot harvest in Block B. And it's had 10% injection for maleolactic."

As they walked around inside the barn, Jancy listened to his explanation of this or that, and then asked intelligent questions. Michael was convinced she was a highly knowledgeable winemaker.

After that he walked through the vineyard with her, explaining what varieties were where, and how many rows of each he had. They started in the oldest block—called Block A—and worked their way across the vineyard through Blocks B, C, and D. To his surprise, Jancy told him at one point that she had also been an assistant vineyard manager at the Napa winery.

"I could more or less speak Spanish, so it wasn't long before the owners let me manage the Hispanic workers. After a couple years, not only had I become fluent in the language, but I also had learned pretty much everything about how the vineyard needed to be managed."

As the hours passed by, it turned out to be one of the most enjoyable afternoons Michael had ever spent as he gave Jancy the grand tour. When they were done, she asked him, "I'm thinking of sticking around for a few days to check some things out. Anywhere good to eat?"

"Well," he began, "there's a café downtown that's so-so. The old A & W drive-in has new owners and is now called the Rocket-In drive-in. Plus, there's the Roundup Saloon but I definitely don't recommend that place."

"Hmmm, not much choice," she commented.

"For accommodations, there's a motel on the south side of town," Michael continued. "A bit weather beaten, though. Seen better days. They say a Super 8 is going in next year, so folks are looking forward to that. Then there's the old historic Watilla Hotel downtown. It's still open but in sad shape. The Chamber of Commerce and the historic society are trying to get a group of investors to buy it and renovate it, but so far there have been no firm commitments. Too expensive, I guess."

Jancy absorbed this information and had a thoughtful look on her face for a moment. Then she brightened up and asked, "Do you mind if I crash with you?"

Michael was taken aback by the suggestion but quickly recovered. "Uh, well, yeah, sure," he managed to say.

"Great!" she immediately replied. "I could fix us something to eat and you could open up a bottle so I can sample another one of your wines."

"Another?" he asked, perplexed.

"Yeah, I've already tasted your Syrah, remember? The competition?"

"Oh yeah," Michael sheepishly admitted, but then recovered. "Okay, how about my '79 Cab? There's still a few bottles of that left."

"Looking forward to it!" Jancy enthusiastically replied.

$$*\qquad*\qquad*$$

Michael helped her move her two duffle bags into the schoolhouse and up to the upper floor where he lived. Jancy immediately took to the old structure, gushing over all the woodwork, the wood floors, and especially the library on the main level that he had converted into a tasting room.

"This has so much character!" she marveled while standing in the middle of the room. "And I love the touch you've added by putting a few old books on the shelves! This is wonderful!"

"Yeah, I suppose it is," he replied. "But it's nothing like what I want to do someday. I'd sure like to do a full-blown restoration. But that'll take a lot of money. More than I'll ever likely have, unfortunately."

Jancy, however, was upbeat. "You'll do it someday, Michael," she said confidently. "It'll happen."

She remained upbeat during dinner as well despite its sparseness, and didn't seem to mind that Michael only had some cheese and crackers on hand, as well as a few cans of chunky style soup. Jancy was intensely interested in his wines, so he began with his unoaked Chardonnay.

"Umm! This is the way Chardonnay should be!" she complimented him. "Refreshing, crisp, lots of nice citrus flavors."

They quickly moved on to a sample of his Viognier as they ate the cheese and crackers. Jancy liked this wine, as well, and related her experience in Napa making Viognier. "The climate isn't quite right," she informed him. "We were never able to get the crispness you've got in yours, nor quite all the lush orchard fruit notes."

Despite his initial protest, Jancy insisted on sampling the off-dry version. She declared it excellent. "Viognier is a wonderful grape to do off-dry," she declared.

Michael, however, scoffed and muttered, "I vowed not to make any damn sweet wine and here I am, not only making it, but it's my number one seller, for Pete's sake!"

Jancy found this funny and laughed. She raised her glass in a toast and said, "Here's to sweet wine! It tastes like money to me!"

Michael was forced to smile and reluctantly raised his glass as well. After taking a tiny sip, Jancy offered some advice. "You know, Michael, a good winemaker offers a range of products. You can't sell just what you yourself like. Your customers will have all kinds of different tastes."

"That's true," he admitted.

"In fact," she continued, "you'd be smart to make a late harvest. The Viognier is absolutely perfect for that. Offer all three versions: dry, off-dry, and late harvest."

Michael's forehead was furrowed as he listened to her. "I've sort of been thinking about that," he conceded. "I've been wanting to experiment with a late harvest wine, but I haven't had much experience with that sort of thing."

"I have!" Jancy immediately replied.

This startled him because she had made the statement not as simple fact, but in a tone of voice that conveyed complete confidence that she was an expert.

"You have?"

"Yeah. I could show you."

He cleared his throat. "What do you mean? You'd come back here in the fall?"

He saw the look in her face, the way her eyes were engaging his and sparkling. He instinctively sensed she was up to something. "I could be your assistant here," she said matter-of-factly. "Starting tomorrow."

This was Michael's introduction to Jancy's nature of making up her mind about something and then seeing that it happened. He suddenly realized that when she had driven up to his winery in her used Jeep, she had already decided to stay…and to stay with him.

He took a deep breath. "Well, that's great but I can't afford to hire you. I hate to admit it, but I really don't have much money."

He might as well have saved his breath; he had already lost. Jancy quickly put him straight.

"You don't have to pay me," she began, "Just provide room and board. Plus maybe a little wine. You can surely afford that!"

He shrugged and simply replied. "Yeah, sure."

Jancy's eyes were dancing with mischief as she continued. "You can teach me how to grow grapes in this climate, and we can learn from each other in the cellar. I learn your techniques, and you learn mine. It's a win-win."

Michael discovered he couldn't say no. Not to this gorgeous creature, and especially when those eyes of hers were engaged with his. "Ok, deal!" he simply replied as Jancy flashed a smile that showed her brilliant white teeth.

*   *   *

The rest of the evening proved to be extremely informative. The more wine they sampled and sipped, the more they talked about themselves. He learned she was three years younger than he which meant she was 28. More importantly, he discovered she came from a broken family, that her father was well off but that he and her mother were estranged, living separately.

"My folks live apart but don't divorce because of the huge fight there's be over the money," she informed him. "As long as my mother receives a comfortable income each month, she doesn't try to sue the pants off my father."

"Hmm. That's too bad."

"That's why I'll never marry," she stated flatly. "You can't have a divorce fight if you don't get married in the first place."

"Don't you think it's a little premature to say you'll never get married?" Michael probed.

"Hell no!" she snapped back. "Tried it once. That was one big goddamn mistake!"

This statement took him by surprise. "You were married once?"

'Yeah. Right out of high school when I was 19," she informed him. "Got divorced the next year. Caught him screwing another girl. What a fight that was! My worthless husband made life hell for my folks threatening to sue them for support. Can you believe that?! He wanted alimony! They finally came to an agreement to pay him off. I think that was his plan all along. Marry me, wait a year, then try to get money from my folks. What a prick!"

"Wow, I'm sorry that happened to you," Michael replied gently.

"So now you know," she replied. "No getting married again for me. And no kids, either. Thank God for the pill!"

An uncomfortable silence followed for a moment before Michael cleared his throat and changed the subject, "Say, why don't we finish by opening that Cab we were talking about?"

Jancy immediately perked up. "Okay, sounds good!"

After opening and pouring each of them a generous taste, Michael decided to ask her a question that was on his mind. "You said you wanted to check some things out around the area. What did you mean by that?"

"Oh, nothing," she replied dismissively. "Just curious about some things around here, that's all."

Michael stared into his wine glass as he thought for a moment, turning her statement over in his mind. The more he thought about it, the more he became convinced of what Jancy was up to. She had come to Watilla to explore starting her own winery.

*   *   *

When it came time for bed, Michael got out an air mattress, inflated it, and set it up in a spare room near his. He got sheets for it and a couple pillows as well. When Jancy said she was okay, he told her to use the bathroom first. Several minutes later it was disconcerting to see her come out wearing only a white strap tee shirt and low rise thong panties. Her sexy, long legs were on full display.

Michael had been in similar situations in the youth hostels he had often stayed in during some of his time in Europe. But this was totally different. She wasn't a stranger in a mix of young people. There were only he and she present, and they had become very familiar with each other already. And she was incredibly sexy.

She padded past him, smiling, and said good-night as she entered her room. He blew out a breath of air and shook his head. Good God

Almighty, this day had been unreal! His entire world had been suddenly turned upside down.

He went to bed that night with his mind in turmoil, turning over again and again the events of the day. He decided to shut the door. He usually slept with it open but it was too easy to turn his head to one side and look into Jancy's room where he could see her skimpily clad body lying on the air mattress.

The next couple weeks passed in an enjoyable manner as Jancy learned the rhythm of Michael's winery and what needed to be done each day. But some days she would disappear for a couple hours, 'on business' as she would say if he asked what she was up to.

At the start of the third week of her stay, they shared a dinner one evening that she had prepared—she was the cook now—and one of Michael's fabulous Syrahs. Later, just after he had turned in for the night, his bedroom door suddenly opened. Jancy entered, topless but with her panties on. She had a coy, sweet smile on her face as she slipped beneath his covers.

No words were spoken between them. Instead, they gazed at each other, a big, wide smile on her face. It was a smile that didn't show her teeth, and Michael was to learn that when she was silent and just smiled at him like that, he would know she was in a special mood.

After a moment, she reached beneath the sheet and slipped her panties off. He immediately stripped off his pajama top and bottom, and when they both were totally naked, she kissed him lightly on the lips and began caressing him, arousing him. He responded by kissing first her lips, then her petite breasts. A moment later they suddenly began kissing passionately, their ardor increasing by the second.

After a moment, they broke apart, both breathing heavily, and Jancy mounted him. The two lovers began engulfed in a rhythm of erotic lovemaking. As they rocked and thrust back and forth, that same coy smile remained on her face as she looked down on him. Michael gazed back up at her, totally transfixed by her blue eyes. Every minute or so, he would pull her face down to his so he could kiss her while her long blonde hair hung down and made a tent around his head.

It was an incredible lovemaking experience for him as they changed positions several times, each position new to their experience with each other. When they finally finished, spent, he saw on the bedside clock that an hour and a half had passed. How had that happened, he wondered in amazement. He and she had been completely unaware of time, each eagerly drowning in the passion of the other.

Michael shifted and got on top of Jancy, allowing just enough of his weight to gently rest on her so that her small, swollen nipples pressed into his chest. He touched his nose against hers, gazed straight into her deep, liquid blue eyes, and nuzzled her nose for a moment. As she continued to smile looking up at him, he whispered, "You're incredible."

She whispered back, "No, you're incredible."

Chapter 7

Three Hills Vineyard

Watilla, Washington
1982/1983

After that first night of making love, Jancy shared Michael's bed from that point on. They often slept in the nude, frequently making love for the first month as he and she explored their passion for each other. She may have been a feminist, but she also had a healthy sexual appetite. A liberated woman, in the terminology of the times, a lady who dictated life strictly on her terms.

One day, almost two months after she had arrived, she made an announcement that greatly surprised Michael. "I'm starting a vineyard!" she informed him, excitement in her voice.

As he was quickly learning, this also was classic Jancy: she kept things entirely to herself until she had made a decision, then she acted.

"Really!" he reacted, caught off guard. He had suspected, of course, that was what she had been up to –scouting out a vineyard site somewhere around Watilla. And he had encouraged her, anxious that he no longer be the lone grape grower and winemaker within at least an hour's drive.

"Yep!" she confirmed. "I'm closing on the purchase in three weeks."

He saw her blue eyes dancing and he knew there was more to her story. "Okay, great," he replied. "Where at?"

She punched him playfully in the chest and said, "Right next to yours!"

"You're kidding!" he exclaimed, taken completely by surprise. He had not known that the land next to his vineyard had been for sale.

"Nope!" she replied. "No kidding! You and I are going to have vineyards side by side!"

She seemed pleased with herself, as if she had sprung an unexpected surprise, which, in fact, she had.

"Wow, that's crazy!" It was the best that Michael could come up with. He couldn't think of anything else to say at the moment. After several seconds, though, he gathered his thoughts and began to probe for more information. "Okay, you bought some land next to mine. How much?"

"80 acres!" she replied, more excited than ever, virtually bubbling over with too much energy.

Michael could only stand there, transfixed with shock. "80 acres!" he cried. It was absolutely unreal.

"Yep," Jancy replied, smiling broadly. "I bought everything over to Dead End Road."

Michael blew out a breath of air as he thought about the immense amount of property she had just purchased. "You mean you now own everything from my vineyard all the way over to Dead End Road?"

This was truly amazing news. He took a moment and visualized in his mind the situation. His property bordered School Bridge Road, a north/south road. His tasting room—the old schoolhouse—stood a short distance before the bridge over the Watilla River. His vineyard rose up from the schoolhouse, south to north, on the ancient alluvial terrace for a distance of an eighth mile, and it gained roughly 50 feet in elevation. Next to it, going east, the alluvial terrace extended quite a ways. In fact, if you went roughly a half mile you would come to Dead End Road, another north/south gravel road that ended at the Watilla River because there was no bridge across it. Jancy was going to buy that immense piece of property.

He ran both hands through his hair. "Wow, that's incredible!" he said to her. "How the heck did this come about?"

"I've been working with a local real estate agent," she informed him. "Like they say, I made an offer that couldn't be refused."

As they talked, Michael learned that Jancy had made an attractive offer for the land, and that her father had bankrolled the purchase. She would also be purchasing an old farmhouse that stood across the road from where her vineyard would be. She wanted it for a future tasting room.

"He told me that this was it as far as money goes," she remarked about her father. "He said raw land always had value, so he didn't mind buying it for me. But he also made clear that he wouldn't put any money into a vineyard or a winery. That was up to me if I wanted to take that risk."

"You're surely not going to plant the whole 80 acres are you?" Michael asked, refusing to believe that she could afford to buy that many vines, or that she could even manage such an immense operation.

"Of course not!" she replied as if he were crazy. "A vineyard of 20 to 30 acres will be more than enough to supply grapes for my winery. The rest of it I'll lease out to others who want to start their own winery, too."

"Others?"

"Yeah, sure," she replied confidently. "I'm sure there'll be others eventually. Don't you? I thought that was your dream."

"It is, it is," Michael quickly confirmed. "It's just that no one is showing up yet."

"They will," Jancy replied, certainty in her voice. "Just like I did. You'll see."

It was a nice thought but he wasn't sure he shared her optimism.

*   *   *

A couple weeks later they met in Jonas's office to discuss a business plan for Jancy. To Michael's surprise, the accountant was excited. He had bought into Michael's contention that the Watilla Valley would someday be a wine region producing wines as good as California.

"J Phillips Cellars," Jonas repeated after Jancy told him the name of her winery. "Sounds classy, refined. I like it!"

Jonas also liked the idea of Jancy leasing out a good portion of her land to future growers and winemakers. In fact, he even encouraged Michael to expand his vineyard another five or ten acres by leasing from Jancy.

"This site of yours seems to be producing excellent grapes," he informed Michael. "Act now to expand while the land next to you is bare, before Jancy plants for herself. Assuming, of course, that she's willing to lease to you."

Jancy replied she was. "I have no problem doing that," she told Jonas. "Michael can have up to ten acres if he wants, then I'll plant the next 20 to 30. That'll leave 40 or more left over to lease out to future wineries that locate in the valley."

Two weeks after that they were in Bill Burton, Jr.'s office discussing Jonas's feasibility study. Jonas was with them as well. It was good that he was, because Bill was hesitant.

"Jonas, are you sure about this?" he asked, doubt written all over his face. "I mean, Michael is struggling. I wish both his balance sheet and cash flow were stronger. He can hardly make the loan payments. Now, I'm being asked to bet on another vineyard and winery."

Jonas, however, was not to be off. "Listen Bill, I was in Portland last month at a regional CPA seminar catching up on my continuing educational units. I brought along bottles of three of Michael's wines – two red and one white. I took them to an evening hospitality event in one of the hotel suites that was being sponsored by a vendor. And guess what?"

Burton raised his eyebrows. "Um, they liked them?" he guessed.

"I should say so!" the accountant exclaimed. "They were knocked over! They couldn't believe they were Washington State wines. They said they could have been from California, from Napa or Sonoma. I'm telling you, Bill, Michael is dead on when he claims this part of Washington will one day be wine country as good as anywhere else."

Michael was pleased at Jonas's praise, but he saw the doubt in the banker's face. Sighing heavily, he conceded, "Okay, I'll run this by the loan committee. But listen, it's not the risk to the bank I'm primarily concerned about. These loans are 90% guaranteed by the SBA, and we have the land itself as collateral, so we're covered. It's just that if this all goes bust, then these young people will bear the failure and lose everything they're working for."

It was a sobering statement and Michael reflected on it for a moment. He cast a sideways glance at Jancy but she was all perky looking. Glancing back at him, she smiled and said, "We're going to make it happen. I know it!"

*   *   *

As summer began yielding to autumn, the 1982 harvest got under way. Michael employed the amigos again, this time a dozen strong. Agreeing to Jorge's suggestion, Michael made it a family affair, and the workers' wives and children all came out to help. It was a boisterous, fun time as the children helped their parents, the older, taller kids cutting clusters of grapes off the vines, the younger ones carrying the small tubs full of grapes over to the collection wagon attached to a small farm tractor.

In the winery, Jancy assisted with the processing and fermenting of the grapes, along with Jorge, Antonio, and Luis. Having been taught by Michael, they were knowledgeable enough now that they were, basically, assistant winemakers.

In fact, Michael good-naturedly told them they were official cellar rats now, and he and Jorge had fun trying to translate this term into Spanish. Since the word for rat was feminine in Spanish, that simply wouldn't do, so he and Jorge settled on the word 'mouse,' because that word was masculine. And so, the Mexicans helpers became the *ratones ocupados,* - the busy mice. When they were told, everyone had a good laugh and some good-natured ribbing ensured.

At the end of each week of harvest, everyone would gather on Saturday night at the Buena Tierra for beer and all manner of Mexican food. Usually, Michael and Jancy were guests of honor, and so they ate and drank on the house.

As winter set in, the white wines aged in their stainless steel tanks, or neutral oak barrels, while the reds were put to bed in new or slightly used oak barrels. Both Michael and Jancy took off for a couple weeks over Christmas and New Year's to spend time with their respective families and relatives in California.

Back at the winery in January, they spent the next several months working with the wines to clarify them, and to do barrel tasting of the reds. This was necessary to determine whether a varietal wine—made from a single grape variety—would be made, or whether a blend of some sort would be done.

This was where science stopped and art began – determining the exact blending ratio. Would the Syrah this year be blended with 5% Viognier, or 7 or 8, or even 10%? What would be the exact combination of the five grapes going into the Bordeaux style blend?

And, was the Cabernet Sauvignon good enough on its own, or would a bit of Cab Franc or Petit Verdot enhance it?

Each year was different, depending on the weather conditions during the growing season, and how the grapes developed and matured. Because of this, Michael never experienced the same exact winemaking conditions two years in a row, and he knew this was where good winemakers were separated from mediocre ones. Within wide limits, a good winemaker could make great wine no matter what Mother nature gave him or her.

When spring came around, Jancy got busy with the amigos in planting her vineyard. She consulted with Dr. Cline on the varieties and bought accordingly. Rather than plant a little at a time, she chose to put in 10 acres of vines the very first year. She was just too anxious to get going. The work took a whole month.

When Michael asked her out of curiosity if she had a name for her vineyard, she replied, "Three Hills."

"Why Three Hills?" he asked, puzzled. There certainly weren't any hills on her property. Her answer surprised him.

"Because when I stand on my property I have a nice view off in the distance of three large foothills of the Blue Mountains."

Michael had virtually the same view from his vineyard, but it had never occurred to him to name it after the view. But to each his or her own, he thought. And so, there were now in the Watilla Valley two vineyards: School Bridge and Three Hills.

*   *   *

A special wine was made in the fall of 1983 – a late harvest Viognier. Under Jancy's enthusiastic direction, the grapes for this wine were left out in the vineyard after the other Viognier had been harvested, then they were harvested after attaining just the right amount of sweetness. At that point, the grapes were more like raisins than plump globes full of juice. But they were raisins loaded with sugar.

Michael found that the actual production of the wine wasn't that much trouble. It was more of a pain in the ass than his other wines, but not that bad. The main difficulty, he realized, lay in harvesting at just the precise time. The resulting wine would either be good or not good, depending on just when the grapes were brought into the cellar.

However, he did have to buy special half-size bottles to bottle the wine, and these weren't cheap. He knew that late harvest wines, by tradition, were bottled in 375 ml. bottles rather than the standard 750 ml.

One day in February, after the wine had been bottled and labeled, he remarked to Jancy, "You know, if this stuff sells, the profit margin will be a whole lot greater."

"Well, yes!" she replied, "That's the whole point of making late harvest wines! It's more work and time, so you can charge a higher price but put it in a smaller bottle."

Michael nodded as he delicately sipped a sample after opening a bottle. He and Jancy had sampled throughout the production process, of course, but you had to cross your fingers until you actually opened a bottle and confirmed the wine still tasted the same.

"I actually like this," he conceded. "The Viognier aromas and flavors come through strong, even more intense than the regular. Plus, the sugar is not too high that it puts me off."

"Yeah," Jancy agreed as she sniffed and took a sip. "It's lovely. And the sugar at 6% is just right. It's a great wine to enjoy with crème brulée."

"Hey, why don't we make that for dinner tonight!" Michael said excitedly as the thought popped into his head. "We'll celebrate our new late harvest wine with a proper dessert for it!"

That evening Michael grilled burgers which they enjoyed with one of his Cabs, that being all they could afford on their meager budget. Jancy tried her best with the crème brulée, and Michael had fun caramelizing the tops with a small propane torch.

The dessert paired perfectly with the late harvest Viognier and when they had finished it, Michael declared, "Hey, this evening's been a success!"

"Yes, but it hasn't been perfect," Jancy remarked, which brought a frown to Michael's face. Then his expression quickly changed as he saw the coy smile on her face. Minutes later they were in the bedroom enjoying each other.

*   *   *

In April 1984 Michael entered a number of his wines in the 1st Annual Pacific Northwest Wine Competition held in the Sky City Restaurant near the top of the Space Needle in Seattle. Although he won several medals, it was the late harvest Viognier that garnered a double gold as the best dessert wine. Then, in the best of show voting, the judges voted it the overall best wine of the competition.

Once again, there was a flurry of inquiries from various newspapers, and even from one of the Seattle TV stations. The story was perhaps even bigger than any other about Olde Schoolhouse Cellars because the competition had taken place in Washington state, and in the city of Seattle.

It was all good publicity, of course, but the most significant development involved a thirty-year old judge with short curly hair who was determined to find out just what in the world was going on in Watilla.

Chapter 8

Tommy

Olde Schoolhouse Cellars
May 1984

About a month after the Seattle competition, Thomas O'Donnell satisfied his curiosity by turning up at Old Schoolhouse Cellars. He had just turned thirty years old and had a tall, lanky physique capped by short, rusty-brown hair that was naturally curly. His long face was open and friendly looking despite his sharp, slightly bent nose.

He introduced himself as Tommy O'Donnell and readily shook Michael's hand with a big smile and a "Glad to meet you!" When introduced to Jancy, it was evident in his look of surprise that his reaction was, holy cow, what's a babe like you doing here? But he managed to politely greet her.

The visitor explained that he also had winemaking experience. "I'm the assistant winemaker at a place south of Salem, Oregon," he said. "But they're obsessed with Pinot Noir and I want to work with a full range of grape varieties. It seems you folks are doing something really special here in that regard and I'm thinking maybe this would be a good place for me to go off on my own and start my own label. It's something I've been dreaming about for several years."

Michael cautioned him that it was just he and Jancy for the time being. "But I'm telling you," he added, "someday there's going to be a nice little wine district here. Because of how my vineyard has thrived, I've heard that two farmers are planting their own vineyards just north of town. Seems like things are starting to bubble around the valley."

Michael and Jancy showed Tommy around the cellar and explained the operation. "We affectionately call our cellar The Barn," Michael informed him. "For the short-term future, Jancy will be renting space in it until she gets her feet under her and can afford her own facility. Plus, she's buying grapes from me and paying to use my equipment so she can have wine to sell until her vineyard starts producing in a couple years."

Tommy nodded as he listened. The wheels in his head were already spinning with ideas of how he could take advantage of the situation as well. He held his peace, though, as his hosts led him out into School Bridge Vineyard. Michael explained the different varieties he had and how many rows of each.

"Wow, 20 acres!" Tommy exclaimed. "Impressive! You have a nice little gold mine here."

But Michael simply shrugged. "I've found out my ideas are bigger than what the real world is ready for. I'm having trouble selling my wine – at any price. It's all I can do to keep my head above water."

But Tommy was optimistic. "Napa and Sonoma are really taking off, and they say the Willamette Valley is going to be a great area, too. Americans are getting more into wine and even folks in this part of the country will begin discovering you."

Jancy, however, pointed out a problem. "There's a fad right now with that White Zinfandel crap. You wouldn't believe how many visitors to the tasting room ask if we make it."

"God help me, but I'd make it if I could!" Michael interjected. "Anything at this point to make a buck. But we can't grow Zin in this climate."

Tommy nodded. "Yeah, I wouldn't think you could. I've heard there are years in California when they don't finish the Zin harvest until nearly January. You guys here just don't have that much time to ripen it, despite the longer days in summer."

Then he added, "Don't get down about White Zin, okay? I think it's actually a good thing because I believe it'll turn out to be a transition wine for most folks. Get them drinking any kind of wine, I say, and then we can move them along to the better quality stuff as their palate matures."

Michael could only hope Tommy was right. After walking a large part of the vineyard, they took him over to the schoolhouse. He was impressed with the building. "A stroke of genius!" he remarked to Michael. "I love this place! There's nothing that interests the public more than a tasting room that's unique and unusual. You've certainly have that here."

*   *   *

Michael and Jancy treated Tommy to a dinner of chili that evening in their cozy kitchen on the upper floor. Samples of Michael's whites and reds were opened and tasted as the evening progressed. Tommy' observations on each one seemed intelligent and insightful as the three winemakers discussed the finer points and nuances of each wine.

Tommy seemed to fit right in, as if he had been friends for a long time with Michael and Jancy. Along towards 10:00, when everyone had plenty of wine and were liable to express thoughts they might usually be more reticent about, Tommy gave voice to the thoughts he had been turning over in his mind since he had arrived.

"Okay, this may sound crazy," he said, looking at Michael, "But I'm thinking of moving here and starting my own operation. How would you take that? Would you feel I'd just be competition you can't afford?"

Michael, however, surprised him with his response. Leaning forward on the table, he expressed his philosophy about making wine in the Watilla Valley. "We need a critical mass," he began. "We need at least a dozen wineries—all of whom able to make quality wine—before people will take notice of us. We need to become a destination so folks from Portland, Seattle, Spokane, or wherever, will feel like driving here. You can't have just one or two places for them to visit. They need enough wineries that it'll take a day or two. Then they'll feel like it was worth their while."

Jancy vigorously nodded in agreement and added, "But we have to have owners who can make good wine, or at least hire someone who knows how to make good wine. We have to have a reputation for quality."

Tommy took a final sip of the Cab he had been drinking. "Well," he announced, "so far you're making darn good stuff."

"Thanks," Michael replied.

"You know, Michael," Tommy continued, "that's a very generous outlook on life you have. Most people would have the attitude of stay the hell out of here and leave me alone."

Michael vigorously shook his head. "No, we can't think like that," he declared emphatically. "We have to help each other. Anyone who comes here to set up shop. We have to help them. We have to be generous. Only by being supportive of each other, will we all be able to succeed and build a nice little wine industry. Then we'll all prosper."

*   *   *

Michael got out the air mattress once again and put up Tommy in the spare room for the night. The next day he took off to drive over to the Tri Cities for a visit with Dr. Cline.

"I just need to hear for myself," he explained to Michael and Jancy. "My folks will have to support my living expenses for a few years until I start selling wine, so this way I can say I talked to an expert."

Before he left, though, he secured Jancy's verbal agreement that he could lease some of her property that she didn't intend to plant. "You can have up to 40 acres," she informed him.

But Tommy dismissed such a large quantity. "I just need 10, 12, maybe 15 acres," he replied. "I want to be strictly small time, a boutique winery, as they now say. You and Michael can do 5,000 to 6,000 cases a year if you want, but I'll be happy at 3,000."

Tommy also obtained Michael's verbal okay to use The Barn to produce his wine. After he had departed, Michael turned to Jancy and said, "See how this goes? I establish a vineyard and a winery. Then you and Tommy come along and buy grapes from me for the short-term, and rent my facilities and equipment as well. That's extra income for me that'll help keep me afloat."

Jancy understood the concept. "And when Tommy and I get established, we'll be helping out those who come after us."

"Exactly!" Michael exclaimed, glad that she understood. "That's why we must always help each other. We need more vineyards and more production facilities. It's like dominoes falling. One thing leads to another and everyone benefits."

Michael began to benefit when the 1984 harvest started coming in. He selected what he considered to be the best grapes for himself, and then sold the rest to Jancy and Tommy. There really weren't any bad grapes produced from his vineyard, but as the owner he retained the right of first choice.

He reserved 50% of the harvest for himself with Jancy and Tommy splitting the remainder between them. This allowed Michael to keep his wine production more in line with what his sales were, but allowed Jancy and Tommy to make some serious quantities of wine for their labels.

Jancy's label was J Phillips Cellars, a name she had previously decided upon. Tommy came up with Fíona Cellars. "My ancestors were Irish," he explained, "and the Irish root word for wine or grapevine is Fíon, so viola, Fíona Cellars."

"I like it!" Jancy exclaimed, delighted.

"Yeah, I like it, too," Michael admitted. "It's sort of mysterious, like what does Fíona mean, people will ask. And when you tell them, they'll say, hey, that's clever!"

"Well, I hope so," Tommy replied. "At least that's my theory right now."

*   *   *

As they became good friends, the three winemakers came to affectionately refer to themselves as the Three Musketeers, the ones fighting for the winemaking reputation and honor of the Watilla Valley. Michael had his tasting room in the schoolhouse which he finally had declared an historic building. Jancy used the small farmhouse but continued to live with Michael and be his lover. Tommy bought the farmhouse at the end of Dead End Road which he used as both a tasting room and living quarters.

They all lived simply and on restricted budgets. Their favorite pastime was eating dinner together in the schoolhouse, where they enjoyed the wines they each had made as they ate and socialized. During the year, Tommy' California girlfriend came out to live with him but left after several months, the isolation and lack of cultural amenities of southeast Washington not to her liking.

"She didn't think dining at the Pendleton Steakhouse was haute cuisine," he joked, referring to a landmark western steakhouse located an hour's drive south in Pendleton, Oregon.

Also in the fall of 1984 Michael joined the Watilla Chamber of Commerce since he had a little more income now from selling grapes and leasing part of The Barn. The Chamber had been after him to join ever since he had set up his winemaking operation and now he consented.

"We'll put you in the agricultural category," the Chamber rep informed him. "That way, your dues will be at the lowest rate."

Not to be outdone, Jancy also joined. Tommy, however, took a pass, at least for the present. "When I'm making money, then I'll think about it," he declared.

Business continued to be slow in the three tasting rooms as spring 1984 arrived and Jancy and Tommy had a few white wines to sell. Each of the three winemakers would excitedly tell the others when a visitor stopped in who had been referred by one of them. Their goal was to get every single customer to also stop by the other two tasting rooms. Often they succeeded.

In addition to his work, Michael was instrumental in organizing a winemaker's group called the Greater Columbia Valley Winemaking Association, a fancy sounding title for a group of a dozen struggling winemakers. They represented the entire total operations from Yakima over to the Tri Cities, and then over to the Watilla Valley.

Except during crush, as harvest season was known, the group tried to meet once a month. They took comfort from one another's struggles and travails, and shared tips as well as trends in the world of winemaking. Sampling and commenting on each other's wines was an important part of each meeting. It was their best guarantee of quality because they were all very frank in their comments and criticism.

One of monthly rituals at these meetings was carping about *Wine Explorer* magazine and its owner, R.R. Parkston, the internationally famous wine critic.

"He doesn't even know we exist!" was frequently the major complaint. "The only thing he knows is French and Napa wines," was another complaint.

"I've been mentioned several times in *W.E.*" Michael told the group during one of their meetings. "But just little tiny mentions due to some medals I've won at a major competition. Mr. Parkston knows we exist. The question is, does he care?"

Another development during the year was Michael being invited to be a wine judge, and at more than one competition. He was invited to a Napa County judging, and then also to the 2nd annual competition in Seattle. His reports to the Columbia Valley group were on the depressing side.

"At the Napa event," he reported, "some of the judges actually challenged my credentials. How could I know anything about real winemaking, they asked. But, fortunately, there were a couple people who knew of my awards at events like the competition in San Francisco."

"Unbelievable!" one winemaker said, shaking his head.

"Yeah, it's sad," Michael replied. "Some of the folks actually thought we're making fruit wines here in Washington. You know, all the apples and cherries grown here. They asked, how could we grow wine grapes? When I told them this is one of the best places in the world to grow grapes and make wine, they scoffed in disbelief."

"Well, screw them in Napa," Jancy declared with her typical frankness. "I know what pissheads they can be. I used to work there."

But Michael, to everyone's surprise, defended them. "No, in general they're not bad people," he said. "It's just that they're full of themselves because all the wine critics fawn over them. Publications like *Wine Explorer Magazine* focus on Napa when writing about American wine."

"So what the hell can we do to change that?" one of the others asked.

"Just keep plugging away," Michael replied grimly. "Just keep making great wine and entering competitions. The world can't ignore us forever."

Chapter 9

The 1985 Reserve Syrah

Olde Schoolhouse Cellars
1985

The year 1985 proved to be a busy one. Tommy planted his first vines, choosing to limit his vineyard to an initial three acre block due to his limited finances. Jancy, meanwhile, finished her plantings in Three Hills which brought her total to 22 acres. In addition, Michael expanded his School Bridge Vineyard by leasing five acres from Jancy and planting them in various non-French varieties such as Sangiovese, Tempranillo, and Touriga Nacional.

"I'm expanding my portfolio," he explained to the other two. "I'm adding the finest red grapes that represent Italy, Spain, and Portugal."

"Ah, I see a bottle of American Chianti on my dinner table in a few years!' Tommy exclaimed as he joshed his friend.

Michael simply shrugged. "Dr. Cline claims these grape varieties should do well here in addition to all the French ones I've planted," he explained. "So, I'm going to find out one way or the other. If they thrive, then I'm going to challenge myself as a winemaker and see if I can't make some great non-French reds."

Jancy was curious in what Tommy would call his vineyard. "You know," she said to him one day, "just because you don't own the land, there's no reason you can't have your own name."

"Yeah, I've thought about that," he admitted. "If it really doesn't matter to you, then I think I'll call it Mianta which is Gaelic for Aspirations. Sort of like saying Irish Dreams."

"Sounds perfect," she replied. "God knows, we all have aspirations trying to establish ourselves here!"

And so, just south of Watilla, there were three vineyards in a row: School Bridge, Three Hills, and Mianta. In addition, two local farmers had each planted 10 acres of grapes on the north side of town, having decided to experiment for themselves after visiting with Cline and obtaining his guidance.

During the summer the Watilla Chamber of Commerce twice referred individuals to Michael for advice on setting up winemaking operations of their own. "The Columbia River Valley is starting to get some attention," one of the men informed him. "And I'm looking to get out of the rat race in Seattle, so I thought owning a nice little winery somewhere would be a great pastime for my retirement."

Michael answered with the same joke he told to anyone asking him for advice. "You know what they say, if you want to make a small fortune in the wine business, then start with a large one first!"

Although he welcomed the possibility of new operations in the valley, he made sure that the people involved realized exactly what was involved, and the extended time period necessary to eventually succeed.

*   *   *

During the summer Michael brought up a topic with Jancy that had been weighing on his mind for some time. "You know," he began one evening as they sat after dinner sipping wine, "we've been together for a long time now. Do you ever see us getting married?"

Taken by surprise at the question, Jancy simply replied, "Nope."

"I know you've said you'll never get married again, but don't you think this is different?" he asked. "Aren't you and I a different situation?"

Frowning, Jancy asked, "Why are you bringing this up?"

Shifting in his chair, Michael replied, "Well it's just, you know, something we haven't really talked about. I'm 35 now and I'm not married and I don't have kids, so it's just something I thought we should talk about."

Jancy's voice took on a defensive note. "I told you once that I don't want to have children, either. I'm never going off the pill."

Sighing, Michael sought to keep the conversation from becoming an argument. "I know, I know," he conceded. "It's just that sometimes things change over time and I thought we should talk about it again."

Giving him a severe look, Jancy asked, "Are you not happy with us anymore?"

"No! No!" Michael exclaimed, shaking his head. "I love you just as much as ever."

"And the sex is still good?"

Michael nodded his head, "Yes, of course it is."

"Then, if you still love me and the sex is good, that's all that matters," she replied evenly, carefully searching Michael's face.

Sighing again, Michael responded by saying, "With the dream we're both pursuing of building successful businesses, I was thinking that maybe we could also be building a family. Maybe not this year, but sometime."

"Do you want me to move out?" Jancy suddenly asked.

"No!" he protested.

"I can always do that, you know," she continued, a hard edge now to her voice. "If you want to start a family, then I can move out and you can go find a local girl to marry."

Michael held up his hands. "Listen, Jancy, no, I don't want you to move out. I told you, I love you. I want to stay with you."

"Well, you asked me two questions, Michael," she replied. "Do I want to get married and do I want to have kids? The answer is no, and no."

Michael blew out a breath of air, a defeated look on his face. "Okay, okay. I just wanted to bring the subject up. Now we've discussed it and I know where things stand, so I don't have to wonder anymore."

"Don't ever propose to me, either" she warned him. "I'll say no. You can count on it. So please don't hope that I might get sentimental by a surprise proposal."

Michael nodded as he understood that he and Jancy would never get married or start a family. It saddened him but he tried not to be resentful. She was a very attractive woman and a good life partner in all other aspects. Instead of a family, he would keep his life's focus totally on establishing a thriving wine business in the Watilla Valley.

*   *   *

During the fall harvest, Michael decided to make a reserve wine as part of an expanded marketing strategy. If it turned out that the wine was, indeed, superior, then he could make other reserve wines and start a wine club like they were doing down in California. It was a trend he hoped to profit from.

Although the term 'reserve' on the label of an American wine had no meaning, many winemakers really tried to make their reserve wines special. Usually, that meant selecting the best grapes for the wine, hence the term 'reserve.' The best grapes were reserved for a specially produced wine. When bottled and released for sale, the wine would be sold at a higher price point than the rest of the product line.

As Michael considered his vineyard, he thought of the quality of his vines. It seemed that a portion of the Syrah vines in both Blocks A and B produced especially good grapes. But which block to use? He talked it over with Jancy.

"Use them both," she told him. "Ferment them separately and barrel age them separately, then do barrel tasting and figure out a blending ratio." To her it was straightforward. Michael, however, balked.

"I want to use just one lot of grapes, not two different ones," he said.

"Why?" Jancy asked, her face screwed up in puzzlement. "Who cares?"

"I care!" Michael exclaimed. "I want to do a single lot, reserve wine."

She threw up her hands in exasperation. "If it was me, I'd do a blend and not worry about it."

Michael thought about it for a few days, then decided to seek Tommy' advice. The next day he got both him and Jancy together in The Barn. He explained the dilemma to Tommy.

"I agree with Jancy," he informed Michael. "Just use the best grapes you have and don't worry about where they come from."

"See?" Jancy piped up.

The lanky Irishman stroked his chin, turning a thought over in his mind. "You know, Michael," he said, "I've heard of adding a little Petite Sirah to regular Syrah to both increase the depth of color, and to boost the robustness of the wine. You have a couple rows of it, so maybe you can also experiment with tasting how some of that works."

"I can't believe what I'm hearing!" Michael replied, shaking his head. "By the time you two get done with my wine, it'll be some sort of Frankenwine patched together from a little bit of this, a little bit of that!"

Tommy, however, held his ground. "The Feds don't care," he pointed out. "The only thing that matters to them is that you have at least 75% Syrah in a bottle labeled Syrah. The other 25% can be anything else. Hell, you could add apple juice if you wanted!"

Jancy giggled. "Yes! Let's try adding a little apple juice while we're at it!"

Michael shook his head and turned away. "You two are disgusting," he muttered in mock contempt.

As the 1985 harvest proceeded, Michael began to come around to the others' point of view. He selected the best Syrah grapes from both Block A and Block B and fermented them separately. He kept to his standard practice of co-fermenting with 5% Viognier but kept both lots of the wine completely separate.

As he fermented his Petite Sirah, he kept an open mind about what he would use it for. As winter passed and his red wines barrel aged, he and Jancy conducted a series of barrel tastings. Michael valued her sense of taste and smell, suspecting that it was superior to his. Using a long, curved glass wine thief, they would extract a small sample of wine from a barrel and release it into their glasses. They swirled the wine, sniffed it, swirled again, sniffed again, all the time commenting on what they were smelling.

Next, they drained their glasses into their mouths, swishing the wine around for several seconds before spitting it out. After exchanging comments on the taste and finish, they moved on to the next barrel and repeated the process.

By spring Michael and Jancy had conducted two barrel tastings for the reserve wine and decided on a ratio of 60% Block A to 40% Block B. He and she also decided on adding 7% Petite Sirah to the blend, making the 1985 Reserve Syrah 88% Syrah, 7% Petite Sirah, and 5% Viognier.

The final decision to be made was how many barrels should be made. "I think I should do three," Michael commented. "It's going to be higher priced, so it'll sell slower. I don't want to be stuck with a lot of inventory that'll hang around for years."

Jancy disagreed. "I think you should go for four barrels," she said. "The wine is promising to be very good. In fact, I'd say exceptional. If you win a gold medal in Seattle or California, or both, you'll be sorry you didn't make more."

Michael couldn't fault her logic. "True," he simply replied. "Four barrels it is."

The two winemakers racked off enough of the component wines to blend four barrels worth of the Reserve Syrah. "I think I'll also age it for an extra six months beyond what I do for the other reds," he told Jancy.

She merely shrugged. "Suit yourself. It's your reserve wine, not mine, so make it how you want it to be."

*   *   *

The next two years passed by quickly as the three winemakers continued their struggle to earn a living. Tommy managed to plant another four acres of vines, bringing his small vineyard to seven acres. He supplemented his wine production by buying grapes from the two vineyards north of town in order to make enough wine to sell.

Times remained tough but things were slowly looking up. The economy nationwide was humming and Americans were consuming more wine. Traffic at the three tasting rooms increased incrementally year to year.

Michael and Tommy became good friends and worked closely with each other. Jancy, on the other hand, was establishing her own production facility over at her farmhouse. She had paid for a metal pole building to be erected, a concrete floor poured, and a crush pad poured as well. She was slowly buying her own equipment.

Michael didn't mind this since his Barn was pretty crowded and congested with three winemakers all making their own wine. Tommy expressed an interest in perhaps leasing from Jancy instead of Michael since his vineyard was much closer to her new facility than The Barn.

"Go for it," Michael advised him. "If she's reasonable on the costs, then it makes more sense for you to be over there than here. I'll miss working with you, though."

"Ah, hell, I'll always make some wine here," Tommy replied. "Somebody has to supervise you to see that you get it right!"

This was typical of their kidding each other.

In April 1987 Michael entered his '85 Reserve Syrah in the Seattle competition. It blew away the other Syrah entries and, in addition, took a double gold as best red in the Northwest. This reinforced his growing reputation as a top quality producer, but the problem remained that his tasting room was far away from a major population center.

It was true that there were now several other vintners in the valley, all small start-up operations. One had planted a vineyard and the others bought grapes. But yet, there just wasn't enough reason for large numbers of wine enthusiasts to travel to Watilla, Washington.

After the Seattle double gold, Olde Schoolhouse Cellars did experience a small uptick in visitor traffic. Michael got all kinds of people. Some were snobbish, some just wanted a free drink, but most were pretty ignorant of wine. Michael enjoyed talking to the novices and explaining about his wines, how they were made, and the differences in one grape variety from another.

The visitors he liked the least were the know-it-alls who occasionally stopped in. Incredibly, they often lectured him on wines and winemaking. He was always relieved when they left.

One Saturday a stocky, fifty something man with a short, neatly trimmed beard stopped in right as Michael opened the tasting room. He was dressed in a sport coat but no tie. Instead, he wore a solid colored shirt without a collar underneath. Michael knew that this was now a fashionable way for professional men to dress. He pegged the guy for a professor from State.

"Hello! Welcome!" Michael greeted him.

"Good afternoon," the visitor replied cheerfully as he surveyed the tasting room.

"First time here?"

The man turned to look at Michael. "Yes, indeed," he confirmed, then added, "I love this room! I'd say this is really an old schoolhouse."

"Yep," Michael confirmed. "1915."

The visitor nodded approvingly. "A stroke of genius, making it into a tasting room."

After a further minute of small talk, Michael asked the man if he were there to do a tasting. "Yes, of course!"

He gave the visitor a glass and then turned around to retrieve a bottle from the small counter fridge behind him. "This is my estate Chardonnay," he said as he poured a small amount into the visitor's glass.

The man looked down at his glass, then back up at Michael. "Is this all I get?" he asked with a frown.

Since he didn't charge a tasting fee, Michael tended to pour light for visitors. "Ah, here, I'll add a touch more," he said as he added another splash.

The visitor held the glass at an angle for a moment, peering through the wine, noting the clarity and color. Next, he set his glass down on the counter and gave the wine a vigorous swirl. He then immediately raised the glass to his nose and sniffed it. "Ah!" was all he said as he set the glass back down on the bar and swirled it yet again, and then took a second sniff.

After satisfying himself on how the wine smelled, the man drained the sample into his mouth and swished around, frowning and concentrating on what he was tasting. After several seconds, he reached over to the dump container near him, drew it to him and expertly spat out the wine that was in his mouth.

Michael watched in fascination as the visitor next withdrew a small notebook from inside his sport coat, as well as a pen, and began dotting down notes. After a moment, the man looked back up and said, "Okay, we can move on, please."

Michael brought over another bottle and prepared to pour a sample. "This is my dry Viognier," he informed the visitor as he prepared to pour a more generous amount than he had the first time.

The man, however, refused to let him. "Aren't you going to rinse me first?" he protested.

Michael gave him a look of surprise; no one had ever been that fussy before. "Oh, sorry, I don't usually do that."

The visitor gave him a look of incredulity. "How on earth do you ever expect people to properly evaluate your wine if you don't rinse in between?" he demanded.

Michael immediately categorized his visitor as a wine snob. Yep, he was a know-it-all professor, either in state or out of state. He sighed as he took the visitor's glass, poured a small amount in it, swirled the wine around, and tossed the contents into a nearby bar sink. He then re-poured the Viognier.

The visitor carefully evaluated the wine as he had previously with the Chardonnay, taking notes once again. This piqued Michael's curiosity. "I'm sorry, I never introduced myself," he said as he extended his right hand to the man. "I'm Michael Ross."

The visitor shook his hand. "My close friends call me Casey," he replied. "It's just my nickname. Like in Casey Jones, the railroad guy." Then he added, "It's a private joke from my college days."

"Oh," Michael said, thinking to himself what a strange guy this was.

The tasting proceeded as Michael went through several of his wines: Merlot, Cabernet Sauvignon, Bordeaux style blend, and regular Syrah. Casey found the Syrah, in particular, interesting.

"Hmmm, reminds me of a Northern Rhone without the minerality. More fruit-forward, of course, but still, there's that wonderful smokiness and leather, that delicious blend of fruit, all combined with a nice touch of spiciness."

"You're familiar with Rhone wines? Michael asked, now more curious than ever about his visitor.

"I should say so," Casey replied. "I've been there."

"Really! I worked in a winery there for a year," Michael informed him. "In the Côte Rotie."

"Hmmm, that's impressive," Casey acknowledged. "You certainly learned a few things while you were there and made productive use of your time. Tell me, what Domaine did you work at?"

"Garçon," Michael replied. "Domaine Garçon."

Casey nodded. "Yes, that sounds familiar. I believe I stopped in for a visit. Who was the winemaker?"

"Jacques," Michael answered. "Jacques Garçon. He was the grandfather."

Again, Casey nodded. "Yes, I think I remember who you're talking about. I think he may have been the one who gave me a tour of the cellar operation."

Michael instantly had an increased respect for his visitor. "You've met Jacques personally?" he asked in amazement.

Casey nodded. "Yes, if memory serves me correctly. I also remember how impressed I was with the wines."

The two men talked for several minutes about France before moving on to the next wine. Over the course of the next half hour Michael learned that Casey lived in a place called Reston in Northern Virginia just outside D.C. And Casey learned about Michael's growing up in Santa Cruz and working at a winery there for many years.

Finally, Michael introduced the next wine. "This one I'm really proud of," he informed Casey. "This is my '85 Reserve Syrah."

Casey's face lit up. "Ah! The double gold winner in Seattle last month!" he said excitedly. "This is why I really wanted to stop in here on my way to Salt Lake City."

Since Casey was obviously a man of culture and wine knowledge—and perhaps occasionally a wine judge—Michael took his glass and replaced it with a clean one. "I want you to try this with a fresh glass."

Casey nodded approvingly. "Yes, indeed. Thank you."

Michael poured a generous sample and watched Casey go to work. "Gorgeous, deep concentrated color!" he announced as he peered at the wine.

"Yes, the wine is made from my best Syrah grapes, plus there's a bit of Petite Sirah in there as well."

This surprised Casey. "Petite Sirah! That took some courage, I would say. You certainly didn't learn that in the Rhone!"

"No, I didn't," Michael confessed. "That's what nice about working in the States. There are very few legal restrictions on blending and things like that."

Casey simply nodded as he swirled the wine and then sniffed it. "Oh my, what a wonderful nose! Rich tobacco and leather, along with a generous helping of bacon cooking in the skillet."

Michael swelled with pride. This was exactly what he had been trying to accomplish with the concept of a reserve wine. He had put all his winemaking skills to the test in order to craft the best possible wine he was capable of making.

Casey now tasted the wine, swishing it around in his mouth longer than he had any of the previous wines. After spitting it out, he announced, "That is pure magic in a glass, Michael. Lots of plumy notes, along with juicy ripe raspberry and blackberry. Plus, absolutely delightful elements of allspice and pepper. Well-structured tannins. And the finish! The wine just doesn't want to say goodbye!"

Although Michael tried to maintain his composure, he couldn't help grinning. "Thank you! I have the same experience myself every time I try it."

After writing down extensive notes, Casey looked up at Michael and said evenly, "That is an extraordinary wine. Although it's young yet, it's one of the best American wines I've tasted in a long time. Congratulations."

A moment later, Michael served Casey with a sample of his late harvest Viognier which also elicited favorable comments from the visitor. After that Casey placed his order. "I'll take a case with me. Please give me two bottles each of everything I tried except the for the off-dry Viognier. I really don't care for that style of wine."

"I know, I don't either, but it helps pay the bills," Michael explained.

Casey sighed. "Yes, I know. It's unfortunate but that's the way things are. However, I have a theory. I believe that the success of coffee shops such as Starbucks are making Americans aware of nuances of flavor in beverages. And I think that's especially important for young people. I predict that both wine and craft beer will enjoy a renaissance in the coming years."

*   *   *

The next month, June, Michael received a call from a young lady who informed him she was working on a short article for *Wine Explorer Magazine.* "We want to inform our readers of the basics of the budding Columbia Valley wine region," she explained. "I hope you don't mind if I stop by for a brief interview and some photos."

"No, not at all!" Michael happily replied.

He welcomed any publicity about Washington Sate wines, and especially any mention of his own area, the Watilla Valley. Over the next couple minutes he and the caller finalized a date and time for her to stop by.

Two weeks later, in the first week of June, the magazine writer arrived at Olde Schoolhouse Cellars. She was older than Michael had first thought from talking to her over the phone. Perhaps late 30s. Which was good, actually. She would be no novice.

He found out that she had, in fact, been writing for more than 10 years for R.R. Parkston, the publisher and executive editor. And, as he and she talked, he learned that she was quite knowledgeable about wine – both American and European.

The interview lasted a good two hours as they chatted in Michael's tasting room, sipping small samples of his wines all the while. Afterward, he led her on a tour of his vineyard, and then later of The Barn. The lady recorded much of what he said, either by a small tape recorder, or by taking shorthand notes.

In the end, she photographed him in the tasting room, in the vineyard, and in The Barn. She was especially fussy about the photos in the latter. "I want to pose you standing next to an upright barrel, a glass of wine in hand, the bottle on top of the barrel, and a wall of aging barrels in the background.

"Okay, sure," he replied. "I assume you want me to have a red wine?"

The lady immediately answered, "The '85 Reserve Syrah, of course!"

"Alright, let me go get one from my inventory cellar in the schoolhouse. Should I bring the double gold medal as well?"

The writer's reply surprised him. "No, no medal. Just bring a bottle and a glass."

And so Michael posed as the lady wished, a raised glass of the wine in one hand. After the first shot, she admonished him, "Try to smile better, okay? Pretend like you're really happy to be a winemaker and being photographed like a celebrity."

He tried his best, fearing though that he probably was appearing foolish. Relieved when the session ended, he answered a few further questions about other winemakers in the area. "There's Jancy Phillips and Tommy O'Donnell a short ways from here."

"Yes, I'm aware of them," the lady informed him. "Any others?"

Michael told her about five other winemakers who had set up shop in the past couple years. "Three of them are planting vineyards nearby, and the other two are going to operate for the time being just buying their grapes."

Michael also gave her the names and addresses of nearly a dozen other winemakers west of the Tri Cities. When she thanked him and prepared to depart, he asked her, "When will the article appear?"

"Not sure," was the lady's reply. "Soon, I would guess. I'm always working under a tight deadline! So, probably next month. Can't guarantee that, though."

*   *   *

The July issue of *Wine Explorer* contained no mention of Olde Schoolhouse Cellars or any other Washington State winery. Michael, Jancy, and Tommy were disappointed, all three of them having been interviewed, although Michael's interview had been the longest and most extensive by far.

The following month the August issue was a rude letdown. Jancy and Michael looked at it as soon as they received it in the mail. The cover was a breathtakingly beautiful color photo of Napa County vineyard countryside, and the banner headline read: Is Napa Destined To Reign Forever?

Inside, they read the cover story in which R.R. Parkston waxed eloquently about Napa County wine, especially the Cabernet Sauvignon. *"Cab is king in Napa and, indeed, Napa Cab is the best to be found outside of Bordeaux,"* they read in dismay. *"One must ask the question,"* the article continued, *"Is Napa wine destined to reign supreme over the American wine scene for the foreseeable future. Indeed, perhaps forever?"*

Jancy opened her mouth, stuck a finger in it, and pretended to vomit. "What crap!" she announced.

Michael's face colored as he frantically paged through the magazine, finding no trace of any article on him or the Columbia Valley. "Sonofabitch!" he said in a raised voice. "Napa, Napa, Napa! I get so goddamned tired of hearing about that place!"

"Mr. Parkston wouldn't know a Washington Sate wine if it bit him in the ass," Jancy observed in sympathy.

Michael threw the magazine down in disgust. "Fuck R.R. Parkston!" he said bitterly.

"Yeah," Jancy chimed in. "He doesn't know jackshit. If he'd ever take his head out of his ass, then he just might see there's more to the world than French wines or Napa Cabs!"

*   *   *

Although it was late afternoon in Watilla, it was early evening in Reston, Virginia, where Ralph Roger Parkston had just finished a fine dinner during which he had enjoyed his favorite wine: a first growth, left bank Bordeaux. It was one of the most expensive wines in the world, but as a so-called international wine critic, he was the recipient of numerous wines at what he called, 'deep discounts.'

Settling into a recliner in his study, he snipped the end off a Cuban cigar that a good friend had smuggled back from a trip to Bermuda. After lighting it and puffing on it several times, he retrieved a small glass from an end table next to his recliner and sniffed the aromas of a Late Bottled Vintage Port. After sipping it, he smiled in satisfaction. Life didn't get any better than Cuban cigars and fine Port.

If he had been made aware of Michael's distress over the August issue of his magazine, Mr. Parkston would have smiled and uttered one of his favorite sayings: "Thus the fool falls so easily into the trap!"

The fact of the matter was that he had set Michael up. Not only that, he had also set up the entire world of wine. Parkston knew that there was nothing so subjective as wine. Everyone had their own opinion. If you wanted to enliven a dinner party, simply ask what was the best wine. It wouldn't take long for a lively debate to break out.

He also knew that controversy and sensationalism sold newspapers and magazines. And he was certainly capable of stirring up a controversy to increase the popularity of his magazine. After setting up everyone with his little Napa County controversy, he would shortly create an even larger one. Within the month, R. R. Parkston would set off a bomb that would send shock waves through the wine industry around the entire planet.

Chapter 10

One For The Ages

Olde Schoolhouse Cellars
September 1987

Michael would remember for the rest of his life exactly what he was doing when the September issue of Wine Explorer arrived in the mail. He and Jancy had just returned from spending Labor Day weekend in Seattle, one of their favorite haunts. Now they were back at work, walking the rows of Chardonnay in his vineyard, examining the ripening clusters. They carried small, hand-held tubes called refractometers.

Every so often they would select a grape at random and squeeze it until several drops of juice fell onto the open prism at the end of the tube. The clear covering for the prism was flipped down and the opposite end of the tube with its eyepiece was held up to the eye. Pointing the refractometer to the sky to allow natural light to pass through the prism, the user could read a number inside—technically called Brix—which denoted the percent of sugar in the juice.

As Michael and Jancy well knew, Chardonnay was a tricky grape. Harvest it too soon and you wouldn't get the optimum acidity or all the delicious ripe flavors that Chardonnay was famous for. But let the Brix get just a little too high and you ended up with a flat, flabby wine that tasted of over-ripe fruit and was off-putting to discerning wine drinkers. In some years you might have just one or two days to harvest Chardonnay at its peak, thus timing was everything.

At 11:30 Jancy decided to go down to the schoolhouse. "I'll go make us some sandwiches," she told Michael, "so why don't you come down around noon and we can have lunch."

"Okay, sounds good!" he agreed.

After she had departed, he worked his way up the row, pausing from time to time to select another grape from a cluster and read its Brix. Twenty minutes later, he had walked up to the top of the row.

He took a moment to survey the landscape from his high vantage point. Looking south he could see quite a bit of the Watilla River as it ran east to west. His schoolhouse was off to the right, roughly 3/8 of a mile away. He noted that the Rural Route carrier was coming down School Bridge Road.

Michael watched as the carrier's car stopped by his mail box and deposited mail into it. The car drove off and crossed the bridge over the river. Almost immediately, Jancy emerged from the schoolhouse; she must have heard or seen the carrier stop. He continued to watch as she walked out to the road to the mailbox. Even from this distance her golden hair was radiant in the bright sun and he smiled.

And then Michael's life changed forever. Jancy extracted the mail, glanced briefly at it as she turned to walk back to the schoolhouse. Suddenly she began shouting what sounded like, "Oh, my God!" and jumped around, waving something in her hand above her head.

She raced back to the schoolhouse where her battered old Jeep was parked. Michael watched in astonishment as she scrambled up on the hood and began jumping up and down, shouting his name: "Michael! Michael!" while she continued waving whatever it was above her head.

Good Lord, he thought, what on earth was wrong? He shouted back to her that he was coming in, not sure if she heard him or not. Running downhill through the vineyard between two rows of grapes, he arrived a moment later breathing hard. Jancy jumped down from the hood and ran to meet him, holding what looked like a magazine in front of her.

"Michael! Michael!" she cried, "Oh, my God! Look! Look! Number one!"

He stared at the magazine cover, not immediately comprehending. His image, prominently displayed, was smiling back at him.

"My God, Michael!" Jancy cried out again, "you're number one!"

He took the magazine from her and looked the cover over. It displayed the photo where the lady writer had posed him in The Barn back in June. He was holding up a glass of wine, smiling, with the bottle standing nearby on top of an upturned wine barrel.

The banner headline read, **'Our Annual Top 100 Issue.'** Below it, a smaller headline read, **"#1 Olde Schoolhouse Cellars – A Perfect Syrah."** As Michael continued scanning the cover, he read the script next to his photo: *'Michael Ross with his 100 Point Reserve Syrah.'*

"Jesus Almighty!" he exclaimed as he looked up at Jancy. "Please tell me this isn't a dream!"

She grabbed him and kissed him. "One hundred points!" she exclaimed. "A perfect 100!"

Michael opened up the magazine to read further, but Jancy stopped him. "Let's go inside and open up a bottle and enjoy it as we read this together!"she urged.

"Great idea!" he immediately responded, and they both ran inside and up the stairs to the tasting room. At the bar Jancy grabbed a bottle of the '85 Reserve Syrah and used a corkscrew to remove the cork. She quickly poured two glasses.

"I completely forgot that the September issue is always the Top 100 issue," Michael confessed. He slowly shook his head and whispered, "Good God!"

He quickly found the lead article near the front of the magazine. It began with an introduction that provided an overview of the annual list of the best wines in the world – at least in the opinion of R.R. Parkston. *"This year's list is, as always, very impressive and represents truly outstanding wines from around the globe,"* it began before continuing, *"From a pleasant and surprising discovery in the Columbia Valley, to a well-crafted Chateauneuf du Pape, this year's list of the top wines represents the very cream of the crop of the world's best winemakers."*

After reading further, Michael and Jancy turned the page to the list itself. Michael's wine was honored with an entire page, while the opposite page was divided equally between #2 and #3. Succeeding pages were divided into four wines per page.

They began reading Michael's page. A large photo on it showed him in his vineyard while a smaller photo was of a bottle of the '85 Reserve Syrah. The text of the story was a flowing river of praise for Michael, Olde Schoolhouse Cellars, and the Reserve Syrah.

"On only six previous occasions over 17 years of publication have we ever awarded any wine a perfect 100 points," the story began. *"But our evaluation of Olde Schoolhouse Cellars' 1985 Reserve*

Syrah convinced us that it was time once again to bestow such a high and prestigious honor."

"Wow!" Jancy exclaimed. "This is only the seventh time they've ever awarded 100 points!"

It wasn't unusual for *Wine Explorer Magazine*—or other publications, for that matter—to score a wine 90, 91, or 92 points. But wines that scored 95 points or more were fairly rare, and 98 or 99 points were extremely unusual. However, a perfect 100 points was virtually unheard of, and any such wines became legendary and were talked about for decades. The debate in the world of wine regarding the validity of the 100 point system was beside the point for Michael on this day. He hadn't realized it yet, but he had instantly become a legend.

He and Jancy continued reading Parkston's description of the Reserve Syrah. *"Michael Ross, winemaker and owner, has utilized his training in the Côte Rotie to craft a stunning American Syrah, one that simply takes your breath away."*

"The nose is everything—absolutely everything—that one could ask for in a perfect Syrah: intoxicating aromas of tobacco, freshly cooked bacon, and rich leather, mixed with wonderful hints of allspice, cloves and sassy pepper.

The palate confirms the nose and adds a delicious pluminess underlain by a foundation of ripe berries, cassis, and a pepperiness that sparkles in the mouth. The tannins are well-structured, thus creating the perfect balance and backbone for a wine that is so enjoyable now with dinner, but will lay down for a decade or more before reaching its full potential."

As if all this isn't enough, the wine yields even more with a finish that lingers, reluctant to ever say farewell. This Syrah is truly one for the ages and shows the startling potential of the Columbia River Valley to produce world-class wine."

Michael could only shake his head in near disbelief. "I knew it was good," he chuckled, "but not this good!"

All thoughts of lunch had evaporated as he and Jancy discovered an article on the Watilla Valley wine business further on in the magazine. It had been written by the lady who had visited and interviewed them in late spring and was titled, *The Columbia Valley Begins To Shine.*

Olde Schoolhouse Cellars was the lead in the story, but Jancy's J Phillips Cellars and Tommy' Fiona Cellars were also featured, as well as roughly a dozen wineries west of the Tri Cities.

After reading the article, Michael suddenly had a question. "What does R.R. Parkston look like?"

Jancy frowned a moment, then brightened up. "Look in front of the magazine," she suggested. "There's usually a note from the editor."

He flipped to the initial pages of the magazine and, sure enough, there was a *Letter from the Editor*, along with a small photo that revealed a head shot of Parkston. As Michael stared at the photo, he suddenly exclaimed, "That's him! That's the guy who was in my tasting room last spring!"

Jancy found it strange that he wouldn't have recognized Parkston's name. "He didn't use his real name," Michael replied defensively. "He introduced himself as someone else. Let's see…oh yeah, Casey. He said he was Casey, like in Casey Jones the railroad legend. Said it was some sort of private joke."

Jancy immediately made the connection. "His initials," she pointed out. "R.R. His initials are the same as for the word railroad."

Now it made sense. Ralph Rogers Parkston had visited Michael's tasting room in person and he hadn't realized it. "I never met the guy before, so how was I to know?" he protested.

As she poured herself a second glass of the now famous Reserve Syrah, Jancy made another connection. "I think Parkston had become intrigued by the results of the Seattle competition," she offered. "After all, he needs to keep on top of what's happening in the world of wine. So, he stops in your tasting room, is very impressed with your wines, and decides to delve deeper into what's happening here in the Columbia Valley. He sends one of his writers here to do a story because when he got back home he decided to score your wine really high. He knew he needed background material due to the fact that few of his readers would know anything about Washington State wine."

Michael also poured himself a second glass of wine and pondered Jancy's observations. "Hmm, I think you're right," he agreed. Then he chuckled, "Folks will sure know now that we exist!"

He and she clinked their glasses together and took sips of the wine. Jancy's intense blue eyes were dancing and sparkling as she looked at

Michael over the rim of her glass. "My lover has become famous," she said, smiling.

They kissed again, and then again. Michael saw the classic, coy smile on full display on Jancy's face that she exhibited every time she was in the mood to make love. He set his glass aside and then took hers and put it aside as well. Drawing her to him, he wrapped her up in his arms as they began kissing nonstop.

Moments later they had run upstairs to their private quarters where they stripped down in the bedroom and began making love with a fierce intensity. Charged up with excitement from the magazine articles, and put into a special mood by the wine, it was as if they were making love for the first time, their passion for each other urgently needing to be satisfied.

They explored each other's bodies, running their hands all over each other, Jancy moaning and emitting small gasps as Michael brought her to her first climax. They continued kissing and caressing each other, and then moments later they both climaxed together.

Resting briefly, Michael lay on top of her, carefully supporting his weight as he stared into the liquid blue pools of her eyes, his nose nuzzling hers. "I love you," he whispered, as he always did during such moments. And, as she always did, Jancy smiled and whispered back, "I know," the closest she would ever come to saying "I love you, too."

*   *   *

They would have had a second round of lovemaking but the downstairs phone rang. "Let it ring," Michael said as he nuzzled Jancy's nose again. "That's what we have an answering machine for."

Jancy closed her eyes and savored Michael kissing her breasts. As he did so, the answering machine picked up. But before they could begin again, the phone rang a second time. Now Michael was concerned.

"Someone's trying hard to get hold of us," he observed, assuming the caller was the same person who had just called the first time.

The answering machine picked up again and they waited until it clicked off. Silence filled the schoolhouse again for a moment and Michael smiled. "Okay, now where were we?"

The phone, however, suddenly rang again. "Damnit!" he exclaimed irritably as he rolled off Jancy. "I suppose I should see what the hell's going on. Hope it's just my folks trying to get hold of me and not some sort of bad news."

He got out of bed and padded over to the closet where he pulled out a bathrobe and put it on. Jancy did the same and followed him downstairs to the tasting room. Michael walked around behind the bar and picked up the phone.

"Olde Schoolhouse Cellars," he answered.

The caller identified himself as a man from Seattle. "How much are you selling your '85 Reserve Syrah for?" he asked.

Taking a plunge, Michael told him, "$24.95." To him, the price was a bit outrageous. His next most expensive wine was $19.99. But that was the point of having a reserve wine. He wanted to see if he could sell it at a nice profit margin.

The caller, though, seemed doubtful. "You're talking about the 100 point Syrah that's featured in this month's issue of *Wine Explorer's Top 100*?" he asked.

"Yes, that's correct," Michael replied.

"Okay, I'll take 10 cases then. Put them aside for me and I'll be there in the morning."

Stunned, Michael managed to say, "This is Tuesday. We're only open Fridays through Sundays."

"Alright, make that 20 cases. Now will you open for me tomorrow?" the man demanded.

Michael was taken completely aback. The sale would amount to nearly $500 after taking into account the 20% case discount. His previous record single sale amount had been a little under $100 .

"Uh, yeah, I guess so," he managed to stammer.

"Good!" the caller replied. "I'll be there by noon. Name's Caldell. Jim Caldell."

Michael thanked him and hung up. The phone immediately rang again. Michael answered it and found himself talking to a guy from Portland. He wanted five cases. When Michael told Jancy about the calls, she suggested he open up the tasting room the next day to the public."

"I think you're going to get a lot of visitors," she predicted.

The phone rang yet again. When Michael answered it, the operator was on the line asking him if he would accept a collect call from New York City. "Hell, no!" he answered and abruptly hung up, irritated. "This is nuts!" he exclaimed.

Jancy gently squeezed his arm. "This is nation-wide, Michael," she concluded in awe. "Think about it. The magazine has a subscriber base that's nation-wide. There are even a couple foreign editions: England and France."

He ran his hand through his hair, trying to think. "God, I need to figure this out!"

Michael changed the recording on the answering machine to let callers know that, for the present, the tasting room would be open daily from noon to 5:00 p.m. He also informed callers that he was located five miles south of Watilla on School Bridge Road.

He and Jancy then went upstairs to get dressed. As they did so, the private phone rang in their kitchen. Michael rolled his eyes and shook his head in disbelief before answering it.

"Hello?"

It was Tommy. "Hey!" he said excitedly, "Have you guys see this month's *Wine Explorer*?"

"Yeah, we were just looking at it," Michael replied. "Quite a shock, isn't it?"

"Congratulations, buddy!" his friend exclaimed enthusiastically. "You hit the jackpot!"

The two friends talked for a couple minutes as Michael told Tommy about the deluge of calls coming in. "Can you believe the phone in the tasting room is ringing nonstop?"

"I think all hell is going to break loose," his friend predicted. "You better get ready for it because I think a tidal wave is headed your way."

*   *   *

That evening they had dinner in their kitchen with Tommy after Michael invited him over for what he called a strategy session. He and Jancy had splurged from their near empty bank account and had bought steaks at a local grocery in Watilla. A bottle of the now famous Reserve Syrah was opened to go with the steaks.

"Listen, Michael," Tommy said as they were eating, "people go nuts over wines that score really high. And they'll go into a feeding frenzy for a 100 point wine."

Jancy shook her head. "Wine scores shouldn't mean much," she protested. "Wine is so subjective. One person's opinion isn't really valid."

"Valid or not," Tommy replied, "the reality is that the 100 point system is driving wine sales now. And you've been suddenly caught up in it."

Turning to Michael, Tommy warned, "You're going to be mobbed starting tomorrow. I predict people will be desperate to buy the Reserve Syrah. You should think about its price and how much will go into the library."

He was referring to a winery's library of past production. Most winemakers held back a number of cases in order to taste the wine as the years went by to see how it developed and whether it held together or fell apart.

"The price is $24.95," Michael informed his friend.

"Make it more, a lot more," Tommy immediately replied. Then he gave his friend some sage advice. "You'll probably never have this opportunity again for the rest of your life. You need to take maximum advantage of it."

Michael shifted uncomfortably in his chair and glanced at Jancy. "Okay, I'll think about increasing the price."

"And the library?" Tommy pressed.

"What do you think?"

"A dozen cases, at least."

"Jesus!" Michael exclaimed. "Are you serious?"

"Yep," Tommy confirmed. "You've got one of the rarest wines on earth right now. Believe me, you'll want to keep a nice amount in storage, both for reference to compare with future vintages and to just enjoy once in awhile."

Michael ran a hand through his hair and blew out a breath of air. "Oh, man, I don't know."

Jancy reached over and squeezed his hand. "You need to keep a decent amount. Tommy's right."

After several seconds of silence, Michael suddenly informed the other two, "I know one thing for certain. Each of you is getting a case."

Tommy, however, immediately disagreed. "No way, man, no way!" he protested. "That's being way too generous."

"You and Jancy gave me advice that made the wine what it is," Michael pointed out. "So I'm offering you each a case, gratis. I've made the offer. Walk away from it if you want; it's up to you."

Jancy intervened to offer an amenable solution. "Take the case," she urged Tommy. "You were the one who suggested using some Petite Sirah, so you're partly responsible for Michael's success. Besides, he and I can share. We can sample the wine year to year from whatever we put away in the library."

Tommy gave in and consented to receiving a free case of what would undoubtedly be one of the most sought after wines in the entire world – at least until next year's Top 100 list came out. And so, the three friends spent until midnight sipping wine and excitedly chatting about the day's momentous development and what it might mean for their future.

*   *   *

Early the next morning Michael made several calls. The first was to Jorge to ask him if he could come up with a couple women to help out in the tasting room for the foreseeable future. "I just need them to retrieve wine and put it in boxes for customers," he explained. "Plus, it would be ideal if one of them knew how to operate a cash register and make change."

Jorge assured him he knew of two suitable ladies who could be out at the tasting room by noon. "Make that 10:00, okay?" Michael asked. "It's not even 8:30 yet and I've got five cars out front waiting for me to open. I think today I'll open the doors early."

Another call went to Jonas. The CPA was flabbergasted at the news as Michael explained the situation. "That's tremendous!" the accountant exclaimed. "Congratulations!"

"Thanks, but I have a question for you," Michael told him. "How the heck much should I charge for the wine?"

Jonas didn't hesitate in his answer. "Don't increase it by a lot," he warned. "There are laws against gouging the public, so you'll have to be careful."

"Okay, that's good to know," Michael replied. "My posted price right now is $24.95. Can I increase that at all?"

"Yes, of course you can increase your price," Jonas responded. "That's always a prerogative of a business owner. But you have to be careful how you do it. If you do a price increase, make sure that it's across the board. You can use a percentage if you want, but you'll be on firm ground if your entire product line has a price increase."

"Okay."

The accountant continued. "I suggest you determine how much you want to charge for the Reserve Syrah and then increase all your other products by the same percentage."

"Alright, gotcha, "Michael acknowledged. "Thanks for the advice."

"And, Michael?"

"Yeah?"

"Here's some advice that I urge you to follow: Don't accept checks, especially from anyone out of town. You'll end up being sorry if you do. Just cash and credit card, okay?"

"Alright, we'll see. Thanks for the advice!"

"No trouble at all," Jonas said. "Now go out there and make a ton of money. I'm looking forward to doing your books at the end of this month."

The last call Michael made was to Tommy. "I'm opening at 10:00," he warned his friend. "And Jancy will be at her tasting room by then as well. I'm going to recommend to every single customer who comes today that they also stop in at her place and your place. I want us all to make money off this craziness."

"Okay, thanks!"

After that, Michael had one final decision to make – how much to limit each customer. "Exactly how many cases do you have?" Jancy asked.

"I bottled 90 complete cases," he answered. "There are 86 left plus one partial case." Then Michael suddenly corrected himself. "No wait, 85 cases. Tommy took one."

She thought for a moment before asking, "And have you made up your mind about the library?"

He shrugged. "Three cases, I guess."

Jancy nodded. "If you get the traffic you're expecting, then I would limit purchases to 3 bottles per customer."

"Wow! Only three?"

"You'll be better off selling to a bunch of customers than to just a handful," she advised him. "I wouldn't be surprised if someone showed up offering to buy all 85 cases. But you want your name out there in the world, so lots of small sales will ensure that people all over the Northwest, and the west coast, will see your label."

Michael nodded as he thought about it. It made sense but there was one problem. "What about the guy in Seattle who wants three cases? Seems like I sort of agreed to that when I talked to him on the phone yesterday."

"Tough shit for him," Jancy replied in her typically earthy, no-nonsense manner. "Tell him it's three bottles or nothing. If he doesn't like it, tell him he can kiss your ass."

Michael chuckled. "You'd really say that, wouldn't you?"

"Damn right I would!" she retorted, her blue eyes blazing. "It's your wine, your business. You make the rules."

"Okay, okay," Michael replied, seeking to calm her down. "I'll see how it goes."

He kissed her good-bye and she left to drive over to her tasting room in the farmhouse she had bought and remodeled. Meanwhile, he spent the next hour stocking the shelves behind the tasting bar quickly going over things with the two women who showed up shortly before 10:00. One was Luis's wife and the other was a daughter of another amigo who had graduated from high school and worked evenings at the supermarket in town working a cash register.

By 10:00 there were more than 20 cars parked in front of the schoolhouse, both in the small parking lot and out along School Bridge Road. Michael opened the doors and welcomed everyone inside.

The tasting room quickly filled up and he was forced to alter his normal procedure. Instead of tasting through his product line, he offered only three wines. If anyone wanted to taste any others, he would comply. But he wouldn't open any of the Reserve Syrah. It had been a tough decision that he had struggled with it. But, damnit, if

R.R. Parkston had declared it a perfect 100 point wine, then there was no need to have folks taste it and waste precious wine.

No one much complained; they were there for one reason only and that was to get their hands on his Reserve Syrah. He sold it for $29.95 per bottle, a price he never would have dreamed he could sell a wine for in 1987.

He did concede a 20% discount if customers put together a mixed case, but that didn't seem to matter. They wanted his 100 point wine and that was about it. The rest of the product line didn't really matter. After a couple hours, though, he got a little smarter and pointed out that his regular Syrah was from the same vineyard.

"If you want another wine that's from the same exact vineyard," he would declare, "then you should buy the regular Syrah, or Cab, or Merlot. That way, you can brag to your friends you've got wines from the same vineyard that the #1 wine in the world came from."

That tactic immediately sparked sales of his other wines as people anxiously wanted anything associated with the wine that topped *Wine Explorer's* list. The only glitch during the day was the guy from Seattle who thought he was going to get three cases, not three bottles.

He and Michael got into a heated argument about it which came to a head when Michael said, "Listen, I got a ton of phone calls yesterday. I can't remember what I said to who, but there's a mob of people here today and I want everyone to have a chance to buy some of the wine."

"Goddamnit, you promised me three cases!" the guy replied heatedly. "I'll sue you if you don't fulfill your promise!"

The more the man argued, the more stubborn Michael became. "By the time you sue me, there won't be a single bottle of the wine left," he pointed out. "Then you won't have any."

In the end, he and the man finally reached a compromise in which he relented and sold the guy three mixed cases, each case containing three bottles of the Reserve Syrah. Although the customer didn't like it one bit, he accepted it as the best deal he could make.

Michael watched in amazement as the guy pulled out a wad of $100 bills and peeled off five of them. He made change and helped carry the cases out to the customer's car. When it had driven off, Michael though, good riddance!

By the end of the day, he was exhausted. He hadn't had a break all day, nor lunch either. But the craziness finally ended by 6:00 and he was finally able to shut and lock the doors.

Chapter 11

Ronni

Olde Schoolhouse Cellars
Autumn 1987

The three months between the world learning of Michael's perfect 100 point wine and the annual meeting of the Watilla Chamber of Commerce were heady ones for him. His tasting room was flooded each and every day with people from all over the world. Although most visitors were Americans, he did have people visit from France, England, Italy, and Spain, as well as from down under – Australia and New Zealand.

Absolutely everyone was anxious—even desperate— to purchased his '85 Reserve Syrah. Unfortunately, he quickly sold out. By the end of September it was gone. He had initially resolved to save three cases for his library, but that had turned into two, and then, reluctantly, he sold more until he had only a single case left. Even then, he agreed to sell six more bottles to an assortment of wine columnists from major U.S. newspapers who stopped in to interview him and obtain a bottle of his fabled wine.

In the end, he cut off sales while he still had four bottles left, having decided he would save them for himself to enjoy on extremely special occasions in the future. In the meantime he continued selling his inventory of other wines at a brisk pace until he had virtually sold out of everything he had ever made. Jonas, of course, was ecstatic at the revenue that was rolling in.

Less enthused, however, were his friends Jancy and Tommy. Although they were profiting from Michael's fame, not every one of his customers had bothered to visit their tasting rooms.

"They only wanted to get their hands on your 100 point wine," Jancy bitterly observed. "It didn't matter that R.R. Parkston had rated my Bordeaux blend 93 points."

Tommy confirmed Jancy's experience, but remained upbeat. "I just have to think that people are now aware of who we are and over the next several years they'll be visiting and exploring our area," he told the other two after that first week of craziness.

Michael agreed. He was confident that the Watilla Valley was now on the map, so to speak. More and more people would visit as time went by. Just as critical, more winemakers would set up shop in the area now that the wine industry knew world-class wine could be made here.

Despite Michael's overnight success, he had a problem that was proving tough to deal with, and that problem was Jancy. For some reason she had changed and he found it disconcerting. They had been together so long now that he easily detected her new moodiness. She was irritable most days and pretty much uncommunicative.

He tried to talk to her about it, but she just snapped at him and put him off. Was she jealous of his success? He could easily envision that. Or, more ominously, was she seeing someone else? But then, one day in late October, another possibility presented itself – that she was sick with something.

"Are you feeling okay?" he asked her at breakfast one morning.

Surprised at his question, Jancy answered, "Yes, I'm fine. Why?"

Michael shrugged. "I was just wondering. You haven't been yourself lately and I thought yesterday morning I heard you sick in the bathroom."

"Well, you heard wrong," she replied tersely. "There's nothing wrong with me."

"Well, okay, I was just wondering."

And that was that. Jancy remained moody and uncharacteristically uncommunicative. He knew something was clearly bothering her and it was beginning to tick him off. They had been a couple for a number of years and he thought they should be able to talk about anything.

*   *   *

After Michael's stunning overnight success, the city of Watilla suddenly discovered they had a small but thriving wine industry in their midst and that it had attracted national attention. Several weeks after *Wine Explorer's* Top 100 list had come out, the Chamber of Commerce decided there was no better candidate for their Business Person of the Year honor than Michael Ross of Olde Schoolhouse Cellars.

When he took the call, the Chamber president himself gave Michael the news. "As you're aware because you're a Chamber member, our annual meeting is always the first Saturday evening of December," he related.

"Yeah," Michael confirmed. "I was at it last year. It's sort of an annual review of the business climate in Watilla wrapped up inside a Christmas party."

"If you recall, we also honor one of our members who's had notably success the past year," the president continued. "And this year we can't think of a better business person to honor than you."

Pleasantly surprised, Michael could only think to say, "Well, thank you! This is a nice surprise."

"I hope you don't have any conflicts with the date," the president replied. "We like to have our honoree in attendance to accept the plague we have made up, and also give a little speech. You know, telling us about your business. Stuff like that."

"I'm not much of a speaker," Michael confessed.

"Not to worry," the president assured him. "Just a few words is all. No need for anything more than a minute or two if you want."

Michael replied that that sounded okay, so he and the president wrapped up their conversation. Afterward, he smiled and shook his head. When it rained, it poured as the old saying went. First the magazine, then all sorts of wine columnists stopping by to interview him and write stories for major newspapers across the country, and now the Chamber honoring him.

That wasn't all, however. Down in California, it was as if an earthquake had hit and had sent shock waves ripping through the wine industry there. Michael found himself invited to give a talk to a group of leading winemakers who were interested in promoting Rhone varietals.

"Oh my God!" he reported excitedly to Jancy after he had returned from his trip. "I can't believe I met guys like Joseph Phelps and Fred Cline! Oh, and John McCready of Sierra Vista, was there, too. He's really excited about Rhone grapes in the Sierra foothills area. They're all interested in making the public aware of Syrah, Viognier, and all the other Rhone grapes."

Jancy, however, didn't seem very impressed. "That's nice," was all she commented.

That got Michael steamed. Now he knew it was professional jealousy that was eating at her. She had turned down the opportunity to accompany him on the trip—she was from California, for Pete's sake!—and that had really surprised him. It was obvious that she couldn't take all the attention being heaped on him.

*   *   *

It was no surprise to Michael that Jancy refused to accompany him to the Chamber's annual meeting. "I don't care for those dress-up parties," she simply said. "I'd just be out of place."

Michael had learned there was no debating or arguing with her. She was a woman who simply decided what she wanted or didn't want, and then acted accordingly.

The gala affair was held in the once glorious ballroom of the historic but ailing Watilla Hotel. The peeling paint on the walls and water stains on the ceiling were mostly hidden, however, by all the festive holiday decorations adorning the room.

As soon as Michael arrived—decked out in a rented tux— businesspeople began pumping his hand and congratulating him. Many of them had stopped in his tasting room back in September to purchase a bottle of his 100 point wine.

There was a cash bar set up, but Michael was informed it was gratis for him. "Get whatever you want," he was told. "It's on the house for our guest of honor!"

He ordered a cocktail and began sipping it. All sorts of people wanted to talk to him, to get his opinion on wine, and to solicit business from him. He disliked this aspect of the annual meeting, especially the insurance agents who were always trying to invite him to lunch to discuss his "business insurance needs."

One person, however, caught his attention: An attractive, single young lady by the name of Roxanne came over and introduced herself. "My friends call me Ronni," she informed Michael as she gave him a sweet smile.

Ronni was quite something; in fact, pretty much the opposite of Jancy. While Jancy was blonde, Ronni had raven black hair. Instead of deep blue eyes, Ronni had enchanting dark ones. Jancy never wore makeup; Ronni was tastefully made up, her eyeliner in particular caught his attention.

Jancy would never wear an evening gown; Ronni had on a sleek, black gown slit way up on one side to reveal a shapely leg. She wore heels as well; Michael doubted Jancy had ever owned a pair. Ronni had on an intoxicating perfume; Jancy rarely used any. And where Jancy was on the petite side in the breast department, Ronni was very well endowed, as was evident by her eye-popping cleavage on display due to a plunging neckline.

"I seem to be empty," Ronni pointed out, holding up her cocktail glass. "Buy a girl a drink?" she asked, raising her eyebrows.

"Sure, no problem," Michael immediately replied. "What are you having?"

"Seven and 7," she replied, and he got her glass refilled a minute later.

"So, you're pretty famous," she remarked to him after taking a sip of her new drink.

"Yeah, I'm sort of like a rock star in the wine industry," he bragged. It was a phrase that he had taken a liking to recently as more invitations had come in asking him to speak to this or that winemaker's group in this or that part of the country.

Flashing her eyes and smiling, Ronni pointed out, "And here you are having a cocktail!"

"Um, yeah, I'm having a Cosmopolitan," he admitted, somewhat sheepishly. "Change of pace from always having wine."

Ronni was immediately interested in his drink. "Oh, can I try a sip?" she asked, batting her long eyelashes as her eyes engaged his.

"Uh, sure," he readily agreed, giving her his glass. He watched as she raised it to her lips and took a sip while her eyes stared at him over the rim of the glass.

"Yum! That's good!" she exclaimed, handing him the glass back. Her red lipstick had left very obvious print marks of her lips on the glass.

They chatted for a couple minutes as Michael fought a losing battle of trying not to glance at the inviting cleavage right in front of him. He quickly finished off his drink, suddenly realizing that this lady was interested in him.

"Oh, baby, you need a refill!" she immediately declared. "Be a dear and get me a Cosmo, too."

Michael complied and he and she spent the next twenty minutes in deep conversation as they each finished off a couple more drinks. As the liquor began taking effect, Michael became more voluble and animated as he answered Ronni's questions about his winery and winemaking operation. At one point she asked, "Do you ever give private tours?"

"Uh, yeah, sometimes," he admitted.

"Oh, goody!" she exclaimed in glee. "Can you give me one? Maybe one day next week? I'd be so excited if a famous winemaker like you would give me a personal tour!"

Shifting his weight, he agreed. "Sure, I can check and let you know what day would be best." He knew it would have to be a day that Jancy wouldn't be around . If Jancy ever caught sight of Ronni…well, there certainly would be hell to pay.

Ronni set her glass down on the bar and asked the bartender for a pen. Taking a bar napkin, she wrote down her telephone number. "Give me a call, baby," she said as she smiled and handed him her number.

*   *   *

When it came time for dinner to be served, Ronni made sure she was seated next to Michael at a table near the front of the room. As they ate, he and she kept up an animated conversation. Michael was especially pleased that all the wines served to the guests in the ballroom were from Olde Schoolhouse Cellars.

Ronni was effusive in her praise of the glass of dry Viognier she had with her appetizer and salad courses. Later, she complimented him on the Cabernet she enjoyed with her steak.

"You have to be the absolute best winemaker ever!' she exclaimed at one point.

Feeling very mellow at this point, Michael replied, "Well, you do have to be pretty darn good to make a 100 point wine. Only a handful of people anywhere in the world have ever done that."

It felt so self-satisfying to him to be able to make those kinds of statements. And the more he drank, the more he enjoyed bragging. Whether or not the other guests at the table found him smug, or even worse, he couldn't recall later. Between the alcohol and Ronni's deep cleavage, he paid virtually no attention to anything or anyone else.

While dessert was being served, the Chamber president walked over to the podium on a small stage at the front of the room and began the meeting. After several routine reports on Chamber activities during the preceding year, the time arrived to honor Michael.

"Ladies and gentleman," he began, "it's time for us to recognize our Business Person of the Year." Ronni placed a hand on one of Michael's thighs and squeezed it as she smiled at him and winked.

"Chamber members and guests," the president continued, "this past year has seen an extraordinary development and honor bestowed on one of our members by an internationally acclaimed magazine. Mr. Michael Ross of Olde Schoolhouse Cellars came here in 1975 and saw virtually unlimited potential in the Watilla Valley to become a world-class wine region. With little financial resources, but tons of optimism, he planted the first vineyard in this area the following year."

The man was just relating information that Michael had provided him at a lunch they had had the previous week, but it was nevertheless music to his ears.

"Michael began making wine and worked diligently year after year," the president continued, "crafting unique and extraordinary wines that began winning major awards at prestigious competitions. In 1985 he crafted a legendary wine, described by *Wine Explorer Magazine* as 'truly one for the ages.' Earlier this year, the magazine awarded it a perfect 100 points, only the seventh time in its publishing history that it has done so."

The man held up a copy of the magazine for all the room to see. Ronni kept squeezing Michael's thigh in excitement, constantly flashing him a big smile. Clearly, she enjoyed being next to him, basking in his reflected glory.

Lowering the magazine back down, the president wrapped up his speech. "Ladies and gentlemen, it is truly extraordinary to honor a man who has single-handedly started a brand new industry in our region. Please help me welcome Michael Ross to the podium."

Michael stood and walked the short distance to the stage while the room erupted in applause as everyone stood up and clapped. He shook the beaming president's hand, then accepted a plague as a photographer snapped a photo.

When the president turned to leave the podium, Michael found himself facing the roomful of people who were reseating themselves. He had thought out beforehand some comments to make, but now he was tipsy and his mind a little foggy.

He managed to thank the Chamber, and then quickly added his appreciation for all the folks who had stopped by over the years and bought his wine. He told them his old joke about a small fortune/large fortune. After a moment of chuckles throughout the room, Michael began warming up to his audience.

"The comments by our Chamber president about this area becoming a wine region are true," he informed the crowd. "By my count, we currently have five vineyards with a combined area of approximately 80 acres and eight winemaking operations. Believe it or not, I expect over the next decade that these numbers will rapidly increase."

Michael paused a second for effect before continuing. "In fact, I wouldn't be surprised if ten years from now we have two dozen or more winemaking operations, as well as a couple hundred acres of vines. That would make an industry producing roughly 50,000 cases of wine each year."

Michael saw the looks of surprise and disbelief on many of the faces at the tables. He wrapped up by giving the audience a mild warning. "Mark my word," he advised them, "what we have today is only the beginning of a small tidal wave that's coming. The Chamber and the town should work diligently to foster and encourage the growth of this new industry."

With that, Michael relinquished the podium to the president, stepped off the stage, and walked back to his table as the room again applauded him. As he sat down, Ronni squeezed his arm and whispered, "Great speech!"

*   *   *

After a few more business items, including the installation of incoming officers, the Chamber president adjourned the meeting. Minutes later a band began playing as folks refilled their drinks, socialized, and danced.

Michael got a couple of new cocktails for he and Ronni, and she hung around while a number of people congratulated Michael and chatted with him briefly. After a while, though, Ronni was anxious to dance, so he escorted her to the dance floor.

After a couple of swing numbers during which he enjoyed dancing with her, the band switched tempo and began a slow dance song, much to Ronni's delight. She hung onto him tightly, and he found himself enjoying the feeling of her large breasts pressing against his chest.

"Hmm, I could do this all evening," she murmured in his ear.

"Yeah, this feels good," he whispered back.

And she did feel good. After five years of living with Jancy, it was almost strange to find himself enjoying the company of another woman. Ronni must have felt the same way because after the dance ended she took his hand to lead him away.

"Here, come with me," she said as she lead him over to the exit doors of the ballroom.

"Where are we going?" he asked, puzzled.

"Somewhere private," she answered.

Out in the grand foyer, Ronni lead Michael off to the right and around a corner. After a short walk down a side hall, they arrived at a small side alcove with a couple chairs and a coffee table.

They were alone now, the only sounds were muffled notes of music drifting by them from back in the ballroom.

"This is a smoking alcove," she explained. "A place where two or three people could gather to smoke and talk when they wanted to be alone."

"Well, we're certainly alone," Michael observed.

Ronni stepped up to him and he just naturally took her into his arms. He pulled her tight to him and held her. He suddenly found himself kissing her, and there was no doubt about how she felt. Ronni eagerly kissed him back and, after a moment, ran a hand around to the back of his head and pulled his face down to her cleavage. Michael kissed the inviting flesh of her breasts.

"God, yes!" Ronni moaned.

A moment later they were passionately kissing, oblivious to anything else. After a minute, Ronni broke off the kissing. "We need to get a room!" she murmured as she stared up at him.

Blowing out a breath of air, Michael slowly shook his head. "I don't know," he replied softly. "I've had a lot to drink."

Ronni ran a hand down to his private area. "Isn't everything working tonight?" she teased him.

"As far as I know," he replied. "But it's late and as much as I've enjoyed being with you, I should be going."

Pouting, Ronni asked, "Do we still have a date for that private tour you promised?"

"You bet," he assured her. "I'll give you a call in a couple days."

*   *   *

Michael was fairly certain later that he was legally drunk when he left the hotel. He made it out of town okay, however, and then down the five mile deserted stretch of School Bridge Road to his schoolhouse home.

Nearly midnight, he tried hard to quietly make his way up two flights of stairs to the upper floor residence. In the bathroom he undressed from his formal clothes and left them in a pile in a corner. Good thing Jancy wouldn't have to wash them; she would undoubtedly smell perfume on them.

Just to be on the safe side, he showered to get rid of any further traces of Ronni's perfume on him before sliding into bed beside Jancy. She stirred slightly and murmured, "You've sure been making a racket!"

He slept in the next day, finally getting up around ten with a hangover. Later on in the day Jancy told him, "I have a doctor's appointment next Saturday in the Tri Cities. Any problem with that?"

"No, I don't think there's anything going on to interfere," Michael answered before asking, "Why do you need to see a doctor?"

"Just a routine female exam," she replied.

Her answer seemed a bit odd, so he followed up with another question. "Why not see someone local instead of driving all the way over there?"

"Because I rather see a woman doctor," she immediately explained.

Well, okay, that made sense, Michael thought, so he didn't think anything further about it. But when Jancy left a few minutes later to run over to her winemaking building, Michael took the opportunity to call Ronni.

He left a message when she didn't answer. "Hi, this is Michael," he began. "Listen, this coming Saturday would be a great time for you to come over for a tour. Say about 10:00?"

He suddenly realized that it would make an awkward conversation if Ronni called back when Jancy was home, so he added, "And there's no need to call back unless you can't make it. Thanks. Bye."

It was sort of the truth and sort of a lie. But with Jancy making her wine at her own facility these days, he was growing dissatisfied with her cold attitude of the past few months. Maybe seeing another girl a few times would give him a better perspective on things.

When Saturday rolled around, Jancy took off for her medical appointment in the Tri Cities and, a half hour later, Ronni showed up. Michael met her at the schoolhouse front door and he gave her a hug.

"Hey, it that all I get?" she teased him.

He quickly kissed her. "Ah, that's more like it!" she said with a big smile.

"Hey, before we go inside, let's go over to what we call The Barn and I'll show you where the wine is actually made," he suggested. "After that, we can try some of it in the tasting room."

"Okay, sounds good!" she replied enthusiastically.

Michael walked her down the short access road to the large fruit barn that he had converted into his winemaking operation. Going inside, he showed Ronni around and explained what was going on in the various barrels and stainless steel tanks.

"Does anyone else work here?" she asked, seeing that they were the only ones in the building.

"Oh, yeah," Michael assured her. "I have two full-time and three part-time employees. None of them work on weekends except during September and October when things are crazy because of the harvest. Plus, I have a full-time vineyard manager who uses as many as a dozen temporary laborers depending on the time of year."

"I can't believe how many barrels you have!" Ronni marveled as she looked around. "This is impressive!"

"Yeah," Michael agreed. "It's getting more complex every year."

After twenty minutes, Michael had pointed out pretty much everything he wanted to. Selecting a long curved, glass wine thief from a nearby bench, as well as two glasses, he walked over to one of the barrels that wasn't stacked high on a storage rack.

"Let's try some of the reds that aren't ready yet for long-time storage," he said as he handed the glasses to Ronni.

He removed the bung from the top of the barrel and inserted the thief, then quickly pulled it out with a sample of the wine. "This is the new Cabernet Sauvignon," he informed her as he removed his thumb from the top of the tube, allowing wine to be released into the glasses.

After sipping it, Ronni remarked, "Hmm, tastes very different than I thought it would."

"Yeah," Michael agreed. "It's new wine and I need to rack and filter it before putting it to sleep, as I like to say, for about 12 to 14 months. But, a winemaker always barrel samples before finalizing a wine. I may age it as is, or blend a little something in it, or wait until it's aged and then blend. I have choices, as you can see."

He barrel sampled a number of times over the next fifteen minutes until he and Ronni had had about a glass and a half of wine. Having gone through all his different reds, he suggested they go to the tasting room. "You can have anything you want," he informed her.

When they got to the tasting room, Michael helped Ronni take off her coat. He noticed how nice her large breasts stretched out the long-sleeved, tight fitting sweater she was wearing. Damn, this woman looked nice!

"Okay, what would you like?" he asked.

Instead of looking over the bottles of wine on the bar that Michael had previously set out, Ronni stepped up to him and slid her arms around him and looked up at him seductively. "You said I could have anything I want, right?"

Before Michael could answer, she kissed him. Gazing into her eyes, he said softly, "I guess I did say that, didn't I?"

Ronni pressed her breasts against him and they began kissing. After a moment, she slide her hand down to his private area. "This is what I want," she whispered between kisses.

Michael quickly became aroused as they continued to passionately kiss. As Ronni used her hand to rub and feel him becoming aroused, he began gently squeezing her breasts, enjoying how they felt.

A moment later, Ronni broke off the kissing to urgently exclaim, "God, baby, do you have a bed around here?"

Heady with passion, Michael quickly thought what they could do. He didn't want to take her upstairs, so he suggested, "I have a couch over there by the wall."

*   *   *

Meanwhile Jancy had changed her mind about keeping her appointment for a consultation at the Planned Parenthood office in the Tri Cities. Halfway there, she had pulled off the road and had sat, thinking, for ten minutes until she had reached a decision.

"I don't need to keep my options open," she had murmured to herself. "This is my baby and I'm having it for me, not anyone else. This is for *my* future."

Executing a U-turn, she had headed back to Watilla. Now, pulling into the drive for the schoolhouse, she noticed an unfamiliar car in the parking lot. Being an hour before Michael opened the tasting room to the public, she idly wondered who it might be. Probably another wine writer.

Parking by the back door, she intended to go inside for a quick change of clothes before driving over to her own tasting room and open it up for business. She trotted up the side steps leading to the main staircase, then rounded the end of the handrail and started up the main stairs. She immediately heard a strange commotion coming from the tasting room.

Reaching the landing at the top of the stairs, she briskly walked through the doorway of the tasting room, alarmed by the noises she heard. Glancing to her right she was shocked to see a naked woman riding on top of a man, her large breasts wildly bouncing around.

It took a second for her shock to resolve the fact that she recognized the naked man beneath this woman.

"MICHAEL!" she screamed.

Ronni whirled around and saw Jancy standing a few feet away. "Oh, hello!" she said pleasantly.

"MICHAEL!" Jancy screamed again. "You son-of-a bitch!" With that, she whirled around and ran out of the room.

Michael struggled to get Ronni off him. "Get dressed!" he ordered. "You have to leave!"

"Darn!" Ronni replied as she got off him and stood up. "We were having the greatest time ever!"

"I have to go!" Michael gasped breathlessly as he hopped around trying to pull his pants on. Quickly dressing, he waited with irritation until Ronni got all her clothes on, then escorted her down the main stairs to the front door.

"Call me, baby," she said as she walked through the door he held open for her.

Michael mumbled something and said good-bye. Closing and locking the door, he raced back upstairs to grab a coat, and then raced back down the two flights of stairs to the back door. Locking it as well, he ran to his brand new Blazer and fired it up. Backing out the drive, he gunned the truck and drove off.

Reaching the crossroad north of the schoolhouse, he turned right and sped down the road a half mile to the small farmhouse that Jancy used as her tasting room. He stopped briefly and ascertained that her old battered Jeep wasn't around, either at the farmhouse or in back by the metal building she used for her own winemaking operations.

Back out on the road once more, Michael sped down to the next intersection and turned right onto Dead End Road. He drove the quarter mile to Tommy's place and there he saw Jancy's vehicle parked out front.

He pulled in and braked to a stop. Jumping out, he ran to the farmhouse's front porch, bounded up a short set of steps, and pounded urgently on the front door.

"Tommy!" he shouted. "It's Michael!"

A second later Tommy opened the door. "What the hell's going on, man?" he wanted to know.

"I'll explain later," Michael replied as he brushed past Tommy.

Off to one side was the front room, a sort of parlor. Jancy was sitting on a sofa, tears streaking down her face. Seeing Michael. she snarled, "Get out of here!"

Walking up to her, Michael tried to defuse the situation. "Look, we need to talk. I can explain."

Casting him a look of complete incredulity, Jancy shot back, "You can explain? There's nothing to explain!" Then, shouting, she cried out, "I walked in on you fucking another woman!"

Tommy hovered at the room's entrance, looking distressed, not knowing what to do or say. Michael blew out a breath of air and tried to think. "Look," he offered, "I'm not proud of what happened, but there is some background you need to know."

Again, Jancy cast him a disbelieving look. "This wasn't the first time?" she exclaimed.

"No, no, no!" Michael quickly corrected her. "But you need to understand how this came about."

She shot him a severe look. "Please leave," she said in low voice. "Leave or I'll fucking go out of my mind and scream my lungs out until you do!"

Tommy immediately took several steps into the room, desperate to defuse the situation. "Look," he pleaded, "Let's all of us just calm down for a moment. Obviously something very traumatic just happened."

Jancy looked up Tommy. "Traumatic? You better believe it!" Then, pointing an accusing finger at Michael, she added, "He was just banging another woman in his tasting room!"

A pained look crossed Tommy's face; he was at a complete loss of what to do. Michael, meanwhile, sensed that nothing could be worked out at the moment, so he purposefully glanced at his watch.

"Look, it's only an hour before all three of us have to have our tasting rooms open for business," he observed. "Let's take care of business and then Jancy and I can talk this evening."

Chapter 12

Jayson

Watilla, Washington
1987/1988

As the afternoon passed, Michael served a steady flow of customers in his tasting room while mentally fretting over what he would say later to Jancy. It all for naught, however, because a little after 6:00 Tommy called. He didn't have good news.

"Jancy just showed up and says she doesn't want to see you tonight. Says she's not ready to talk yet."

"Damn!" Michael exclaimed softly.

"And listen," Tommy continued, "She asked me if I had a sleeping bag and a few other items. She was thinking of camping out in her farmhouse tonight and I said, hell, just stay here in my spare room. So she took me up on the offer. Just for the night."

"Tommy," Michael replied with consternation, "She and I need to talk."

"I don't know," he replied. "I think it'd be better if you two did that tomorrow. When a woman get pissed off, it's best to let things settle down and everyone sleep on it."

"I really feel like I need to talk to her now," Michael countered.

"Well, you can do what you want," his friend replied. "But I really think you need to let things cool off. She's not in a good mood, believe me."

"Maybe you're right," Michael conceded. "We'd probably just end up shouting at each other."

"By the way, she wants to stop over briefly to get a change of clothes and a few items like a toothbrush. But she doesn't want you there."

Michael sighed heavily. "Damnit!" he muttered. "I suppose I can make a run into town for some groceries. Tell her I'll be gone for an hour between 7:00 and 8:00."

Tommy excused himself for a moment. When he came back on the line, he reported, "She wants you to promise you really won't be there."

Michael fought to control his temper. "Yes, damnit, I'll really be gone," he replied tersely.

An hour and a half later, he returned to the schoolhouse from his trip into town. When he got upstairs, he looked around and saw a couple toiletry things in the bathroom were gone. As for Jancy's clothes, he really didn't keep track of how many jeans, tees, blouses, or sweater she had, so he wasn't sure just what she had taken.

That night he had trouble getting to sleep, tossing and turning past midnight. It was the first time in five years he was sleeping alone in his bed. The schoolhouse had been his and Jancy's home. Now it was just an old, creaky building. And it had a haunted feeling as well because his mind subconsciously hoped that Jancy would walk through the bedroom door any moment.

The next day, Sunday, slowly dragged by as Michael busied himself in the morning and then again served customers in the tasting room in the afternoon. Because of the holiday season, his business was brisk as a number of customers from Seattle, Spokane, and Portland stopped in.

After he closed at 6:00, he called Tommy. "Hi, this is Michael," he began. "Is Jancy coming over here, or do I go over there?"

"I'm not sure," he replied. "If she shows up here, I'll give you a call."

"Okay, thanks."

Before Michael could hang up, however, Tommy added some shocking news. "She and I talked for a while last evening. She was really frustrated and had to get some things off her chest and I guess I was the one she wanted to unburden herself on. In the course of our conversation she revealed she's pregnant. She didn't think you knew."

Stunned, Michael could only say, "Pregnant?"

"Yeah, she's almost four months along."

"She never told me!" Michael blurted out. "Damnit, Tommy, she never said a thing about that!" Then, suddenly thinking that maybe Jancy had a motive to keep quiet about it, he asked, "Am I father?"

"Of course you're the father!" Tommy exclaimed.

"Okay, okay," Michael replied. "God, why the hell didn't she say anything?"

"She told me why but, you know, that's something she needs to say to you in person," his friend replied.

"Yeah, you're right about that!"

Michael was getting a little steamed now. If only he had known, then he wouldn't be in the mess he was in. He kept his emotions in check, however, and simply replied, "Well, give me a call if she stops in."

"Will do," Tommy promised.

Michael spent the next half hour pacing and prowling around his tasting room, his mind in turmoil. The fact that he was fathering a child was the most incredible, unexpected development. He mentally cursed himself for his stupidity. And for his vanity. His success and fame had led him to think too much of himself. He had temporarily lost perspective on his life.

The quiet of the room was suddenly broken by the phone ringing. It was Tommy again. "She's here," he informed Michael. "You can come over and talk to her. She doesn't want to go over there. Sorry."

Ten minutes later Michael was knocking on Tommy's front door. His friend let him in and led him into the kitchen where Jancy was sitting at the table, a half glass of red wine in front of her. Instead of looking up and greeting him, she just sat there staring down at the table.

Tommy cleared his throat and said, "I'll go in back to my production building and hang out there for awhile so you two can have some privacy."

After Tommy left, Michael sat down across the table from Jancy. Taking a deep breath, he said, "I can't change what happened; I can only apologize. You don't know how sorry I am."

Jancy, however, kept staring down, her eyes fixed on her wine glass. Michael nervously tapped his fingers tips against each other as he carefully chose his words. "I understand you're pregnant," he said quietly.

"Yes," she simply answered in a wooden voice.

Several seconds of silence passed until Michael asked, "When were you planning on telling me?"

Jancy suddenly looked up and shot him a severe look. "When I came back yesterday," she answered," a trace of bitterness in her voice. "But I didn't get the chance."

Again, a moment of silence passed before Michael continued his questioning, trying hard to keep his voice gentle. "Why didn't you tell me?"

"Because I wasn't sure," she replied. "I thought I wanted to start a family but I wasn't sure. A couple weeks ago I made an appointment with Planned Parenthood to discuss an abortion. That's why I went to the Tri Cities yesterday. I changed my mind on the way, however, and came back home." Then she quickly added sarcastically, "A little too early, as it turned out."

Michael blew out a breath of air and ran a hand through his hair. "You were really thinking of an abortion?"

"Yes," she confirmed. "It would have served you right."

"Served me right?" he asked, stunned. Then, his anger rising, he asked in a raised voice, "You would have killed a baby to get back at me? I can't believe that! I can't believe you'd be that kind of a person!"

Jancy glared at him. "You're right," she said, an edge of anger in her voice now. "I'm not that kind of a person. But I feel angry enough to have done it, to have aborted and started over with another guy."

Michael was tempted to reply but kept his temper in check. Instead, he sighed heavily and tried to think how to proceed. "Okay, I'll thank you for not going through with the abortion," he said. "Now, we need to talk about how we go on from here."

Jancy, however, made no reply. Michael shifted uncomfortably in his seat before saying, "I'm asking you to please come home. I love you; I can't go on without you."

Jancy's reply was a dagger to his heart. "I'm not coming back," she simply replied.

Now Michael became frightened. He knew her well and how hard-headed she could be. "Oh, God, Jancy, please don't say that!" he pleaded. "We don't have to be intimate from now until the baby is born. Hell, we don't even have to sleep in the same bed! But please come back."

Jancy fixed him with a hard look, her intense blue eyes ice cold. "Michael," she asked, "how many times have you banged her?"

Taken aback by the question, he quickly replied, "That was the first time! Honest, Jancy! I had given her a tour of The Barn, and then we went to the tasting room to try some samples but things got out of hand and something happened that should have never happened."

After hearing his answer, she immediately followed up with a second question. "I see. How many other women have you screwed behind my back?"

He raised his hands up in mock surrender. "None!" he exclaimed emphatically. "None!"

A moment of silence passed. "Michael, even if I came back, and even if I could bring myself to trust you again," she said in an even, low voice, "I will never, ever, be able to get out of my mind the image of you and her naked and she being on top of you. I will never get over picturing that in my mind."

He sighed heavily and slowly shook his head. "I still don't know why you tell me you were pregnant," he complained. "If you had, none of this would have happened! Why didn't you say something? If this was accidental, you still could have talked to me."

Jancy picked up her glass and took a sip, then out it down again before answering. "It wasn't an accident," she explained. "You had said previously you wanted a family someday, so at the end of July I felt good enough about our future that I went off the pill. I never dreamed I could get pregnant so fast! I think it may have been the day when we got the magazine with the news you were number one on the Top 100 list."

Michael nodded. He remembered very vividly how they had made wild, passionate love that day. "So why the thoughts of an abortion?" he asked, puzzled.

"Because you changed," she accused him.

"How?" he wanted to know.

"How?" she asked incredulously. "You're the rock star of the wine world, for God's sake! Sometimes I think if I ever hear that term again, I'll kill you!"

Michael's face colored. He had to admit it was how he had referred to himself a number of times over the past three and a half months.

"When you were at the Chamber meeting Saturday evening, did you give me any credit? Did you give Tommy any credit?"

His face continued to be deeply colored; Jancy was hitting home with her criticism.

"When you talk to other wine groups," she continued, "especially in California, do you give credit to Tommy and I?"

His embarrassed look answered her question. "No?" she asked, driving a knife in him like a prosecutor who knows he has a witness trapped. "Who do you think helped you? Do you happen to remember that you and I barrel tasted and you depended on my recommendations for the blend? Do you happen to remember that it was Tommy who made the suggestion to incorporate a little Petite Sirah?"

"You're right," Michael admitted. "I haven't given credit when I should have."

"Now I can accept the fact that a magazine has to have one person—and one winery—for an award," Jancy continued, "but that doesn't mean you can't try to tell the world that it was a three person effort."

Michael continued nodding agreement. "But the fact of the matter is, you haven't," she stated. "You've become an egotistical ass. The so-called 'rock star.'"

He sighed heavily, fighting back tears. Shrugging, he whispered, "I can't argue against what you say."

Jancy picked up her glass again and drank the rest of the wine. "You're going to California to talk to another winemaker's group next week, right?" she asked.

"Yeah," he confirmed.

"While you're gone, I'm going to move out," she informed him, then warned, "And don't change the locks to prevent me. I'll just break in."

*   *   *

When Michael made his trip to California a week later, he gave credit during his talk for the first time to Jancy and Tommy for their valuable advice in creating the perfect 100 point 1985 Reserve Syrah. By then it was too late, as he discovered upon returning home. Every single trace of Jancy had disappeared from the schoolhouse. It was as if she had never existed, and he felt a profound sadness.

A couple days later, Tommy stopped by The Barn with an update. His friend made a habit of stopping in from time to time, for Michael and he had become good friends. They particularly enjoyed kidding and teasing each other nearly every time they got together.

This day, however, the mood was sober, for Tommy had surprising news. "Hey," he said to Michael after they had exchanged greetings. "I need to tell you that Jancy is renting my spare room until the baby comes."

Seeing Michael's surprised look, he hurriedly explained. "She looked at some places in town to rent, but decided she was going to buy some second-hand furniture, appliances, and so on in order to make her farmhouse livable. I said, heck, I'd rent my spare room pretty darn cheap, and she would have use of the kitchen, to boot, so she agreed."

"I see," Michael replied, tersely.

"Listen, Michael," Tommy emphasized, "there is nothing between her and I, nor will there be. She'll be strictly a renter." Then he added, "I just know that when the baby comes, she'll be more amenable to getting back together with you. Time heals everything, as they say."

Michael pondered this for a moment before slowly nodding his head. "Yeah, that's probably for the best," he told his friend. "She should have someone around her, especially at night, when the due date approaches."

"That's what I was thinking, too," Tommy agreed. "Plus, I can remain a pipeline between you two."

Michael nodded again. With sadness in his voice, he observed, "You know, I tried to make the best wine possible. And then suddenly one day I achieved everything I could have hoped for, but in the process I lost what I loved most."

*   *   *

Michael spent late December in California with his parents where he received a Macintosh computer as a Christmas present. His father was excited about the future of technology and told his son, "You need to get with the high tech revolution!"

Michael returned to Watilla after the New Year. The annual cycle of life began once again in 1989 with the vines in the vineyards barren and dormant, slumbering through the winter. In spring they came back to life, budding out.

Vineyard manager Jorge was back with his crew of amigos to prune the vines which then put forth their new growth. All of Michael's blocks of vines had matured several years earlier and were now at their peak of production.

He saw almost nothing of Jancy during this time, except at a distance when she was working in her vineyard. He had tried calling her a couple of times, but she had never returned his calls. Tommy kept him apprised that all was going well with the pregnancy.

On June 10 Michael received a phone call while he was eating breakfast. Tommy was on the other end. "Jancy's in labor!" he reported excitedly. "I'm taking her to the hospital right now!"

"Ok!" Michael replied, his heart suddenly pounding. "I'm on my way!"

Fifteen minutes later he met Tommy at the maturity ward of the Watilla Community Hospital. "She's inside in a room where a nurse can keep an eye on her," his friend informed him. "Even though her water broke, the nurse says she's nowhere near dilated enough for delivery. So it's a waiting game."

Michael learned to his dismay that Jancy had instructed the hospital staff neither he nor Tommy was allowed to see her. He decided to wait around anyway. After all, this was his child being born. Tommy, however, saw no further need to stay, so he left after wishing Michael well.

Nine long hours later a nurse came out to the waiting room and told Michael, "You may go in. She's had a boy."

When Michael entered the room where they had put Jancy for her stay, he saw her lying on the bed, worn out and tired. Beside her wrapped up in a blanket was the baby.

"Hi," he said softly.

Jancy turned from looking at the baby to look at him. "Hi," she said in whisper.

Michael walked over and sat down on the edge of the bed. He smiled as he gazed at the little bundle. "How are you doing?" he asked her.

Jancy didn't answer his question but said instead, "His name is Jayson." Then she spelled it out for him.

"Hmm. Is that a name in your family?"

She kept gazing at the baby, a small smile on her lips. "No, I just like it," was her simple explanation.

Michael retuned the next day for a visit but was only able to spend several minutes with Jancy. Her mother had arrived from California and was hanging out in the room for the day and her attitude made it clear that he was just in the way.

The next day when he visited, he insisted on seeing Jancy in private. While he was holding Jayson in his arms and marveling at how small a newborn baby was, he broached the subject of reconciliation. He tried to frame his thoughts as delicately as possible.

"I hear you're getting released tomorrow," he said. "Don't you think it's time to come back home? We're a family now. We have a son. And I've done my penance. Believe me, I've been lonely these past five months and have lived with so much regret."

Michael held his breath waiting for what Jancy would say. "You know what I told I could never get out of my mind," she replied without emotion. "I may have eventually forgiven you if I had found out some other way about your unfaithfulness. But I walked in during the act. I'll always remember that."

Handing little Jayson back to her, he asked, "So what's your plan? What are you going to do? Move back to California?"

Jancy gave him a sharp look. "California?" she said in disbelief. "I came here to Watilla to make it on my own. It's been a struggle but things are getting better. No, I'm not going back to California. I'm building a business and a future for myself." Then she quickly added, "And for my son."

Although dismayed by her reference to 'her son,' Michael breathed a sigh of relief. Jancy would be staying in the area and that meant Jayson would as well. He would be able to see his son, to watch him grow up, and to interact with him.

"Where will you stay?" he wanted to know.

Holding Jayson and stroking his head, she replied, "With Tommy for now. Later, I'll get my farmhouse remodeled so I can live in the back part while continuing to use the front part as a tasting room."

*   *   *

Two weeks later Michael was in downtown Watilla in the office of an attorney. The news he was receiving wasn't good.

"The problem is, you two weren't married," the man explained. "You have very little legal basis for visitation rights."

"But I'm the father, for crying out loud!" Michael replied in consternation.

"Yes," the attorney acknowledged. "but an unmarried father. Therefore, the mother has automatic custody and any legal visitation rights for you must be awarded by a court."

Michael's face colored as his anger rose. "You mean Jancy can refuse for me to see my own son?" He couldn't believe such a thing possible.

"That's correct," the attorney confirmed. "In such a situation you still have rights, but you must go to court and have the court hear the case. The court will then determine the extent of your visitation rights."

Michael sighed in defeat. The attorney tried to be optimistic. "Look, it may be in your best interests to work out an informal arrangement with Ms. Phillips. Going to court will be very expensive – for both you and her."

Michael blew out a breath of air as he tried to think. He rubbed his eyes for a second, then looked at the attorney and asked, "What if she decides to move out of state?"

The man cleared his throat and replied, "Well, that's the downside of an informal agreement. A court-ordered visitation arrangement would address issues like that."

"How much would it cost to go to court?" Michael wanted to know.

"In most cases, $5,000 to $10,000," was the reply.

"And she would have roughly the same costs?"

The attorney nodded. "Yes, going to court in these cases is always expensive – for both parties."

Then he added, "Listen Michael, I would advise you to seek an informal agreement with Ms. Phillips, but in writing. I can draft a straight-forward agreement that would have the same force of law as a contract would."

Michael nodded. "Go ahead and do it. But listen, make it fair for both of us, okay?"

"Of course."

Michael left the office in a bad mood. He had screwed up, yes, but he felt he shouldn't have to pay for it the rest of his life. Instead of going back to his winery, he stopped in at the Roundup Saloon. Being late morning, he intended to get a bite of lunch.

When he took a seat at the bar, however, he ordered a beer first. The lady behind the bar could see something was bothering him. When she delivered the second beer to him, she asked, "Bad day?"

"Hmmfh! I'll say!" he replied. "Just got done with a meeting with an attorney."

"Oh yeah, it's a bad day then, "the barkeep sympathized.

Michael eventually ordered a burger and a third beer. Thirty minutes later when he had finished, he looked over at the White Caucasian Appreciation Society sign on one wall. All these years and it was still there.

As he pulled out some cash to pay his bills, he nodded his head towards the sign and commented, "Mexicans need not apply, eh?"

The lady barkeep made a face. "They all belong in Mexico!" she said in disgust.

Taking his billfold out again, Michael extracted a $20 bill. "How much for that sign?" he asked. "Will $20 do it? I want to buy it."

The lady looked at him as if he were crazy. "You want to buy that sign?"

"Yeah."

She gave him a hard look. "Listen, mister, it ain't for sale."

Pausing a second, feeling angry at the world, Michael made a decision. "Oh yeah? Well I'm buying it anyway. Here."

He threw the bill on the bar and turned to walk over to the sign. The lady yelled at him, "Hey! I told you it's not for sale!"

He ignored her. Grabbing hold of the sign, he ripped it off the wall and then savagely smashed it on a nearby table, breaking it apart.

"Hey, goddamnit!" the lady yelled.

Michael turned around and snarled at her. "If you put up another sign like this, I'll return and smash that one, too!"

"Get out of here you pervert before I call the cops!"

Michael walked out of the saloon feeling an immense amount of satisfaction. At least he could feel good about something this day.

Chapter 13

Jana

Watilla, Washington
1988/1989

As things turned out, Michael found himself entering a new stage of life – a life without Jancy. She made it clear that the split with him was permanent, so he concentrated on maintaining access to Jayson. After a couple months, however, this suddenly proved to be a very manageable situation due to Tommy's intervention.

Just before the '88 harvest was to commence, Michael's good friend stopped by with some very interesting news. "Jancy wants to stay with me rather than do all that work to get her farmhouse in livable shape," he reported. "She rather rent from me than live on her own."

Seeing the concern in Michael's face, Tommy quickly assured him, "It's strictly a rental arrangement. There's nothing romantic about it, nor will it ever be."

Then, to his surprise, Tommy handed him a sheaf of several papers. "This is the visitation agreement your lawyer drew up," he said. "Jancy signed it."

His friend went on to explain. "I told her she couldn't stay at my place unless she came to an agreement with you over Jayson. I said I wasn't going to be his father; that you were. I want you to be involved in raising your son. You're Jayson's dad, not me. I'm just going to be Uncle Tommy."

Michael slowly nodded as he thought it over. "This might actually be for the best," he told his friend. "You'll be able to keep me up to speed with what's going on until Jayson starts walking and talking.

And it keeps Jancy here. I've been afraid she might think of moving back to California."

Tommy shook his head. "No, she's determined to make a name for herself here. I really get the feeling she thinks of Watilla as home now. I think that's why she took your, uh, indiscretion so hard. She was starting to see herself as a businesswoman as well as a mother with a family."

Michael sighed. "Yeah, you're probably right."

Over the next several months, Michael enjoyed seeing his son develop and grow, although his visits were short and not very satisfying since Jayson couldn't yet relate to his surroundings very well.

As the holidays approached, he received an unusual phone call one day. The Chamber president was on the other end. "Hey, Michael, how are you?"

"I'm fine. How about you?"

"Oh, great, just great," the man replied. "Busy these days, you know, getting ready for the annual meeting. Hope you'll make it."

Michael wasn't so sure he would. Ronni might be there again and he wasn't ready to have to fend her off. The president continued. "Say, are you free for lunch next week? Tuesday? I want you in on a brain storming session with a couple other people."

"Um, I'm free as far as I know. What's up?"

"Well, you know we have this little community college here in town that has auto mechanics and business classes," the Chamber president explained. "They've even added a couple computer classes."

Michael knew of the Watilla Community College and approved of its mission, although the institution was pretty small and was housed in an old building on the east end of town.

"Well, anyway, some of us got to talking the other day and were kicking around the idea of the college offering a winemaking class. Maybe even a class on vineyard management, too. What do you think of that?"

His eyebrows arched in surprise, Michael thought for a moment before replying, "Offhand, it sounds like a good idea."

"Good, good!" the president replied enthusiastically. "You know, we've got, what, almost a dozen winemaking operations in the area now, plus the Chamber keeps getting all sorts of inquiries. Seems like maybe we should capitalize on this interest and start educating some of our young people about the wine business."

"Yeah," Michael agreed. "I think that's a great idea."

"Okay!" the man replied. "How about we talk more on Tuesday? Say 12:00 at the Roundup Saloon?"

"Uh, I don't go to the Roundup anymore," Michael informed him without explaining about his little altercation the last time he was in that place. "Let's meet somewhere else," he suggested.

The Chamber president thought for a moment. "Hey, I know! Nancy Sloan has a new place downtown on 2nd. Called the Vineyard Café or something like that. Nice little cozy establishment."

"Sound good to me!" Michael replied, and then the two men ended the call.

Over the next couple days, and through the weekend, Michael thought over the idea the president had run by him. The more he thought about it, however, the more he was dissatisfied with it. What would be accomplished by a single class on wine making? Or vineyard management, for that matter?

The whole concept of the Community College was to train young people in some useful skill to keep them from moving out of the area after high school. What was the use of knowing just a little about winemaking? No, Michael thought to himself, a much bolder approach was called for.

When Tuesday rolled around, he drove into town and parked not far from the meeting place. Getting out of his truck, he noted that downtown Watilla was changing. The town was growing and new businesses were opening up in storefronts which had been empty and boarded up.

The newly opened Vineyard Café & Bakery was a case in point. There was also talk of an organic gourmet food store of some sort. Michael smiled to himself. He was seeing the beginnings of a possible revival of the small city as a wine industry developed outside of it.

Inside the Vineyard Café, Michael was greeted by aromas of freshly baked goods, fresh brewed espresso, and aromas of just made soups and sandwiches. In the back he found the Chamber president sitting at a small table with two others: a professionally dressed black lady, and a middle-aged man in a coat and tie.

"Hello, Michael!" the Chamber president greeted him, standing up and extending his hand. The other gentleman also stood and shook his hand as well as the Chamber man introduced him, "Bill Shelton, the college's executive director."

The lady was introduced to him as well. "This is Sheila Washington from the governor's office of community education."

Michael shook her hand and expressed his pleasure at meeting her. Everyone then sat down and for the next ten minutes they engaged in small talk until they ordered sandwiches and soft drinks.

Clearing his throat, the Chamber guy got down to business. "Well, Michael, it seemed that you were on board with our idea when you and I spoke last week," he began. "Any further thoughts?"

Michael shifted in his seat, cleared his throat as well, and replied, "Actually, yes. I've given this a lot of thought and I've got an idea to run by you folks."

Turning to the college man, he asked, "Bill, your objective at the college is to teach young people a skill they can make a living at, right?"

"Yes, absolutely," Shelton replied, nodding vigorously.

Michael continued. "So, tell me about auto mechanics. How does that work?"

"Well, the kids take a year learning hands-on, either auto or diesel mechanics," Shelton explained. "It's their choice. We also offer a year's hands-on for learning auto body work. In addition, we're adding starting next year a couple courses in ag equipment maintenance and repair."

"Uh huh," Michael nodded as he listened. "The whole point is to learn by doing?"

Shelton nodded. "Oh yes! That's our philosophy. We're not going to send these kids out into the world unless they know what they're doing. We're proud of our reputation at the college that our graduates are ready to go from day one when they hire on with someone."

Michael briefly glanced at the three people sitting with him. "In that case," he said, "I'd like to propose something along the same lines."

"We're all ears, Mr. Ross," Ms. Washington said, her eyebrows arched in expectation.

Michael took a deep breath and plunged ahead. "Okay, it's my firm conviction that the 1990s will see a boom in the wine industry in

Washington," he informed the group. "The central Columbia Valley is bubbling like crazy right now. From Yakima to the Tri Cities, we're seeing more and more vineyard land planted and winery operations started. Some of that activity is happening right here in the Watilla Valley, too. But, I think we haven't seen anything yet."

"But, Michael," Shelton interrupted, "just how much wine can be made? Aren't we in danger of reaching a saturation point?"

Michael firmly shook his head. "No, not by a long shot," he declared. "When you compare per capita wine consumption of this country to places like France, Italy, and Spain, well, we'd need a thousand new wineries overnight even if we suddenly were to drink only a third of what the Europeans do."

"Yeah, but what's the chances that Americans will start drinking more wine?" Shelton wanted to know.

Michael understood the man's position. Shelton something concrete to hang his hat on before committing his institution to a new direction.

"We're already seeing the change," Michael countered. "I'm seeing more young people in my tasting room. It's not just folks in their 50s and 60s. Young professional people—the so-called Yuppies—are starting to branch out and consume more wine and beer. They've got the disposable income and they want to live a more sophisticated lifestyle."

"So what are you thinking, exactly?" the black lady wanted to know.

"If you're going to do this," Michael said evenly, "then do it right. Create a winery. Have a vineyard. Put up an industrial building next to it with a crush pad. Go the entire 10 yards."

"Wow!" exclaimed Shelton. "I certainly wasn't thinking of anything like that."

"Geez, Michael," the Chamber man said, "You certainly think big!"

But the black lady was intrigued. "Explain some more, please" she urged.

"Look," Michael continued, "A winemaker cannot succeed without making a quality product. You have to sell to the public and that means you need to establish a reputation for quality. So, there's no better way for enology students to learn this than to actually have to sell what they make to the public."

"But who would buy wine from a community college?" the Chamber president wanted to know.

But Michael was dogged in arguing his idea. "That's the whole point," he countered. "The program would have to be top notch, offering a good product at a reasonable price. People will buy. And once you establish that the college can make great wine, then you'll have all sorts of people wanting to get into the program."

"So, you're saying a program like you envision could attract people from outside this area?" Ms. Washington asked.

"Absolutely," Michael replied with conviction. "Look, where else can you go to learn viniculture or vinification without paying a ton of bucks for a four year college degree? If you offer a two-prong enology program—viniculture and vinification—then students will learn both how to grow high quality grapes and how to turn those grapes into quality wine."

"Hmm, I like this idea," Washington commented. "What you're advocating is a real world, hands-on program where students could graduate ready to go straight to work for a winery."

"Yep, absolutely," Michael confirmed. "Students would learn how to plant grapes, prune them, train them, manage them throughout the growing season, and then how to properly harvest them. After that, they would go through the entire winemaking process, including bottling and selling to the public."

"We're talking about quite an undertaking to get something like this off the ground," Shelton pointed out. "And a lot of money."

"I'd be happy to help with the paperwork to get a bonded winery established, and to teach a class or two," Michael informed the group. "Plus, you have other winemakers and vineyard managers in the area who could also help teach."

"I like this idea and I think I could arrange for some grant money to get the program off the ground," Washington informed the other two. Then, looking at Shelton, she added, "Bill, why don't you get together with Michael and draw up a proposal outlining how you would do this, along with the associated costs?"

*   *   *

Michael and his friend Tommy worked over the next couple months with Bill Shelton to draw up a detailed proposal for the establishment of a two year winemaking program at the community college. They eventually decided to call it Viticulture & Enology, signifying that the emphasis would be on both growing wine grapes—viticulture—and all aspects of winemaking—enology—that students would have to master. Local growers and winery owners would be encouraged to offer internships to students prior to their graduation

They decided to call the proposed college winery Watilla Community Cellars. Michael and Tommy suggested the college purchase 20-30 acres of suitable land just outside of town for the vineyard.

"You can plant a half acre a year as part of the program," they told Shelton. "The vineyard and the program can grow hand-in-hand. The larger the vineyard becomes, the more work will be required, but you'll have more and more students over time."

At Michael's urging, Shelton utilized Jancy to assist with marketing materials, especially for attracting female students. "We women usually have a better sense of smell and taste than men," she informed him. "But you hardly will find a woman winemaker anywhere. This is a perfect opportunity to begin changing that!"

By year's end, Sheila Washington had secured funding from the governor's office of community college development for the start-up money required. Land was purchased and construction of a small but adequate winemaking facility was scheduled for the spring. Classes would begin in the late summer.

*   *   *

As the new year of 1989 began, Michael found himself enjoying being around Jayson more and more. By spring the little boy was not only crawling, but also trying to walk. He had mastered Da-da and Ma-ma, and was able to say Tom-tom when referring to Tommy.

On Jayson's first birthday in June, Michael joined Jancy and Tommy at an ice cream parlor in Watilla where they held a small birthday party for the little tyke. During the party Michael took the opportunity to congratulate both of his winemaking colleagues on the good ratings that *Wine Explorer* magazine had given to several of their wines. Tommy had scored an impressive 94 points on his Merlot, while Jancy scored 95 points on a Viognier, and an eye-popping 97 points on a red blend she called *Adagio*, which she explained in ballet means a combination of slow movements that exhibit ease and grace.

Later on at the end of September, Jancy made the Top 100 list in the magazine, coming in at #17 with her *Adagio*. Michael was still ineligible for the list since R.R. Parkston had a policy that once you made the list you were not eligible to be reconsidered for three years. This policy both prevented anyone from dominating the list, plus increased interest in the magazine since each year's list was totally new.

On the Saturday morning after Thanksgiving, Tommy stopped by the barn for a visit after first calling and making sure Michael would be around. "Hey," he said to his friend after greeting him, "I need to talk to you in private about something."

"Okay," Michael replied cheerfully, "let's go to the tasting room and open up a bottle. I've got two new releases you can give me your opinion on."

Tommy, however, shook his head. "I don't think you're going to like what I have to say," he informed Michael ominously. "In fact, you may not consider me a friend anymore."

Michael hesitated a moment before replying. Sighing heavily, he took his friend by the shoulder and turned him towards the door. "Oh, hell, let's go have a drink anyway," he urged Tommy. "If I lose you as a friend, then what would I do? Go hang out at the Roundup Saloon after work each day?"

He said it in a joking manner but, deep down inside, Michael knew he would sorely miss Tommy coming over and visiting several times a week. Besides, he had a feeling what his friend was going to say and it wouldn't really be a surprise.

After opening up a bottle of what he called Block Two Syrah, Michael poured a half glass for both of them. After they had sat down at one of the bistro tables near the bar, Michael listened as Tommy critiqued the wine.

"Very nice nose," his friend began after swirling and sniffing his glass. "Lots of that bacon-frying-in-the-pan element." Taking a sip, he swished it around in his mouth a couple seconds before swallowing it. "Hmm, very true to the grape," he complimented Michael. "It's a thoroughbred Syrah, alright. Lots of plums and ripe dark fruit, plus hints of cloves and pepper. Damn near as good as anything you make from the Block One section."

Tommy's references to the blocks in Michael's vineyard reflected the change in designation that Michael had made. Instead of A, B, C, D, and E, he now referred to them as numbers. It just sounded better to him when he labeled the wines as Block One, Block Two, etc.

After a minute of chatting about the wine, Tommy turned serious. "Well, I should get on with it," he began as Michael gave him his full attention. "First, Jancy and I were wondering if you'd like to have Jayson stay overnight occasionally. You, know, start getting him used to sleeping here."

Michael nodded as he listened. "Yeah, that's be nice," he responded. "You know that I have the spare room upstairs already made into a little boy's bedroom. He plays there whenever he visits, and he's taken naps on the bed, so he's familiar with the room."

"Good, good," Tommy replied, shifting his weight in his chair. Michael observed that his friend was clearly uncomfortable.

Looking down at the table, he continued. "There's no easy way to say this, Michael." A second of silence followed before Tommy blurted out, "Jancy's pregnant again."

"I see," Michael said in a even voice, trying to betray no emotion.

Tommy looked up at his friend, a stricken look on his face. "I'm sorry, Michael! I really am!"

Instead of becoming angry, though, Michael surprised his friend by saying, "Hey, don't be sorry. This is supposed to be good news."

But Tommy was filled with guilt nevertheless. "Goddamnit, Michael, I never intended for things to become romantic!" he exclaimed.

Michael simply shrugged. "I figured it would get that way after she decided to stay at your placed after Jayson was born," he confided to his friend. "It was just a matter of time."

Tommy rubbed one hand across his forehead as he looked downward, avoiding eye contact. "I haven't been a very good friend," he confessed. "I've been trying to pretend things were different for the past six months or so, hiding the truth from you. But now I can't hide it anymore."

Michael reached across the small table and gave his friend's arm a friendly squeeze. "Hey, buddy, snap out of it!" he urged Tommy. "You can feel as guilty as you want, but I'm not angry. Hell, I'm not even upset. What would be the use? It is what it is"

Tommy looked up, his eyes red from holding back tears. Michael sat upright and said with a smile, "Hey, if it'll make you feel better, I can give you a good cussing."

Tommy finally cracked a smile. "Yeah, I'd probably feel better if you did."

Seeking to break the emotional atmosphere hanging over them, Michael switched gears. "Did she tell you ahead of time?" he asked, curious.

"Sort of," Tommy replied. "She asked me one day if I ever thought I'd like to have a family. I said, sure, but then we never talked about it anymore until one day three or four months later she tells me she's expecting."

A wry smile broke out on Michael's face. "Classic Jancy," he observed.

Tommy smiled and nodded. "Yeah, that's for sure," he admitted. "Like you've said before, she thinks things over, decides what she wants to do, then just goes and does it."

After several seconds of silence, Michael asked, "So, have you two ever talked about getting married?"

Tommy emphatically shook his head. "She's told me not to even think of proposing! She claims she'll never, ever get married."

Michael sighed. Was there a more headstrong woman anywhere, he wondered. Then, curious again, he asked, "When's she due?"

"She figures around the first of July as best the doc can calculate," his friend answered.

As Michael thought about this, he had to smile. The due date correlated closely with the September issue of *Wine Explorer* that listed J Phillips Cellars in the Top 100 list. He slowly shook his head. It was déjà vu.

*   *   *

The year 1990 brought the establishment of Watilla Community Cellars and the planting of its first vines on a site just northeast of the city. Next to the new vineyard, a metal industrial building was constructed for winemaking, as well as an annex for classrooms. Everything was on schedule for classes to start in late August.

During the night of the 4th of July, Michael received an anxious call from Tommy. "Can you get over here right away? Jancy's water broke and we're getting ready to take off for the hospital."

Michael threw on his night robe, raced out to his truck, and was over at Tommy's five minutes after the call. He accepted a sleeping Jayson into his arms and returned back to his place as Tommy and Jancy drove off for town.

Around noon the next day, he received a follow-up call from Tommy. "Well, she had a baby girl," he informed his friend. "The name will be Jana."

After congratulating him, Michael commented. "Seems like Jancy has a thing for names that start with J."

Tommy chuckled. "Yeah, you're right. You know what I think? I think she's ensuring that there'll always be a J to run J Phillips Cellars. Jayson. Jana. Someone whose name begins with a J will always run the business."

Michael agreed with his friend's conclusion, then added, "I'll stop by tomorrow and give her my congratulations in person. Can't wait to see your daughter!"

Jayson stayed with him for the next four days which Michael enjoyed immensely. As he thought about the future, he was sure that Jayson would end up living part time with him now that Tommy and Jancy had a child of their own. In fact, Michael even began to hope that Jayson would live full time with him once the little boy started school.

Live was just about perfect for Michael. He was doing extremely well financially, had more and more access to Jayson, and in little more than a month he would begin part-time teaching duties for the new wine program at the community college.

Three weeks after Jana was born the national news carried a story of the president of the United States signing into law the Americans with Disabilities Act. Michael was familiar with it because of his involvement with the Chamber which had sought over the past couple months to educate its members about the law's implications.

As far as Michael could tell, he didn't have anything to worry about even though his schoolhouse tasting room presented a formidable barrier to handicapped persons due to the large main staircase. But the law had exceptions for businesses that would suffer a financial hardship to accommodate disabled persons. In addition, there was an exception for historic structures if accommodation would significantly alter the nature of the structure.

He planned to add a handicapped parking space or two out front of his tasting room but that would be it, though, as far as accessibility went. He was confident there was nothing else he needed to be concerned about in that regard.

Chapter 14

Maggie

Olde Schoolhouse Cellars
1990 – 1992

Autumn of 1990 was a hectic time for the three pioneer winemakers. Not only was there the hectic business of the harvest and processing grapes, but the community college began its winemaking and vineyard management classes. Response to it had been surprisingly strong.

"We thought we would get a couple dozen inquiries," Shelton informed Michael one day, "but we were amazed to get over 200. Almost half of them actually sent in an application, so we had to be selective in whom we admitted. Ms. Phillips was invaluable in assisting us with that process."

Michael was glad Jancy had been involved. Too bad she had her hands full with the new baby; it prevented her from actually teaching any classes. But he and Tommy were instructors in several classes, plus the college had hired a fulltime instructor who was a retired winemaker form California.

On the vineyard side of the program, Dr. Cline had recommended an experienced horticulturalist with vineyard experience that the college had also hired full-time. In addition, Jorge had agreed to be a part-time instructor to lend his experience with raising and caring for vines in the unique conditions of the Watilla Valley.

In the spring of 1991, Michael organized the first meeting of the Watilla Valley Winemakers & Growers Association. He learned from this effort that there were now 15 winemaking operations of one type or another in the Watilla Valley, plus nine growers who raised grapes but didn't make wine. Total acreage of vines was approaching 200. For Michael, this was a satisfying vindication of his original vision that a wine industry could be created in the region.

In March the group had its first meeting on a Sunday evening in Michael's tasting room. The first order of business was for everyone to introduce themselves to the group. During this process, Michael and the others met a middle-aged couple who were making wine by renting part of an old storage building out at the Watilla airport.

"There's more than a hundred acres of old World War II era buildings out there," the husband reported. "It used to be an Army Air Corps facility: barracks, admin offices, and storage buildings of all kinds. The Pentagon declared it surplus about 15 years ago and the city took ownership. There are maybe a dozen other little businesses out there now."

"Do you raise any grapes?" another winemaker wanted to know.

"No," the guy replied. "Right now we're buying our grapes, both from here and from further west. Horse Heaven Hills and the Yakima Valley."

"Are you the ones that people are talking about that are going to open a tasting room downtown?" someone else wanted to know.

"Yes!" the wife confirmed. "Instead of putting a lot of money trying to convert part of our industrial space to a nice tasting room, we figured we would open one right in the downtown area. That's where the people are anyway. Why try to get them to drive out to the airport industrial park when they're already eating and staying overnight downtown?"

"Hmm, I see an emerging business model," Michael said, only half joking. "Rent cheap space in the industrial park to make the wine, and then sell it from a cozy tasting room right smack in the heart of downtown."

After a little more conversation about this subject, Michael turned everyone's attention to marketing materials. A committee of three volunteers was formed to develop a color brochure promoting the wine industry of the Watilla Valley. Included would be a map showing the locations of existing wineries and/or tasting rooms for anyone who contributed financially to printing the brochure.

The final order of business was agreement that monthly meetings would continue through August, after which they would be suspended due to the demands of the harvest season. The thinking was to start them up again in January of the following year.

When the new year arrived, Michael started a new tradition at the April meeting – blind tasting. "We should do a different blind tasting each month comparing our wines to others from around the world," he explained. "That's the best to improve our winemaking."

The first blind tasting involved seven Chardonnays, three local and four from elsewhere. Bottles were kept in paper bags to keep the identity of the wines hidden until everyone had tasted and voted on them. The results were eye-opening when the wines were revealed.

"The Chardonnay with the highest point total is…a Chablis!" Jancy announced as she pulled the bottle out of the paper bag. After a moment of comments from the group, she continued on. "Second place is…a white Burgundy!"

She was pleased when a moment later she announced her own Chardonnay was number three. Dead last was a Chardonnay from California. Michael immediately jumped in to offer his opinion on the results.

"Look at these results," he said. "What do they say?"

"That we as a group like unoaked Chardonnay," one of the other winemakers answered.

"Exactly!" Michael replied excitedly. "Chablis is famous for its steely character. No oak imparts all those wonderful green apple and citrus elements. And, the same for the white Burgundy. The true expression of the grape is coming through, the exact opposite of the last place Chard which is oaky, buttery plonk from California."

The group chuckled at his putdown of California Chardonnay. He continued on. "Look at the number three wine. After the two French ones, Jancy's was the one we liked next best. She hardly uses oak, right?"

Michael was looking at her when he asked the question and she immediately gave the technical facts of her wine. "Yes, I used 20% new oak, 50% neutral, and 30% steel. Plus, just a touch of maleolactic."

She was referring to maleolactic fermentation, a second fermentation process in winemaking that uses an injection of bacteria to convert harsh, naturally occurring malic acid into soft, buttery lactic acid that is prevalent in dairy products.

"I think we have an opportunity here to further distinguish this region. If we do our Chardonnay mostly in steel, or at least only neutral oak, and skip the maleolactic for the most part, we'll have a wonderfully crisp, refreshing white wine with nice acid levels and that expresses the true nature of the Chardonnay grape."

"But everyone likes California Chardonnay," one of the others protested. "Wine drinkers in this country like that oaky, buttery aspect."

Michael, however, was not deterred. "That's because California winemakers have got people used to that style," he countered. "We have an opportunity here in Washington to offer a better alternative. Let California make what they make, but we'll offer consumers something they haven't had before: a true Chardonnay. I'm convinced they'll like it."

This started a lively debate over the merits of making Chardonnay one way versus another. Michael, however, pointed out something no one could argue with. "What's the best Chardonnay in the world? Chablis, right? Also several unique appellations in other parts of Burgundy, but consumers recognize the word 'Chablis.' When people come into your tasting room and you offer them an unoaked Chardonnay, tell them it's made in the style of the best Chablis. People respect French wine, so we'll market to them on that basis. We need to be different than California."

*   *   *

In June Michael, Tommy and Jancy celebrated Jayson's second birthday, and then in July they celebrated little Jana's first birthday. Michael's relationship with Jancy had finally warmed up; she would actually speak to him these days without him having to speak to her first. He attributed the thaw to the fact that he accepted her and Tommy being a couple, and also to expressing his happiness that they were a family.

In fact, all of them were now a sort of extended family. He was connected to Jancy by Jayson, while Tommy was connected to her by Jana, and he and Tommy were good friends.

Even though they were a family, Tommy and Jancy continued to make wine separately. She concentrated on making J Phillips Cellars a premier brand, and she now had more than 25 acres of mature vines. Tommy continued his Fiona Cellars label and had increased his acreage to 15 but said he wasn't going to plant any more. His operation was as big as he wanted it to be.

I'm a true boutique winery," he would say to folks who stopped by his tasting room. "I handcraft small lots of premium wine."

In September the 1991 Top 100 list came out in *Wine Explorer*. Tommy was the first to see it and immediately called Michael. "Hey, have you seen this month's *Wine Explorer* yet?" he asked anxiously.

"Uh, no," Michael admitted.

"Well, hey, you're #47 this year! R.R. Parkston thinks your dry Viognier is among the best there is."

Michael sighed. "Damnit, I'll have to place a limit on it otherwise it'll sell out in a week."

Tommy, however, had more news. "Guess how many other Viogniers are on the list?" he teased.

"Uh, none?"

"Just one," his friend informed him. "And it's #72. Guess where it's from?"

"I wouldn't have the slightest idea," Michael admitted. How the hell could anyone guess which wine Parkston would deign to bless, he thought to himself.

"Condrieu!" Tommy told him.

"Holy shit!" Michael exclaimed. "Are you sure?"

"Yep," his friend assured him. "Your Viognier placed higher than a Condrieu. How about that?"

Michael was well familiar that the world's best Viognier was considered to be made in the Condrieu region of the northern Rhone Valley. In fact, his year of winemaking in France in the Côte Rotie was right next door to the Condrieu region, just like how Napa and Sonoma Counties lie next to each other.

"I'm telling you, Michael, those French winemakers are going to be pissed!" Tommy exclaimed with glee. "First your Syrah scores a perfect 100 points, then your Viognier places higher than a Condrieu." Chuckling, he added, "You're making them look like chumps!"

Michael knew better, of course, because the Top 100 list was always filled with many French wines every year, but he smiled anyway at his friend's enthusiasm. And, admittedly, it did feel good that R.R.

Parkston would think so highly of his Viognier. He shouldn't have been surprised, though, because Michael had learned to appreciate the Syrah and Viognier of the northern Rhone while he had been in France. He had brought back his knowledge and appreciation to the States, then had built on it with his own style. Since Parkston was a huge fan of French wines, it was no mystery that he liked Michael's Rhone varietals so much.

Placing once again in the Top 100 list of the world's most popular wine connoisseur magazine generated even more interest in Olde Schoolhouse Cellars, and once again the tasting room hosted overflowing crowds. Michael's greatest satisfaction, however, was in knowing that the publicity was good not only for him, but also for the entire valley. All the other winemakers would benefit from increased business as people traveled to Watilla to visit his establishment and then discover that other wineries were in the area.

*   *   *

The following year, in the spring of 1992, Maggie Higgins decided to personally check out Olde Schoolhouse Cellars. As a Watilla resident, she was familiar with several of Michael's wines, having enjoyed them in a couple of the local eating establishments. She had not, however, ever visited the tasting room.

Now she summoned the courage to do so, having decided that she every right to visit his place of business just like anyone else. Her sister Karen, who was her caretaker, drove her out on one delightful late April Saturday afternoon.

When they arrived at the schoolhouse, the parking lot was crowded but they were relieved to see an empty handicapped parking spot. "At least they have handicapped parking," she observed.

As Karen guided the car turned into the parking space, its tires crunched on the loose gravel of the unpaved lot. Shifting into PARK, Karen turned towards her sister and asked, "Are you sure you want to try this? I've heard there's a pretty nasty stairway inside."

Being paralyzed from the waist down and confined to a wheelchair, Maggie tried hard to put on a face of optimism as she went through life. "Where there's a will, there's a way," she replied with a half smile. "Besides, it's my birthday and this is something I've wanted to do for a long time."

At forty years of age, Maggie Higgins was still an attractive woman. Her light-colored red hair contrasted sharply with her piercing green eyes. Although she wasn't a vamp, her finely sculpted cheekbones, pretty smile, and enchanting eyes combined to give her a sex appeal that naturally made people, particularly men, want to help her.

Sighing, Karen shut the car off and got out to retrieve Maggie's wheelchair from the trunk. Placing it by the passenger door, she assisted her sister in settling in. The loose gravel made pushing the chair forward difficult, if not impossible, so Karen rolled it backward over to the sidewalk that led from the parking lot straight up to the front door of the schoolhouse.

Once Karen had Maggie up on the sidewalk, she turned the wheelchair around and let her sister propel herself forward unassisted. At the entrance, three low steps led up to a set of double wooden doors. A couple of visitors, just leaving the building, assisted Karen with pulling the wheelchair backwards up the steps and through the doors.

Inside the small foyer, the two sisters took stock of the situation. "Oh, my," sighed Karen as she looked up at the imposing staircase that led to the tasting room on the next floor. "There's no way I can pull you up those."

"Well, please go up there and inform them I require assistance," Maggie replied in a matter-of-fact voice. She wasn't going to be deterred, having made it this far. Karen left her sitting to one side and climbed up the steps to the tasting room. Maggie looked down at the set of side steps in front of her and noted the restroom sign below.

"Hmnpf, even the ladies room is a challenge to get to if I had to use it!" she muttered to herself.

Karen returned a minute later. "They're getting a couple men from the winery out back," she informed Maggie. "They'll carry you up."

After a wait of roughly ten minutes, two of the amigos—Cesar and Julio—came up from below on the other side staircase. Although their English was limited, they readily understood what Karen was trying to tell them. They picked up the wheelchair and carefully and slowly carried it backward up the grand staircase. Maggie maintained a tight smile on her face as she hoped they wouldn't stumble and drop her.

Safely at the top, she thanked the amigos and wheeled herself into the tasting room. As with everyone else who visited Olde Schoolhouse Cellars, she was impressed and delighted with the historic nature of the room.

"Aunt Denise actually went to this school," she commented to Karen. "It's nice to see how well preserved it is."

As nice as the tasting room was, however, it presented its own obstacles. The bar, of course, was too high for Maggie, but so were the bistro tables scattered around the room. Not that it mattered; the room was crowded as usual on a Saturday afternoon and there was virtually no room either at the bar or at a table.

"They should have a special place for visitors who are disabled," Maggie commented.

Karen parked her off in one corner and went to the bar to obtain some assistance. There were two ladies and one young man trying to do their best to handle the crowd and, after a wait of several minutes, one of the ladies came over with two wine glasses and a tasting menu.

It took a long 45 minutes for the two sisters to taste five wines. Being off in the corner, they were neglected due to how busy the tasting room was. Karen kept having to flag down one of the three helpers to get a taste of the next wine.

When they were finally done, Maggie purchased a bottle of Block 2 Syrah at a price of $29. Then she and Karen went through the process of getting back to their car. Once again, they had to wait until the two amigos were summoned, then Maggie endured being carried in her wheelchair back down the grand staircase and out the door.

Once Karen finally had her seated back in the vehicle, she commented, "Well, that certainly was a bit of an ordeal. I hope you enjoyed the visit."

"It's a very nice place," Maggie replied. "But the service is bad and the wine too expensive."

*   *   *

The next month, in May and on a Thursday morning, Michael was working in the Barn as Antonio and a couple of other amigos ran the bottling machine. Another amigo, who had been working outside, came in and informed Michael that he had a visitor.

"Who is it?" he asked.

The amigo shrugged. "A man who says he has something important for you."

"Sounds like a damn salesman," Michael groused. He hated salesmen; they were always coming around despite the signs that proclaimed NO SOLICTING.

"He says he's not a salesman."

"Hmnpf, then he's an insurance salesman," Michael said in contempt. Insurance salesmen were constantly soliciting him, but in their minds they didn't consider themselves to be salesmen even though they were.

Michael told his worker to let the guy in, but he was prepared to tell him to hit the road as soon as he began his pitch. A short, stout man in an ill fitting suit stepped into the Barn and doffed his bowler hat as Michael approached him.

"Are you Mr. Michael Ross, owner of Olde Schoolhouse cellars?" he asked brightly.

Michael, however, was in no mood for pleasantness. "Yes, I am," he confirmed. Then, pointedly, he asked, "What do you want?"

The man smiled and pulled out an envelope from his inside suit jacket pocket. "Well, sir, I have something for you," he said as he offered the envelop to Michael.

Michael accepted it and immediately asked, "What's this?"

Smiling, the man replied, "I'm a process server and you've just been served." Doffing his hat again, he added, "Have a good day!" With that, he quickly scuttled out of the building.

'What the hell?" Michael muttered as he opened the envelop. There were a several papers folded up inside, so he unfolded them and scanned them. He saw the words, 'Complaint,' 'Superior Court,' 'Americans with Disabilities Act' and 'Margaret Higgins.' What really opened his eyes wide, though, was the figure $750,000.

"I think I'm being sued!" he said to himself in disbelief.

The very next morning he was in downtown Watilla at his attorney's office. The gentleman was a lawyer he used from time to time for routine business matters. After intently reading the entire complaint, the lawyer put it down and said, "Yes, you're correct, Michael. You're being sued for $750,000 for non-compliance with the Americans with Disabilities Act."

Michael couldn't understand why, though. "I thought I was exempt from the ADA," he complained.

His attorney, however, contradicted him. "No, no business has a blanket exemption. There are only situational exemptions. In other words, on a case by case basis."

"Well, I've been told that an existing business doesn't have to comply if it imposes a financial burden," Michael pointed out. "There's what's called reasonable accommodation. And I've done that. I've provided a couple handicapped parking spaces."

The lawyer pursed his lips for a second. "I guess reasonable accommodation is open to interpretation," he replied. "We've been involved with two cases here locally the past year. One involved providing a wheelchair ramp and the other involved issues with a restroom."

"Okay," Michael conceded, "But I know for sure that historic structures are exempt and my schoolhouse is registered as an historic building. If I put in an elevator or something like that, then, hell's bells, I'd have to tear up the entire schoolhouse and that would completely destroy the historic nature of it!"

The attorney nodded. "I'd say offhand that that would be your best defense. But, listen, let me research this more and we can meet again next week and plan our strategy. I've never been involved with an ADA case quite like this one, so let me check if there's any case law yet regarding historic structures. We have a month before we have to respond to the complaint, so we can take our time and put together the best response we can."

Michael was still smoldering over the unfairness of the whole thing. "This is probably some activist suing local businesses hoping for an out of court settlement," he said bitterly.

The attorney, however, frowned and disagreed. "No, I don't think so," he said slowly. "If memory serves me right, this Margaret Higgins is the daughter of a couple who were in a horrible car accident. Had to be twenty years or more ago. They were killed and she had her back broken, or something like that. If she's who I think she is, then she's wheelchair bound."

Crap, Michael thought to himself. It was easy to get angry over the lawsuit when he thought it was some money-grubbing activist. But if the lady really was paralyzed, then that was a different matter. Still, it was unfair of her to sue him.

He and his attorney agreed to meet the following week to work out a response to the lawsuit. On the drive back to his winery, Michael still stewed over this crappy turn of events. His business had prospered and he had, in fact, completely repaid the loan from Bill Burton's bank. He still needed a line of credit, though, to smooth out cash flow throughout the year, so he wasn't exactly well off. He had a little money in the bank, but $750,000, God that would be disastrous if he had to come up with such a huge amount of money.

As he thought about it, he realized he would have to steel himself for the looming court battle. Margaret Higgins might be paralyzed, but that was too bad. He would have to fight her in the coming weeks and months. With his business at stake, he couldn't allow himself to feel any sympathy for her.

Chapter 15

Court(ship)

Watilla, Washington
1992/1993

After mulling things over in his head during the weekend, Michael decided that the best defense against the lawsuit was a good offense. That's what the old saying was, anyway. He looked up Margaret Higgins' address and, at 9:30 on Monday morning, stopped by her house in a quiet neighborhood in Watilla. He had thought of calling first but then decided she wouldn't agree to see him if he did.

He parked on the street by the house, a nice looking, older two-story frame home with a front porch and a tidy lawn. He walked up the short sidewalk that led to the porch. He noted the wheelchair ramp off to one side as he trotted up the steps.

Ringing the doorbell, he waited a moment until a lady who was maybe in her late forties opened the door. "May I help you?" she asked, a curious look on her face as she looked him up and down. Michael had decided to dress nice for this occasion, so he had on a polo shirt, dress slacks, and polished loafers.

"Good morning!" he greeted her cheerfully. "Would Ms. Higgins be home?"

"Which Ms. Higgins do you wish to see?" the lady answered, her facial expression becoming more neutral.

Michael was taken slightly aback at the question; he wasn't aware that two women with the same last name lived in the house. "Ah, Ms. Margaret Higgins, please," he answered, still managing a smile.

"And you would be?"

"Ah, Michael Ross."

The lady's face suddenly took on a look of concern, if not alarm. "The owner of the winery?"

"Yes, that's correct," he admitted.

Now a scowl took over the lady's face. "You should leave," she said pointedly.

Behind her, Michael saw movement and then realized it was a lady in a wheel chair approaching the door. "Karen," she said, "please ask Mr. Ross what he wants."

Karen turned around and replied to her sister in a low voice, but Michael still was able to hear her say, "He shouldn't be here and we shouldn't talk to him."

Michael knew he had to act fast. "Margaret?" he called out. "May I please have just a minute of your time?"

"Please ask Mr. Ross to come in for a minute," he heard Margaret say to her sister.

With a look of exasperation, Karen turned back to Michael and opened the door for him to come into the house. Once across the threshold, he came face to face with Margaret Higgins. She wasn't at all what he expected. Instead of an elderly woman, he encountered an attractive, smiling face with emerald green eyes greeting him good morning. She appeared to be maybe forty or so, and had reddish hair. Overall, she was a nice looking woman despite being in a wheelchair.

Michael said good morning back to her and quickly explained why he had come. "You've filed a lawsuit against me and I just wanted to learn the circumstances that motivated you to do so. I'm a reasonable guy who'd rather get along with folks than get into a dispute. The sooner I can understand exactly what the problem is, the sooner I can take steps to rectify it."

Margaret consider him for a moment while Karen hovered nearby. Breaking out into a smile again, she said, "Why don't we sit down and discuss this over coffee or tea?" Then she hastily added, "As long as the conversation remains civil, that is."

Michael held up a hand and replied, "I promise to keep the conversation civil."

"Maggie, this isn't a good idea," Karen interrupted. "You and Mr. Ross are legal adversaries."

Ignoring her, Maggie turned to Michael and asked, "Coffee or tea?"

"Ah, coffee, please," Michael answered "With a bit of cream or milk."

Turning to her sister, Maggie said, "Be a dear and please bring Mr. Ross some coffee. Oh, and I'll have another cup of tea."

Giving Maggie a severe look, Karen turned and headed to the kitchen. Maggie turned her wheelchair around and led Michael into a small living room off to one side. She wheeled herself up to a coffee table and indicated Michael should sit in a cushioned chair across from her.

"Well, Mr. Ross," she began, her green eyes twinkling with mischief, "we'll see if you keep your promise."

He immediately interrupted her. "Please, call me Michael," he said smiling. "Calling me Mr. Ross makes me feel old!"

"Well then, Michael, please call me Maggie."

He felt himself falling under her spell. Those eyes of hers, her smile, the way she regarded him as she looked at him, it all combined to have an effect upon him. He realized it would be difficult for him to ever become upset with her.

"Okay, Michael," she replied. "Let me begin by saying I've filed a lawsuit against you because, quite simply, your establishment is not accessible to disabled persons such as myself."

Michael nodded and cleared his throat. "I take it you've actually visited my tasting room?" It was important to him to find out if she had visited in person or was just filing a lawsuit against him because he made an easy target.

"Oh, yes, I certainly have," she confirmed. "On the 10th of last month."

"Please tell me about it," he urged.

"It was a dreadful experience!" Maggie replied. "To begin with, your handicapped parking spots are all well and good, but no one can move a wheelchair across loose gravel. Your parking lot needs to be paved."

"Hmm," was all Michael responded as he shifted in his chair.

"After struggling to get to the sidewalk," she continued, "I was then confronted by those three steps in front of your front door. Karen managed to pull me up those, but then, goodness, that big staircase of yours! My, what an obstacle!"

Maggie proceeded to describe how two of the amigos had carried her up, and then later carried her back down. But before she could tell Michael more, Karen arrived carrying a tray with his coffee, and with Maggie's tea and hot water.

"Thank you very much," he said as a coffee cup was set on the table in front of him, along with a spoon and a small container of cream. He poured a little of it into his coffee and stirred it as Maggie dipped a tea bag into her cup of hot water.

"Anything else?" he asked as he took a sip of coffee.

"Oh, yes, indeed," Maggie immediately replied. "Your tasting bar is too high for someone like me, as are those bistro tables. We were relegated to a corner and, as bad as that was, the service was absolutely disgraceful! It took nearly 45 minutes just to taste five wines."

Michael winced. "Ouch."

"My sister and I were neglected, Michael," she continued, looking at him critically. "Your staff was too busy with other customers to pay proper attention to us."

"I'm sorry," he replied with feeling. "That shouldn't have happened."

"It's obvious you don't know what goes on in your own tasting room," Maggie pointed out to him. "I find that very surprising for a small business owner."

Michael maintained his composure in the face of her biting comment. "It's true that I'm rarely in the tasting room anymore when it's open to the public," he admitted. "Sounds like that needs to change."

He took another sip of his coffee before asking a question that he knew wouldn't be well received. "Why do you think suing me will help the situation?" he wanted to know. "As I understand it, I'm basically exempt from the Americans with Disabilities Act, not only for the financial burden it would impose, but also because my schoolhouse is a registered historic structure."

Maggie, however, was having none of his line of reasoning. "Well, Michael," she replied as she set her teacup down, "I believe, first of all, that you can well afford it. Your wine is very expensive, at least by Washington State standards, and you do quite a bit of business at your establishment."

Michael's face colored as he listened to Maggie but he maintained his stoic composure. He knew he was being tested to see how he would react.

"Second of all," she continued, "historic buildings are not exempt as long as modifications would not significantly alter the nature of the structure. I've had an architect look at your schoolhouse and he thinks an elevator can be installed on the back side of the schoolhouse without compromising the nature of the building."

"You've had an architect look over my schoolhouse?" Michael asked, surprised.

Maggie smiled and her eyes twinkled as she replied, "Yes, I have. You don't realize it yet, but you could have a very accessible facility that almost any disabled person could visit."

Michael knew that she already had the costs figured out. "And did your architect make an estimate of the cost?" he asked.

"Yes," she confirmed. "Roughly $150,000 for the elevator and another $50,000 for modifications needed to the structure itself to accommodate the elevator. Plus, I really think you need to pave your parking lot. That's another $20,000 to $30,000. Add in a better sidewalk, one that would branch and also go around back to the elevator, and you have approximately $250,000 for the total cost."

Michael sat back in his chair a she absorbed the information. Now he knew the worst, and it was a lot better than the $750,000 of the lawsuit.

"Just because the price of my wine seems high to you doesn't mean that I have $250,000 lying around," he pointed out. "And suing me for three times that amount will guarantee the modifications will never get done."

Now it was Maggie's turn to feel a bit uncomfortable and she sighed. "Yes, I know. That was our attorney's idea. He said it was standard to sue for punitive damages in addition to the cost of the remedy."

Michael stroked his chin for a moment as he thought over the situation. Before he could make any reply, Maggie spoke up again. "You know, there's grant money on both the state and Federal level that could help reduce the total costs. I'd be more than happy to explore that avenue for you if you'd like. I write all kinds of grant applications for the local schools and non-profit groups."

"Really?"

Maggie shrugged. "Yes, it's one thing I can do by sitting at home," she confided." I work on my computer and am able to earn some semblance of a living."

Michael was intrigued. He liked Maggie and how she had a practical down-to-earth nature. To her, there were no insurmountable obstacles, just challenges to overcome. He took another sip of coffee and carefully put his cup down.

"Maggie, I tell you what. I'd like to meet with your architect and have him explain in detail what his ideas are. Would that be okay?"

Her face immediately brightened. "No, I wouldn't mind at all! That would be very considerate of you."

Michael nodded. "Okay then, let's set up a meeting. And, why don't you also look into those grants?"

*   *   *

A week later an architect from the Tri Cities drove over to Watilla and met Michael at the schoolhouse. Maggie and Karen drove out as well. It was eye-opening experience for Michael. Being the gentleman, he insisted on helping Maggie and pushing her wheelchair. He found out first-hand the extreme difficulty of trying to maneuver in the loose gravel of the parking lot.

Once around back the building, he listened as the architect explained his idea for an exterior elevator. Later, he and the gentleman went inside while Maggie and her sister remained outside. Up in the tasting room, the architect spent some time looking the situation over. Off in the side room that used to be a study hall, he liked what he saw.

"Michael, I believe we can open up the exterior wall here for the elevator doors," the man explained. "This would make excellent access to your tasting room. Disabled people could enter and exit the elevator away from the crowd at the tasting bar. That would make for a nice flow of foot traffic. Your normal customers would come and go via the staircase while, in here, in this separate room, disabled customers would come and go with no hassles."

Michael nodded. It seemed to make perfect sense. He also talked to the architect about designing modifications to the tasting bar itself in order to have a lower section for wheelchair patrons.

"I believe you could add a short extension on the left hand side," the man suggested. "Say, about five or six feet in length. That'd be enough to accommodate two wheelchairs side by side."

After that Michael led the man downstairs and they discussed the restroom situation which presented a problem. Michael's inventory room was located where the elevator would be. As he talked things over with the architect, he suddenly got an idea.

"Let's go outside," he urged. "I think I might have the answer."

Outside again with Maggie and her sister, Michael revealed his idea. "The wedding business is getting to be significant for the local wineries," he began. Indeed, Jancy had already put up a spacious, permanent tent next to her tasting room, enclosed with walls and capable of being heated and cooled.

"I've been thinking of constructing a little cottage type building here in back the schoolhouse," he informed the others. "It'd be for brides to get dressed prior to the ceremony. Why not just make it larger to include restrooms on one end with exterior access? The restrooms would be completely handicapped accessible. We'd just run a side branch of the wheelchair sidewalk over to this new building."

The architect immediately envisioned what Michael was talking about. "That's a great idea!" he replied approvingly. "The restrooms in the schoolhouse would be a nightmare to retrofit and make accessible. This is a much simpler solution, and a better solution. New construction is the ideal way to address accessibility issues."

Later on the group was treated to lunch by Michael at the Vineyard Café in downtown Watilla. The architect laid out an estimated budget of $350,000 which included the bride's cottage. Michael approved it and wrote out a check for $3500 to have specifications written and design plans drawn up.

"Maggie and I will work on securing funding as soon as possible," he informed the architect. "I want to get this project going as soon as possible."

*   *   *

A week later, Michael found himself back at the Tri Cities National Bank where he had secured his original business loan almost 15 years earlier. It had been several years since he had last seen Bill Burton Jr. and he wasn't surprised at all that the banker was now president of the bank.

"Yeah, Dad finally retired," the banker admitted with a smile. "Plays golf nearly every day down in Arizona."

"Rough life!" Michael joked.

Michael was surprised when Burton informed him just how much the bank was involved in the winery business. "We've got loans and accounts with nearly 20 wineries now, both here locally and over in your area."

Michael nodded. "The industry is really taking off in Washington," he agreed. "I'm glad you're part of it."

Burton chuckled. "I still remember the day this kid turned up in my office and said he was going to make wine in Watilla. That was quite a surprise!"

Michael chuckled, too. "And I'm still rather amazed that you had faith in me."

After a minute of further small talk reminiscing about Michael's early days establishing his vineyard and winery, the two men got down to business. He explained what he wanted to do and how he was going to try to pay for part of it with grants. Surprisingly, Burton was very receptive.

"Listen, Michael, let's proceed like this," the banker suggested. "The bank will loan you everything you need for the project so you can get started with construction, then when you get the grant money, just turn it over to me to reduce the size of the loan."

"Okay, thanks!" Michael replied, surprised by the readiness of Burton to act.

"We like these kinds of loans," the banker explained. "When the bank examiners do their annual review of our operations, they always check to see if we're fulfilling the 'community responsibility' part of our charter. So, we like to have a certain percentage of what's called socially responsible loans in our portfolio."

"Hmm, okay," Michael responded. "Glad I can help out with that!"

After their business was concluded, Michael left the bank and drove over to the architect's office where he informed him that the project was going ahead full steam. Then Michael drove over to Jonas' office and chatted with his CPA.

"Sounds like a good investment, Michael," the accountant informed him after listening to an explanation of the project. Then he added, joking, "You've been too profitable for the past seven years and used up all your tax losses that were being carried forward. It'll be good to have some write-offs again so you can stop paying taxes for a few years!"

Jonas also told Michael about his increasing winery business. Just like the bank, Jonas' firm was doing business with a number of wineries in central Washington. It was yet another reminder to Michael of the snowballing effects of economic activity. The more the winery industry expanded, the more business there was for all the businesses that supported the industry.

When he finally got back to Watilla, Michael immediately called Maggie and gave her the good news.

"That's wonderful!" she exclaimed. "This is so exciting!"

"Yeah, I think we should celebrate," he suggested.

"Absolutely!" she agreed.

"How about we have dinner? I heard that the Vineyard is has expanded their hours to include dinner now, not just breakfast and lunch."

"That sounds perfect!" she replied.

They agreed on a time for Michael to stop by and pick her up. His Blazer made it easy to carry her wheelchair, plus he had a couple grab bars on the passenger side that made it convenient for her to help swing herself into the passenger seat as he helped her up out of the chair.

Once in the café, Michael suggested a bottle of Champagne to start. "You certainly won't have to twist my arm on that!" she laughed. "I love bubbly wine!"

After the server opened the bottle and the cork came out with a pleasant pop, she poured the foaming wine into two flute glasses for them. Michael raised his in a toast. "Here's to a completely accessible tasting room at Olde Schoolhouse Cellars!"

Maggie clinked her flute against his as she replied, "Yes! A new day is about to dawn at your winery!"

As they both took a sip, their eyes were locked on each other. Michael realized once again how Maggie's emerald eyes sparkled when she was happy. It had the same effect on him as Jancy's eyes used to have, except the color was green rather than blue.

As Maggie put her flute down, she cleared her throat and said, "Now, I've some good news for you."

"Oh, yeah? About what?" he asked, wondering what she was going to tell him.

Leaning forward, she said in a low voice, "I've put the lawsuit on hold. When the project is completed, I'll drop it completely."

Michael nodded as he absorbed the news. "Good. Thanks."

Maggie sighed. "You know, I should never have filed it. I should have talked to you first. I apologize for that."

He waved a hand dismissively. "No, there's no need for an apology. It doesn't matter."

"Still, I should have talked to you first. It's just that I was so upset over my visit."

"That won't happen again," he assured her. "I've added another person to the weekend staff in the tasting room, and I've talked to them about how we can serve our customers better."

After they had placed their orders for dinner, Maggie had a question to ask. "You have a computer, right?"

"Oh, yeah, sure," he replied. "In fact, I'm on my third one now. Seems like the technology is changing so damn fast that I have to upgrade every year or two."

Maggie readily agreed with him, then went on to explore a subject she was curious about. "So, I can assume you surf the Internet, right? What they call the World Wide Web?"

He nodded. "Sure. It's amazing what you can find on it these days."

"More and more companies are creating a presence on the Internet with a website," she pointed out. "It's the wave of the future."

"I think you're right," he agreed.

"Have you ever thought about your winery having a website?" she probed.

Michael took a final drink from his flute. "What makes you think I don't have one?"

"I've checked," she shot back, her eyes dancing mischievously.

Michael raised his eyebrows. "So you've been checking up on me?" he needled her.

"You should have a website," she urged him. "It's cutting edge right now. Get on the Internet ahead of the pack and you'll have a competitive advantage."

He nodded as he listened. "Yeah, we talked about that at last month's association meeting," he informed her. "My friends Jancy and Tommy are getting web sites done for them."

"I know," Maggie replied. "I'm doing them."

Michael gave a start. "You're doing their websites?"

"Yes, I am," she confessed. "It's another thing I can do working from home. I learned HTML and how to construct websites. I think in a few years I'll have more business than I can handle."

"So, are you Watilla Internet Solutions?" He had seen an ad in the Chamber newsletter.

Maggie smiled broadly. "Yes, that's me," she proudly admitted. "'Internet solutions for a competitive advantage' is my business slogan."

When their dinners arrived, they ate them while deeply involved in a discussion of what a web site might look like for Old Schoolhouse Cellars. Michael liked her ideas and gave her the go-ahead to begin putting one together.

*   *   *

By August construction was in full swing at the schoolhouse. Prior to the actual digging, Michael agreed to a ceremony hosted by the Chamber in which he and Chamber officials, along with the architect, posed for a photograph, everyone with a shovel in their hands.

The elevator pit was dug and a foundation was poured for the bridal cottage/restroom building. The parking lot was paved over with asphalt and work begun on the sidewalk that would lead to the back of the schoolhouse to access both the elevator and the bridal cottage.

During the first month of work, Maggie and Michael had dinner once a week at the Vineyard Café. They enjoyed each other's company immensely and never lacked for topics of conversation.

By September Maggie had Michael's website finished and up and running. He was greatly impressed with it and told her so. "You've made my business really stand out," he told her. "It really makes me proud to be the owner."

After once a week dinners over four weeks at the Vineyard Café, Michael asked Maggie if she would like to have dinner at a nice restaurant over in the Tri Cities. She readily accepted and they enjoyed a pleasant evening out. Even the drive over and back passed quickly as they conversed nonstop.

When Michael took her home, he helped her out of his vehicle as usual and into her wheelchair. But before accompanying her to the front porch, he knelt down beside her. "I had a really nice time tonight," he said in a soft voice as he gazed into her eyes.

Smiling, Maggie replied in an equally soft voice, "I did, too."

He kissed her lightly on the lips and smiled. "I couldn't help that," he whispered. He kissed her again and then nuzzled her nose with his. "I really like you," he confessed. "I really enjoy being with you."

She stroked the side of his face with one of her hands. "And I really enjoy being with you, too," she whispered back.

Kissing her a third time, he whispered, "I'm going to keep asking you out."

Her green eyes shimmering, Maggie whispered back, "Good!"

After returning home, Michael lay in bed for a time just staring at the ceiling and thinking. He was strongly attracted to Maggie, there was no doubt of that. There was just something about her that made him want to please her, to make him want to look good in her eyes. He pretty much knew he was in love with her, although he had not yet told her.

Maggie Higgins had suddenly blown into his life and dramatically changed it. And for the better. He couldn't believe the big changes he was making with the schoolhouse. He knew he never would have done such an ambitious project on his own. And that was the thing about Maggie. She was good for him; they made a good partnership.

The next time he called her, he suggested driving over to Pendleton and dining at the famous steakhouse. "I can get reservations for Friday evening," he suggested.

"Why don't we make a weekend of it?" Maggie replied excitedly. "We can have a nice dinner on Friday, then on Saturday tour the mill, the tunnels, and see the historic district."

She was referring to Pendleton's well known woolen mill and the underground tunnels constructed in the 1890s for what became a city of Chinese laborers.

"Well, maybe not the tunnels," she quickly corrected herself after realizing they probably weren't accessible for the disabled.

"Uh, are you talking about staying overnight?" Michael asked, unsure if that was what she implied.

"Well, yes," she said. "If you're agreeable."

"Um, yeah, that's be okay," he confirmed. "I'll see if I can reserve two rooms at a local hotel or motel."

"Why two rooms?" Maggie quickly asked, startling Michael. "Won't one do?"

"Uh, are you sure about that?" he countered.

"If you're uncomfortable with the idea, then let's forget it," she replied, concerned.

"No, no," he quickly responded. "That'd be okay. You just caught me off guard."

That Friday evening they drove to Pendleton, Oregon, and dined at the grand western steakhouse with its fabulous interior. Michael was particularly pleased to see two of his wines on the wine list, although he ordered a Bordeaux to go with their steaks.

Afterward they went to the hotel and checked into their room. Once inside it, Maggie asked him. "Michael, you know why I wanted one room don't you?"

He sat down on the edge of the bed and took one of her hands in his. "I think I know why but I'm not sure."

Maggie smiled a sweet smile and explained. "I thought that after a nice steak dinner, some wine, and good conversation, that we could come up here and do what other couples would do."

He slowly nodded. "Yeah, that's what I thought. It's just that I'm uncertain about, uh, you know, exactly how we would do that."

Maggie took her free hand and placed it over his hand that was holding her other one. "You are a gift to me, an incredibly nice guy who treats me like the most special lady in the world."

"And you're a gift to me," he assured her.

"When two people feel strongly about each other, they naturally wish to express their intense feelings as physical love," Maggie continued. "Tonight, that's what I want to do."

Michael smiled as he saw her eyes sparkle and dance. "So, how does this work exactly?" he asked, curious.

"Well, I can't physically feel pleasure like a normal woman," she began explaining. "But there's an interesting phenomenon that can happen that involves mentally transferring the pleasure to another place on the body. My breasts, for instance. I can have an orgasm by concentrating on your kissing and fondling my breasts. Plus, it really helps if you talk to me while we're making love. You know, romantic things."

"I think I understand what you're saying," he replied. A second later a big smile broke out on his face. "I'll see what I can do!"

He helped her get on the bed and they held each other for a few minutes while they exchanged kisses. They slowly helped each other undress and Maggie began stimulating him with her hand as he kissed her breasts.

After several more minutes had passed, Michael was sufficiently aroused to enter her and they began making love. Following her advice, he concentrated on kissing her breasts and stimulating her taut nipples. He alternated that with whispering in her ear that he loved her and that she was the most incredible woman he had ever known.

The technique worked because Maggie began moaning and little gasps escaped her lips. Eventually she climaxed, giving a cry of pleasure as he felt her body shudder. The lovers didn't stop, though, but continued passionately kissing each other. Michael kept moving rhythmically with his thrusts, all the while whispering words of love to her and managed to bring Maggie to a climax a second time.

Later, when they were both spent, he continued to lay on top of her, supporting himself with his forearms as he nuzzled her nose and gazed into her eyes. "Thank you for loving me," she whispered, gazing up at him. "Thank you for being in my life."

Michael smiled and replied, "Thank you for suing me!"

Maggie chuckled. "Who knew? Who knew that this would happen?"

"You did," he said, teasing her as he kissed her. "This was all part of your plot."

"Looks like it worked!" she replied, teasing him back.

*   *   *

After spending a Christmas Eve get together with Jayson, Tommy, Jancy, and Jana, Michael drove over to Maggie's place on Christmas day for a mid-afternoon dinner. Afterward, she gave him a present that from its weight and size seemed to be a coffee table book. When he opened it, he discovered it was indeed a beautiful coffee table book – a worldwide atlas of wine regions written by two leading wine experts.

After perusing it for a few moments, he thanked her with a kiss and commented, "My present is over at the schoolhouse. "Mind if we drive over there?"

Maggie immediately said yes, and off they went. Using the new elevator, he and she arrived on the second floor. When they came around the corner of the study hall and entered the tasting room itself, Maggie was stunned to see a motorized three wheel cart sitting there with a big bow on it.

"Oh, my gosh!" she exclaimed, putting her hand to her mouth. "You didn't!"

"Yep," Michael replied, grinning. "I wanted you to have the latest in mobile fashion!"

He helped her into it and then enjoyed watching her try it out. She drove around the room, weaving around the dozen tables. "This is marvelous!" she exclaimed in delight. Stopping in front of him, she added, "You spoil me!"

Kneeling on one knee by her, he replied as he kissed her, "You deserve it."

A moment of silence passed as they gazed at each other. Suddenly, Michael took her hands in his and asked, "Maggie, will you marry me?"

Caught off guard, she was so stunned she couldn't reply for a second. After several seconds, however, she finally managed to reply, "Did you just ask me to marry you or am I imagining it?"

Michael chuckled. "I love you, you sweet woman. So, yes, I just asked you to marry me. We make a good partnership don't you think? We complement each other in many ways." Then he added, "Not to mention that I'm really crazy for you!"

Tears welled up in Maggie's eyes as her face became a mask of emotion. She managed to nod yes to him. Reaching into his pocket, Michael retrieved a diamond ring and slipped it on her finger.

Chapter 16

Economic Development

Watilla, Washington
1993 – 1998

The spring of 1993 proved to be a memorial time for both Michael and the Watilla region. In March the Chamber and the newly established Economic Development Commission held a joint press conference at the Watilla Hotel for a major announcement. A consortium of investors had decided to go ahead with a 'destination winery' south of the city.

"We've examined the Watilla area and feel the time is ripe for a new winery concept," a spokesman told the assembled crowd. "We're going to build a complex that will combine approximately 60 acres of vineyards, a European style country hotel with restaurant, a golf course, and a winery capable of producing an annual volume of 15,000 to 20,000 cases. It will be designed as a destination for guests to come and stay for several nights as they dine with us, sample our wine, play golf, and visit other area wineries."

The spokesman continued by saying the proposed name was Moritz Cellars and it would be located two miles north of Olde Schoolhouse Cellars on School Bridge Road. That would put it halfway between Michael's winery and the edge of town.

Michael was amazed at the scope of the project. It was certainly ambitious, to say the least. The question that remained to be answered however: could it be profitable? He wasn't sure.

A day later, Tommy dropped by the Barn for one of his periodic visits to help Michael barrel sample several wines. "You know, Michael," he said at one point when they were discussing the proposed development, "I think we just might be seeing something rather amazing taking shape. It could be that this area is going to really take off. I don't think it's going to keep developing slowly as you've been saying."

"No?"

Tommy shook his head. "Nope. I think we're hitting some sort of critical mass."

Michael frowned. "I'm not sure, but I have to admit this Moritz Cellars project is certainly something."

"I'll say!" Tommy exclaimed. "God, $3 million! That's a fortune!"

Michael agreed, and replied, "But I doubt the investors are a bunch of dummies. I wouldn't think they would put up that kind of dough unless they've done their homework and saw potential here."

"A lot of potential," Tommy said with emphasis. "Like I say, this region may be on the verge of major change."

By May the project with all its zoning and utilities issues had been worked out and approved by both the city and county. A construction start date was announced for the first week of June. Work also got under way on planting the first 10 acres of vines.

*   *   *

On Saturday of Memorial Day weekend, Michael and Maggie were married. The ceremony was naturally carried out at Olde Schoolhouse Cellars. In fact, Michael had found that hosting weddings was a profitable addition to his business, so he had had an area between the schoolhouse and the Barn designed specifically for weddings.

Jayson, nearly five years old now, was the ring bearer, and Jana, almost three, was the flower girl. Maggie's brother from New Mexico came up for the ceremony and gave her away, while her sister Karen served as maid of honor. Tommy readily agreed to be Michael's best man.

Maggie's brother escorted her on foot as she slowly drove her motorized cart up to the presiding official where Michael was already waiting. Once Maggie arrived, Tommy brought a chair over for Michael so he could sit side by side with her. The official proceeded through a simple but traditional ceremony. After exchanging vows, he pronounced Michael and Maggie husband and wife.

Afterward, they drove into town to the historic Watilla Hotel for a reception held in the ballroom. After the toasts and the cake cutting, guests went through a buffet line and then to tables to eat.

A band with a male vocalist had been hired to provide live music, and for the first dance Michael and Maggie had selected *More*, a song made popular by crooners such as Andy Williams. The band and its vocalist slowed the music down a bit to a waltz style and since Maggie barely weighed a hundred pounds, Michael held her in his arms while he slowly waltzed to the music.

"More than the greatest love the world has known," the vocalist's deep voice smoothly began, and no one in the old ballroom could help but be affected emotionally. As he continued singing lines like, "No one else could love you more," tears started appearing on several faces. And by the time he got to, "Far beyond forever you'll be mine," there was hardly a dry eye in the crowd.

After the first dance, many of the guests got up and began dancing to the follow-up numbers. A half dozen songs later, though, the dance floor cleared to allow the newly married couple to go solo once again, this time to the song, *A Time for Us*, the love theme from *Romeo and Juliet*.

Tommy wasn't much for slow dancing, but he liked swing, so he and Jancy danced several swing numbers over the course of an hour. Michael couldn't help but notice Jancy and how exceptionally attractive she still was, especially dressed up. She had retained her slim and sexy figure and, of course, her blue eyes and shoulder-length blonde hair. He sighed. If he hadn't screwed up once upon a time, perhaps this could have been their wedding day.

That was water long over the dam, however, and Michael was now beginning a totally new phase of his life. He knew he would be happy with Maggie, and if truth be told, she was just the challenge he needed. Caring for her and making her happy gave renewed purpose to his life which, before the lawsuit, had settled into a boring predictability.

But if Michael thought things were totally over between him and Jancy, he was mistaken. A short time later, Tommy came over to join him at the bar and congratulate him once again. After a moment, he casually mentioned, "Hey, I think a certain lady is waiting for you to ask her to dance."

This statement took Michael by surprise. "Huh? Who?" he asked, looking around the room.

Tommy rolled his eyes. "You really have no idea?"

Michael frowned as he thought it over. "Jancy?" he finally ventured.

Tommy sighed. "Who else do you think I'm talking about? I don't do slow dances, so I'm depending on you to fill in for me," he joked.

Michael was immediately suspicious. "How do you know she wants to dance with me?"

"Uh, she asked me to come over and let you know," his friend replied. "*Moon River* is her favorite slow number, so I put a request in for the band and they'll be playing it shortly." Clapping his friend on the back, Tommy added, "You best get moving."

Michael immediately put his drink down and made a beeline for Maggie where he spent a moment explaining the situation. To his surprise, she was supportive.

"You look so handsome tonight in your tux!" she informed him with a smile. "It'll be a treat to watch you dance with a lady who can actually dance!"

He bent over, kissed her, and thanked her. Turning around, Michael walked over to the far side of the room where Jancy was standing, conversing with a couple of female acquaintances. She raised her eyebrows in expectation as he approached. Clearing his throat, he nervously asked, "Would you like to dance with me?"

He felt he was a bit out on a limb with the question because things were still very frosty between him and her despite all the years that had gone by. He was relieved when she immediately smiled and replied, "Sure!" and then set her drink down.

He escorted her to the dance floor as the band began the first strains of *Moon River* and the vocalist prepared to start singing the well-known lyrics. It felt strange after all these years to be in physical contact with her again, to have his right arm around her waist and his left hand holding her right hand while her left hand rested upon his shoulder. He tried his best to waltz in time with the slow tempo of the music.

After a brief moment, she suddenly said, "I was wrong."

Puzzled, he didn't understand. "About what?"

"About that evening at the Chamber meeting," she replied. "I should have gone with you."

Michael shrugged. "Water over the dam. It doesn't matter now."

"No, I was wrong," she insisted. "And also about keeping my pregnancy from you in the early stages."

Michael shook his head. "We were both wrong. Why don't we let it go at that?"

He raised her arm for an underarm turn and she slowly twirled around, then came back into him. "I forgive you," she also added, looking him straight in the eye. "Your marrying Maggie is such an incredibly nice, romantic story."

Gazing at her, he thought, God, I can't believe how blue her eyes are! Struggling to control his emotions, he shook vigorously his head as he replied, "There's no need to apologize or forgive me for anything."

"Yes, there is," she insisted. "I've held it against you for so many years. Now it's time for a new beginning."

"Okay," he simple answered, not sure where she was going with this.

"I want all of us to be friends," Jancy continued, explaining herself. "We're sort of a big family anyway. You…me…Jayson…Tommy…Jana. We're all connected."

"That's true," he agreed.

"Now Maggie's part of the equation," she continued. "I want all of us to be friends and to be part of an extended family."

"Thank you," he replied as he led her into another underarm turn. "That'll be nice."

As the dance was ending, a severe look came over her face as she admonished him, "Just don't do Maggie wrong," she warned.

Michael held up one hand as he solemnly promised, "Don't worry, I won't."

*   *   *

The next day Michael and Maggie took off on a 10 day driving trip to California. He had a nice custom van fitted with a hydraulic ramp to easily load and unload her powered chair. They started first with wineries in Mendocino County, then drove further south and spent time in Napa and Sonoma. Whenever Michael dropped his name, he and Maggie were usually treated as VIPs and given private tours and private tastings.

Finally arriving in the Santa Cruz area, they spent three days with Michael's parents who had recently retired and moved to the nearby seaside resort of Capitola. Although his folks had attended the wedding, it was a pleasant interlude to go wine touring with them in the Carmel Valley and neighboring Santa Lucia Highlands. They both thought highly of Maggie and her pleasant, friendly personality.

After returning to the Watilla area, the newlyweds bought a home on the south edge of the city that had been previously owned by a retired businessman who had had a disabled, wheelchair-bound wife. He had constructed the house as a single level, completely accessible residence which was perfect for Maggie's needs.

Jayson began kindergarten that fall and Jancy consented for him to live with Michael and Maggie during the week, and with her and Tommy during the weekends. In addition, Michael and Maggie were frequently invited over to Tommy and Jancy's for dinner. Michael and Maggie would return the favor, and eventually the two households fell into an alternating weekend routine for Sunday evening dinners.

With Jayson starting school, Michael knew that in just a few short years he would begin teaching his son the skills of a world-class winemaker. "I can't wait!" he proudly boasted to Jancy and Tommy one day. "He's going to be a chip off the old block!"

"I know exactly what you mean," Jancy replied. "I can't wait to teach Jana!"

*   *   *

The time period from 1994 to 1998 brought many changes to Watilla. The town's population continued to expand rapidly, hand-in-hand with the growing wine industry. Predictions were made that the 2000 census would show nearly 15,000 residents in the small city, up from less than 9,000 in 1990.

Looking back in hindsight years later, it would be generally agreed that the year 1998 was a turning point, for it was the year that the city realized its future was inextricably bound with its wine industry. The Moritz Cellars project was complete and open for business, the community college wine program was booming, the number of

winery operation was fast approaching 50, and the total planted
acreage of vines was nearly 1,000.

The city leaders knew beyond a doubt that the future of Watilla and
the surrounding Watilla Valley would prosper hand in glove with the
wine industry. Although onions continued to be an important crop,
total acreage of strawberries, cherries, and apples continued to rapidly
decline, replaced for the most part by vineyards.

In the fall of 1998, the Chamber of Commerce and the Economic
Development Commission held yet another joint press conference to
announce a major project. The event was held once again in the old,
crumbling Watilla Hotel, but this time the location was appropriate.

The executive director of the Economic Development Commission
announced that a group of investors was buying the hotel with the
goal of restoring it. Nearly $5 million dollars would be spent on a
complete, historically accurate restoration, plus a conference center
would be added on the west side of the structure. One of the principal
partners in the project was introduced to the assembled group, and he
proceeded to explain the reasoning behind the investment decision.

"We've taken a look at the potential of the Watilla area, and we like
what we see," he began. "You folks here have a wine industry in full
bloom. And it's in the potential of that industry that we're making our
investment."

The man continued, offering several amazing statistics. "When we
made projections of the Watilla Valley over the next 20 years, we
came to some surprising conclusions." Everyone in the old ballroom
of the hotel was now hanging on every word the man uttered.

"By 2018 we predict a population of Watilla of 20,000 to 25,000,"
he announced. "We foresee more than 100 wineries in the area which
will bring 200,000 or more visitors each and every year. This
projection, as well as the on-going growth of the community college
and the city, more than justifies our investment. We will fully restore
the ballroom and all seven floors of the hotel, as well as add a 20,000
square foot conference center. The Historic Watilla Hotel will once
again be the crown jewel of the city."

Hearty and prolonged applause greeted this news. For Michael,
standing in the middle of the assembled crowd, it was nothing short of
amazing. The economic snowball was indeed rolling and gathering

momentum, just as Tommy had suspected several years earlier. The change to the city and the region was accelerating.

*   *   *

In that same year Michael discovered that his personal vision of the future might not be realized when Jayson came into the Barn one day. He was 10 years old now and looking more and more like his father. He would be tall like Michael, although because of Jancy's height, he probably wouldn't end up taller. His sandy hair also told of a mix between her blonde hair and Michael's chestnut brown.

Jayson came into the little office Michael had in one corner of the winery. "Dad!" he said in a raised voice, clearly excited about something.

Michael looked away from his computer screen to his son and replied, "Hmm?"

"Did you know you have 211 wine barrels?"

A look of mild surprise spread across Michael's face. "211? Really?"

"Yes!" Jayson confirmed, and he held up a couple of sheets of paper from a yellow note pad. They were covered with hash marks in groups of five – each group having four vertical marks and one diagonal, just as the little boy had been taught in school.

Michael looked over the sheets with some amazement. "You counted all the barrels in here?" he asked, a bit incredulously.

"Yes, I did!" the boy proudly replied. "There are so many of them that I wanted to know how many!"

Michael stroked his chin. "Well, that's something, I have to admit. But, are you sure you counted them accurately?" he teased. "Are you sure there's not 210, or maybe 212?"

"Nope!" Jayson immediately countered. "211!"

Michael scratched his cheek for a second, then suddenly said, "Well, partner, why don't we check? I've got the inventory right here on the computer."

Michael had a bookkeeping program on his office computer that had been installed by one of Jonas' associates. His bookkeeper used it twice a week to keep the books of the business. He opened up a section of the program and checked.

Turning to Jayson, he said, "It says here that there are 223 barrels in here right now." Motioning to the screen, he showed his son the listing of barrels by the type of wine they held. "See? The grand total is 223."

But Jayson wasn't persuaded. "No, Dad. There are 211. I counted them!"

Michael gave his son's hair a tousle with his hand. "Well, then, there's only one thing to do. Let's go out and count them together!"

Jason's face lit up with excitement. "Okay, Dad! You'll see!"

Michael and his son walked down the length of the winery to the far end and began counting the stacked rows of barrels. Michael personally made the count, always double checking that Jayson circled each group of five hash marks to make sure of accuracy. As he scanned his son's work, he noticed something else: The marks were neatly lined up in straight rows. Not only did his son like to count, but he had a sense of organization as well.

Ten minutes later, the count was completed and the total number of barrels was…211. "Well, I'll be doggone!" Michael exclaimed.

"See, I told you so, Dad!" Jayson replied, excited.

To solve the mystery, Michael sought out Mercedes, his assistant winemaker. She was a young woman who was the daughter of Jorge and his wife, Maria. A graduate of the community college's wine program, she was a bright, hard-working young lady who readily soaked up Michael's tutelage.

She proceeded to explain that a number of discarded barrels were lying out back. "We have requests from time to time for half barrels," she explained. "People mostly use them for planters in their yard. For flowers and things like that. So we cut in half the ones that we don't wish to use anymore. Generally they're damaged too much to use any longer."

She led Michael and Jayson out back where off to one side they saw a number of damaged barrels and half barrels. Adding everything up, they arrived at a number close to 223. Mystery solved.

After that incident, Michael's eyes were opened to what the future might hold for his son. When the little type learned that grapes were weighed during harvest, he wanted to keep track of the tonnage of each batch. And by type of grape. Of course, the amount of juice pressed was also weighed, and he kept track of that as well.

In fact, in the fall, Jayson would make a beeline for the Barn every day after school and try to learn what work had been done that day. How many gallons of juice pressed? How many barrels filled for fermenting? How may gallons in the stainless tanks? And on and on.

Shaking his head one day, Michael muttered under his breath, "Good God, my son's going to be an accountant!"

Chapter 17

A Birthday Party

Watilla Valley
1999 – 2001

By 1999 Michael and many other winemakers were using cell phones, an exciting new technology that promised to change how they did business. The city of Watilla, as well as the county, had recently been provided coverage through the construction of a network of cell towers. Although there was no coverage beyond roughly 10 miles outside the city limits, the new technology was eagerly welcomed. Winemakers outside of the city could converse with ease with local suppliers even if they were standing in their vineyards.

A second development of note was *Wine Explorer* magazine doing a feature story on the Watilla Valley in its July issue. Although Michael, Jancy, and Tommy were given special coverage as the 'pioneers,' the comprehensive article made an effort to cover many other winemakers as well. Michael was especially glad to see that the magazine's cover photo was of an expanse of picturesque vineyards with Mortiz Cellars in the background. He was no longer the center of attention and that was just fine with him.

The article noted that while the three pioneer winemakers had extensive product lines, Olde Schoolhouse Cellars emphasis was on Syrah, and that J Phillips Cellars specialty was red Bordeaux-style blends such as its well known *Adagio.* As for Fíona Cellars, Tommy was described as the 'King of Merlot,' and the article went on to describe that Merlot in general from the Watilla Valley was very different than most others, especially those from California.

Michael had noted this fact as well over the years. Watilla Merlot to him was more robust and more full-bodied, and it had very intriguing red cherry/red raspberry elements. But since his interest was primarily Syrah and Viognier, he was content to let Tommy and other winemakers specialize in Merlot. As far as he was concerned, it was all good.

*   *   *

In May 2000 Tommy talked to Michael about a birthday party. "The Big Five-Oh is coming up for you," he teased. "The ladies really would like to have some sort of to-do for you."

By ladies, he meant Jancy and Maggie who had become good friends. Michael had purposefully avoided any celebration when he had turned 40, but now things were different. His life was richer and fuller, so why not celebrate?

"Listen," he said to his friend, "I want it kept low key, okay? No big party."

"Yeah, sure, no problem," Tommy replied. "Let me talk to Jancy and see what we can do."

"Maybe it can be in the tasting room after hours," Michael suggested.

What actually happened, though, when his birthday rolled around in May, was a rather large party held at La Buena Tierra on a Sunday afternoon. Completely renovated and expanded, the Mexican cantina had become quite a busy establishment over the years, serving not only Latinos, but also whites since Mexican cuisine had become fashionable.

Closed to the public for the private party, several dozen adults came to help Michael celebrate his fifty years. There were friends of Maggie and his, as well as a number of winemakers they knew well. And, of course, many amigos were in attendance, too, both those who were employees and those who were seasonal workers in the vineyard.

A DJ provided a mix of music while guests enjoyed a Mexican buffet. Michael was content to drink Mexican beer which just seemed to be the appropriate thing to do. He accepted the congratulations of the guests, enjoyed a birthday cake, and opened a number of gifts and cards.

The next evening—the actual day of the birthday—a private get-together was held in the home he and Maggie owned. The only other ones present were Tommy and Jancy, plus the kids. Jayson was now going on 12, while Jana was nearly 10. Of the two, Jayson was well adjusted and excelled in school. Jana, on the other hand, was a continuing problem for her parents.

She tended to be anti-social and headstrong. She didn't do well in school and frequently had behavior problems that vexed her teachers. Michael wasn't surprised by how headstrong the girl was because Jancy, after all, was her mother. Her daughter was a chip off the old block, so to speak.

As they settled down in the family room before dinner, either in chairs or on the sofa, a couple bottles of wine were opened – one of Michael's older vintages of Syrah and one of Jancy's older vintages of *Adagio*. She helped Maggie serve food nibbles, one a platter of cheeses and the other a platter of charcuterie.

After the adults had toasted Michael, family gifts were presented to him. Jayson's was a new electric cork remover while Jana's was a gift certificate to the Vineyard Café & Bakery.

Tommy was next and he handed Michael a small item the size of a large paperback book. "Hmm, seems like a book," Michael guessed as he accepted it from his friend who had a strange, silly grin on his face. Unwrapping it, he also smiled and shook his head in mock dismay as he saw the familiar black and yellow cover of a popular book series. "*Winemaking for Dummies*," he read aloud, which prompted a hoot from Tommy as the kids laughed and the ladies chuckled.

"I thought you could pick up a few pointers!" his friend kidded him.

Slightly red faced, Michael pretended to be a bit upset as he replied, "Very funny! Very funny, indeed! I'm sure you had a blast buying this at the bookstore!"

"I was with him at the time and tried my best to dissuade him," Jancy said as she shot a disapproving glance at Tommy.

"Well, I'm sure this will occupy a prominent position on my bookshelf," Michael announced sarcastically.

Next, Jancy picked up a large, heavy item neatly gift wrapped and handed it to him. "This is from both Tommy and me," she informed him. "It's a *real* gift," she emphasized.

As Michael accepted it from her, he suspected it was a coffee table book. Carefully unwrapping it, he discovered he was right. He held in his hands a volume titled, *The Complete Guide to French Wines.* Near the bottom of the front cover, he read, *by Ralph Rogers Parkston.*

"Wow, impressive!" he exclaimed as he hefted the book and admired the gorgeous front cover which pictured a charming chateau in Bordeaux surrounded by lush vineyards.

"Look inside," Jancy urged, excited.

Michael opened the book to the inside cover. He immediately noticed an inscription in an elegant, flowing handwriting. He read it out loud. *"To Michael Ross, truly one of the world's great winemakers. Best regards, R.R. Parkston."*

He blew out a breath of air. "Jeez, personally autographed!" he said in awe.

'When we contacted him," Jancy informed him, "he was happy to help us out. And, he said to tell you he wishes you a happy and memorable birthday."

A brief discussion broke out among the three winemakers about R. R. Parkston and his rating system. A few wisecracks were made but, overall, the talk was mostly of memories of certain past issues of the magazine and some of the top wines that had been featured.

When things settled down again several minutes later, Maggie presented a somewhat heavy, rectangular item to her husband. Measuring a little over a foot long, and four or five inches on each side, Michael accepted it and noted it weight. Removing the wrapping paper, he found himself holding a wooden wine box. The name of the winery was burned into the wood: Domaine Garçon.

"Oh my gosh!" he exclaimed. "Do you mean to say that you bought this direct from the winery?"

Maggie beamed as she replied, "Well, I had to work through a distributor who, of course, made arrangements with an importer but, yes, it's from Domaine Garçon. They were happy to donate it."

"Huh, imagine that, they must still remember me," Michael observed with some amazement.

"Open it up, Dad!" Jayson urged impatiently.

Michael slid the front side of the box out of its grooves and revealed the bottle resting inside. He read the label. "Côte Rotie…1983…Domaine Garçon."

"Holy cow!" he exclaimed. "1983! This is one of their library wines!"

He lovingly turned the bottle over in his hands and glanced at the back label. Then he noticed a small envelop lying in the box. His first name was on it, written in a feminine style. Frowning in curiosity, he carefully set the bottle down on the coffee table in front of him and picked up the envelop.

Opening it, he found a short note inside that read, *'Many best birthday wishes, Michael. This was one of our better vintages and the last made by Jacques. You must come visit us sometime! Warmest regards, Jacqui.'*

He was suddenly overcome with emotion as memories flooded back from the time he had spent at the winery. "God!" he exclaimed softly as he set down the note. "It's been so many years! I can't believe they still remember me!"

Closing his eyes for a second, he visualized the grand old mansion, the winemaking buildings, and the vineyards. He suddenly wondered why he had never seriously contemplated returning for a visit.

Michael visualized, too, sweet young Jacqui. It was gratifying to him that she still remembered him, although he didn't admit that out loud. There was no point in telling everyone about his love affair with her.

Jacqui's note seemed to imply that perhaps Jacques had passed away. Jacques, his mentor. Once again he wondered why he had never gone back to France and looked up the old man. Had it been trepidation of seeing Jacqui again? Of her being married and finding himself in an awkward situation? But her note seemed to convey that she would like to see him again.

"Well, hell, this is supposed to be a happy occasion!" Tommy suddenly blurted out, trying to break the mood. "Why don't I go get your grill going so we can have dinner?" he suggested. Then he kidded his friend by adding, "I'm anxious to see you try to blow out 60 candles on your birthday cake!"

As the females moved into the kitchen to set the table and prepare salads, Tommy, Michael, and Jayson decamped to the back patio. Tommy insisted on doing the grilling. "It's your birthday, so let everyone else work!" he happily explained.

Besides, he was anxious to show Jayson how to expertly put criss-cross grill marks on the rib eye steaks that were the main entrée. He fancied himself an expert on grilling meat and was only too willing to show off his skills.

Once dinner was ready, Maggie invited everyone to sit down. After a quick toast with sparkling wine, the salads were eaten. After that, Tommy rose from the table and said, "Let me go get something really special to enjoy with these steaks."

He went over to a counter where a decanter of red wine sat which Michael had not previously noticed. There was also a gift bag with a bottle in it. "I have to admit to a conspiracy," he told Michael when he had returned to the table. "I brought this over earlier, opened it, and decanted it."

Michael gave an inquiring look at Maggie. "Where has this been?"

She smiled sweetly as she replied, "Hidden out of sight!"

Tommy pulled the bottle out of the bag. It was empty, all the wine having been decanted. "Recognize it?" he asked with a smile as he handed it to his friend.

Michael lovingly cradled the bottle in his hands and shook his head in disbelief as he stared at it. "My '85 Reserve Syrah," he quietly answered. Then he admonished Tommy by adding, "You shouldn't have."

His friend simply shrugged. "I was saving it for a special occasion," he explained. "Seems like your 50th birthday is pretty special!"

Michael sighed. "This has certainly been a memorable occasion," he admitted.

"I hope you have some more bottles of that," Tommy added, "because this is my last one."

Michael blew out a breath of air. "I only have one left myself!"

"Well, save it for your 60th," Jancy piped up. "It should still be good in another 10 years."

He shrugged. "Maybe; time will tell."

Tommy was eager to try the wine, so Michael served the three adults and then himself. After another toast, everyone took a sip from their glass after first sniffing the wine. Each person offered their opinion and the consensus was that it was still extraordinary. All of the wonderful elements that had earned the wine a perfect 100 points were still present, but there were also other, more subtle changes that had occurred over the years.

"It's stayed together and matured," Michael observed. "I'm very pleased with how it is. I think I like it even better after 15 years than when it was young."

*   *   *

Just before the grape harvest was due to begin that year, Michael met with Dr. Cline in early August out in his vineyard. He had invited the researcher to discuss something that had been on his mind for some time. Although retired, Cline was still spry and active.

"This looks like the very picture of a perfect vineyard," he observed as he surveyed it with admiration. He and Michael were standing at the top of the vineyard in the oldest section - Block One.

After a moment of discussing the health of the vines, Michael got down to business. "There's roughly a drop in elevation of 35 feet from where we're standing to the toe of the section," he informed Cline. "Then it's roughly another 15 foot drop to the level of the river."

The researcher nodded as he surveyed the scene. "Yes, just eyeballing it, that looks right," he agreed. "And from records of several local water wells drilled over the years, we can assume that the water table where we're standing is approximately 50 feet. And that means only 15 to 20 feet or so at the toe of the vineyard."

Michael nodded. "And we know that grapevine roots can grow at least that deep."

"Oh, yes, indeed," Cline quickly agreed. "Fifteen to 20 feet is pretty standard, and there are known cases of up to 30 feet. Plus, in California, there are claims that some old vine Zinfandel has gone as much as 50 feet deep, but that's not scientifically documented. However, they say they don't irrigate them anymore, so there may well be some truth to their claims."

Michael considered this for a moment, then replied, "It seems as if the bottom third of this section, and also of Block Two, bear a heavier yield of fruit than the upper two-thirds. I think those vines are in the water table."

Cline considered this statement as he slowly nodded. "You may be right. The only way to tell is to not turn on the water to them next spring."

"That's exactly what I was thinking!" Michael replied, excited. "I'd like to convert as much of my vineyard as possible to a non-irrigated status."

"You're looking for a smaller, more intensely flavored berry," the researcher shrewdly guessed. "As good as your wine is, you're trying to do even better."

"Yep," Michael confirmed. "There are places in Europe where they don't irrigate, like Spain for instance. I've heard that they can irrigate the first five years and then the vines are on their own."

Cline stroked his chin as he considered the prospect of 'dry' vineyards in Washington. "You should go for it, Michael," he said as he encouraged the winemaker. Then, chuckling, he added, "If I was still working, I'd be tempted to do a research paper on it! I'd use your vineyard as the experimental plot."

The more the researcher thought it, the more he liked the idea. "Just imagine" he marveled, "an area of the country that receives only seven inches of rain a year with non-irrigated vineyards! That would be something!"

"You should do the paper," Michael encouraged him. "Use my experience right here in Watilla."

Cline slowly nodded as a big smile broke out on his face. "You know, I just might damn well do it! I'll use a couple grad students from the university and we'll just see if we can't come up with a paper to publish in a two or three years."

*   *   *

During the 2001 growing season, Michael had the amigos reconfigure his drip irrigation system so that a portion of it could be shut off when desired. Specifically, he arranged that the lower third of Blocks One and Two would receive no water unless they began to show alarming signs of stress. A little stress was a good thing, and that was what he was after. Too much, however, would be bad.

As the season progressed, Michael was able to avoid watering the shut off areas. His reward was having the vines respond by producing a lower than normal yield, and the berries were smaller. Excited, he fermented the Syrah grapes from the 'dry' area separately from the irrigated ones.

As the weeks and months went by, he enlisted the help once again of Jancy and Tommy as he sought to craft yet another extraordinary wine. His friends assisted with barrel tasting different batches, trying to come up with the ideal blend. Ever since the 1985 vintage, Michael had routinely incorporated a small percentage of Petit Syrah into his Syrah, in addition to the five per cent of Viognier.

The new Syrah that was made in the 2001-2002 winemaking season meant that a new name needed to be created. Marketing demanded it, if nothing else. But for Michael, it was always enjoyable to invent a new name. Maggie finally hit upon one that summed up the situation so well: *Au Naturel*.

"The wine is made from grapes grown in a natural state," she observed. "No artificial irrigation used to provide water to the vines. They obtain it on their own from deep underground."

"Yeah, makes sense," Michael replied. "*Au Naturel*. I like it!"

He gave her a kiss and said thanks. "Now, why don't you work on a suitable label?" he asked.

Chapter 17

A New Partnership

Fiona Cellars
July, 2002

On 5 July 2002 Michael and Maggie were invited to help Jana celebrate her 12th birthday. They drove over to the farmhouse for a family dinner to be followed by birthday cake. Although Jana seemed flattered by the attention, she was continuing to give her parents trouble. She had even run away once, attempting to spend the night at a friend's place before her frantic parents tracked her down.

Jancy, in particular, was consternated that her daughter resented any attempts to teach her winemaking. To Michael it seemed more a case of rebellion than of being interested in something else, as was the case with Jayson. His son was proving to be a math whizz and showed every indication of someday having a career in the financial world.

After dinner, Jancy brought out the birthday cake and lit candles. Everyone sang 'Happy Birthday' to Jana who seemed embarrassed by the attention. But when it came to her being urged to blow out the candles, she seemed resentful and only did so grudgingly.

For her birthday present, Michael and Maggie gave her a beautiful, expensive, glass wine thief in hopes of spurring her interest in vinification. She held the long, curved tube in her hands and examined it with some curiosity, although she had, of course, seen her mother and father use one countless times. It was more a case of her being a little in awe of having her very own.

"Now you can do your own barrel sampling!" Michael remarked, using an upbeat voice.

"Yeah, that's pretty cool!" Tommy chimed in.

But Jana merely shrugged. "I guess," she simply replied. "Whatever."

"Uh, can you tell Maggie and Uncle Mike thanks?" Jancy prompted her.

Jana gave them a quick glance and a quiet, "Yeah, um, thanks."

Jancy brought out coffee for the adults and milk for the kids after which everyone enjoyed a piece of the cake. When they were finished, Jayson and Jana were excused and they quickly ran to her room to play a game on her desktop.

With the kids out of the room, Tommy cleared his throat and glanced at Michael and Maggie. "I'd like to discuss a business proposition that Jancy and I have thought about quite a bit," he announced.

Michael's eyebrows shot up in curiosity. "What's up?" he asked.

Tommy turned to Jancy. "I'll let you explain," he said to her. "I think it best if they hear it from you and know you fully support this."

Facing Michael and Maggie across the table, she took a sip of coffee and then proceeded to tell them some surprising news. "We're moving our operations—combining them in many ways, actually—and would like for you to be a part of the new business."

Michael looked straight across the table at Jancy and she gazed back at him without the slightest sign of discomfort. Well, well, he thought to himself. She's willing to go into business with me, so I guess I've truly been forgiven.

"There's a number of reasons for us to physically move our businesses and combine them," Jancy explained. "First, you know that there are now nine wineries along my road, so the competition has increased. Tommy is affected as well, of course."

Michael nodded in understanding. "My estimate is that the total number of wineries in the valley is somewhere around 75 now."

"Yeah, no kidding!" Tommy piped up. "And there's no end in sight, either. We need to be more visible."

'Secondly," Jancy continued, "our production operations are outmoded and cramped, and our tasting rooms are outdated."

"So where would you move?" Maggie asked, her curiosity as piqued as her husband's.

"To Schoolhouse Road, about three-quarters of a mile north of the schoolhouse," was Jancy's surprising answer.

Michael immediately visualized in his mind the exact spot Jancy was talking about. The same terrace on which he and she and Tommy had planted their vineyards continued across Schoolhouse Road in a northwestern direction. Less than a mile north from the schoolhouse the road climbed up the terrace.

"I can picture the spot exactly," he informed Jancy. "It's absolutely perfect for a tasting room! Visitors would have a nice panoramic view to the south and southeast."

"Yes," she agreed. "It'd be a gorgeous view which is why Tommy and I are excited about the idea of building there."

"And the ground would be some of the best for growing grapes," Michael observed. "In fact, I've been surprised that nobody has staked out a claim on it yet."

"Well, somebody has now," Tommy told him. "We've taken out an option on 80 acres!"

Taken somewhat aback, Michael let out a low whistle. "Man, you're kidding!"

"Nope," Tommy replied, smiling. "We want to buy an 80 acre tract along the road and extending west, following the terrace. The tasting room, of course, would be right by the road."

"What do you envision for a tasting room?" Maggie asked, intrigued.

Jancy jumped back in the conversation, so excited that she could hardly contain herself. "It'd be as high as a three story building but would actually be divided into only two levels. The bottom one would be concrete walls and floors with a high ceiling for our combined winemaking operations, and a crush pad would be located right out back. The upper level would be a stylish wood and glass theme tasting room with floor to ceiling windows. Plus, there'd be a spacious private event center for wedding receptions and other special events."

"Wineries have become popular sites to get married," Tommy interjected. "You know that as well as anyone, Michael. It's good money, so our new center will feature the best venue in the county."

"Center?" Michael asked, a bit puzzled.

"Yeah," his friend replied. "Casa del Vino. That's the name we're going to call the place. The place—the house—of wine. Three wineries, one location."

"Three wineries?"

Jancy jumped back in. "Yes, we hoping to offer visitors wine from our three wineries: mine, Tommy's, and yours."

"And we hope you'll transfer your operations to the center as well," Tommy added. "It'll be state-of-the-art. All modern equipment. And enough capacity for a combined output of 50,000 cases a year."

Maggie reached out and placed a hand on her husband's arm. "Are you suggesting Michael give up the schoolhouse?" she asked, her voice full of concern.

Tommy shrugged. "If he wants to, but we have no problem if he doesn't. His wine can be offered at both his place and the center. After all, he is the legend."

Michel shook his head. "No, I can't see abandoning it," he stated firmly. "It's an iconic fixture now. People come from all over to taste wine in a 1915 schoolhouse."

Over the next half hour, the four adults looked over preliminary architectural plans that Tommy had retrieved and unrolled on the table. They revealed a breathtaking, thoroughly modern facility sited prominently on the edge of a hill—in reality the top of the geologic terrace that ran through the region—and overlooking the shallow valley to the southeast.

"What is all this going to cost?" Michael asked when Tommy and Jancy had finished explaining all the details to him and Maggie.

Jancy glanced at Tommy and he, in turn, took a deep breath, exhaled, and replied, "Roughly $3 million."

"Man-oh-man!" Michael exclaimed softly.

"The land just by itself is nearly a half million," Jancy informed him.

He glanced first at her, then at Tommy, and asked, "Do you intend to plant all of it?"

Tommy nodded vigorously. "Yes, eventually. We'll do it in phases, of course. But that's what makes this whole deal a win-win. Not only will we have the largest, most modern wine production facility in the Watilla Valley, but we'll have virtually unlimited grapes to sell to all the start-up wineries."

Michael pursed his lips and slowly nodded. It seemed to be a smart business move.

"You know that there's going to be more than 100 wineries in a few years," Tommy reminded him. "They're starting up at the rate of seven or eight a year. Most of them have a business model of renting an industrial space and buying their grapes. Mostly from Horse Heaven Hills, Red Mountain, Yakima Valley. There's a critical shortage of good grapes right here in the Watilla Valley."

Again Michel nodded in agreement. Just then, Maggie spoke up. "You forgot one aspect of the new business model, Tommy," she said. "Opening a tasting room downtown."

"Yes! You're exactly correct!" he agreed. "I can't believe how the downtown is changing! Main and 2nd is the epicenter of an area with a dozen tasting rooms. And more on the way."

"Okay, this is all well and good," Michael said, indicating the plans on the table. "But why do you want me in on this? I'm doing just fine on my own, so you don't really need me."

Jancy spoke up. "Tommy and I like to think of it as a family venture," she began. "We hope one day in the future to turn the winemaking responsibilities over to Jana, and we hope that perhaps at that time Jayson can manage the entire business."

Now Michael understood. This whole new venture would, among all the other benefits, also be a way for Jancy to secure a prosperous future for her children. Let them run the business in ten, twenty years.

"Plus," she added, "there's something very fitting that the new Casa del Vino will be a joint partnership of the three original Watilla Valley winemaking pioneers, and featuring wine made from the three original vineyards."

A wiry, little smile appeared on Michael's lips. "I've created a monster!" he joked.

*   *   *

Two weeks later, Michael was back in Kennewick for yet another visit with Bill Burton, Jr. Maggie, Jancy, and Tommy were along as well. When he had called to make the appointment, the lady answering the phone had seemed hesitant.

"What is the nature of your business with Mr. Burton?" she had asked.

"I wish to discuss a business loan," Michael had replied, wondering what the matter was.

"We have five commercial lending managers," the lady had informed him. "I'll get of them on the line for you."

But Michael had quickly replied, "I would like to see Mr. Burton personally, not someone else. He's my banker."

Clearly, something was wrong. After a pause, the lady had asked his name again and then had excused herself for a moment. Twenty seconds later, she was back on the line and this time her voice had been more friendly. "Yes," she had briskly acknowledged, "Mr. Burton said he'd be delighted to speak with you. When would you like to come in?"

An appointment had been set up and the lady had notified him that the bank was in a new location. She gave him directions.

Now, today, Michael drove up to the location and found a new, gleaming glass and steel office building that looked to be six or seven stories tall. "Impressive!" Tommy exclaimed as he hopped out of the front passenger side of the van.

"Your bank certainly seems to doing well," Maggie commented as Michael got her situated in her electric power chair.

"It made all its money off of us!" Tommy commented to her in jest.

Once inside, the group found itself in an expansive lobby with a polished marble floor. A security guard greeted them and directed them to a nearby receptionist. "Mr. Burton is on the sixth floor," she informed them. "His executive assistant up there will take care of you."

Up the elevator they went to the sixth floor. Exiting, they walked out onto plush, powder blue carpeting. A receptionist greeted them with a smile. "Mr. Burton is expecting you," she informed them. "His office is down the hall and on the right. Mr. Bringhurst is already there."

A minute later the group entered Burton's office and found themselves in a spacious executive suite with floor to ceiling windows overlooking the city. Not far away, the Columbia River was clearly visible.

"Michael! Good to see you again!" Burton greeted him with a big smile as he stood up. Moving around from behind his walnut desk, he strode over to the group and shook hands. Michael introduced him to Maggie who offered her hand and the banker gently shook it. He did the same with Jancy, and then gave Tommy a firm handshake.

Jonas greeted everyone with an infectious smile, genuinely happy to see the three winemakers again, and pleased to meet Maggie.

"Nice building!" Tommy remarked as everyone took seats.

"Yeah, everyone here at the bank likes it," Burton replied, then admitted with a somewhat sheepish smile, "We were a little afraid that it might appear a bit ostentatious, but I think the architect did a good job of marrying esthetics with a sense of power and security."

"You've literally come up in the world!" Michael joked, referring to the office's sixth floor location.

Burton chuckled. "I guess I have." Turning more serious, he added, "Dad is fully retired now; he only comes up here from Palm Springs for board meetings. The only numbers he ponders these days are his golf scores!"

"Who's president then, you?" Michael inquired.

"Well, I have to admit that, yes, I'm president of the bank now," Burton replied. "And my son now works here, as well. In commercial lending. In fact, I'm going to buzz him and have him sit in on this meeting. Once this project is approved, he'll be handling things from our end and serve as your point of contact."

"A changing of the guard," Michael observed with a smile.

Burton again chuckled. "Yeah, time has a way of moving on, doesn't it?"

Jonas suddenly spoke up. "That reminds me, I'm retiring," he announced. "This feasibility study on your new project will be my last piece of business with you folks."

The three winemakers chatted and reminisced with the accountant for several minutes as they expressed their appreciation for his work over the years, and their hopes for him to enjoy a happy retirement.

After Burton's son came in to join the meeting, everyone got down to business. The parameters of the project were discussed until Burton and Jonas were clear on what the winemakers were proposing. Jonas promised to get right to work on it and have his report in five or six weeks. With that, the meeting ended.

*   *   *

The year 2002 was notable for a significant event that would affect the city for decades to come: the renovation of the hotel was completed. After four years and several million dollars, all five stories of the historic Watilla Hotel were fully restored to their original state, except for updating for wiring, plumbing, and fire safety.

In addition, the former ballroom was converted to a full service restaurant, and the former restaurant was converted to a spacious lounge and bar. Next to the hotel, a three story wing was added where guests could stay in modern, luxurious rooms. A grand ballroom was also constructed that was large enough for functions of up to 800 people.

The grand opening was held in October and coincided with the first annual Community College fundraising event. Over twenty local winemakers offered tastes of their wines in the grand foyer, surrounded by silent auction tables. Later in the evening, dinner was served in the ballroom and afterward the chief operating officer of the hotel spoke prior to the live auction.

After thanking the assembled dignitaries present, he got down to the crux of his remarks. "Ladies and gentlemen," he began. "Our vision for this hotel, and our willingness to invest the amount of money that we have, revolves around our expectations for this community."

Pausing a second for effect, he continued, "And let me say, our expectations have been met. If anything, they've been exceeded. The city of Watilla is growing even faster than we projected, and the business base has expanded quite nicely along with the growth in the population. In addition, visitors to the city and surrounding area are increasing at a rapid pace as well.

"These visitors come here increasingly for one reason: to tour our wonderful wine district. The money they spend on food and lodging is becoming an important part of the economic base of the city. The management of this hotel foresees this trend to continue. In short, we're bullish on Watilla and on its wine industry."

At Michael's table, Maggie reached out and squeezed his hand and smiled at him with admiration. He smiled back, immensely satisfied.

Chapter 18

A Grand Opening

Casa del Vino
April 2004

Looking back, Michael would realize that the ten year period that began with the year 2002 would be a decade that encompassed profound, fundamental, and rapid change in his life. "I thought at the time I was settling into a comfortable middle age!" he would later reminisce. "But then everything began rapidly changing, starting with CDV."

The CDV—Casa del Vino—conceived by Jancy and Tommy two years earlier, became a reality in April 2004 with its grand opening. Standing in the spacious tasting room, Michael had to admit that Jancy had achieved a masterful job of interior design. The openness of the room was emphasized by blonde aspen wood flooring and floor-to-ceiling glass windows trimmed in shiny stainless steel.

The tasting bar was a polished slab of highly polished tree trunk machined to have a bit of a curve to suggest a wave. The room was styled throughout in what she called 'Nordic chic' which emphasized design elements of light-colored wood. Stainless steel wine racks lined the wall behind the tasting bar holding over a hundred bottles, divided into three sections representing each winery.

CDV was indeed a three-way partnership, but with a catch. One section of the wine racks was devoted to Jancy's label—J Phillips Cellars—and another section devoted to Tommy's label—Fíona Cellars & Vineyards—but the third section held a new label.

Michael had decided to keep his Olde Schoolhouse Cellars label unique to the historic schoolhouse tasting room, so that was where customers had to go to taste and purchase his famous wines. But for

Casa del Vino, he had created a new label called 3R's which stood for Refined…Remarkable…Reserved. Although he remained the master winemaker for his business, the 3R's wines were made chiefly by his assistant winemaker, Mercedes.

For the grand opening, the Chamber of Commerce performed their usual ribbon-cutting ceremony with several Chamber officials posing for photos with the three pioneer winemakers. Bill Burton, Jr. and Jonas had also been invited to participate and were in attendance.

But when it came to the speeches, Michael declined, preferring to let Jancy and Tommy do most of the talking. Reporters for several local and regional newspapers, however, cornered him for interviews.

One asked how he felt about the fact that the Watilla Valley now sported more than 100 wineries and whether the industry could continue growing. "The industry is maturing," he responded. "The Casa del Vino is one sign of that. Although many small labels are still starting up, we're beginning to see some consolidation taking place. Just last year a major beverage company purchased three wineries throughout the Columbia Valley, including Mortiz Cellars here in Watilla. It's a natural evolution."

"What's next for you, business-wise?" another reporter wanted to know.

Michael shook his head and chuckled. "Just to continue making the best wine I can and to enjoy life," he answered. "My wife and I average a cruise a year, so that's the only plans I have – to just continue to make wine and travel."

After the ribbon cutting, speeches, and photos, the assembled crowd enjoyed catered hors d'oeuvres in the large special events room that adjoined the tasting room. Behind the tasting bar, Michael, Jancy, and Tommy chatted with guests as they poured samples of their wines. After an hour, three hired servers took over to allow the winemakers to mingle.

At one point, Michael stood before one the large windows with Maggie beside him and admired the sweeping view of the landscape outside. He saw his schoolhouse in the distance by the river. He knelt down next to his wife and they clinked their glasses together before taking a sip.

"You know," he said to her, "seeing my schoolhouse over there makes me realize how far I've come. In fact, how far the entire industry in the county has come."

"You should be very proud," Maggie replied. "You're the reason all of it exists."

Michael shrugged. "Somebody else would have started it if I hadn't," he pointed out. "But, God, what an idealist I was back then! I was too dumb to know better. I just plunged ahead and tried to get something started. I only wanted to make great wine and thought this was the place to do it."

"And you right," his wife replied, smiling, a look of admiration on her face.

Later, Michael made his way outside on the deck that fronted the tasting room. It was hot inside and he had spotted Tommy outside.

Joining his friend, he joked, "Hey, Skinny, doesn't Jancy feed you anymore?"

Over the years Michael had occasionally made a wisecrack about his friend's slight build. Whereas most people gained weight as they became older, Tommy remained tall and slender. But it seemed that he had lost weight over the past year or two.

Tommy gave a heavy sigh and replied, "Oh, hell, it's everything that's going on. Besides the normal demands of business, we had all the planning for this place, plus the hassles of installing all the new equipment and moving our old operation in. On top of all that, Jana's driving us to out wit's end."

"What's going on now?" Michael wanted to know, concerned.

Blowing out a breath of air, Tommy admitted, "She's barely passing her classes for one thing. We're not sure she'll even be able to start high school in the fall. And, she and a couple friends got caught sharing some marijuana. She had to appear before a juvenile judge who suspended the charges provided she keeps out of trouble."

Michael sighed. "Sorry to hear that."

Tommy sadly shook his head. "Jancy and I are leaving on a two week vacation soon and thought maybe of having Jana stay with you, but I don't think we can burden you with her right now. She's just too much trouble."

As Michael mulled over what he had heard, he listened as Tommy continue on about how Jancy and Jana regularly got into rows, shouting at each other in anger. "They're like oil and water," he concluded.

"No," Michael quickly countered. "They're too much alike."

This got a chuckle out of his friend. "Maybe you're right!"

*   *   *

The next day Michael had a request for Jayson regarding Jana. "Can you contact her and have her come over to the Barn after school tomorrow?"

'Sure," he son agreed. "What's up?"

"I'm not sure yet," he admitted. "But I want to talk to her. Just don't let her parents know, okay?"

At 4:00 the next day Jana showed up at the Barn. Once she had found Michael inside, she asked, "You wanted to see me?"

Nearly fourteen, Jana was on the verge of becoming a rather tall, slender, good-looking young lady. She had inherited her mother's gorgeous blonde hair, and temperament as well. She was dressed as typical teen in worn jeans purposefully ripped in several places. A small metal stud pierced one eyebrow.

"Yeah, thanks for stopping by," Michael answered, critically looking her over. "I've become concerned about some things I'm hearing about you and wanted to talk a bit about it. I'm hoping I can help."

Jana averted her gaze downward, clearly ready to shut him out. "I have a question for you," he informed her. "Do you want to learn to make wine?"

She merely shrugged without answering. After a second of silence, Michael said, "That's not an answer. Do you want to learn to make wine?"

Without raising her head, Jana simply muttered, "Don't know."

Michael stroked his chin as he pondered what to say next. Clearing his throat, he said, "Jana, look at me."

She slowly raised her head and glanced at him. "If you want to learn to make wine, I'll teach you. It'll be our little secret; your folks don't need to know."

He saw the change in her as her face brightened. "Really?"

"Yeah, really," Michael confirmed. "But you have to want to learn. And to work hard. If you do, then I'll let you make any wine you want: white, red, rosé, or a blend. I'll even let you call it whatever you want and I'll let you design a label for it. It'll be your wine and it'll be for sale after it's bottled."

This clearly impressed Jana. "I'd have my own wine to sell?"

"Yep, your very own. I'll teach you how to select grapes so you can decide which ones to use, then you'll go through all the steps to turn those grapes into wine."

"And we'll do this without my mom knowing?"

As Michael suspected, Jana was rebelling against her mother teaching her anything, even winemaking. "Yes, like I said, it'll be our little secret. I'll just tell your folks that you're working over here as cellar rat doing odd jobs that I'm paying you for. I can say that I'm having you learn all the thousand and one things that have to be done in a winery to keep things ship shape."

Michael could see that Jana was warming up more and more to the idea. Suddenly, a light bulb went off in his mind as he realized what he could use as supreme motivation for the teen.

"You know," he commented to her, "your mother has her *Adagio* red blend that's so well known. It's always highly rated and has been on the Top 100 list. Maybe it's time someone challenged her and gave her a run for the money."

He saw the look of realization spread across the teen's face and he had to suppress a smile. "You mean, make my own *Adagio*?" she asked.

"Yes, exactly!" he replied enthusiastically. "You'll choose the blend and the name, so it'll be your own creation. But if you like the idea, I'll help you make a wine that'll knock your Mom's socks off. She won't be Queen of the Block anymore. There'll be a new sheriff in town."

He saw immediately that he had hit a home run with his psychological ploy. He could channel Jana's resentment and rebellion into a project that would showcase her ability.

"But there's two conditions attached to my offer to teach you and let you make your wine," he warned the girl. "First, no more bad grades. I want you to finish this semester with a better effort, then starting in the fall I want you to maintain a B average. Nothing lower than a C.

You don't have to get all A' s, just maintain a B average. And second, no more getting into trouble. I don't want to hear a single thing about you making any trouble for anyone, okay?"

Jana agreed, so eager was she to get started on showing up her mom. Michael thanked her and told her to show up the next day to begin what he referred to as the 'Stealth Wine Project.'

A few days later, he had to endure Jancy's wrath that her daughter was going to be working in his cellar. He defused the situation by telling her, "Look, she'll do all the gofer stuff and help with cleanup. Things like that. She'll learn the lingo and see how things are done, all while earning a little spending money. After a year or two, she'll be all set to learn actual winemaking from you."

It was half truth, half lie. He disliked not being completely honest with Jancy, but if he couldn't turn Jana's life around, then there might never be another opportunity for positive, productive mother-daughter interaction.

When Jancy and Tommy learned about the good grades and behavior conditions of Jana's employment, however, they felt better about leaving her with Michael for three weeks in June while they took a much needed vacation.

"We're going to go to Portland first," Tommy informed his friend. "Then south through the Willamette Valley tasting as many Pinots as we can. From there, on further south to visit Crater Lake before crossing the state line and visiting Redwoods Park."

"And then California wine country?" Michael inquired.

"Heck, yes!" his friend replied enthusiastically. "We've done well enough here in Washington that we don't need to continue making California the enemy anymore."

Michael chuckled. "True," he admitted. "So, how far south are you going to go? Santa Barbara?"

"Yes," Jancy confirmed, jumping into the conversation. "We're going to go all the way to L.A. in order to spend a few days there, and then return by way of the Sierra Foothills. I've heard a lot of good things about that wine district."

As events turned out, Jana was well behaved while her parents were away. In fact, she readily took to cellar work despite the long hours. Michael also spent time with her in the vineyard every week so she could see the changes that occurred from one week to another.

Jana also proudly used her glass wine thief as Michael taught her about barrel sampling and making decisions on blends. His suspicions were confirmed that the teenager appeared to have a lot of her mother's talent in her. She seemed to take to winemaking naturally; she just needed to learn from someone who wasn't a parent.

*   *   *

In early August, Ralph Roger Parkston settled into his well-worn but comfortable recliner after having dinner. Over the objections of his adult daughter, he lit up a Cuban cigar as was his life-long habit, and then took a satisfying sip of well-aged Port. He had kept up this evening custom despite recently having undergone heart surgery.

Over the years he had put on weight and his thick mane of hair had turned silver gray. Now nearly 70, he had only this year turned over the demanding day-to-day operations of *Wine Explorer* to his daughter. She was visiting from San Francisco, where the magazine was published, in order to come to a decision on a business matter.

"So, you want me to make the decision?" he asked.

"Yes, please," she replied impatiently. "We really need to get cranking on the September issue."

Taking a draw on the cigar, he blew a cloud of blue smoke that swirled upward towards the ceiling. "Hmnpf, it seems we face a quandary without precedent," he commented.

"That's the decision," his daughter replied, pointing out the obvious. "The question is, do we set a precedent – either way?"

Parkston pondered the situation for a moment before asking, "Is the wine worthy of the honor? That's what I always asked myself."

"Yes, of course it is!" his daughter answered, exasperated. "Any of the top three finalists could be chosen, you know that. You tasted each one yourself, Dad."

Taking another sip of the Port, Parkston dwelt a moment weighing the options, slightly amused. No winemaker in the history of his magazine had ever been honored twice with having the number one wine in the world. Nor had any winemaker ever been honored twice with a perfect score of 100 points.

Slightly amused by the situation, he reflected for a moment on the implications before rendering his judgment. "Just because nobody has been recognized twice with such an honor, doesn't mean that they're not worthy of it," he announced. "Or, that we shouldn't honor them thus."

"So, you're saying both number one and a hundred points?"

Parkston smiled. "Yes on being number one," he confirmed, but quickly added, "But only 99 points. I was too generous to him the first time."

Chapter 19

Tre Ballerini

Olde Schoolhouse Cellars
August 2004

At least this time he was tipped off in advance. When he hung up the phone after receiving the news, Michael walked into Maggie's study where she was working on her computer, busily engaged in her web site business. He bent down and kissed her, then announced, "Just got off the phone with *Wine Explorer* magazine. I'm going to be number one in the world again, for Pete's sake."

Expressing delight at such an honor, Maggie asked him why on earth he wasn't more excited. "There'll be another feeding frenzy at the tasting room," he sighed. "I'm not sure I need that hassle in my life anymore."

"But it'll be the best possible PR for the entire Watilla Valley AVA," she pointed out, using the initials for the legal designation—American Viticultural Area—that the Federal government used for the Watilla wine district.

"True," he conceded. "All the other wineries, and the city in general, will benefit."

Then Maggie asked out of curiosity, "So, which wine rocked them this time?"

"The *Au Naturel* Syrah," he answered, referring to the wine made from grapes that he had experimented with by not irrigating them. He had followed Dr. Cline's suggestion and had turned off the water to the oldest and lowest sections of his School Bridge Vineyard.

"I knew it was an outstanding wine, but not this good!" he commented, chuckling. Blowing out a breath of air, he added, "A writer and photographer will be here on Thursday for a story and photos. I'd like you to be in the photo they use for the cover. You and me together."

Despite her protest, Michael held firm that his wife be part of the story. And this time around, so would Jancy and Tommy. When the *Wine Explorer* folks showed up several days later. Michael was pleasantly surprised that the entourage included Parkston himself who had aged considerably since he had last visited Olde Schoolhouse Cellars.

"I just had to drop in again," the legendary wine critic quipped. "You keep popping up on my radar!"

The old man heartily shook Michael's hand, then took Maggie's, bent over, and kissed it. "Pleased to meet you Ms. Ross," he said. "Your husband is one of the great winemakers of the world."

He politely shook hands with both Jancy and Tommy, and then listened as Michael explained their involvement with crafting the wine. Parkston nodded in understanding. "The cover will focus on the winery," he informed the group, "so I want just Maggie and Michael on it. But inside, the lead story of the top 100 will kick off with the *Au Naturel* and that's where we can have a group shot of those responsible for it and give attribution as appropriate."

As the next hour passed, the magazine's head writer interviewed first Michael and Maggie, and then obtained a couple of quotes from both Jancy and Tommy. Meanwhile, the photographer killed time by taking shots around the inside of the tasting room. When the interviews ended, he eagerly got down to work, posing Maggie and Michael at one of the tables, glasses of wine in front of them.

"This way, seated at the table, Maggie will appear as normal as anyone else," he commented.

This clearly pleased her as the photographer took shots of her and Michael smiling the way he wanted them to. But R. R. Parkston had published his magazine for more than 30 years and he knew a thing or two about presentation.

"Hell's bells!" he suddenly groused. "This *Au Naturel* wine is about the vineyard! About the grapes produced without irrigation. We need to go out there and take photos!"

This created the problem, however, of what to do about Maggie. "Bring the damn table and chairs outside!" Parkston barked. "Put them in the vineyard!"

Although the photographer seemed doubtful, he had no choice but to obey Parkston's command. Once outside, however, the photographer became inspired as he looked around. "Put the table here at the end of this row of vines!" he said excitedly. "Maggie and Michael, please sit down at it. Have your wine glasses in hand and raised just a little off the table."

They complied, smiling at each other as they posed for the photographer who, crouching, furiously snapped away with his digital camera from several different angles. Next, he had Michael stand behind Maggie. Michael complied, and this proved to be the best angle of all: Michael standing beside his wife, casually leaning against her chair while holding his glass. The photographer furiously snapped away, slightly adjusting Maggie's pose, or Michael's, as he collected a couple dozen images.

Fifteen minutes later, he reviewed the digital images with Parkston. Grunting from time to time, the old man finally selected just the right image. "Here!" he announced. "This one! This is our cover!"

Satisfied that he had both the cover story and photo, Parkston next asked Michael to lead the group over to the production area, the so-called Barn. Inside, Parkston instructed the photographer to take a group shot of the three winemakers in front of a floor-to-ceiling rack of wine barrels.

Once he was satisfied that the photographer had obtained just the exact pose that would look great in the magazine, the legendary wine critic instructed his employees to wrap things up. He bid farewell to everyone, declining Michael's invitation to stay for dinner in town. "Thanks," he said politely, "but I need to get back to the airport and fly to San Francisco. My daughter and I will begin finalizing next month's issue tomorrow."

A half hour later, Michael watched Parkston's corporate jet streaked across the sky high over School Bridge Vineyard on its way to the Bay area. It was the last time he would see the man who had been responsible in a major way for his success.

*   *   *

A little less than a month later, the September 2004 issue of *Wine Explorer* announced to the world the unprecedented honor of a winemaker having twice scored the number one wine of the world. This time Michael was prepared with extra staff and a firm two bottle limit on purchases.

'This is the most extraordinary wine ever," he told Maggie. "At least in the public's opinion. I want as many customers as possible to be able to purchase it."

He set the price at a relatively modest $59, discounted to $49 for his wine club members. These loyal customers were known as 'The Senior Class,' a designation suggested by Maggie several years earlier. They were urged to purchase the *Au Naturel* in advance of Labor Day because of a 'special announcement' that would be made at that time about the wine, although Michael was prohibited by the magazine from saying exactly was the announcement would be.

When the issue did come out, the cover featured Michael and Maggie exactly as in the photo Parkston had selected: she seated at the small table in front of the vineyard appearing to be about to take a sip from her glass of wine. Behind her, Michael stood with one hand on her shoulder while his other hand held a wine glass half full of red wine.

The major headline on the cover announced, 'The Top 100 Wines of 2004.' Across the bottom of the cover, the subheading read, 'Olde Schoolhouse Cellars Scores #1 Once Again.' Inside, the Top 100 article began with Michael's 2002 *Au Naturel* Syrah and extolled its finesse, its sense of *terroir*, its unique nose and palate, and its overall achievement of winemaking perfection.

Michael smiled as he read, "This singular achievement of Olde Schoolhouse Cellars, and the winemakers involved, cements once and for all that the Watilla Valley is among the premier wine regions of the world. If you wish to enjoy the best wine being made today, you need to put this unique region of southeastern Washington on your wine touring itinerary."

It took only two weeks for the inventory of 375 cases of *Au Naturel* to sell out. This time, Michael was wise enough to set aside three cases for himself to enjoy over the next 20 or 30 years. To his everlasting regret, he had no more of his first #1 wine - the fabled '85

Reserve Syrah. As far as he knew, no one else did either. Sadly, it was only a memory now.

He spent the next two months besieged by reporters, writers, and journalists of all types interviewing him for this or that newspaper, magazine, TV station, or blog. His sanity was preserved by his favorite activity – making wine. And these days, he had Jana to teach.

To Michael's great surprise, Jana had decided against making a red blend to challenge her mother. "I don't want to show up my mom," she informed him. "I just want to show her I can be a good winemaker."

"Then, what do you want to make?" he asked, more curious than ever about what might motivate her.

"What do you think of a white blend, instead?" she asked. "Would that be any good?"

Michael was immediately enthusiastic. "Yes!" he answered, excited. "That would be an awesome choice!"

Jana listened as he proceeded to explain, "There aren't enough being made in this part of the country, in my opinion. There are so many wonderful white grapes to work with!"

He proceeded to tell her of eight different white grapes that grew in the area. "What about our vineyards?" she asked. "What would be a good blend from the three vineyards of our families?"

"Well, let's find out!" he replied, eager to get started.

As the 2004 harvest proceeded over the following two months, he and Jana looked over the grapes as they were brought in to the Barn, frequently selecting grapes at random to taste. They also tasted the juice after crushing, and Michael showed her how to decide which fermenting and aging method to select for each variety.

The following February, Michael led Jana through tasting the different wines; not just the whites but the reds as well. The teenager became proficient at using her wine thief and seemed as happy as he had ever seen her.

And Jana kept up her end of the bargain. Her grades were much improved and she stayed out of trouble for the most part. By the time the school year was winding down in April, her white blend was ready to be bottled. Michael led her through a final tasting to determine exactly what the wine would be.

The young girl settled on neutral barrel Chardonnay, stainless steel Viognier, lightly oaked Roussanne, and stainless steel Riesling. The final proportions was determined solely on her own tasting of various experimental blends in the small lab of the Barn.

Michael was impressed that Jana ensured the blend was composed of grapes from each of the three vineyards: School Bridge, Three Hills, and Mianta. For the bottle design, she worked with Maggie to come up with a design of three grapevines intertwining with each other in a vertical position.

"They represent the three vineyards," she informed Michael. "The vineyards of you and my mom and dad."

Michael nodded in approval. "And the name?" he asked, anxious to hear what she had come up with.

"I'm going to call it *Tre Ballerini*," she announced. "That's Italian for 'three dancers.' The grapes that went into the wine came from the three vineyards, so it's like they're doing a dance at a performance. Each one interacts with the others to create a beautiful whole."

"Hmm, yes," Michael agreed, impressed. "It's called synergy – the whole together is greater than the sums of the individual components. I like it!"

Jana then added, "Since my mom's best wine has an Italian name and refers to dancing and music, I also wanted my wine to be like that as well."

"It's a stroke of marketing genius," he replied with a smile as he squeezed her on the shoulder.

A month later when Michael, Maggie, and Jayson were invited over to Jana's home for dinner, he brought a case of the new wine with him but left it in the van. Selecting one bottle, he put it in a paper bag.

Inside the farmhouse, he set it on the kitchen table after everyone had greeted each other. "Ah, our mystery wine for the evening!" Tommy immediately observed, a big smile on his face.

It was a game they frequently had played over the years: he and Jancy and Tommy. One of them would provide a bottle of unknown wine for their get-togethers and the other two would have fun trying to guess what it was. It could be anything, and from anywhere in the world. In recent years, the game also involved Jayson and Jana as their parents sought to educate their palates.

"I thought we could try this before dinner," Michael suggested. Jancy had already set out wine glasses on a side counter.

"Come over and get your glass!" she cheerfully called out, eager to get started.

Michael had known from his first contact with her that she was what wine experts called a super taster, someone with a superior sense of smell and taste. Because of this, it was no surprise that she enjoyed the game more than anyone. In fact, she excelled at it.

Once everyone had a glass and had seated themselves, Michael removed the cork and poured a sample taste for everyone, carefully keeping the bottle hidden in the bag. For the next several minutes, each person concentrated on their wine, first examining the color and then sniffing it.

"Interesting," Tommy commented without committing himself. "This white has a wonderful nose."

Jancy ventured the first guess. "Definitely a blend," she stated. "There's simply too many floral and fruit elements for it to be a single grape. I can really pick up Viognier and Chardonnay. And...something like Riesling or close to it."

The game was officially on. Going around the table starting to Jancy's left, each person had to confirm or offer a different opinion.

"Yep, I agree," Tommy announced. "It's a blend."

Jayson nodded his head. "I agree."

Jana stared down at the table and simply shrugged. "Now, don't just shrug your shoulders," her mother admonished her. "Give us your opinion."

"Yes, a blend, I guess," was all the teen would say. Jancy sighed but said no more.

Maggie passed. "I'm sorry, but I got a peek at the bottle, so I know what it is," she admitted, telling a little white lie in an attempt to not give away where the wine was made.

Michael wasn't in the game since he had brought the wine, so it was back to Jancy to his left. Taking her first sip of the wine, the look of pleasant surprise was evident on her face. "Definitely New World," she declared with certainty. "It doesn't have an Old World nose or taste." Then she added, "And, it's very good!"

Tommy eyed Michael suspiciously, strongly suspecting where the wine had come from. "Yes, I agree," he said. "New World. And I'll add, Northwest U.S."

Jayson wasn't sure what to say. "Is Australia New World?" he asked. "I forget."

"Yes, it's considered New World," Michael assured his son.

Jayson's face brightened at this information. "Then I say Australia! It's got so many unusual characteristics, it just has to be from somewhere strange."

"Oh boy! A disagreement!" Tommy spoke up with glee. "How about you, Jana?"

She shrugged her shoulders again. "I don't know."

Michael immediately held up a hand as Jancy was ready to pounce on her daughter. "That's okay," he said. "That's fair. If someone doesn't know, then they don't know."

At the end of the table, Tommy smiled broadly as he watched the interaction of his daughter, his friend, and Jancy. Now he knew.

It was back to Jancy. "I think it's one of those strange blends they make over in the Willamette Valley," she announced with certainly. "Except this time it's unusually good. They're finally learning how to make wine correctly!"

"I disagree!" Tommy declared. "This is a new wine that Michael has made!"

Clearing his throat, Michael confessed, "I have to admit, it's from Olde Schoolhouse Cellars. It's a new white blend."

Jancy glanced at him, a frown on her face. "A new creation from Mercedes for the 3R's label?"

Instead of replying, Michael pulled the bottle out of the bag for everyone to see.

"Wow! Awesome label!" Jayson remarked.

Jancy took the bottle from Michael and examined it. "*Tre Ballerini*," she said softly as she looked over both the front and the back label. "No information on the blend, so this is proprietary, I take it?" she inquired.

"That's right, he confirmed. "It'll change from year to year depending on what the winemaker decides."

"The winemaker?" she asked, noting that Michael had failed to mention a name.

"Yes," he replied with a smile. "She's sitting across from you."

"Oh my gosh!" Tommy exclaimed upon hearing this. Turning to look at his daughter, he said to her, "Jana, you made this wine? That's impressive! Holy cow!"

Looking down at the table, her face coloring red, Jana simply replied, "Uncle Mike showed me how."

Michael, however, threw up his hands. "I only showed her the technicalities!" he protested. "Jana crafted the wine herself. She selected the grapes, selected the blend, did all the work. It's her wine, pure and simple."

Jancy looked with admiration at her daughter seated across the table from her. "Jana?" she softly called out. When the teen looked up, Jancy said, "You did good, honey. Real good."

Then the dam burst and Jana brightened and became extremely talkative, telling all about her winemaking adventures of the past year. "You can follow the grape!" she announced at one point with excitement. "You taste it when it comes in from the vineyard, and then you can follow that taste through the crushing, the fermenting, the aging. Each variety has its own distinctive taste and you can follow it through the whole process!"

When her daughter had explained what the grapes were in the blend and why she had chosen them, Jancy commented, "That's what I couldn't identify – Roussanne! I rarely get a chance to taste it." Turning to Michael, she added, "You're one of the few who grows any in the entire Northwest. Perhaps now that Jana has shown how it can be used, others will plant it as well."

It was praise that the teenager soaked up, pleased that she had impressed her mother and father. Later on, after dinner—during which two bottle of Jana's wine were consumed—Jancy and Tommy took Michael aside to express their gratitude.

"You've performed a miracle," Tommy told him. "She's a different person these days. Heck, I think she'll make honor roll this quarter for the first time ever. That's amazing!"

Jancy took hold of Michael's arm. "Thank you," she told him softly. "I really appreciate what you've down with her. She can continue working with you as long as she wants."

Michael knew that was a major concession from her. However, he shook his head. "I think she's ready to learn from her parents now," he replied. "She can continue making her white blend at my place if she wishes, but you and Tommy need to begin teaching her how to make reds. I'm confident she'll do real well."

*   *   *

In July Michael met with a couple from Seattle who had contacted him earlier and arranged a private meeting with him to discuss an investment they were making in Watilla. He only agreed to the meeting after bluntly questioning them and receiving their assurance they weren't trying to coax money from him.

On a Saturday morning before the tasting room opened, he met with them over a private tasting of six of his wines. He was mildly surprised to see that the couple were ethnic Latinos and looked to be in their early fifties. The gentleman introduced himself as Ricardo and his wife as Alexandra.

As they sampled the first wine—Michael's Reserve Viognier— Ricardo revealed that he and his wife had recently retired from the Microsoft Corporation. "I was marketing director for northern South America outside of Brazil which, of course, speaks Portuguese instead of Spanish, so the company felt more comfortable with a native Brazilian to head up things there," he explained. "Northern South America was a natural fit since I'm from Peru. So is my wife, by the way."

"We met at Berkeley as grad students in the 80s," Alexandra interjected, "and found out we were both from Peru." Then she added, chuckling, "We had to leave our country in order to meet each other!"

Ricardo continued, "My wife was a lead project leader for the Windows Explorer team, so we were both part of the Microsoft family. For a very long time. And, of course, we all know how well Microsoft has done. My wife and I have been fortunate to have done very well financially, especially with our stock options."

"So why invest in Watilla?" Michael asked them, more curious than ever.

"We wish to do something completely different in our retirement while we are still young enough to be able to manage a rather demanding business," Ricardo answered. "We've actually been to

Watilla a number of times and have, in fact, visited this tasting room several times. We think highly of your wines."

Alexandra added, "Our daughter graduated from the wine program at the community college two years ago. She's now an assistant at Moritz Cellars."

Michael was impressed. Moritz Cellars had done very well over the years and had a reputation for excellent wine. Their daughter must be very bright to have been hired by the winery.

As he next poured a sample of Jana's *Tre Ballerini*, he asked, "So what business are you starting?"

"It's an existing business that we wish to remake into a wine bar and bistro," Ricardo replied. "We've been impressed with downtown Watilla and what a transformation it's undergone. Statistics the Visitor's Bureau has supplied us are eye-opening. The city has truly become a tourist designation."

"Yes, indeed," Michael agreed. "I believe there's about a dozen tasting rooms downtown now."

"Eleven, to be exact," Ricardo informed him. "With two more due to open next year."

Michael nodded. It was almost mind-boggling to him how much the city had changed. Everything was centered these days around the wine industry.

When he inquired further about what they intended, Alexandra filled him in. "We're going to renovate a business at 2nd and Main into a wine bar and bistro. We're going to call the wine bar Los Vinos, and the bistro Cocina Casera."

"Hmm, home cooking," Michael immediately translated.

"Yes!" Ricardo confirmed enthusiastically. "It'll feature a modern take on traditional cuisine of the Andes prepared by a well-regarded chef we're bringing in."

"Many of the recipes will be from my mother and grandmother," Alexandra added with enthusiasm. "Adapted, naturally, for the American palate."

"The bistro and wine bar will have a separate entrance on Main Street," Ricardo explained, while a traditional lounge and bar will have its own separate entrance on 2nd."

"Wait a minute!" Michael interrupted, suddenly puzzled. "What business are you buying? There's nothing large enough at that location except The Roundup Saloon."

"Yes, that's what we're buying!" Ricardo replied, smiling with pride. "The front will be remade into a wine bar and bistro, while the back with its separate entrance will be remodeled and renamed The Roundup."

"We don't like the term 'saloon,'" Alexandra confided, wrinkling her nose. "Too tacky. We'll redo the bar area into a contemporary, Western-chic style to appeal to a younger and more sophisticated clientele."

Michael could only slowly shake his head and marvel at what he had just heard. "I'll be damn," he said quietly "The Roundup Saloon is going to have Spanish-speaking owners!"

"Hmm, what?" Ricardo asked, puzzled.

Waving a hand dismissively, Michael simply replied, "Oh, nothing. It's a long story."

As Michael stood up and retrieved a bottle of his regular Syrah to pour samples of, Ricardo cleared his throat and said, "Well, we need to come to the point of our visit. The fact is, we would like to feature Olde Schoolhouse Cellars in our establishment. We'll have dozens of Northwest wine on our wine list, have no fear of that, but yours will be the most prominent. In addition, we wish to feature your name and the name, Olde Schoolhouse Cellars, in our advertising. You're a world famous winemaker, you know. Legendary, really."

"We'll pay a premium on your wholesale price, of course," Alexandra added.

As Michael mulled over what his visitors were proposing, an idea came to him. "Tell you what," he suddenly said. "I have an even better idea for you."

He proceeded to outline how they could advertise from the angle of featuring wines of the three original pioneering winemakers of the Watilla Valley. "We're all still personally involved in our wineries," he pointed out. "And we've all garnered plenty of awards and accolades."

As he and his visitors discussed this further, they warmed up to the idea. As Michael poured two more wines for them over the next twenty minutes, a general agreement was reached on the outline of a plan to advertise and market the grand opening.

"I'll talk to the other two tomorrow," he assured Ricardo and Alexandra. "I'm sure they'll be excited about it."

Chapter 20

A Tribute to Greatness

Historic Watilla Hotel
Autumn 2005

After Labor Day weekend, the lady who was the current president of
the Chamber of Commerce called Michael. "As you know, our annual
meeting is always the first Saturday of December," she began. "I hope
you're planning to attend this year."

Michael wasn't thrilled about the prospect since he had been to
many of these events over the years and didn't get much out of them
anymore. "Ah, I don't know," he told her. "Probably not."

"Well, you better!" she chided him. "We're going to do a tribute to
the pioneering winemakers of the Watilla region, especially you and
Olde Schoolhouse Cellars. You sort of need to be there, don't you
think?"

"Oh, no," he groaned in response. "Please don't do this. I really
don't need anybody to do any tribute about me."

The lady was the owner of the Vineyard Café & Bakery and had
slowly grown her business over the years. As such, she knew how to
overcome obstacles. "Well, you just dust off your tux, because I won't
take no for an answer," she replied sternly. "We at the Chamber feel
bad enough that we neglected the 25th anniversary of your start here
in Watilla. We sure as heck aren't going to miss the 30th!"

Michael sighed. "I actually planted the first vines in 1976," he
protested, "so you're off a year. You'll have to consider this for next
year."

"Nice try," the lady replied, chuckling. "but we've already talked
this over. We want to honor the beginning of the industry as the year
the first winemaking pioneer arrived." Then she added in jest,

"Besides, if we wait until next year, then you'll just have an excuse to be elsewhere and that would spoil all the fun! Nope, it's this year, Michael."

As they chatted for another minute, he learned that the Chamber was also going to honor Jancy and Tommy. "It seems like the three of you just naturally go together," she informed him.

"Yes," he confirmed. "We all arrived within a few years of each other, back in the days when people thought we were crazy to try to grow wine grapes in this part of the country."

"Ok, good!," the lady replied. "The Chamber's community outreach committee will work with the Economic Development folks to put together a program."

To Michael's dismay, she added, "Better start thinking about what you'll say because we'll be wanting some sort of a speech from you!"

*   *   *

A month later, the Chamber assisted with a grand opening ceremony for the Peru couple's new business. By prior agreement, Michael was on hand for an hour to personally autograph bottles of his wine that Los Vinos carried.

Afterward, he and Maggie and Jayson hung around to have a bite to eat. They found the new establishment to be very upscale and chic, far beyond anything they would've expected for Watilla, even just ten years ago.

The front of the business was taken up by Los Vinos, a cozy, well-lighted, room with a dozen small tables and a gleaming bar made of polished Andean marble. The back-bar featured a large mirror outlined in chrome, and bordered on each side with chrome, floor-to-ceiling wine racks. One side held bottles from various Pacific Northwest and California wineries, while the other contained bottles from around the world. Dozens of wine glasses hung from chrome wine glass racks suspended above the bar.

Michael liked the overall appearance of the chic décor, but he and his wife and son were even more impressed with the bistro that was easily accessible from the wine bar. Cocina Casera was decorated in a modern style as well, with glass top bistro tables and honey oak colored chairs, all setting on a floor of imported stone tile.

One sidewall provided an expanse of large windows to allow views of the passing world outside, while the opposite sidewall showcased a large, hand-painted mural of South American vineyard laborers harvesting grapes in handmade reed baskets with the snow-capped Andes Mountains in the distant background.

Ricardo insisted on comping their meal. "Order anything you and your family wish," he informed Michael. "It's on the house. I'm anxious to see what you think of our cuisine."

"Is your wife the chef de cuisine?" Maggie asked.

"Oh, no!" Ricardo quickly replied before boasting, "We have the top chef from Lima in our kitchen! The recipes are from Alexandra, but Chef Alberto adapts them for preparation by his team."

"How did you get the top chef in Lima to come here and work for you?" Michael asked, curious.

Ricardo rolled his eyes and sighed. "The economy, you know, is not as good as it was. And the political situation, well, there are increasing problems with drug trafficking as well as protests against mining projects."

"Yes, I've read some news items about that," Maggie commented.

Ricardo continued. "So, Alberto sees better opportunities for his family in the States." Then he confided, "It was not difficult to get a visa for him. After all, who is qualified to cook Peruvian cuisine but a native of Peru?"

Michael chuckled. "Yes, that's true!"

"I will leave you now to peruse the menu and order," Ricardo said. "Later, however, you must come into the back and see the new Roundup Bar & Lounge. I believe you'll be equally impressed with what we've done with it."

*   *   *

On the first Saturday of December, the annual meeting of the Watilla Chamber of Commerce took place in the Grand Ballroom of the Watilla Historic Hotel. Michael and Maggie arrived in the middle of the social hour and, as they entered the cavernous room, they were greeted with a giant banner hanging at one end reading, '**Celebrating 30 Years of the Watilla Wine Industry.**'

Looking handsome and feeling comfortable in a tux after having worn one to a number of Chamber annual meetings over the years, plus to his wedding and on several cruises with Maggie, he easily engaged in conversation with friends and colleagues.

Maggie was looking especially radiant in a shimmering, dark-burgundy gown that accented her fashionably styled red hair. Green emerald earrings matched her equally enchanting emerald colored eyes. She also easily fell into conversation with whomever she met.

Both she and Michael were converged upon by a large number of other attendees who offered greetings. Everyone knew he was the man of the hour; from that point on he and Maggie were treated as celebrities. They were advised that all three of the cash bars were free to them for the remainder of the evening.

They met up eventually with Jancy and Tommy who spent ten minutes chatting with them. Tommy, for the first time in his life, wore a tux and endured Michael's ribbing over it. Jancy was dressed in an elegant black evening gown and had had a stylist do up her long blonde hair in curvy waves. As always, she radiated a natural beauty.

"Listen, buddy," Tommy confided to his friend, "it's up to you to speak for all of us tonight because there's no way I'm getting up in front of this crowd. They say there's 800 people here!"

"God, almighty!" Michael exclaimed as he blew out a breath of air. He cast an inquiring glance at Jancy.

"Don't worry, I'll get them warmed up!" she teased him.

'So, you're speaking, too?"

"Yes," she confirmed, smiling mischievously. "No way I'm missing a chance like this to promote Casa del Vino!"

"Good for you!" Maggie spoke up. "There'll be a ton of money in this room tonight! Go for it!"

At 7:00 an announcement was made for everyone to be seated at their respective tables for dinner. Michael, Maggie, Jancy, and Tommy found themselves escorted to a table in front of the room, just off to one side of the stage and speaking podium. The Chamber president and her husband, as well as the city's economic development director and his wife, completed their table.

Michael was pleasantly surprised to see three bottles of local red wine on their table: his '03 Reserve Syrah, Jancy's '02 *Adagio*, and

Tommy's '03 Reserve Merlot. In addition, his recent vintage of Viognier and Jana's *Tre Ballerini* were on ice in chilling buckets.

"Nice wine!" he commented to the Chamber president. "You spared no expense!"

"Yes, all the wine served tonight is locally produced," she acknowledged. "In fact, there should be a Watilla winemaker seated at each table in the room, along with his or her wine for enjoying with dinner."

"Oh, that's very thoughtful!" Maggie remarked. "That way, the winemakers can talk about their wine with the people at their table."

"Yes, that's the idea, exactly," the president confirmed. "The more we got into planning this event, the more enthusiastic we became."

An hour and a quarter later, the Chamber president excused herself and climbed the three steps up to the stage and positioned herself behind the microphone on the lectern of the podium. She called the room to attention to begin the business proceedings. After a half hour reviewing the highlights of the year, she quickly called in succession the new incoming officers to the stage for recognition.

After that she introduced the economic development gentleman who came up for a short speech. Taking a sheet of paper from the inside pocket of his tux jacket, he cleared his throat to speak.

"Ladies and gentlemen, let me spend a few minutes reviewing some interesting information before we introduce our distinguished honorees," he began. "It's appropriate that on this, the 30th anniversary of the founding of the Watilla wine industry, we acknowledge its impact."

The man paused a second for effect before continuing. "In 1975 a wine industry did not exist anywhere in the greater Watilla Valley. There was nothing. Nada. Not even a single grapevine, much less a vineyard. Then, one day, a young man by the name of Michael Ross arrived and, as they say, the rest is history."

Once again, the man paused and looked out over the crowd for dramatic effect before delivering statistics he had complied for the occasion. "Today, December 2005, there are 107 bonded wineries with a total annual economic impact of $50 million."

Looking up once more, he spoke to the crowd without notes. "Let me say that again: the annual economic impact of our wine industry is $50 million. That's astounding! That figure includes wages from employment, sales of wine, taxes generated, sales of supplies from vendors, professional services rendered to the wineries, tourist dollars spent on food and lodging, and so forth."

Continuing to speak without notes, he itemized the benefits from the industry. "In 1975 the population of Watilla was a little less than 5,000 folks. Today, our city has grown to more than 25,000. We have a new and expanded hospital; our historic hotel has been completely renovated, along with the addition of this spacious, beautiful new ballroom we're in tonight; we have a dozen other smaller hotels; and our downtown business district thrives with tasting rooms and eating establishments such as the Vineyard Café and the brand new Cocina Casera. For Pete's sake, we even have a Wal-Mart!"

Waiting a moment for chuckling to die down before continuing, he revealed new information to the assembled guests, "And I can tell you tonight that I recently assisted a prominent Pacific Northwest chef in obtaining suitable retail space in the general downtown area. He was raised and trained in France and is relocating to our city from the rat race in Seattle to open what he intends to be a well-regarded French restaurant and catering service. He told me our world-class wine industry was what attracted him."

Pausing, the man wrapped up his speech. "Well, I could go on, but you see my point. Watilla is the epicenter of a thriving, vibrant wine region. Speaking earlier this evening with Michael Ross, it seems there are roughly 5,000 acres of wine grapes under cultivation. According to him, there's probably potential for another 5,000. Does that mean a doubling of the number of wineries in the future? Perhaps. Just perhaps, we haven't seen anything yet."

With that, the man stepped away from the microphone and turned to hand control of the meeting back to the Chamber president. He took his seat to hearty applause, having suitably warmed up the audience for the honors soon to be bestowed.

The Chamber lady addressed the room after the applause had stopped. "Ladies and gentlemen, we will now honor the first pioneering winemakers who came here with a hope and a prayer and a belief that the land around Watilla could produce fine wine."

She turned and picked up a very large plaque from a small table behind her. "The Chamber had three of these beautiful plaques made up for our honorees. By prior agreement, we'll go in reverse order of the timeline and begin with Mr. Thomas O'Donnell, the owner and winemaker of Fíona Cellars. He's also a general partner in the new and very beautiful Casa del Vino tasting room south of the city.

"Mr. O'Donnell specializes most of all in Merlot and has put the Watilla Valley on the map as a top producer of award-winning Merlot. *Wine Explorer* magazine honored him several years ago in its Top 100 wines of the world list for his Reserve Merlot."

Pausing a moment, the Chamber president looked at Tommy and, with a smile, said, "Mr. O'Donnell, will you please come up here and accept this token of our appreciation?"

Tommy got up and walked towards the stage as the room applauded him. After accepting the plaque and being photographed, he turned uncomfortably to the microphone.

"Wow, I've never stood before so many people before!" he began, and a wave of chuckles rippled through the audience.

"Um, I'm not much of a speaker," he began, "so just let me say thanks for honoring me and Jancy and Michael tonight."

Turning to look at Michael, he added, "And let me say, I wouldn't be here except for Michael Ross." Pointing towards Michael, he said, "Thanks, buddy, it's been quite a trip!"

And that was the extent of Tommy's speech. He stepped away from the microphone and gratefully beat a retreat back to the table. In the meantime, the Chamber lady spoke again after applause died down.

"Next, I wish to honor Ms. Jancy Phillips, owner and winemaker at J Phillips Cellars, and also a general partner in Casa del Vino. Ms. Phillips has gained world-wide recognition with her *Adagio* Bordeaux-style red blend. As with Mr. O'Donnell, she's been honored on *Wine Explorer's* Top 100 list.

"And I can also inform you that Jana Phillips, Jancy's and Mr. O'Donnell's daughter, is also a winemaker, following in her parents' footsteps. I feel confident that J Phillips Cellars will be making world class wine for decades to come."

After pausing a brief second, the lady turned towards Jancy and said, "Please help me welcome Ms. Jancy Phillips."

The crowd applauded once again in appreciation as Jancy got up from the table and made her way to the stage and the podium. As with Tommy, she accepted a plaque and was photographed. A moment later, she stood before the microphone.

"I wish to thank the Chamber for this honor," she began. "And I wish to acknowledge all the other winemakers present here tonight who have built on the initial foundation that I and Tommy and Michael first established."

Pausing a moment, she composed her thoughts before continuing. "I agree with what Tommy just said: I also wouldn't be here today if it weren't for Michael Ross."

Turning towards Michael, she flashed him a bright smile. "I was just a young lady working in a frustrating job making wine in Napa Valley when I came across a wine from Washington winning a top award at a Bay area competition. I thought, what in the world is going on in Washington?"

The crowd chuckled in appreciation. Jancy smiled again and then continued. "When I arrived here shortly after that, I couldn't believe that Michael was working all alone. There were no other wineries; just him. Just him and his vision that great wine could be made here in Watilla. So I thought, well, this guy might be crazy, but he's passionate about what he's doing. Oh yeah, I thought he was kind of cute, too!"

This elicited laughter from the assembled guests and Jancy paused a second. As she did, she flashed another smile at Michael. "Well, anyway," she continued, "one thing led to another and before you knew it, the three of us were happily making all the wine we could and trying to stay one step ahead of the bill collectors. And then, one day, Michael made the cover of *Wine Explorer* magazine. From that point on, the Watilla Valley was on the map for wine enthusiasts."

Jancy paused once again to collect her thoughts before wrapping up. "Today, I've achieved everything I could have dreamed of. I have a well-known wine label, I've made the Top 100 list, and I'm blessed to be part owner of the beautiful and unique Casa del Vino winery and tasting room. It's a one-of-a-kind establishment, offering an assortment of wines made from grapes grown in the three original vineyards that were established 30 years ago. Please visit it if you haven't had the chance yet."

Having made her plug for her new business as she had promised, Jancy ended her remarks by thanking the Chamber and the economic development commission. She shook hands again with the Chamber lady and left the stage to another round of applause.

Once the room quieted down, the president stepped back up to the microphone, her face beaming. "It is now my distinct honor to introduce a man most of you already know, and whose name is becoming legendary throughout the winemaking world."

Pausing a minute, the Chamber president looked down at her notes to continue. "Mr. Michael Ross received his winemaking training first in California, then later served a one year apprenticeship in the famous Côte Rotie district of the Rhone Valley of France. Sensing that the climate and soils in this region were conducive to growing wine grapes, he purchased land for a vineyard in 1975. Returning the following spring, he planted the first vineyard in the Watilla Valley."

The lady looked up and surveyed the crowd before continuing. "Almost from the beginning, his wines began winning awards in prestigious competitions. Over the years, the wine world took notice and Michael ended up achieving an honor no other winemaker in the world has duplicated: he's been honored—not once—but twice, by *Wine Explorer* with the number one wine in the world. The first occasion was for his 1985 Reserve Syrah while the second occasion was for his 2002 *Au Natural* Syrah."

The lady hesitated a second as murmurings broke out in the crowd as guests made comments to their tablemates about Michael's two #1 wines. Continuing, she added, "Michael is also a general partner in Casa del Vino and, unknown to most folks until now, is the principal investor in Champenoise Cellars, a new winery established last year that will be devoted exclusively to producing Champagne-style sparkling wine from local grapes. He tells me that a tasting room will be opening in the spring in the downtown area."

Stopping a moment to allow for a ripple of murmuring as people digested this news, the Chamber president wrapped up her introduction. "I could go on about Michael, talking about his work with the community college for instance, but we have limited time here tonight."

This remark evoked yet another laugh from the audience which the lady let run its course. When the room was quit again, she simply announced, "Ladies and gentlemen, please help me welcome to the stage one of the world's outstanding winemakers."

As Michael rose and made his way to the stage, the room not only erupted in applause, but also with a standing ovation. Cheers and whistles broke out as the enthusiastic crowd paid homage to the man they knew was responsible for the tremendous economic success that Watilla had experienced.

Accepting his plaque of appreciation and pausing to be photographed, Michael carefully put it down on the table behind the podium before stepping up to the microphone. He stood and let the room quiet down. He began with a disarming remark, "Jeez, in the beginning I just wanted to make wine so I didn't have to go out and buy it!"

The crowd erupted in hearty laughter and he took a deep breath, letting some of his nervousness bleed away. Feeling better, he continued after the room settled down once again.

"Thank you for this honor," he began. "Thank you for honoring not only me and Jancy and Tommy, but also all the other winemakers. I understand that the winemakers here tonight didn't have to pay and all of us appreciate that."

As he surveyed the room, he noticed several of his colleagues raising their wine glasses in silent tribute to him. Taking another deep breath, he let it out and continued.

"I couldn't agree more with what my good friend Tommy O'Donnell said: it's been one hell of a trip!" A tittering of chuckles rippled through the room as he added, "And Jancy Phillips, let me tell you, you kept me sharp over the years. Your determination and drive to make the best wine in Watilla forced me to stay at the top of my game."

He smiled at her and she smiled back as she nodded, and then said aloud, "The game's not over yet!"

As the crowd chuckled, Michael further composed his thoughts before continuing. "Let me acknowledge a person who hasn't been mentioned yet, but who was instrumental in my decision to gamble on the Watilla Valley. And that is Dr. Wilbur Cline, whose ground-breaking research on growing wine grapes in the greater Columbia Valley has made him the godfather of the Washington State wine industry." Looking up at the crowd, he called out, "Dr. Cline, please stand and be acknowledged!"

In the middle of the room, an aged and white-haired Cline rose from one of the tables as the assembled guests broke out in applause and then stood in tribute to the legendary researcher. Looking slightly embarrassed, he gave a little wave of his hand, then sat back down.

After everyone had sat down again, Michael continued. "After this meeting is over, I urge you to talk with Dr. Cline for a couple minutes. He can tell you a lot of stories about the blooming of the wine industry in this part of the state."

After acknowledging the researcher, Michael got to the crux of his remarks. "Let me say that I've been appreciative over the years of the assistance I've received from the Chamber. It's been an invaluable organization in promoting both the general wine industry and also the wine program at the community college.

"And let me also say that I agree with remarks made earlier. I foresee a day when 10,000 acres of grapes will be under cultivation and there will be more than 200 wineries established in the county. The economic impact will be north of $100 million, meaning that the Watilla Valley will increasingly be a major wine tourist destination."

Pausing to allow the crowd to digest this information, he continued a second later. "Why do I confidently say this? Because of the reason I came here in the first place. You have a unique climate and unique soil conditions that are conducive for growing premium quality wine grapes. And that means high quality wine. You can't have great wine without great grapes. You start with the grapes and try not to screw up what nature has blessed you with. And if you do it right, you end up with wine that discerning consumers are searching for. I'm confident that further accolades and awards will be forthcoming over the years for Watilla Valley wines."

Stopping to take a deep breath, he simply concluded. "Ladies and gentlemen, thank you once again."

He stepped back and turned to leave the stage. The room again burst into a thunderous standing ovation as he made his way back to the table. Both Tommy and Jancy, fighting back tears, stood and greeted him with a hug before he took his seat next to Maggie, whom he also hugged and exchanged a kiss with.

*   *   *

Shortly after his speech, the Chamber president adjourned the meeting and an area was cleared for a dance floor. A band quickly set up for live music as Michael shook hands and chatted with various winemakers and business people.

At one point, he finally got a minute with Cline. "Hey, thanks for the acknowledgement," the researcher said. "But, hell, don't call me the godfather, for Christ's sakes!" he admonished Michael good-naturedly.

"I wouldn't be here without you," Michael countered. "My success has derived from your initial encouragement."

The two men conversed for several more minutes before parting. After another half hour of talking with people, Michael found Maggie at his side. "Hey, how are you doing?" he asked.

She raised up a cocktail glass and replied, "Happily getting a little drunk from all the free liquor!"

He bent over and kissed her. "Just don't get arrested for DUI!" he said in jest, referring to her power chair.

Maggie reached out and squeezed his hand. "That was a good speech you gave."

Michael shook his head. "Oh, I don't know. It could have been better. And longer."

His wife disagreed. "The best speeches are the short ones," she pointed out. "Think Lincoln's Gettysburg address."

He chuckled. "I guess you're right."

Cocking her head a little to one side, Maggie asked, "Why don't you do a little dancing before we go? It's a good band."

Michael shrugged. "I don't have anyone to dance with unless you want to."

"No, no," she replied. "It's too crowded." Then she added, "And don't give me that line about not having anyone to dance with!"

"Hmm?"

Maggie raised her eyebrows and said, "Well?" as she cast a glance off to one side.

Michael looked in that direction and saw Jancy standing there who suddenly cast a glance at him. He sighed. "Sure you don't mind?"

"If I did," his wife replied, "I never would have married you."

He squeezed her shoulder. "You're something else, you know that?"

"So are you," she immediately shot back with a smile.

He waited a few minutes until the band began a slow number and then made his way over to Jancy. She turned to him with an inquiring look. "May I?" he asked.

"Sure!" she replied with a smile. He led her out to the dance floor to begin dancing.

Once again, it felt strange, but good, to touch her, to hold her. As they gently swayed to the music, she murmured, "This evening brings back memories doesn't it?"

"Yeah," he agreed. "Both good and bad."

She gazed directly at him, her blue eyes luminous and liquid. "No, only good memories," she countered. After he had led her into an underarm turn and she had come back into his arms again, she whispered, "We're too old to have bad memories anymore. There are only good ones."

Chapter 21

Auld Lang Syne

Olde Schoolhouse Cellars
2006 to 2011

These should have been the halcyon years for Michael, and they were in many ways. He found himself widely acclaimed as one of the preeminent winemakers of the country, always in demand for an interview from someone or another of the media.

He was also the head of a small business empire. His Olde Schoolhouse Cellars winery continued to be hugely profitable, selling carefully crafted wines at premium prices. He personally supervised the production of the Reserve Syrah, the perfect 100 point wine that had initially made him famous.

"I've never forgiven myself for not saving more of it," he lamented more than once to colleagues, adding, "I don't know of anyone who still has a bottle. A couple years ago some collector in New York emailed me that he had enjoyed the bottle he had saved for all these years. Since then, I haven't heard from anyone else."

"Maybe old R.R. Parkston still has a bottle squirreled away," one friend opined.

Michael had simply shrugged and replied, "Who knows?"

It now seemed to Michael that the perfect wine had been only a fleeting phenomenon; it had appeared suddenly like a blazing meteorite, then just as suddenly it had been gone, existing too briefly to be fully appreciated.

He still had nearly a case of his other number one wine, however – the 2002 *Au Naturel* Syrah. And Maggie still had her case, as well, which would ensure that they both would be able to share and enjoy at least one bottle every year for the foreseeable future.

In addition to his elite wines, Michael also did well with 3Rs, his second label sold at Casa del Vino. Mercedes was becoming a top, award-winning winemaker in her own right and handled the primary winemaking responsibilities for the product line. In fact, the volume of wine, as well as the number of products, for both labels necessitated the employment of two assistants who worked under her and Michael's supervision.

As for Casa del Vino, Jancy's and Tommy's vision for an upscale, combined winemaking operation and tasting room was paying off handsomely. Like Michael's schoolhouse, the place was always crowded in the high season from April through October. It had become one of the top venues in the valley for weddings and receptions, which meant that it was immensely profitable as well.

"We're booked solid for the next year for weddings! " Jancy informed Michael and Maggie one day. "It's absolutely crazy trying to keep up with it!"

"But crazy good," Maggie pointed out, and then advised, "Enjoy the good times while they last!"

Michael's other business enterprise, Champenoise Cellars, was off to a promising start. Although he was only the investor—he wasn't about to tackle learning the difficult skill of how to make Champagne-style wine at this point in his life—he did employ an experienced winemaker who had learned his trade in California working for a top name sparkling wine producer before they had been acquired by a French company.

Michael had purchased a storefront in the heart of downtown for a tasting room after a shoe store had gone out of business. His winemaker made the wine in an industrial building out at the airport from grapes purchased throughout the central Columbia Valley.

The first year's release featured a sparkling Viognier which was well received. The second year, another *blanc de blanc* joined the product line, this time made from Chardonnay. And just for the heck of it, Michael made the decision to add a dark sparkler the third year.

"The Aussies are doing it Down Under from the Syrah grape," he explained to friends. "So why not do it here in Washington State where we have world-class Syrah?"

He called the nearly black-colored, sparkling wine *Black Elegance* and featured a label with an artistically drawn tall blonde wearing a strapless black evening gown glancing back seductively over her shoulder. It was a big seller and revealed that Michael was still a pioneer, showing everyone else that new frontiers could still be explored.

Because of his business success, the city's economic development people sought his input on a redevelopment plan for a small area of old warehouses just three blocks off of downtown.

"These old fruit storage and processing buildings can be renovated and redeveloped into retail shops," the executive director told him. "Our downtown is getting maxed out with tasting rooms, so we need a new area to concentrate on."

Michael agreed. "The city itself is increasingly becoming a wine destination," he observed.

"Yes, indeed," the director agreed. "It used to be that folks came here to tour wineries outside of town, but now they also come here to spend a day downtown cruising form one tasting room to another. We foresee making this new area into a sort of upscale wine center to attract even more wine enthusiasts to make a special trip to Watilla."

Michael nodded. "I think you're on the right track. Another section of town with its own cluster of tasting rooms surrounded by wine bars, restaurants, and boutique shops is a great idea. It's smart redevelopment."

*   *   *

In 2008 Jayson graduated from high school and enrolled in Washington State University at the home campus in Pullman. The young man chose to pursue an undergraduate degree in accounting with a minor in business information systems. Michael's old friend Jonas, now mostly retired, had assured the young man that he had a position in his firm in order to gain the experience required to qualify for the CPA exam.

A handsome young man, Jayson was now taller than Michael and equally intelligent. He still functioned as Casa del Vino's business manager, but during the school year could only work on weekends. It was his ultimate goal to someday open a business management consulting firm specializing in the wine industry.

Although Michael very much wanted his son to eventually take over his growing business empire, he had to settle for the fact that Jayson would make his own way in the world. Like father, like son, he ruefully reminded himself. Jancy reinforced this.

"He is who he is," she pointed out matter-of-factly. "Love him for who he is: a very intelligent, hardworking young man. He's a son we both can be proud of."

Having learned earlier in life to accept unusual situations and make the best of them, Michael once again adapted to the realities of circumstances. His son not only would not be a winemaker, but not even work in the family business.

As for Jana, she was turning out quite well, her rebelliousness gradually fading away. The autumn following Jayson's graduation from high school, she began her senior year while continuing to work part time at the Barn making her *Tre Ballerini* wine. But she also worked part time with her parents as well, gradually mastering the complexities of making truly fine red wine.

Michael was pleased when Jancy didn't object to her daughter's plans one year hence to enter Watilla College's wine program. "There's always something new in winemaking," he pointed out to her. "As much as we like to think we know it all, we don't. It's good for young people to be exposed to the latest developments in vinification."

*   *   *

In early 2009 word came that Ralph Rogers Parkston had passed at the age of 82. The wine world quickly paid tribute to perhaps the most well-known wine critic of all. Every major wine publication printed its own eulogy praising him. Certainly, his lifetime of work had made him both legendary, but also controversial as well. His 100 point system of scoring wines had been debated for years as to its validity, and even Michael, who had benefited as much as anyone from it, acknowledged its shortcomings.

"Say what you want about the 100 point scale," he mentioned to colleagues at a monthly meeting of the Watilla Valley winemakers association, "but the world of wine revolves around it. We've seen all the copycats that have sprung up over the years. Nearly everyone scores on the 100 point system today."

"It's just a marketing scam," a colleague shot back. "It made Parkston rich and famous, but it'll never be objective, no matter who uses it. Wine is the most subjective thing there is. Everyone's tastes are different and for one person to score a wine on only how he or she enjoys it is a gross disservice to the winemaker."

'You're right, my friend," Michael admitted. "But we live in the real world and in that world consumers have been trained to buy a wine based on the 100 point scale. It's absurd, but it's reality."

Others joined in the discussion. "I've heard of wine shops and restaurants that won't even carry wine anymore that doesn't score at least 90 points on somebody's scale," another winemaker informed them. "That's crazy when you think that Parkston himself said that wine he rated at 80 points or above was worth drinking."

"To go even further," Michael said, jumping back into the discussion, "it's just as absurd to rank the top 100 wines of the world every year. Despite being so honored twice, I'm against that kind of thing. Sure, I had a number one wine, but did that mean it was the very best of all? Not at all. It was good, but not the absolute best."

"Goddamn marketing," someone muttered. "It sells magazines."

"Yep," Michael agreed. "It creates controversy and that sells. It also sells wine. Restaurants and wine shops all tout any wines they carry that happened to make the top 100 in any given year."

Despite the discontent of winemakers the world over with the 100 point system, R. R. Parkston had made more of an impression on the wine business than perhaps anyone else. His funeral back east was well attended and publications around the globe lauded him. Michael wondered if the world would ever see anyone like him again.

More bad news came later on, in midsummer, when Jana spilled the beans about her father. Not being able to keep a secret anymore, she confided in distress one day, "Dad's on kidney dialysis. Three times a week."

Michael had suspected for several years that something wasn't right with Tommy but he hadn't brought it up with Jancy. Instead, he had asked Maggie to approach her on a girl-to-girl basis but, even then, Jancy had pretended all was well.

"What's wrong with your dad?" he asked the girl.

Jana shrugged. "Something about leukemia. That's why mom and dad have been making a trip to San Francisco each year. To the university medical center. UCSF."

Michael nodded slowly as he thought back over the past several years and the trips Jancy and Tommy had made. They had probably been for bone marrow transplants, chemotherapy, and follow-up checks.

"What's the prognosis?" he asked. "Do you know?"

Jana simply shrugged again. "Don't know."

Sighing, Michael reached out and squeezed her on one shoulder as he sought to reassure her. "Your dad looks pretty good to me, so I think the prognosis is probably good as well. As for the dialysis, people can live for a very long time doing that."

Although he said this to reassure Jana, deep down he doubted. People who had kidney failure generally didn't live more than several years. And Tommy had a certain gauntness to him these days. He had always been on the thin side, but now his face gave away the fact that something was wrong with him.

For the time being, Michael decided not to question his friend about his health. If Tommy hadn't told him by now, then it was an issue he didn't want to share.

*   *   *

Tragedy struck on a day in early September during the hustle and bustle of the harvest when he suddenly lost Maggie. One day she suddenly without warning experienced a massive stroke that left her in the hospital in a coma. After five days, Michael reluctantly made the decision, along with her sister Karen, to end life support. Medical imaging tests revealed that she was, for all practical purposes, brain dead and would never come back to consciousness and awareness.

For the first time since he had been a youth, Michael cried as he watched his wife stop breathing and, a moment later, a nurse announced there was no heart beat. It was hard to believe that 16 years had passed so quickly since they had been married. At times Maggie's disability had made life difficult, but he and she had always maintained a positive attitude and, together, they had overcome any obstacles.

After discussions with both Karen and her brother, Michael consented to having Maggie interred next to her parents in the Watilla city cemetery.

"I don't have any family ties to Watilla," he told her family members. "I'll probably end up being laid to rest in Santa Cruz with my parents when the time comes, so she belongs here in Watilla. If there's really an afterlife, then we'll meet again someday in heaven's vineyard."

He received a gratifying amount of emotional support from not only Jancy and Tommy, but the kids as well. In fact, a couple months later, Jana announced that she was going to make a wine in memory of Maggie.

"Maggie always liked a nice Rosé," she explained. "So I'm going to have Uncle Mike help me make one."

Michael, naturally, chose his favorite grape—Syrah—for the Rosé which was actually the classic grape to use. Rosé had originated in the Provence region of France and Syrah was one of the traditional grapes to use to make it.

Departing from tradition, Jana chose to make the wine a tad off dry with a half percent of residual sugar. Michael and the others understood perfectly when she announced that the wine would be called *Sweet Remembrance*.

"It'll be just sweet enough to justify the name, but not enough to be considered a sweet wine," she explained. She also chose to leave the skins in contact with the juice just long enough to produce a lovely salmon colored wine.

In the spring of 2010 the wine was released for sale and it quickly sold out by summer which really wasn't surprising. When customers visiting the tasting room learned that the wine was named in honor of the owner's late wife, and that all proceeds went to paralysis research, they readily bought it.

Also that summer the first retail shops opened at the newly developed Vineyard Square in the former fruit warehouse district of Watilla. Although Michael attended the grand opening, he declined an invitation to speak.

The new development featured a wine bar, two tasting rooms, a bistro, and a couple of specialty retail shops. The Chamber president announced during the dedication that the development would eventually consist of over 20 establishments, many of which would be directly related to the local wine industry.

Afterwards, Michael stopped in at La Buena Tierra to have a late lunch with Jorge and his wife. Although his Mexican friends were in their late 60s, they both continued to work. Jorge still functioned as the overseer of Michael's vineyard, as well as the more recently planted vines at Casa del Vino. And Marie still over saw the cantina's kitchen, although these days it was more in a quality control position.

They conversed in Spanish of bygone days when the first vines had been planted in 1976 and the cantina had been a cozy little bar and café serving Marie's recipes. Michael reassured them that their daughter Mercedes was continuing to prove herself as an outstanding winemaker at Olde Schoolhouse Cellars.

When the lunch was finished and Michael left, he realized how the torch was being passed to another generation. Mercedes was for all practical purposes taking over completely from Michael, and Jana would soon be graduating from the community college with her winemaking degree, ready to take over from Jancy.

And speaking of Jancy, she had just recently told him about her and Tommy's plans for their retirement house. "We're going to build it overlooking our original vineyards," she informed him.

"It'll have a commanding view overlooking the river valley and the foothills of the Blue Mountains in the distance."

"Sounds very nice!" Michael remarked appreciatively.

"It's going to be our dream home," she continued. "Gourmet kitchen. Large deck. A spacious grand room. Home theater. It'll be one of the finest homes in all of the Watilla Valley."

"And I can guess you're going to be the interior designer."

"Yes!" Jancy enthusiastically replied. "Tommy has already designed the floor plan and we've talked to a contractor, so I'm in the process of figuring out the interior look. It'll be a lot like Casa del Vino."

Michael was further reminded of the passage of time later on in the summer when he heard the news that Dr. Wilbur Cline had passed. He attended both the memorial service and the funeral for what the media was calling the godfather of the Columbia Valley wine industry.

It saddened Michael greatly that the otherwise unassuming researcher was gone from the scene. Would there even be an Olde Schoolhouse Cellars if he had not met the researcher back in 1975? Perhaps not. Michael's determination to plant a vineyard had been due to Cline's confident reassurance that wine grapes would thrive in this part of the country.

"And the rest is history," Michael summed up to a colleague after telling the story of how he and Cline had planned Watilla's first vineyard, beginning with five acres."

"It's truly been a remarkable journey for a kid from California who became convinced he could make wine in Washington State," he summed up with a chuckle.

*   *   *

In October the annual fundraising gala was held on the first Saturday evening for the community college's wine program. Michael attended as, indeed, he always had since the very first one. His winery was represented with a tasting table in the grand foyer, along with 24 other wineries that had been invited to pour samples before dinner. Jancy, Tommy, and Jana were there as well at their Casa del Vino table.

After pouring samples for a half hour, Michael left the work to his helpers and mingled with the crowd, chatting with numerous guests whom he knew. Later on, he sat at a table of eight for dinner in the ballroom with Jayson and his current girlfriend, as well as Jancy, Tommy, and Jana. The other two at the table were Maggie's sister, Karen, and her husband.

Michael was dismayed at Tommy's appearance, his gauntness more pronounced than six months earlier. His dinner was specially prepared to take into account his dialysis situation. Michael noted that Jancy seemed less than her usual self.

An hour later, dinner was almost over and an announcement was made that a live auction—the highlight of the evening—would begin in 30 minutes. As attendees finished their dessert, Michael stood to stretch and then walked towards the foyer. He wanted to mentally go over a short speech he would make just before the live auction announcing his donation of $100,000 for the establishment of the

Maggie Higgins Memorial Scholarship, the interest of which would be used to pay the first year's tuition of a deserving student enrolling in the wine program.

Just as he entered the foyer, however, Jancy was at his side. When he turned to look at her with a questioning glance, she asked, "Walk with me?"

"Sure."

Hooking her left arm around his right one, she said, "Let's go outside."

Exiting the foyer doors, they walked a few steps outside into the parking lot and the cool night air. Above them, the clear sky revealed a rich tapestry of stars. Letting go of his arm, Jancy wrapped her arms around her, as if trying to keep warm.

"What a beautiful sight!" she observed, looking up at the stars.

"Yes," Michael agreed. "It's one of the benefits of living in this part of the country. Crystal clear night air."

She turned her back to him and he saw her shoulders rise and fall with a sigh. Something was wrong.

"I don't think you wanted to come out here to look at the stars," he remarked softly.

Jancy shook her head. A moment later, she turned around, her arms still wrapped around herself. Michael couldn't help but instinctively feel a need to comfort and protect her. Despite being in her late fifties, she was still a beautiful woman, but now she looked forlorn and lost.

"What's wrong" he asked gently, determined to get to the heart of the matter.

Sighing again, she simply said, "Tommy's dying."

Taking in a big breath of air and then blowing it out, he shook his head. "Damn!" he said, almost under his breath.

"I'm going to need your help," she informed him. "I'm going to need help getting through this."

Michael nodded. "Of course." Then, a second later, he asked, "How much longer does he have?"

She shrugged. "We really don't know. Maybe only a couple months. Maybe six months if we're lucky."

A long silence passed before Jancy suddenly stepped forward and hugged herself to him, laying her head on his shoulder. Michael held her as she began sobbing, letting her cry because he couldn't really think of anything to say to make things better.

After a minute, he whispered, "Let me know what I can do. Call me when you need me. Whatever I'm doing, I'll drop it and come."

After a good cry, Jancy finally released him and stepped back, wiping tears from her face. "When we go back in," she said, trying to compose herself, "Tommy will know we talked and that you know, so it'll be okay to talk to him about it. In fact, I want you to. That's one way you can help me. Tell him you'll be with him all the way to the end."

"Of course," he promised.

*   *   *

As winter passed and spring of 2011 arrived, Michael spent as much time during the day as he could with Tommy. He also found himself tightly entwined with his family, often having diner two or three times a week with him, Jancy, and Jana.

Tommy continued to decline until he barely worked anymore, generally preferring to sit and watch the activity going on either at Casa del Vino or the Barn. One valuable contribution he could still make was barrel tasting which involved spitting out samples after each taste, thereby mostly avoiding ingesting alcohol which he wasn't supposed to drink.

Michael and Jancy eventually convinced him to sit in a wheelchair when at the production facilities. This allowed him to easily move about each winery without becoming fatigued. He could still walk, but not far or for long, so the wheelchair worked out well when barrel sampling.

Although Michael became increasingly concerned for his friend as winter went by, Tommy seemed to rally with the coming of spring. He seemed to take particular delight in March when he watched the bottling line at Casa del Vino bottle Jana's new vintage of *Sweet Remembrance*, and then a week later at the Barn her new vintage of *Tre Ballerini*.

And he enjoyed one last St. Paddy's Day celebration, this time at Los Vinos which, despite having Peruvian owners, sought any excuse to host a special party to attract customers. Michael joined his family at the wine bar and reminisced about their trials and tribulations over the years as a wine industry took root in the Watilla region. Tommy even sipped a bit of green beer as he talked about his enjoyment of producing a Merlot different from the typical California variety.

"You certainly made some great wine over the years," Michael acknowledged. "You showed the world there was a different, better kind of Merlot than the stuff produced in California. You proved Merlot can be a very special, elegant wine with body and character."

"Yeah," piped up Jana. "People got the wrong idea from that movie when they said, 'Don't give me any fucking Merlot!'"

Although she got the quote a little wrong, the group understood her reference to the movie *Sideways* and the prejudice of the main character for Pinot Noir.

"Don't give me any fucking Pinot Noir!" Tommy shot back, and everyone had a good laugh.

After a moment, Michael asked his friend, "So when are you bottling your Merlot?"

Tommy straightened up, clearing his throat. "I think next week. We'll do a single vineyard from my grapes, and then another one from Jancy's vineyard."

"As usual, I'll take a case of both," Michael replied. "You haven't had a bad vintage yet. It's your great contribution to the reputation of this region."

Turning philosophical, Tommy observed, "A man could do a lot worse for a legacy."

Michael knew his friend's real legacy, however, was his daughter. He felt deep down inside that Jana would become a legendary winemaker in her own right.

*   *   *

On a Friday in late April Michael received a call from Jancy. "I hope you can stop by for dinner Sunday evening," she remarked, her voice emotional, almost breaking. "It'll be the last one we have at home as a family. Tommy's going to hospice Monday morning."

Sighing heavily, Michael assured her, "I'll be there."

At six that Sunday evening, he and Jayson stopped in at the farmhouse for the dinner. Jana met them at the door. "Mom and Dad are in the kitchen," she informed them, letting them in.

Tommy was already seated at the table while Jancy was busy finishing up the cooking. Smiling wanly, Tommy greeted them and shook hands without standing. It was obvious to Michael that his friend could no longer stand on his own.

"Glad you could make it," he said to them with an effort, his voice weak.

Jancy came over and said hi as she hugged first Jayson and then Michael. "Wow, something smells great!" Jayson remarked.

"Beef rib roast," his mother replied. "Always's been Tommy's favorite. It's absolutely awesome with Merlot."

Michael looked over with great interest the array of wine bottles on the table before Tommy. "Looks like I didn't really need to bring anything," he joked as he pulled out a bottle of *Au Naturel* from a gift bag. It was the '02 vintage that had been honored as the number wine of the world.

Tommy managed another smile. "Jancy said I could have anything from the library."

"Impressive!" Michael exclaimed as he examined a 1987 bottle from Jancy's first vintage of *Adagio*.

Picking up another bottle, he saw it was an '89 Merlot, one of the first that Tommy had made. "You know," Michael remarked, "this collection of wine right here on the table represents some of the best the world has ever seen."

Tommy nodded, and then managed a smile as he joked, "Hell, I should arrange to die more often!"

Several seconds of pained silence followed before he added, "Well, that joke didn't over very well did it?"

Michael put the bottle down in his hand and stepped over to Tommy and gave him an affectionate squeeze on the shoulder. "Sometimes you just have to be humorous to make life bearable," he said gently.

A little later dinner got under way. Tommy managed to take a sip of wine now and then, as well as a few bites of food. The group found that conversation went best when they talked shop, discussing what was going on at the wineries. It was the only way to make the evening bearable, and it had the added benefit that Tommy readily added his thoughts and opinions.

An hour and a half later, dessert had been served and dishes were being cleared. Jayson and Jana got up to help Jancy, leaving Michael at the table to talk with his friend. After several minutes, Tommy held up his hand to stop the conversation. Michael suddenly noticed that the house seemed empty.

"The others are down in the cellar for a few moments to leave us alone," Tommy informed his friend. "I told Jancy I wanted to talk to just you about a couple things."

Michael suddenly became very alert, dreading what his friend might want to discuss. "First thing," Tommy began, "I want to ask you to look after Jana and Jancy after I'm gone. They're both taking this pretty hard."

"Of course," Michael immediately replied. "Absolutely."

"They're both so much alike," Tommy continued. "Headstrong as hell. And they keep things bottled up inside too much. Keep an eye on them."

"You know I will," Michael reassured his friend.

"Make sure you help them with the financial affairs. I have a will, but just the same, they'll need some help sorting everything out."

"Jayson will be good for that," Michael pointed out. "And he has the expertise of Jonas's firm if he needs it."

"Good. That's good."

A moment of silence passed before Tommy spoke again. "There's something else, too," he managed to say, emotion in his voice. "Jancy will need someone. Maybe not right away, but later on."

Michael nodded. "I'll be there for any support she needs in the short run, but I think she'll do just fine on her own in the long run."

Tommy shook his head. "You don't understand," he replied. "I'm saying it's okay if you two get back together. You know, someday. You're practically like a father already to Jana, so who else would be better for Jancy after she goes through her grieving?"

But Michael vigorously shook his head. "That is not something fit for discussion here tonight!" he protested. "I'm ancient history. If she ever decides to have someone else in her life, then there'll be all kinds of choices for her."

Tommy picked up his glass and took a sip before carefully putting it back down. "I'm saying it's okay if it's you, goddamnit. If you and her don't get back together, then I'll make it a special point to haunt you from beyond the grave!"

Sighing, Michael didn't argue any further. "Okay, okay, you made your point," he said. "Now, let's talk about something else."

The next day Tommy was transferred to the local Watilla hospice where Michael visited him every afternoon. That was when his friend would be wheeled out to the courtyard in his hospital bed so he could enjoy the sun propped up in a sitting position.

The two friends would talk and reminisce for a couple hours each visit until Jancy, usually with Jana, came to be with Tommy to spend the late afternoon and early evening with him. This pattern of visitation lasted nine days until he slipped into unconsciousness. Five days later he died.

Michael wasn't that surprised to learn that his friend had desired a natural burial, even to the extent of not having a casket or simple coffin. After a memorial service in town, his body was laid to rest at a spot along the boundary line of his and Jancy's original vineyards. He was lowered into a four foot deep grave wrapped in a simple burial shroud. A large stone with a simple plague on it was added a few days later to mark the location.

Chapter 22

Mystery Wine

Vista Mozzafiato
2011 – 2012

A month after Tommy's funeral, Michael and Jayson were invited over for a family dinner to celebrate Jana's imminent departure for California. After graduating with honors from the wine program at the community college, she'd been accepted for a year's internship at a large Sonoma winery.

Having a well-known mother for a winemaker had aided her application, as did Michael's letter of recommendation. The young lady, however, had also earned her way by virtue of her outstanding coursework.

Michael knew Jana was keenly interested in biodynamic vineyard management, as well as organic practices for both vineyards and winemaking. This interested him as well, since both he and Jancy had discussed converting their vineyards to biodynamic practices. However, they were reluctant to do so without expert guidance.

"I don't want to risk ruining my vineyard by turning it over to nature," he informed colleagues. "If I go the biodynamic route, it has to be extremely well planned out."

"It's about having the right kinds of birds and bugs, isn't it?" he was asked.

"Well, actually, it's a lot more than that," he replied. "You have to create a unique ecosystem that can support the vineyard without having to use toxic chemicals like herbicides and insecticides. That means a whole suite of plants like flowers, bushes, and shrubs that allow the beneficial birds and insects to thrive."

At the dinner, Jana talked excitedly about her upcoming internship. "The winery was one of the first in California to be biodynamic," she explained. "If you remember, *Wine Explorer* did a big story on them a couple years ago."

"Yeah, I recall that very well," Michael told her. "It was the cover story for that issue."

"I can't believe they're letting me stay a whole year!" she exclaimed. "I'll get to see what they do for the entire 12 month growth cycle. That's awesome!"

"Well, don't let them keep you!" Jancy half kidded her. "We want you back here someday, remember."

Afterward, when dinner was finished, Jayson departed for the Tri Cities and Jana left to meet up with a couple local friends. Jancy invited Michael to linger over a glass of wine. They made small talk for a while about Jana as Michael sensed that Jancy wished to talk about something but was reluctant to do so.

Finally, though, she cleared her throat and asked, "Can I ask you a personal question?"

Michael's eyebrows raised as his face took on a questioning look. "Sure."

Swirling the wine in her glass, Jancy glanced up at him and asked, "Over the time since Maggie died, why haven't you gotten together with someone else? After all, you're still a handsome man, not to mention being a famous winemaker with an iconic winery. You'd be quite a catch for a woman."

Taking a breath and letting it out, Michael pondered his reply. After a moment of staring into his glass, he replied, "Hmm, well, I have had opportunities, that's for sure. I guess it boils down to the fact that I've fallen in love with three women in my life. I had to give up the first, I lost you, and Maggie was taken from me. I just haven't felt like I have the energy to start all over again with someone else."

Another moment of silence passed before Jancy commented, "Well, for me, I'm thinking I'm too young to quit on life. Even though Tommy and I never married, I'm a grieving widow right now. But I won't be forever."

Michael nodded in understanding. "Life moves on," he simply observed. "In one way or another, we all need to move on."

"I'm going to grieve for one year," Jancy informed him, looking directly at him. "I'm going to take a year and live with my memories. I'm going to have the new house finished as a tribute to Tommy. That'll keep me busy, keep me occupied for a while. But after that, like you say, I'm going to move on with my life."

"Finishing the house would be good," Michael agreed, although he wondered what she was going to do with such a large place.

"It's going to be something!" Jancy said excitedly, her face brightening as she thought about a subject dear to her. "I'm going to call it Vista Mozzafiato – the house with the breathtaking view."

Michael smiled as he mentally pictured the site where earthwork had started before Tommy died. Since then, however, work had been halted. Now he was glad to hear Jancy was a going to have it start up again. With Jana gone for the next year, Jancy would need something to keep her busy and energized.

*   *   *

The year passed rapidly as Michael busied himself learning all he could about converting to biodynamic and sustainable practices. He Skyped on an almost weekly basis with Jana, and she also provided information to him via email on what she was learning.

He had become her surrogate father as he found their conversations sometimes veering off into other directions as she sought his advice on personal matters such as auto maintenance, personal finance, and even, once in a while, on boys and why they acted the way they did.

He saw Jancy only a handful of times. With Jana gone, he wasn't invited over anymore for Sunday dinners, although she did accept several invitations to go out to dinner with him when their son Jayson was in town.

Vista Mozzafiato was completed in the spring of 2012 and immediately became the talk of Watilla. Rumor had it that the estate cost over a million dollars with everyone wondering what the inside looked like. Michael wondered, too, but didn't receive an invitation from Jancy.

In early May of that year he commemorated the anniversary of Tommy's passing by sending a card and note to Jancy, as well as laying a large bouquet of lilies on his friend's grave site. Other bouquets were there as well, along with several notes expressing that he was not forgotten.

Later in the month, Jancy and Jana joined him and Jayson at Cocina Casera to celebrate both his 63rd birthday and Jana's return to Watilla. During the dinner Jancy mentioned that she planned a house warming party soon and that Michael would be invited.

The invitation came on a Tuesday in early June when he received a text message from her: *"r u free Sat 4 house warming party?"*

He texted back: *"Sure. What can i bring?"*

"just yourself. 6ish. enter code 8987" was her reply.

Michael smiled when he saw the code which he assumed was for a security gate. He briefly wondered if the code meant anything or was just something easy to remember. In any event, when Saturday arrived, he drove over to her new place and, sure enough, he encountered a security gate with a punch button box. After entering the code, the gate swung open.

He drove a short distance alongside a vineyard on a paver brick driveway that ended in front of the house in a circle that enclosed a small fountain ringed by flower beds. He smiled when he saw Jancy's old battered Jeep standing off to one side by a three car garage. She never had gotten rid of all these years. She had driven it to Watilla from California when she had first arrived in the valley and had kept it ever since even though she rarely drove it anymore.

The house was an impressive, two-story, Italianate structure in the neoclassical style with a mauve stucco exterior and a roof of red tiles. The middle third of the house was recessed between two wings and was fronted by a colonnaded entrance that led visitors up to a palladium glass door bordered by a large palladium window on either side.

This porch-like area was covered by a colonnaded veranda on the second level fronted by a white balustrade. Each of the left and right wings of the house contained a row of three grand palladium windows on the first level, and white-framed, square double windows on the upper level. The top of a chimney could be seen above the roofline.

After parking three-quarters of the way around the circle, Michael got out of his vehicle, whistling softly and shaking his head as he eyed the structure before him. The house conveyed the appearance of both elegance and wealth, its message clearly stating that no ordinary person lived here.

He could guess that there was a third, lower level visible only from the back since the house was built on a slope. There was probably a walk-out from that level covered by an expansive deck.

When he went up a flight of five steps and rang the door bell, Jancy answered it a moment later. "Hey, hi!" she greeted him, flashing her trademark smile.

Michael saw she was barefoot and dressed in jeans and a pink, lightweight V-neck sweater. "Gosh, I feel overdressed," he commented as they briefly hugged and he offered her a gift bag with a bottle of wine in it.

Wearing dress slacks and a casual sport coat over an open-collar shirt, he wondered if maybe Jancy hadn't dressed yet for the party. Suddenly worried, he asked, "Am I early?"

"You're dressed just fine," she reassured him. "I like the way you look when you're dressed up."

"Oh, okay."

"And, you're right on time," she reassured him as she turned and led him into the home's great room.

Michael took in the high vaulted ceiling above him and the massive stone fireplace that was the centerpiece of one of the walls. As he followed Jancy into the open kitchen, he wasn't surprised to find it a gourmet cook's dream with stainless steel appliances and a large island with black granite countertops.

On one of the back counters by the stacked ovens, he noticed what looked like a small beef roast sitting out, waiting to be roasted. This prompted him to wonder about the party. It seemed like something wasn't quite right. Despite what Jancy had said, he strongly felt that he was early for the party.

Off in the side dining room, he spotted a brown sack on the table with the rim of a wine bottle barely visible. "Ah, looks like mystery wine!" he commented, smiling. How many times over the years had he and she and Tommy played that game? More than he could possibly remember.

"Yes!" Jancy confirmed from behind him. He turned around as she entered the room carrying two empty glasses. "I can't wait for you to try it!" she exclaimed with a big smile.

She seemed in high spirits—even excited— as she set the glasses down on the table. "We should wait for the others," Michael commented. "I don't want to start before the other guests."

Jancy pulled out a chair for him to sit. "There are no other guests," she replied, matter-of-factly. "Just you and I tonight."

Taken aback, Michael was at a loss for words for a moment as he sat down. Jancy pulled out another chair and positioned it right next to him as she sat down, so close that their shoulders almost touched.

"I suppose I shouldn't really be surprised by anything you do anymore," he said, slowly shaking his head and smiling.

She glanced at him, returning his smile with her another of her own before reaching for the bag. "Here, let's get started!" she said impatiently. "I can't wait for you to try this!"

She's really charged up this evening, Michael thought to himself. What the heck is she up to? And, what's so special about this wine that she's invited only me?

Jancy poured out a small quantity of the mystery wine into his glass and handed it to him. Michael was shocked when he accepted the glass and saw what the wine looked like. "Wow, this stuff has some age on it!"he commented as he eyed the light rusty/reddish liquid.

Jancy was practically squirming in her chair, barely able to contain her excitement as he frowned and examined his wine. "Looks like 20 years or more to me," he commented. "Possibly even older!"

He swirled the wine around and then sniffed it. "Hmm, not a strong nose which isn't surprising given the age."

Glancing at Jancy, he asked, "What the heck have you got here? Your first vintage of *Adagio*?"

Arching her eyebrows, she replied, "So, you're sure it's New World?"

Sniffing the wine yet again, Michael nodded his head. "Yes, I think so. There's no minerality and there are still some traces of fruit to it."

Jancy merely smiled as he continued pondering his glass. Taking one final sniff, he reached a tentative conclusion. "There are also traces of tobacco and leather, maybe some bacon. Very faint but they're there." A second later, he added, "I'm beginning to think it's a Syrah, not a blend."

Taking a sip, Michael was further surprised as he swished the liquid around in his mouth before swallowing it. "This seems to be a well-made wine!" he opined. "It still has some fruit to it, a touch of pepper, maybe. And some hints of tannins. This wine has had enough backbone to hold together over the years." Then, seeing her smiling at him, he asked, "What the devil have you given me?"

Jancy leaned slightly towards him so that her shoulder touched his. "You know this wine," she whispered.

Blowing out a breath of air, he frowned again, puzzled. "I know this wine?"

Instead of answering, Jancy merely nodded, smiling.

Now the mystery deepened. He assumed the bottle came out of her personal cellar and was one of her wines. But she was acting as if it was one of his.

"Is this one of my early vintage Syrahs that you're kept squirreled away?" he asked, really curious now.

"You know this wine," she whispered once again. "You know what it is."

Suddenly, like an electric shock, it hit him and he made the connection. He shook his head in disbelief, emotion suddenly welling up inside of him. "It's not possible," he managed to say.

Jancy, however, continued smiling coyly as she slowly nodded her head, her blue eyes shimmering. Michael put his glass down, leaned back in his chair, and rubbed his forehead as he glanced at her. Reaching for the bag, she pulled out the bottle and there, right in front of him big as life, was his '85 Reserve Syrah - the perfect 100 point wine.

He pinched his eyes, trying to keep tears from trickling out. "I didn't think any were left," he said hoarsely, barely able to speak.

Jancy poured a half glass for him as well as one for herself. "I was saving it in case you died before I did," she explained. "I wanted to enjoy it a year or two afterward in honor of your memory. But then, this past year, I changed my mind and decided it would be much more enjoyable to share it with you while we're both still around."

She raised her glass in a toast and said, "Here's to a perfect wine."

He raised his glass as well, and then they both took a sip. A moment later, Jancy leaned closer so her shoulder touched his once again. "Do you remember what we were doing when we heard the news?" she asked.

Reaching back into his memory, a smile spread on Michael's face as he recollected that momentous day. "Yes, I do," he answered. "We were working in the vineyard when you left to go make lunch in the schoolhouse. As you were almost there, the mail carrier stopped by and delivered the mail, so you went out to the mailbox and retrieved it. Suddenly, you started shouting and making a commotion, and I wondered what in the world was the matter."

Still leaning against him, she whispered, "And then what did we do?"

Still smiling, Michael continued. "I ran down to you and saw the magazine and couldn't believe it. I was simply struck dumb, but we were both so excited that we went inside, opened a bottle and sipped it as we read the article."

Leaning against him even more now, she again whispered, "And then what did we do?"

Michael turned slightly to glance at her. They were so close now that their cheeks were almost touching. He saw her smile, the look on her face, the sparkle in her eyes, and he knew what she wanted him to say.

"And then we went upstairs and made love," he whispered in reply.

Slowly nodding agreement, Jancy added, "Passionately."

Michael also nodded as he recalled in his mind that day of long ago. Jancy straightened up and took another sip of wine.

"I would like us to enjoy this precious wine for the next 10 or 15 minutes and let it work its magic on us," she stated. "Then I want you to make love to me."

*   *   *

They weren't young anymore, so their approach was a bit more practical. Jancy first put the roast in the oven and set the temperature control as well as the timer. "It'll take 90 minutes for it to cook," she informed him. "That should be just about perfect for us!"

She led him to the bedroom where they made love for the better part of an hour. For Michael it was both a new experience, and yet a familiar one. It was strange but exciting to be able to caress Jancy's body again, to smell her, to kiss her, to make love to her.

After the first rush of passion had been sated, they settled into a slow, sensuous rhythm, whispering words of love to each other, trying to make up for so many years of being apart. When they were finished, Michael lay on top of her, his weight barely pressing against her, his nose gently rubbing hers.

"God help me, but I still love you," he barely whispered.

Looking up at him with her brilliant blue eyes, Jancy smiled and whispered, "I know," as she had so many times in the distant past whenever he had told her he loved her. But then she unexpectedly added, "I love you, too."

Shocked to hear the words she had said she would never utter, Michael raised himself up a bit higher and stared down at her with a smile. "Watch it," he kidded her, "you're slipping in your old age!"

She slid her hands around the back of his neck and pulled him down to her and kissed him. Tears trickled out of her eyes as she looked up at him, her face a mask of emotion. "Don't hurt me again," she managed to whisper.

"I won't," he whispered back.

A few moments later they showered together, enjoying one last time caressing each other's bodies. Afterward, they dressed and went to the kitchen where Jancy finished the preparation of dinner. When they had finished off the half bottle, she poured their glassed full again from a carafe into which she had poured the first half of the bottle before Michael had arrived.

Raising his glass, Michael offered a toast. "A perfect wine for a perfect evening."

Jancy raised her glass in response and replied, "To a perfect evening."

After they had finished both dinner and Michel's perfect Syrah, Jancy surprised him by saying, "You'll stay the night, of course."

Leaning back in his chair and feeling very mellow, he cocked his head at her and sighed. "You know I will." A second later he added, "Hells bells, you know I'm putty in your hands and I would probably do whatever you wanted."

Propping her head sideways and supporting it with one of her hands, Jancy smiled back at him and simply replied, "I know."

Chapter 23

First the Answer, then the Question

Vista Mozzafiato
June 2012 – June 2013

Over the next several weeks, Jancy invited Michael over with increasing frequency. Although they didn't always end up making love, he generally stayed the night. Their hanging out began to follow a routine: together, they would make dinner, enjoy it with a good wine, then retire to the deck to sip wine and enjoy the warm evening as the sun set.

On one such evening in mid July, they were sitting side by side in lounge chairs, glasses of wine in hand, when out of the blue Jancy announced, "You should move in." It wasn't a question, but more of a strong suggestion.

"Hmm? Are you sure?" Michael replied, a bit surprised, as he turned his head and glanced towards her.

"Yep," she immediately replied. "This house is too big and lonely without a man in it. Even when Jana moves in downstairs this fall, it still won't feel right."

Then, after a brief pause, she added with a coy smile, "Besides, I'm getting used to you being around."

Michael turned his head back to look straight ahead, gazing out upon the expanse of green vineyards in the near distance. "As long as you're sure," he replied softly.

"I'm sure," she confirmed without hesitation.

He gave the new arrangement a two month trial to satisfy himself that things were working out. As the weeks passed, it became evident that he and she still retained the same strong attraction for each other as when they had first met. Reassured, he finally put his house on the market and moved the rest of his personal belongings into Vista Mozzafiato.

The kids took the new living arrangements as well as could be expected. Jayson could have really cared less because Michael and Jancy were, after all, his parents, so if they lived together now, then that was simply natural.

As for Jana, she accepted the new situation mostly because it involved a new house that she had not been raised in, nor had ever shared with her parents. Besides, Michael had served as a surrogate father during important times in her life and that made the transition easier for her to accept. Everyone involved agreed that she should continue calling him by the convenient term, 'Uncle Mike.'

There were more changes to the family situation. Jayson had surprised his parents the previous year when he had announced at his college graduation he wasn't interested in becoming a CPA. "Although I like accounting," he had informed his parents, "I really don't want to be doing people's taxes all my life. I think a more exciting career would be as a business consultant or manager."

Michael and Jancy had immediately embraced this new direction in his life. They had been discussing a new corporate structure for their various businesses anyway, so it made perfect sense now to retain the services of a prominent business law firm to hammer out the framework of a holding company. All of the family's assets would be managed under the umbrella of the new company with Jayson as the chief executive.

Olde Schoolhouse Cellars, Casa del Vino, J Phillips Cellars, and Champenoise Cellars would all be operating divisions of the new company. After much spirited debate, a name for the new company was settled upon.

"This is the passing of the torch," Michael pointed out to Jancy when he protested having his name involved in any way. "A new generation is taking over. This is all about Jayson and Jana, not you and I. We should just keep it simple and call it J & J Vintners."

"But it's about more than just winemaking," Jayson protested. "We're selling wine as well."

"Ah, here's where the wisdom of your elders comes into play," Michael teased his son. "When I was in France, I learned that the meaning of the word vintner originally referred to a wine merchant. Today, of course, we use the word to mean winemaking, but originally it meant wine merchant."

And so they settled on J & J Vintners except that Jancy had the last word when she announced, "You know my sense of style. Drop the & from the name. Just call the new company J J Vintners. It's cleaner and more elegant."

"I know the perfect slogan!" Jana suddenly interjected. "Purveyors of fine wine!"

As the legalities were being finalized, Michael made a move to expand his business empire—now in reality the family's business empire—by starting yet another new business.

"Those of us who were the first winemaking pioneers cooperated with each other and helped each other," he reminded everyone. "Today, it's even more daunting to get started in the winemaking business, so I'm going to start a co-op."

"A coop?" Jayson asked. "You mean, have a number of winemakers band together?"

"Yes, exactly," Michael confirmed. "It'll be like a business incubator. We'll own the building and the equipment and lease it out to several budding winemakers who'll jointly use it. Plus, we can give them expert advice on brand development and marketing."

Instead of using an old barracks or storage building at the airport industrial park, Michael elected to buy several vacant lots there and construct a brand new building. Jancy designed the exterior appearance to give the overall appearance of stylish functionality. Inside, the structure was designed to accommodate up to 10 winemakers who were just starting out.

The business was named the Watilla Wine Co-operative and was incorporated as a non-profit organization with Jayson as chairman of the board of directors, and Michael and Jancy as two of the five board members.

In other changes to the family business, Jana became head winemaker for J Phillips Cellars with Jancy as the overall executive winemaker. It was a mostly amicable arrangement as long as mother and daughter kept to the agreed upon division of duties.

At Old Schoolhouse Cellars, Mercedes was promoted to head winemaker with Michael as the overall executive winemaker. Unlike

Jancy, he was completely willing to give the young woman all the responsibility she could handle.

*   *   *

As early September arrived, Jancy and Michael were sitting together one evening on a love seat on the deck, sipping wine and watching the shadows lengthen over the landscape. Everything felt right with the world.

In the middle of this mellow mood, Jancy characteristically gave voice suddenly to a dramatic statement with no forewarning. "We should go to Europe."

Familiar with her mode of decision making, Michael knew she had already made up her mind and that she and he would be heading to Europe something in the future. Sighing contentedly, he simply asked, "Where, exactly?"

"Italy to start with," she replied. "You know how much I like anything Italian."

He chuckled as he thought how much, indeed, she enjoyed Italian themes. The name of their joint venture tasting room, the name of her house, the name of her signature wine, were all Italian terms. Hell, the design of her house was pure Italianate.

"Anywhere in particular?"

Jancy suddenly rose from her seated position and climbed on Michael to straddle his lap and face him. Sliding her hands behind his neck, she answered excitedly, "Yes, Tuscany! We need to rent a Tuscan villa, Just like in the movies! Rent a villa for a month and explore the region around us. Maybe even take a cooking class!"

"And visit wineries," Michael added.

"Yes! We'll visit lots of wineries!" she replied, her eyes shining brightly. She gave him a quick kiss.

A second later, she added, "And of course we'll have to visit France afterward. Starting with the Rhone. We should stop in at Domaine Garçon. You know you have a standing invitation, remember?"

"Yes, I remember."

"Then we can go all over France: Burgundy, the Loire Valley, Bordeaux, Champagne!" she continued with mounting enthusiasm, ticking off the major wine regions of the country. "You're so famous in the industry that all the best wineries will give us private tastings and tours. Think about it! It'll be a dream trip!"

Michael knew she was right. They could go anywhere in the world to visit wineries and be treated like royalty. In fact, over the years, he had hosted numerous winemakers from both the U.S. and other countries as they had sought him out to see what he did to make such award-winning wine.

"So, when would we do this?"

"How about June?" she suggested. "It'd be the perfect time of year to travel Europe. All the vineyards will be green and the weather warm."

"Under the Tuscan sun, hmm?" Michael teased her, citing the name of a movie.

"Yes, under the Tuscan sun!"

He sighed once again and smiled. "Okay, let's plan on it!"

"Alright!" Jancy replied. "I'll get to work on the travel arrangements and accommodations. And you can send emails to the wineries I suggest to alert them you'll be in their area."

*   *   *

In early October on a mild evening that promised an unusually nice sunset, Jancy announced after dinner, "I've been waiting for a really nice sunset like this evening's. Let's go out in the vineyard and watch it!"

Michael poured another half glass of wine for each of them and they proceeded outside. Strolling roughly a hundred yards, Jancy led them to the high corner where her original vineyard met his original vineyard. From this vantage point, they had a sweeping view of the river below them to the south, and a panoramic view of the sunset to the west. Standing for several minutes, they sipped and made small talk.

But as the sun sank so that its bottom rim began to touch the horizon and the sky around it transformed itself into a palette of purples and reds, Jancy took Michael's empty glass and put it down on the ground, along with hers. Turning her back to him, she leaned against his chest. This generated a natural reaction for him to slid his hands around her and hold her tightly.

"It's beautiful," she murmured as they stared at the sunset.

"Yes, it is," he murmured back.

A minute of silence passed before Jancy broke it by asking, "Isn't there something you want to ask me?"

The question surprised him. "Hmm? What?"

"Isn't there a question you'd like to ask me?" she repeated.

Searching his mind, Michael couldn't recollect anything they had discussed recently that had been left unresolved, unless it was their Europe trip. To buy a little time, he joked, "What? Whether you're a natural blonde?"

That got a rise out of her. Spinning around, Jancy gave him a playful punch in his chest as she retorted, "You found that out the first time we made love!"

Then, her face suddenly turning serious, she said, "Isn't there something you've always wanted to ask me?"

Michael frowned as he gazed into her blue eyes which were beginning to shimmer, a dead giveaway that she was up to something amorous. As she saw his look of puzzlement, Jancy slid her hands around his neck and gazed up at him.

"The answer is yes," she said softly.

Still puzzled, Michael stared back at her for a moment, seeing the obvious look of desire on her face. "If you ask the question," she whispered, encouraging him, "my answer is yes."

Frowning slightly, he peered into the liquid blue pools of her eyes. Was it possible, he wondered? Was it really possible that she wanted him to ask *that* question?

As emotion welled up in him, Michael took a deep breath and plunged ahead. "Jancy Phillips," he quietly began, trying to speak without trembling, "will you marry me?"

She released her hands from his neck, stepped back slightly, and cocked her head at him. "I'll have to think about it," she teased, a big smile on her face.

"What?" Michael replied in surprise, confused.

She immediately jumped up to him, forcing him to catch her butt in his hands as she held on and wrapped her legs around him. "I told you the answer is yes!" she reassured him as they gazed at each other, their noses only inches apart.

Jancy quickly kissed him, "But I'm not changing my name."

Michael kissed her back. "I don't care."

"I love you," Jancy whispered.

"I love you, too."

Fifteen minutes later, they walked back to the house, excitedly talking about wedding plans. "I didn't have any warning about this, so I don't have a ring for you," Michael pointed out.

"That doesn't matter," Jancy replied. "We'll select one tomorrow at a jewelry store.

Once back in the house, Michael was curious about the date. "When, exactly, do you think we should tie the knot?"

"Why, June of course!" she answered. "I want to be a June bride!"

"And where are you thinking as the place?"

She shot him a look as if he were dense. "Casa del Vino! Where else?"

But Michael frowned as he heard this. "I thought it was booked more than a year in advance?"

After a second's hesitation, Jancy informed him, "There's an opening one Saturday in June." She turned back to attend to loading dishes into the dishwasher.

Hearing this surprising piece of information, Michael became suspicious. "I find it hard to believe that the most popular wedding venue in the Watilla Valley has an opening in June less than a year in advance," he commented, trying to keep any tone of accusation out of his voice.

"Well, there is," she retorted.

Michael noticed that Jancy kept her back to him. Her eyes would give her away, he thought to himself. That's why she's avoiding looking at me. Something's not right.

"Look," he said, "I don't want to get married at Casa del Vino if it means another couple gets bumped."

Hearing this, Jancy whirled around. "Nobody got bumped!" she said firmly, glaring at him.

From her tone and the look she was giving him, Michael realized she was telling the truth. Suddenly it struck him like a thunderbolt. "The trip to Europe is our honeymoon!" he said in astonishment. "You've planned this all out! You reserved the wedding day a long time ago!"

Jancy glanced away, then turned her back to him again. "Maybe," was all she replied.

Michael quickly walked over to her. "Well, well, well," he teased her. "You certainly were risking a lot on me actually proposing! After planning the honeymoon and wedding a long time back, you had a lot riding on me proposing!"

He was standing beside her now. Turning around to face him, she simply said, "No, I didn't."

"Oh, why not?"

A smile spread over her face as she announced, "I knew you would propose if I gave you the chance."

Raising his eyebrows, Michael replied, "Oh, really?"

"Really."

Sighing, he shook his head and smiled back at her, "Life is really interesting with you, that's for sure," he said, stating the obvious. "First the honeymoon is planned, then the wedding, and then I propose. It's all backwards!"

Jancy raised her eyebrows as she reminded him, "You forgot we started a family first."

"That's right!" Michael exclaimed. "First we started a family, then we planned a honeymoon, then a wedding, and then I proposed."

*   *   *

When the last Saturday of June rolled around, Michael Ross and Jancy Phillips were finally married in the wedding garden at Casa del Vino. Security personnel kept back the public who crowded the deck and grounds that afternoon trying to take it all in. Everyone knew that two founding members of the Watilla Valley wine region were being married and that generated intense curiosity.

Jayson walked Jancy down the aisle and gave her away. As he later told friends, "That was weird giving my mother away to my father!" Standing beside Michael was his longtime friend Jorge who served as best man.

Jana was maid of honor. And, as she told friends, "I used to hate my mom once as a teenager, and now I'm her maid of honor. But I'm cool with it."

The reception took place in Casa del Vino's special events room where guests enjoyed a gourmet catered dinner and live music afterwards. Michael and Jancy stayed just long enough to dance a couple times and politely speak with each guest a moment or two.

As they left, Michael was curious where they were going because Jancy had insisted on making arrangements for where they would stay on their wedding night. When they got into his SUV, he asked, "Okay, where to?"

"Why, to the schoolhouse, of course!" she replied matter-of-factly. "I thought we could share a glass of wine in quiet before heading to our overnight accommodations."

"Sounds good to me!"

"It's where everything started with us, after all."

"Yes, you're right."

But when they got to the schoolhouse and unlocked the door and went up the stairs to the tasting room, Jancy suddenly announced. "I don't really feel like drinking just right now."

"Huh?" Michael didn't understand. "I thought you wanted to come here."

Glancing upward, she coyly asked, "What did we used to do upstairs?"

Michael glanced up the staircase to the upper floor for a second, then looked back at Jancy. "We used to make love up there," he admitted."When it was a bedroom. But it's a special events room now, not a bedroom anymore."

Cocking her head slightly at him, a small smile playing on her lips, she teased him by asking, "Are you sure?"

Frowning, Michael began suspecting he had been set up yet again. "What do you mean, am I sure?"

Jancy turned to go up the next flights of steps. "We should go check it out."

Following her up the stairs to the upper floor, he discovered a queen size bed in the middle of the room. "I don't believe it!" he exclaimed. "When did this happen?"

"A few hours ago," Jancy admitted. "I couldn't arrange it any earlier for fear you would stop in here and find out." Pausing a second, she asked, "Surprised?"

Although he was, Michael replied, "No, not really. Not anymore. Not with you. Just when I think I have you figured out, you throw me for a loop."

Jancy stepped up to him and he readily took her into his arms. "I thought this would be appropriate since this is the exact place where we first made love 35 years ago," she said to him.

Studying her face for a moment, he finally said, "Everything has come full circle."

Gazing up at him, she simply replied, "Yes, it has."

Chapter 24

Old World Meets New

Domaine Garçon
September 2013

The newlyweds spent a month in Tuscany, enjoying sun-bask days visiting wineries, small town markets, and surrounding historic sites. That idyllic interlude was followed by two weeks in the Veneto, a region outside Venice known for its lighter style wines such as Prosecco and Pinot Grigio.

Several trips were made into Venice itself to dine at outside cafés, either in Saint Mark's square or along the Grand Canal. Then it was off to France for an extended journey through many of its famous wine districts. However, several months earlier, Jancy had changed her mind about the order of things.

"Instead of visiting the Rhone first, why don't we begin in Paris in the north and work our way south?" she had suggested. "That way you can work on your French as we go and be able to converse fluently by the time we get to Domaine Garçon."

"Good idea!" Michael had readily agreed. "My French is pretty rusty after more than 30 years."

And so they had taken their time beginning with a week in Paris playing tourists and enjoying one of the world's truly great cities. Afterward, they spent several days in Champagne where some of the best houses gave them private tours and tastings, as well as hosting them at private dinners.

Michael made extensive notes on the finer points of making Champagne to take back home, and he made arrangements for his winemaker at Champenoise Cellars to spend a month the following spring to experience first-hand how the French did their blending to create their fine sparkling wines.

Jancy and Michael also toured the Loire Valley from its mouth to the Pouilly Fumé district, visiting a couple fairytale castles along the way. Then it was on to Bordeaux where they were treated, indeed, like royalty. Several of the world-famous chateaux hosted them to private cellar tours, barrel tastings, and dinners featuring some of the most expensive red wines in the world.

A week later they were in Burgundy, starting first in Chablis to sample world-class Chardonnay. From there they hopped over to the Côte de Beaune and worked their way down the valley to Côtes de Nuits, enjoying world renown Pinot Noir all along the way.

Finally, they arrived in the northern Rhone Valley in the Côte Rotie where Jancy was simply amazed at the steepness of the vineyards on the valley walls. The picturesque countryside featured rock walls and terraces made by hand over the centuries to hold the vineyards on the steep slopes.

"I remember one week in the summer when I helped the crew gather up rocks and gravel at the bottom of the slopes," Michael related. "We shoveled the stuff into buckets and then carried them higher up and dumped them back into the vineyards. It was a never-ending task – rains would wash the rocks down and the workers would carry them back up."

Jancy just shook her head as they drove along. At one point she commented, "Looks like many of the vineyards have vines that are vertically trained."

"Yep," Michael confirmed. "You sort of make a teepee out of poles and let the vines grow upward. It seems to work better on steep slopes."

South of the small city of Vienne, Michael steered their car onto the local road for Domaine Garçon. A couple kilometers later he turned into the lane that led to the winery. A short distance brought them to the venerable 17th century mansion house.

"This place hasn't changed a whole lot," he commented as he drove around a circular flower bed and parked in a small graveled lot next to a stone wall that joined the house to another, smaller building.

"Boy, this looks 17th century! " Jancy observed as she got out of the passenger side and looked around.

The house was an imposing three story structure that roughly resembled a castle. The cobblestone exterior walls had been covered with earth-tone stucco to protect them from the elements and preserve their integrity. Two large chimneys bolstered each end of the house, ending slightly higher than the steeply pitched roof.

Dormers stood out from the roof on the third story. Pointing to one of them, Michael said, "That's where I stayed. There, in that room. Hot as hell in summer and cold as frozen brass in winter!"

Jancy chuckled as he continued. "But what a view from up there! I could see the French Alps on days when the weather was good. They're not that far away. In fact, the city of Grenoble where the winter Olympics were held is close enough that folks around here go skiing there."

Just then the front door of the house opened and a man and woman emerged. For the first time in a little more than 40 years, Michael laid eyes on Jacqui. He still recognized her although she had certainly changed. She was still willowy in stature but her once beautiful, raven black hair was faded and heavily streaked with gray.

"Michael!" she greeted him with a big smile as she walked up. "I would know you anywhere!" she added, speaking French. "You haven't changed!"

He and she exchanged quick kisses on each cheek. Her face was lined and crow's feet were evident, but her eyes still twinkled and danced as she looked him over.

"And you haven't changed, either," he replied, also in French.

This elicited a laugh from her. "Oh, such a lie! But you may lie all you wish!"

Switching to English, Jacqui introduced him to her husband. "Michael, my husband Henri Trudeau."

"Pleased to meet you," Michael said in French as he shook Henri's hand.

"And I am pleased to finally meet you," the Frenchman replied.

Changing once again to English, Michael turned to Jacqui. "I'd like you to meet my wife Jancy." Turning back to Jancy, he added, "This is Jacqueline, the granddaughter of the man who taught me so much about winemaking."

"Please, call me Jacqui," Jacqui immediately said, seeking to put Jancy at ease.

The two women bussed each other and then Henri welcomed her, exchanging quick pecks on the cheek as well. Jacqui turned and motioned to the door. "Please, come in! Our home is most welcome to you!"

Once inside, the guests were ushered through a foyer and past a three story staircase that accessed the upper levels. In the great room of the mansion, Jacqui turned to Michael. "You and your wife will share our main guest room on the second floor." Then, teasing Michael with a twinkle in her eye, she added, "We won't make you sleep in the attic!"

Michael smiled but didn't respond. When he had lived here as a young man, not all the winter nights had been cold. On some nights he had had a certain, ah, 'bed warmer,' as he preferred to think of the situation.

Henri invited them on through the house and out the back door into the rear courtyard that was lined with paving stone. Several tables with chairs were placed about the spacious patio. "We must have a glass of wine and catch up before we have dinner!" he heartily exclaimed in French.

By now Jancy had picked up enough of the language from their travels to figure out the gist of what Henri had said, so she held up her hand to stop Michael from translating. When they were seated, Jacqui disappeared for a moment to fetch the wine and glasses. The men settled into small talk in French which Michael translated for Jancy.

When Jacqui returned a few moments later, she brought a tray with a bottle of white wine and four glasses. She disappeared again for a moment before returning with a platter of three cheeses. Henri took the bottle and removed the cork with a corkscrew.

"Southern Rhone white," he informed Michael as he began pouring the wine. "A splendid blend of Viognier, Roussanne, and Marsanne. One of our specialties in regards to white wine here at Domaine Garçon."

"And the grapes?" Michael inquired, curious.

"We control two vineyards in the area immediately south of Chateauneuf du Pape," he explained, referencing one of the most famous wine regions of the Southern Rhone Valley. "We have leased them for more than 50 years and specify exactly how the grapes are grown. But, to our dismay, our efforts to purchase the vineyards outright have never borne fruit, if you will forgive my poor pun."

It was not an usual situation, for many vineyards in France remained in a family for generations, especially the ones with the best reputations for quality grapes. After ten minutes of sipping the wine and sampling the native cheeses, Jacqui explained the upcoming schedule. Unlike Henri, she was conversant in English.

"Tonight we will have a family dinner," she explained. "Our son Henri, Jr. will be here with his wife, as well as my sister Adele. Our daughter Simone, unfortunately, lives in Paris and cannot get away."

A moment later, Jacqui added, "Michael, you have a certain reputation here. Tomorrow we shall go shopping and sightseeing in Lyon, but the day after, well, there will be a celebration here with you as the guest of honor. Winemakers from the entire region will be here to honor you."

"Sometime during our stay," Michael responded quietly, "I'd like very much to visit wherever Jacques is buried. I wish to pay my respects."

Pleasantly surprised, Jacqui replied, "He is here in the local cemetery. Just a short drive to the village."

Jancy had by this time shrewdly divined the relationship between her husband and the French lady. Interrupting the conversation, she said, "I've always wanted to visit Lyon. Such a historic and important city! How about Adele and I going to Lyon tomorrow? Michael, you can spend the day here visiting the cemetery and going through the vineyards."

There was a moment of silence as the four adults looked at each other. "Are you sure?" Michael asked her.

"Why, yes!" Jancy quickly assured him. "You'd be bored silly while I try on shoes and the latest French fashions. Adele and I can shop up a storm while you catch up with what's going on here."

"Well, then it is settled!" Jacqui announced, then quickly translated for her husband.

Henri simply shrugged his shoulders and affirmed the decision with a simple. "Oui."

*   *   *

Later, Michael and Jancy were given a tour of the winemaking facilities behind the mansion. "Man, things have changed!" Michael exclaimed upon entering a relatively new building and looking over all the modern equipment.

"Yes, that is very true," Jacqui agreed. "Our production is more than twice what it was when you were here."

They were introduced to a short and stout, middle-aged man named Roland who was the winemaker. "We only use the old cellar for aging very small lots of private production reds," he explained. "All of the commercial wine for sale is made here in the newer facilities with the latest sanitary protocols in an attempt to keep the Brett out."

"Really?" Jancy replied, surprised. "I thought one of the essentials of French wine was the so-called barnyard smell."

Roland slowly shook his head, "Ah, that is so true, but times have changed," he explained sadly. "Today, everyone wants a clean wine, filtered and fined, and having some sort of fruit aroma on the nose. But, the Brett gives a wine character and complexity, even affects the taste. In my opinion, the effect is generally to the good."

The discussion among the winemakers was over a wild yeast called Brettanomyces commonly present on grape skins. Michael weighed in with his opinion. "I've read a lot about Brett," he informed Roland. "It seems the effects of the yeast are generally good at low levels, but there is a point—a threshold—beyond which people perceive the effects to be negative."

And so it went as the tour proceeded, the three winemakers engaged in intense but congenial conversations. Two hours rapidly passed before Michael and Jancy had satisfied their curiosity on current winemaking techniques at Domaine Garçon.

At 7:00 Henri drove his guests and his wife into Vienne to a restaurant that he and Jacqui held in high regard. Henri Jr. and Jacqui's sister Adele met them there. They were escorted through the main dining room and into a cozy back room reserved for private events.

After being seated, they were introduced to the chef who informed the Americans that he would be serving a tasting menu of many of his best dishes. When he retired back to the kitchen, a waiter introduced himself before setting up an array of wine glasses before each guest.

Next, the waiter brought out four bottles of wine, three of which were Domaine Garçon: 1985 and 1993 Côte Rôtie, as well as a 2010 Condrieu. In addition, there was a bottle of sparkling wine from another Rhone producer.

"We shall start the evening with a sparkling wine!" Henri informed everyone. "It is made from Viognier."

Champagne flutes were filled by the waiter as his assistant placed small plates of foie gras before each diner. Henri stood up and offered a toast to the American visitors, and then Michael took his turn by offering a toast to his French hosts.

As the evening progressed, the head waiter served Viognier from Condrieu, and then it was on to the reds. Michael and Jancy enjoyed the well-aged Côte Rôtie Syrahs. In addition, southern Rhone blends produced by Domaine Garçon were also served.

The wines were enjoyed with classic French food: gratinée Lyonnaise—onion soup topped with a slice of baguette and a thick crust of melted cheese—as well as another type of soup called pot au feu featuring beef and vegetables. This was followed by a stuffed cabbage dish called choufarci, and then a hearty cassoulet with chunks of coarse-grained sausages called andouillette and cuts of goose meat.

Michael and Jancy were not surprised that dessert consisted of a selection of elegant petits fours, but they were pleasantly surprised when the waiter poured a Beaumes-de-Venise fortified Muscat to pair with the sweet treats.

"It's a Southern Rhone appellation," Henri explained. "We don't pretend to complete with Sauternes, so we simply take the naturally sweet Muscat grape and fortify it with Brandy to come up with our own version of a dessert wine."

"Very, very interesting," Jancy observed after taking a sip. "It's amazing what a variety of wines you find when you travel the world."

*   *   *

The next morning, Jancy and Adele left by auto for Lyon for a day of shopping and sightseeing. Henri also left but, in his case, for the family's business office in nearby Vienne. Jacqui busied herself making a picnic lunch while Michael spent an hour visiting in the winery with Roland.

When Jacqui was ready, she retrieved Michael from the winery and led him over to her Citroën DS3, a chic and snappy looking, silver-colored hatchback. "I've already packed our lunch, so we're ready to go!" she informed him enthusiastically. "And such a beautiful day!"

She put the car in gear and off they went, leaving the estate and following a maze of narrow local roads for ten minutes until they came to the small village of Ampuis. Situated right on the Rhone, it was spread out along a valley terrace just above the river. The surrounding slopes were covered for the most part with vineyards.

Jacqui drove into the center of the village before turning right to follow a narrow street for a short distance as it gained elevation. When they came to an ancient stone church, she pulled into the churchyard and cut the engine.

"The cemetery is in the back," she informed Michael as she opened her door to get out.

He joined her as they walked around to the rear of the church where they encountered a modest-sized graveyard surrounded by a hand-laid stone wall approximately four to five feet high. Jacqui opened a wrought iron entry gate and they walked in.

Michael saw that the cemetery contained a mix of headstones, some rather new while others were heavily weathered and looking as old as time itself. He followed Jacqui as she picked her way over to the family plot marked by a small stone obelisk carved with the word 'Garçon' on it.

There were six graves within the family plot, each having its own small headstone. Michael immediately spotted the one for Jacques and his wife, Marie, and he stepped over to it. Standing silently by it, he gazed upon the name as memories of his mentor came flooding back.

Jacqui stood beside him, perhaps lost in her own memories. "He taught me a lot," Michael quietly said.

"He was proud of you," she replied. "When the news of your success first hit this area, he quite naturally bragged to everyone that he had been your teacher."

Michael glanced at Jacqui and chuckled. "I can just picture him doing that!"

They spent several more minutes by the grave, chatting about their memories of Jacques before departing. As they strolled back to the car, Jacqui hooked her left arm around Michael's right and glanced at him, smiling.

She drove them further down the road to a spot that provided a sweeping overlook of the river valley. Pulling off at an entrance road to a vineyard, she parked the Citroën. "Here is where we'll have our picnic!" she happily announced.

Retrieving a large insulated picnic tote bag from the back of the car, Jacqui handed it to Michael to carry. Also retrieving a large blanket, she led the way to a spot a short distance from where they had parked.

Jacqui had selected a site that provided an excellent view of the broad Rhone River below them while red-tiled roofs in the village contrasted nicely with the blue water. Lush grapevines in terraced vineyards descended down to the village.

"If I was an artist, I'd paint this view!" Michael exclaimed. "It's perfect!"

As they settled down on the blanket that Jacqui had spread out, she pulled out a chilled bottle of Condrieu. "Open this, please," she asked Michael.

As he removed the capsule and began using the corkscrew, he joked, "I had a feeling we'd be drinking Viognier!"

Jacqui smiled and explained, "We're at the edge of the appellation. In fact, one of the vineyards we control is just down the road. The wine in the bottle was made from grapes from that vineyard."

"Nothing like enjoying wine next to the vines that produced it!" he observed.

Jacqui set up their lunch: several cheeses as well as finger sandwiches and fresh table grapes. Michael poured the wine into two glasses that Jacqui had given him. Admiring the delightful light golden color of the wine, he remarked, "It looks delicious!"

Jacqui raised her glass. "A votre santé!"

"A votre santé!" Michael happily replied, saying 'To your health' in French.

Over the next half hour they enjoyed their lunch as they sipped their wine and engaged in conversation. At one point, Jacqui asked, "Do you ever wonder what it would have been like if you had stayed?"

"You mean, if I'd have remained here all my life?"

Nodding slightly, Jacqui simply replied, "Yes."

Michael took a deep breath as he mulled over the question. "Well," he began slowly, "I don't think I would have been happy."

"No?"

"No. I wanted to be a winemaker – a good winemaker. But if I had remained here I never would have been accepted. I would have always remained the outsider, the American who wasn't quite as good as the locals."

"Perhaps," Jacqui said. "Perhaps not."

Michael shrugged. "It doesn't matter. Even if I would have eventually been acknowledged as a master winemaker, the rules and regulations here are too restrictive for me. In Côte Rôtie the red wine is Syrah whereas in Condrieu the white is Viognier, and so forth. Plus, there is no blending beyond certain narrow limits."

"That is true," Jacqui acknowledged. "But it is this way because we know what grapes grow best in each area. That is how we produce such outstanding wine."

Michael chose not to argue the point but, instead, went on to explain why he had been so successful. "In the States we're not so restrictive," he pointed out. "There are few limits on what we can do with wine. I was able to find a completely undeveloped place like Watilla and just experiment to my heart's content."

"And you succeeded brilliantly!" Jacqui replied, smiling.

Michael gazed at her for a moment, taking in her still attractive face, her lively dark eyes, her gray-streaked dark hair. "But there may have been one benefit I would have enjoyed if I had stayed," he said mischievously.

Jacqui's eyes met his for a moment before she replied, "I think I would have liked being married to you." Then she quickly added, "Oh, don't misunderstand me. My Henri is a good man. I have no regrets on that account."

Michael nodded in understanding and then quietly said, "You would have been good for me."

He immediately saw that this pleased Jacqui and it made him ponder how very different his life would have been if he had stayed in France.

Later, when everything had been packed up in the car once again, he and Jacqui walked over to have a better overview of the valley. It seemed natural that they held hands as they walked until they stopped.

As they admired the view, Jacqui turned to Michael and stood so close to him that their bodies almost touched. Quickly giving him up kiss on the cheek, she said, "Thank you for coming here."

*   *   *

The next day was given over to a celebration of the two American winemakers. Owners and winemakers from throughout Côte Rôtie, Condrieu, St. Joseph, and even as far south as the Hermitage district, came to meet and talk to Michael and Jancy.

Jacqui and Henri played gracious hosts, providing a catered buffet in back of their manor house. Michael was pleasantly surprised, and a little amazed, that many of the winemakers had managed to obtain a bottle of one or another of his current releases that they wished him to autograph. And of course, they all wanted to talk shop, to hear directly from him the techniques he used to make his famous wines.

It was no surprise that they all had to speak with Jancy as well, each one enjoying immensely the opportunity to talk with an attractive blonde. All in all, it was quite an afternoon, both gratifying and exhausting.

That evening, Michael and Jancy were treated to a private dinner in the house with just Jacqui and Henri. During the course of the conversation, they invited their French hosts to visit the States, especially Watilla.

"Please let us know," Michael informed them. "You're welcome anytime."

"Yes, we must visit!" Jacqui eagerly agreed. "I'm so curious to see your winery!"

"Well, it's pretty utilitarian," Michael had to admit. "Not like all these lovely centuries old places you have here in Europe. But I do have an historic tasting room you'd like."

Two days later he and Jancy were on a westbound transatlantic flight to Seattle. As she slept beside him, Michael pondered his future. He was returning home—to Watilla—and a wine industry he had created. There were now more than 125 wineries of one sort or another, more than 150 labels, and an annual production that, in terms of total economic impact, was truly staggering.

He had been the pioneer, the visionary. What would he do now with the rest of his life? Were there any other wine challenges left? He knew there was no such thing as a perfect wine, so it was a waste of time to try to make one. For him, the spice of life, so to speak, in the winemaking business was in creating something new.

And what would that something be? As he thought about it, Michael realized that the Watilla Valley had no distillery. If a guy could make distilled spirits, or had access to them, then he could make a fortified wine like Port. Hmm, A Watilla Valley Port-style wine. Or wines, plural. Ruby, tawny, or white, a guy could make them all.

Smiling, Michael settled back in his seat and drifted off to sleep thinking about just what it would take to make fortified wines.

Author's Story Notes

Although my story and characters are fictitious and products of my imagination, I have derived a certain amount of inspiration from real life as follows:

The Watilla Valley in the story was inspired by the Walla Walla Valley in southeastern Washington State. Today, the area produces world-class wine, but a wine industry did not exist there prior to the late 1970s.

Olde Schoolhouse Cellars was inspired by the real life L'Ecole No 41 winery which is, indeed, located in a delightful 1915 schoolhouse. It is situated west of Walla Walla—rather than south of town as in the story—and produces outstanding wines. The site of Michael's winery in the story is actually occupied by the real life Saviah Cellars, another producer of extraordinary wines.

The Dr. Wilbur Cline character was inspired by the late Dr. Walter Clore who has been officially recognized by the Washington state legislature as the 'Father of Washington Wine.' His vision and research made it possible for winemakers and vineyard growers to establish a thriving wine region throughout the greater Columbia Valley in what is essentially a desert environment.

The 100 point rating system in the story is very much controversial in today's wine industry but has become, for better or worse, the standard for how wines from around the world are rated.

The annual top 100 wines of the world list in the story is actually published in real life by *Wine Spectator*, one of the most prominent publications about wine. When a wine makes the list, it often establishes the reputation for years to come for both the winemaker and the winey.

The Watilla Community College wine program in the story was inspired by the real life Walla Walla Community College program. It has grown to become one of the nation's most respected programs for aspiring winemakers to learn their craft.

The western theme steakhouse in the story located in downtown Pendleton, Oregon, really exists and is called the Hamley Steakhouse. It is a must stop when traveling in that part of the country.

Garry Scholz is a former food and wine writer for regional Pacific Northwest publications of The McClatchy Company, one of the nation's leading newspaper and Internet publishing companies. This is his second work of fiction

Garry lives in Alexandria, Virginia, with his wife Donna.